I0557935

SEASON OF THE WITCH

BOOK 2 WHEEL OF THE YEAR MYSTERIES

MICHALEA MOORE

 Eloquent Peasant Books

ELOQUENT PEASANT BOOKS

No portion of this book may be reproduced in any form without permission from the publisher or author, except as permitted by U.S. copyright law. To request permission, contact the author at michalea@michalea.com.

This book is a work of fiction. Names, characters, and incidents are products of the author's imagination or are used fictitiously. Any resemblance to actual events, locales, business establishments or persons living or dead, is entirely coincidental. Certain long-standing institutions, agencies, and public offices are mentioned, but the characters involved are wholly imaginary

Black and White Tarot images: Design Bundles Ltd https://designbundles.net/

Cover art via Canva.com and Fotor.Com

Cover design: Michalea Moore

ISBN: 979-8-9876449-2-8 (paperback)

ISBN: 979-8-9876449-3-5 (digital)

First Edition 2023

Eloquent Peasant Books, 9501 Quail Village Lane, Austin, TX 78758

www.michalea.com

CONTENTS

THE MAGICIAN

Tis now the very witching time of night when churchyards yawn and hell itself breathes out contagion to this world. — Hamlet *by William Shakespeare*

THE MAGICIAN.

Skills • Potential • Power • Resourcefulness • Creativity
New Beginnings & Opportunities

Reversed: Manipulation • Trickery • Insecurity
Imbalance • Lack of Confidence

Once Upon a Time in Hawaii

> *Once upon a time, witches flew, gliding through the clouds, free of earthly constraints. That's the story, anyway. Me? I never sailed on air currents, not like the old ones. The way I saw it, modern witches either soared in their dreams or boarded jets. Cyrus Harper's private jet introduced this witch to a new level of magick. Tonight, I'd go to sleep in Kona, Hawaii. Tomorrow, I'd wake up in the same bed four thousand miles away in Riverton, Illinois. Come on, now! It's the biggest badass magick ever! Or, it's a faery tale wrought by a man I suspected was a dark Fae prince.*

I closed *BoSsBlog*, my *Book of Shadows*. Faery tales end, and no one can fly forever. Gravity came calling as we drove to the airport from the winery Cyrus bought as a vacation souvenir. We circled the Big Island after a blizzard (yes; I said blizzard) closed the Saddle Road over Mauna Kea.

"Hawaii's almost in the rearview mirror. Time for our little talk, yeah," Cyrus said outside Pahala where the road ran between jagged black lava fields and the ocean.

Air whooshed from my lungs faster than a punctured balloon. We should have taken our chances with the blizzard instead of the lava. Old habits and old ghosts die hard, and mine oozed through eons of molten rock gone hard. Feisty from their dormancy, the ghosts were ready to rumble.

"Since we're stuck in the car, now's a good time," he said.

Although we rocketed along at sixty MPH, the distance to the airport stretched out from here to eternity. Had I expected him to forget? Cyrus forgot nothing. If I still had a million dollars to gamble, I'd bet it on him sending a digital reminder.

> **To:** Cyrus
> **From:** Cyrus
> **Note to self.**
>   At 4:37 pm on March 11, discuss the Wheel of Fortune Tarot reading with Maren. Propose major life changes.

The last time we made plans, the police arrested us for murder, and someone tried to shoot us.

WHY RISK IT?

For ten days, my Inner Voice had been on vacation. We'd been careful not to summon her. Not one sentence began with 'when we were accused of murder.' Not a single 'Wasn't jail a hoot?' passed our lips.

Nope, we kept it light. On daring days, we asked, 'Sunbathe by the pool or windsurf?' Now he wanted to make long-term plans?

NOT BLOODY LIKELY! NOT ON MY WATCH.

Yep, Inner Voice was back, rested and ready.

DO YOU KNOW ANY AMNESIA SPELLS?

Nope, not one. Distraction it was. "Great vacation."

POSSIBLY THE LAMEST DISTRACTION THIS DECADE.

"Do I need to drive to the volcano so we can symbolically enact *The Fool's* leap off a cliff?" He grinned and gestured toward the mountains behind us.

OOOH. HE'S GOOD!

While struggling to prove our innocence and asking how to move our relationship forward, my Tarot reading advised a leap of faith.

"The leap was a soul lesson, yeah." Cyrus had a photographic memory when it served his purpose. "Also, what about taking the reins of our power and going after what matters?"

Total freaking recall.

Every nerve twitched. We'd stuffed disaster in a bottle and put a cork in it. Plans decanted the jinx. My grip on the door handle tightened. Whenever I bumped up against a plan, I bolted, but you can't bolt from a car going sixty miles per hour.

Calm down, girlfriend! This is not unexpected!

So why were my lungs burning and my heart racing?

"It also said I needed to focus, which is impossible after three glasses of wine. Wasn't there something about you not always being in the driver's seat?" I reminded the man in the driver's seat.

"Want a turn at the wheel?" He pulled off the road.

The ghosts from my past, as black as the lava, hopped around the alien landscape, imitating the dancers we'd applauded at a luau. They heckled me about watching and waiting for a sign that he had a foot out the door, a sign he saw what everyone saw about me. I drove people away and ran like hell. Not necessarily in that order.

It's what you do best.

"We're supposed to be at the airport at seven," I countered, buying time. "Do you want to miss our flight?"

"It's my plane, babe. It'll leave when I get there."

Right! My soul flew from my body to join the ghosts.

Making plans isn't necessarily a bad thing.

I vowed to go all in with planning a mere eleven days ago. Now, my breath came hard and fast; my brain ate clouds and became fuzzier by the second. The ghosts circled the car, reiterating their warning and drowning out Inner Voice.

Make a run for it before HE does.

My hand clutched the door handle in a death grip.

You know how this story ends. Move it.

Our eyes met; his grin faded. "Uh-oh. Is it hightailing time?"

When you find your soul mate, someone who *really* gets you, nobody warns you he might see you for the shipwreck you are. A thousand bees came to life under my skin. The ghosts waved cautionary pom-poms.

"Take a breath," he said. "Hold it. Now, release."

Cyrus breathed with me until I stopped hyperventilating.

"Better?"

"Yep." I squeezed the word past the macadamia-nut-size lump in my throat. "I'm tickety-boo."

"Fibber." He knew me too well. "We'll talk later."

When we were cruising at thirty-thousand feet and *even I* wasn't daft enough to try hightailing it?

"We'll work on tuning out the chatter in your head." He reached across the console and embraced me, kissing my forehead right where the Third Eye was located. "Everything's gonna be all right, yeah? Even if I have to move the mountain we leap off of."

Like all Fae, Cyrus Harper didn't make idle promises. It's why I loved him.

TWO OF SWORDS

TWO HOURS LATER, WE roared up to Kona Jet Executive Center. After Door-Med scanned our Bio-Bits and pronounced us virus-free, the gates swung open. A dozen uniformed attendants scrambled to unload our luggage (OK, *my* luggage) into a service cart. Cyrus tossed the car keys to another employee, who drove us to the plane waiting on the runway.

We'd entered the realm of Cyrus the Great. The guy in a black sweater and cargo shorts loping toward the jet's airstairs might look unremarkable, but a hundred antennae went up the instant Door-Med scanned him. Not just here at the Executive Jet Center, but everywhere. The mouse-thoughts scurrying inside the heads of gawkers who vied for his attention came through loud and clear. *What's so special about her?*

Damned if I knew. Five months ago, I tried running away from a smelly druid at Cardiff airport, and the terminal layout and staff made it impossible. Thanks to Cyrus, those days were gone. For now.

HOW ABOUT A LITTLE GRATITUDE?

"Hey, you!"

Cyrus turned, pantomiming Who Me?

"Yeah, you, Prince Charming!" I scrambled to catch him and snaked my arm around his waist. I loved the solid feel of his muscles, and I patted his belly. When our eyes locked, my body melted into his. "In case I forgot to tell you, it's been the best. The best trip and the best birthday ever."

He ducked his head, a rare bashful gesture. "You liked your present, yeah?"

HE NEEDS TO ASK?

I shook the Globe-Trotter Square bag; the jeweler's box clattered against my Tarot deck and the essential oils and incense I'd packed before Cyrus hustled me off to Hawaii. "Almost as much as I like you. Almost, but not quite."

Cyrus's smile was weapon *numero uno* on the Defense Against the Dark Arts syllabus. He stopped right there on the runway for a kiss that fogged my brain and vaporized rational thought. No planes were taking off, but I doubted it would have given him pause. I grabbed a second kiss because, witch's truth, he tasted better than honey, fresh chocolate chip cookies, and Veuve Clicquot.

"The world just tilted on its axis," I said when I found enough air to fill my lungs. "You moving that mountain, yet?"

"Doing my best, babe."

His worst was better than most people's best. We were OK. For the moment. Arms around each other's waists, we ascended the airstairs.

A bright-eyed steward with an orthodontia-approved smile asked, "Did you enjoy your stay, Mr. Harper?"

"We had a great time, Linda; thank you." The charm was out in full force today.

Linda took my bag and flashed an ingratiating-myself-to-the-boss's-girl-friend smile. "Cute dress!"

"Thanks." My vintage sundress with Tahitian girls playing ukuleles on a field of black and white flowers boasted a classic fifties silhouette. A full skirt and fitted bodice with side-smocking gave me curves I didn't have. Cyrus squeezed my waist.

Passing through the galley with its savory smells, my stomach rumbled. "Dude! I'd jump your bones every night if you could bottle that smell into perfume."

He snorted. "I'll get right on it."

I inhaled again. "Do it. You'll make another fortune; that smell is sin on a stick."

"Dinner is from La Bourgogne." Linda named a restaurant we'd visited twice. She stowed my bag under a cushy, white leather seat in the Master Lounge. "Wheels up in ten."

In Cyrus-world, it meant 'buckle up, buttercup'. On the way to Kona, I'd learned the hard way no one presumed to order Cyrus (or his guests) to buckle up, but the plane didn't take off until we did.

"I can serve dinner as soon as we reach cruising altitude," Linda said.

"I need to check messages, so hold dinner for a few." He turned his smile on her, then reconsidered, reaching across the table separating us and patting my hand. "But you sounded peckish, Moonchild. Bring out the Brie and the 2019 Ulupalakua Malbec as soon as we're up. That work for you, love?"

"Yep!" Did I mention his jet had a wine closet? More magick. I buckled my seatbelt. Linda disappeared, presumably telling the captain I'd mastered Seatbelts for Dummies.

The jet's ventilation kicked on with a whoosh, blowing my concentration to hell and back. The captain came over the intercom. "We're clear for take-off, Mr. Harper."

The lights flickered. As the plane taxied, the wind whooshed, and the flaps whirred. Every sound was normal, but a thousand times louder without a hundred other passengers to distract me. Two quick, loud thumps came from underneath the plane. I took deep breaths. Cyrus reached across the table and placed his hand over mine, giving it a quick squeeze.

"It's a jet, babe," he said. "The pilot and co-pilot are former Air Force."

Right. Not a twin-engine, six-seater piloted by my father.

The jet ate up the runway like a hot rod on a drag strip. The landing gear thumped into place, and we ascended at a sharp angle. I closed my eyes and imagined myself on a broomstick until Linda came out with a brie and wine tray.

"You're shivering, babe. Linda, please fetch Maren's sweater from the closet." I had a sweater in the closet now? Cyrus poured the wine and tasted it. "Malbec can be a beast, yeah? With this one, you get to know the beast's raw and sensitive side."

Much like Cyrus himself. I toasted the beast.

Cyrus sipped wine, thumbed through his emails, which often ran into the thousands, and deleted them like a boss. I guzzled wine and gobbled baked Brie. The flakey crust, the voluptuous cheese, and the green apple slices were simple, classic, and stupid good. If Cyrus could snack, drink, and check email, I could multi-task, too. I retrieved my bag and took out my tablet.

I reviewed my proposal for turning The Majestic Theatre into a different venue, held my breath, and sent it to Uncle Ira. Dreaded task finished, I emailed my assistant, George, and requested an update on the feud between the Imag-i-Tron guys, my new retail tenants, and the electricians. My mentor, Talia, left a message to remind me to practice my shielding, something she'd been nagging me about since the whole Greier murder mess. Yeah. Yeah. I'll get to it.

The next email came from Alexander Filippidis. Please, Goddess, don't let Alexander be the electrician. George was supposed to handle that stuff.

To: Witch Maren

From: Alexander Filippidis

RE: Did you like your vacation?

Back to reality, dear Maren. You can run, but you can't hide. I thought you'd hit a low point with those losers you hooked up with at The Rusty Spoke back in Austin, but the sad-sack druid proved me wrong. Still, it's rude not to answer his emails. What if the poor schmuck offs himself?

Do you believe Cyrus Harper is trading up? So disappointing, dear Maren!

Regards, Alexander

WHO THE HELL IS ALEXANDER?

Probably someone I used to date.

WHO TOLD HIM ABOUT THE DRUID? OR THE RUSTY SPOKE?

Don't know; don't care. I deleted the message post-haste. Although I never tried to convince Cyrus I was lily white, I didn't flaunt my past either. I chugged the Malbec and held out my glass for more.

"Cassandane says this latest virus shut down the Fredericksburg schools." He filled my glass.

"She didn't give the school district Bio-Bits and Door-Med?" His sister might not be Cyrus-rich, but she damn well could afford to outfit her kids' school.

"Cass lives smack in the middle of conspiracy country." He waved his hands, rolled his eyes, and mimed a crazy face. "Ooh, big bad Cyrus Harper's coming for your brain! Run! Everybody, run!"

When Bio-Bits came out, one tin hat theory claimed they controlled people's minds. A later conjecture alleged Cyrus sent hypnotic messages to users to transfer their money to his account, and that's how he became so rich. NEWSFLASH: if you believed that bullshit, you didn't have enough money to make it worth his while. The stories eventually died; but when Riverton Police subpoenaed Harp data during the Greier murder investigation, they resurrected.

He drained the wineglass in a single gulp and poured another. Usually, emotions ran across Cyrus's face faster than a newsfeed. Right now, he was stuck on livid. "Viv says the emails started again. Probably from email accounts that already had their financial data compromised."

His mouth twisted into a sinister smile. OK, dangerously pissed. He'd mentioned the emails several times in Hawaii.

"Sounds like a job for Yunus." Yunus, the mythical Turkish hacker, was Cyrus's alter-ego in cyber-world.

"Could be," he muttered, but his expression brightened. "Anyway, Cassandane still has her condo on Lake Shore Drive. She schlepped the family and the tutor to Chicago for the duration. It'll be great seeing the kids."

"Who'll take care of her chickens and goats?"

The next eye roll was for me.

WATCH YOUR TONGUE.

Message delivered. A Cyrus explosion at thirty-thousand feet might equal an extinction-level event, so I filled my mouth with brie. When hunger subsided, I pulled the Tarot deck from my bag and shuffled. *What is my guidance for the day?* I drew a card.

Two of Swords: tough decisions, weighing options, an impasse, and avoidance. Right on the money. Tell me something I don't already know!

The blindfold meant the woman was confused. Right on the money, again. Possibly she saw a relationship at a crossroads because she couldn't decide.

PROJECTING MUCH?

The balanced swords suggested I'd better weigh the pros and cons. Rocky islands dotted the water in the card. If water represented emotions and swords the mind and intellect, I needed to use both head and heart. The crescent moon meant trust my intuition.

WAIT! DIDN'T THE WHEEL OF FORTUNE READING SAY THE SAME DARN THING? IS THE UNIVERSE RAPPING YOU ON THE HEAD?

Undoubtedly. But decisions made me vulnerable.

WHAT ABOUT THE EMAIL?

I closed my eyes, letting the engine drone carry me off to a foggy place where indecision reigned supreme and avoidance was the highest art form.

"Hey, sleepy girl."

I floated back. In my absence, the lights had dimmed. Linda had draped a sweater over me and set the table with a white cloth, china, candles, and flowers. With a squint, I could imagine myself in a little bistro. I wiggled into the sweater. As always, Cyrus was right. The cabin was cold.

"You hungry or ready for bed?" The storm clouds had cleared. Animated Cyrus was back with wild gesticulations and broad smiles. "I can go either way."

"When am I not hungry? What did you order?"

"A little of everything we didn't try." He signaled Linda. "We'll have the La Fillaboa 1898 Albariño with the Scallop Salad."

"Did you order the Lavender Hare?"

"I think you mean *Roti De Lapin à la Lavande*, you barbarian, but, yes, dear."

"*C'est magnifique.* It makes tonight *une occasion spéciale.*" I stowed the cards in my bag and retrieved my birthday present necklace. Calling a Cartier masterpiece with twenty-eight flawless pearls, a massive pearl pendant, and twenty-four diamonds a necklace seemed pedestrian.

"Let me help." Cyrus came around the table and fastened it around my neck. "It looks spectacular against your tan."

The necklace was spectacular with or without my tan. The pearls were warm and mysterious, a minor miracle meant to be worn close to the skin.

YEAH, ALEXANDER-WHOEVER-YOU-ARE, SHE DEFINITELY TRADED UP.

"Do you think Wallis wore the necklace when she and the Duke were alone?" Cyrus asked.

"Probably. They dressed for dinner every night. In evening clothes. Even when it was just them."

"Cool." He returned to his seat. Linda served the Scallop Salad and poured wine that looked like liquid gold. He took a sip. "This is nice."

When it came to food and wine, he didn't miss a beat. He'd make a great food critic. I tucked into the Scallop Salad.

"Nice balance of savory and sweet," I said, which he likely already knew.

GEESH, MAREN, YOU'RE TRYING TOO HARD.

The Lavender Rabbit, slow-roasted in white wine with aromatic vegetables and French lavender, put me in the zone. Later, the poached pears stuffed with chocolate knocked off our socks.

When I finished scraping the chocolate from the plate, Cyrus hitched his thumb toward the opposite end of the plane. "Let's talk in the bedroom."

While I brushed my teeth in the *en suite* with a marble sink and a shower, he changed into mohair sweatpants. Tossing an oversized black

Dior sweatshirt with the Fleurs Bibliques motif and matching shorts at me, he said, "Might as well get comfortable."

"When did I buy these?"

"You didn't, but you needed clothes for the plane. You know I hate packing and suitcases."

Oh, boy, did I know. The bitching about packing for Hawaii had been epic. He'd only packed two pairs of shorts, two tee shirts, a sweater, swimming trunks, and linen trousers and shirt. A real hardship for a clotheshorse like him. Maybe he'd bought the coffee plantation with its eight thousand square foot main house and three guest houses, so he'd have a place to leave his clothes.

"You like black, and the sweatshirt is black, yeah," he said. "You like flowers; it has flowers."

"You spoil me." Irrefutable logic. Cyrus spoiled like a pro.

"Not as much as I would prefer." He flopped onto the bed and patted the mattress. "Come over here. I want you in grabbing distance in case you decide to parachute into the Pacific."

"Ouch!" I rolled my eyes. But I had no objection to cuddling; any excuse sufficed. As for the pricey sweatshirt, the plane was chilly, and I couldn't sleep in a sundress, so I wouldn't stand on principle. Twenty seconds later, pearls still around my neck, I snuggled against him.

"OK, Hal, play *I'm a Woman* by Koko Taylor and then Best of Indy Lover Cult."

"OK, Cyrus," the virtual assistant replied. Hidden speakers blasted Koko Taylor growling *I'm a Woman*. A woman who made love to a crocodile. He snaked his arm around my neck in an old-fashioned headlock when Indy Lover Cult came through the speakers.

"Mm-hmm. Romantic, dude."

"Hey, I don't want the crew hearing you yell at me. I've got a reputation to uphold."

"What am I yelling about tonight? Because, honestly, you've been a sweetheart." Plus, I'd finished with my panicked hightailing. For today, at least.

"Change of plans." He held up his free hand in a cease-and-desist gesture. "I know I said we'd be in Chicago just for the concert."

Ah, the Peter Thornhill concert. The rock sensation and Cyrus's good friend had arranged for a gaggle of Lilienthals to join us in prime seats and meet him.

"Frank emailed me." He sighed.

Poor Frank, the Harp CEO, who lived with the disappointment he wasn't Cyrus, constantly checked in.

"He wants me to stick around for the PSEC-Harp integration because the PSEC employees know me. Continuity, yeah?" Harp bought PSEC after we were cleared of murdering its owner.

"Makes sense." My head nodded like a bobblehead. I should have expected something like this. When the police grilled me, they reminded me Cyrus typically spent a week, two at the most, in Riverton. This time, he'd clocked four months. Because of me and, well, murder charges.

"Are we talking two weeks?" I punched his arm to hide any messy emotions. Why not? Chicago offered more fun than Riverton any day. If ghosts haunted Cyrus's house, at least they weren't *my* ghosts. But it wasn't that simple. It never was.

"Longer," he said.

Damn! I was certain we'd left the ghosts and demons on the Big Island, but they'd hitched a ride. They popped through the bulkhead and the jet's metal skin. Capering around, they pinched me with icy fingers.

See. We warned you!

A Greek chorus of demons shrieked with unfettered glee. These demons specialized in the personal and ordinary, not the noble doom of epic poetry. They writhed, pointed their fingers, and spat burning venom. If I'd been a Salem witch, my demons were the hysterical girls. Instead of screeching, "The devil's sitting on Goody Lilienthal's shoulder," they lobbed my worst fears at me.

You blew it.

You overreacted to the 'let's talk' moment in the car.

You can't give a straight answer to a simple question.

He's done with you, girlfriend. He wants OUT.

Brace yourself, and end it with dignity.

Hello, Inner Voice. Little help, please.

"Hey, what's going on in there?" He pulled my head to his shoulder and rubbed my scalp with his knuckles.

"Nothing. It's all tickety-boo," I said. "After the concert, I'll go back to Riverton with Manny and Ivy."

"The places your mind goes terrifies me," he said.

Me, too.

"You think I'm saying goodbye?"

Sometimes, he was psychic, or he just knew my psychoses. "Nothing lasts forever."

"Why do you think that?"

"Seems to work out that way." All my life, I watched forever melt away.

"Let me finish." His arm tightened around me. "I want you to stay for the whole shebang. With Cass home, my mom will want a family dinner. Remember, I warned you my family does the Easter thing."

Gah! What if his brother Darius was coming?

"Cass and Harper want to join you and my mom for tea on Sunday."

Quality time with a sister who didn't like me? Let the good times roll.

"The Harp Board meeting is April twenty-first and second." He rubbed his chin. "I gotta be there."

"Obviously." He was the freaking Chairperson of the Board.

"We meet during the day, but there's dinner on Thursday and a cocktail thing on Friday before everyone flies off. You can be my date, yeah?"

Sweet Goddess. He wanted me to become *that* woman. The woman my sister-in-law Ivy aspired to be. The woman Oma was. The woman my mother pretended to be until it killed her.

"Think about it."

"There must be a million girls who'd be the perfect date. Why me, Cyrus?"

"Why you?" A bark of laughter. He squeezed my hand. "It's obvious."

"Not to me."

After a long pause and a patient sigh, he said. "Dating used to be a normal thing, but After the IPO, it changed. I made a date with this woman I met at the MedFusion conference. A marketing VP. A real power player. We agreed to meet at a restaurant. She was on the phone and didn't see me come up behind her. She was saying, 'Yeah, I met this guy, and I think he needs help spending his money.' We had dinner, and I never saw her again. That became my new normal."

"Your gifts are...uhm, they're a little extravagant." A Patek Philippe watch, diamond earrings from a Russian Countess, chocolates flown in from Paris, and the Duchess of Windsor's necklace would have satisfied any marketing VP I'd ever met. Even a power player.

"I enjoy surprising you, and besides, it's not that much." He shrugged, measuring an infinitesimal amount with his thumb and his forefinger.

I suppose it was a mere drop in the Great Cyrus Ocean, but to mere mortals, it was a fortune.

"When we first met, you didn't know who I was, and you had dinner with me, anyway."

If I had recognized him, would we be here tonight? The MedFusion VP's ghost whispered *doubtful*. I hoped she was wrong.

He rolled onto his back and stared at the ceiling. "No one ever says no to me, you know. No one tells me what I don't want to hear. Except you. I don't think I'm scary, but people fear me. I don't scare you, do I?"

Ha!

When his black moods came on or I imagined him as a dark Fae prince, he scared me plenty. I kept it to myself. "No."

"Good. Before you, I was in prison. A nice prison with almost everything I wanted, but it was still solitary confinement. When I'm with you, I'm not thinking about the past; I'm not worrying about the future. I'm not thinking about anything but you and what we have right here, right now, at this moment."

He slid over me, anchoring me with his weight and inviting me to a familiar place. His lips knew me and reminded me I knew him. Goddess knows he was a master at persuading me all I wanted was to kiss him, kiss him again, and to keep kissing on a runway, in the air, in Riverton, in Hawaii, in Chicago, or wherever. I clutched his shoulders, wrapped my legs around him, and gave him everything. Except an answer.

"I'm not saying no, but it's complicated," I whispered, hoping the jet engine's drone and Indy Lover Cult drowned me out. "Relationships terrify *me*."

"I'm not a relationship. I'm Cyrus." He kissed his way from the hollow of my throat to the triple moon tattoo on my stomach. "I don't need an answer tonight. Remember, your cards said to take a leap of faith."

TOTAL FREAKING RECALL.

"It's easier to make a leap when you're holding someone's hand."

"Right, and we'll have fun." He traced the pearl necklace with his fore-finger. "You'll wear this, and we'll dress up for dinner. On Sundays. Drink champagne, yeah?"

"Seriously?"

"Your grandmother would approve."

Oh, yeah; Oma will approve.

"Maybe we can find a nice tiara for you."

"A tiara?"

"You've got the hair for it."

He meant that we'd make a plan for our life, stick to it; and, by God, have fun along the way.

OK, the message came through loud and clear. Did I believe him? There was the rub. I was the girl where relationships went to die. Deflection time. "We'll need better dishes."

"Babe, I've got dishes that will knock your socks off."

"I'll need evening gowns if we're dressing for dinner."

"I know how you love a little reckless shopping," he said.

"The Duchess was a dominatrix." I rolled him over and straddled him. "At least that's the rumor."

"Did the Duke enjoy it?"

"Seems like." I put my hand over the pearl pendant and gestured toward the closet to emphasize the point. "Does your magick closet have a black leather bustier?"

"An unfortunate oversight, mistress, and one I intend to correct as soon as this plane lands in Chicago."

"I guess we'll make do, pretty boy."

Indy Lover Cult's cover of *Season of the Witch* erupted through the speakers. A song covered a multitude of sins and sounds. I drank in the ecstasy stealing over his face. The way he gasped when we connected, biting his lip when he moved. Goddess, those soft touches as he gathered me close and trailed kisses along my collarbone felt better than sin.

Everything would work out if we could stay in this bed, on this plane forever, but that was as unlikely as the eternal Hawaiian vacation. *Two of Swords* flashed before my eyes. If the woman dropped one of the balanced swords, no matter which one fell, there'd be serious damage.

The Money Won't Spend Itself

Saturday, March 12

"Wake up, babe." Cyrus nibbled my ear. His breath was soft against my neck, his palm flat against the triple moon tattoo he called his lodestar. "We have time for a shower before landing and the mongrel horde's invasion."

Calling my family a mongrel horde was generous. Try a pack of rabid squirrels, trailing tendrils of gossip in their wake. They'd dig for details about our relationship like long-buried nuts to carry back to Oma.

My toe tested the air temp. I burrowed under the duvet. My head snuggled against his chest, setting the tone for the day to his steady heartbeat. "Ixnay on the shower; it's freezing. On your buying spree, did you find any wool slippers?"

"Would I ever forget your popsicle toes?" Cyrus sighed, rolled from bed, and retrieved slippers and jeans from the magickal closet. "Hal, play *Popsicle Toes* by Diana Krall."

The virtual assistant filled the cabin with a bluesy song in which frozen toes became erogenous zones. Cuddles trumped showers.

"Seems popsicle toes have a certain charm," I said.

"Definitely, but Hawaii was one sweet respite."

"Funny. Didn't seem to bother you last night."

"We were still in Hawaiian airspace." He warmed the slippers in the air pocket between us before sliding them on my feet. I never appreciated Cinderella's story until now.

"We're beginning our initial approach to Riverton." The captain's voice interrupted *Popsicle Toes*.

"Get a move on, girlfriend." Cyrus smacked my bottom.

I found the Dior sweatshirt and pulled it on before jumping into jeans and twisting my hair into a messy ponytail. If I looked ratty enough, I might avoid family interrogation, although perhaps no one looked ratty in a $2000 sweatshirt. When I nodded, Cyrus opened the door to the main cabin. I plopped into a seat and buckled up for landing and the family invasion.

The captain announced, "Welcome to Riverton. It's clear and sunny. The outside temperature is 38 degrees."

Kill me now!

Cyrus deplaned to welcome my family. He'd missed (or ignored) the memo stating the Pied Piper led the rats away; he didn't lead them onto the plane.

"Aunt Maren. Aunt Maren." My niece Gertie's shrieks rivaled Banshees as she darted down the aisle and jumped into my lap. "We brought Mrs. Johnson's donuts."

Mrs. Johnson crafted pure sugary goodness. My stomach growled right on cue. I hugged her and kissed the top of her head. "Thanks, urchin."

The Lilienthal tribe led by my brother, Manny, overran the cabin. His wife, Ivy, pregnant belly, and their twin boys, Parker and Porter, followed. My cousins, Ainsley, Ellison, and Julian, brought up the rear. The gaggle would fill up all of Cyrus's bedrooms and need two cars. Hope Mr. Planning-and-Organization was on top of it.

Not. My. Problem. Whew!

My relief lasted two seconds before guilt came down like a hammer. At Oma's Christmas party, I'd promised to have drinks and catch up with Julian. Hadn't happened. New love and murder charges distracted me.

A glance confirmed the cabin had no hiding places; I fluttered my fingers at Julian, who rarely held a grudge and was the least likely to be Oma's stool pigeon. Fingers crossed. "Long time, no see, J."

"Mare, lookin' good."

SERIOUSLY? IN A SWEATSHIRT AND A SLOPPY PONYTAIL?

Ellison and Ainsley — looking hip in black jeans, sweaters, and fashionable hairstyles — devoured Cyrus with their eyes. Who'd blame Cyrus if he traded up for a more conventional Lilienthal girl? One who wouldn't get him implicated in a murder. I smoothed my sweatshirt and felt my birthday present under the fabric.

DIOR, WALLIS SIMPSON, AND FUZZY HOUSE SLIPPERS. STOP FRETTING. NOTHING IS MORE PATHETIC THAN AN INSECURE WITCH.

"Glad you guys could join us." My cheery smile felt stiff. I snagged a donut and glugged coffee.

"Uncle Cyrus!"

Gertie's salutation stopped me mid-bite. When had it become OK for her to call him uncle? I laid the blame at Manny's feet.

"Uncle Cyrus, can we see where they drive the plane?" Parker and Porter joined the chorus. Yep, Manny. He pursued an agenda, personal or business, like a hunting dog. I was an agenda. One dictated by Oma, who intended to have me married and fully integrated into Riverton society.

"A quick peek, then we need to buckle up so we can take off, yeah?" Cyrus marshaled the children toward the cockpit while I died in silence.

"He's so good with children," Ivy cooed and looked straight at me. "I expect he'll be wanting his own before long."

DID OMA TELL HER TO SAY THAT?

Ignoring the barb, I buckled my seat belt, preparing for the longest one-hour flight in aviation history. Manny and Julian took seats across the table from me.

"OK, let's get this show on the road." Cyrus clapped his hands.

The kids raced down the aisle, commandeering the conference table. Ivy smirked and took a seat on the couch by my girl cousins. Cyrus sat beside me and squeezed my hand.

Once we were airborne, the kids clamored for donuts and milk. Linda was a trooper, serving milk, coffee, and a cornucopia of distractions, including coloring supplies, Legos, and game tablets I didn't know were on the plane. Made sense. Cyrus had a niece and nephews, too.

Manny took his first sip of coffee. A slow smile spread over his face. "Oh, man! This is good."

"Kona coffee," Cyrus said. "You can taste the difference. Clean, bright, and sweet."

Ivy's puzzled expression conveyed a sense of superiority. Unlike Lilienthals, even Ainsley and Ellison who smacked their lips over the coffee mugs, she hoarded her good taste for finer things: decorating, fashion, hostessing, and motherhood.

"We toured three coffee plantations," Cyrus said.

"But only bought one." I held my cup like a holy grail. "Plus, a winery in Volcano."

"It was a small plantation. Only twenty acres," Cyrus amended. "Maren needs her coffee fix."

"All for me? Three houses and four thousand coffee trees." Childish, yes. Pleasurable, also yes. Ivy gnawing her lip bloody, priceless. "The big house is dreamy. You can see dolphins and whales from the lanai."

The men, perhaps sensing Ivy's disapproval, moved away and congregated near the galley, waiting for fresh coffee. Or so they claimed. The conversation fragments drifting over the engine noise centered on the pros and cons of carbon-neutral jets, a subject on which they considered Cyrus an expert since we were flying in one.

The women scooted over to the dining table.

WHO SAID SEGREGATION WAS A RELIC?

"Maren, have you met Mrs. Harper yet?" Ivy asked, although she damn well knew the answer.

"It's Doctor Rossellini. She'll rip your head off if you call her Mrs. Harper. Or so I hear." I took some glee in correcting Ivy who prided herself in knowing everything.

Ainsley and Ellison exchanged knowing glances and began chittering about Pieter Thornhill, the gorgeous rock star at the center of the upcoming concert. Ivy wrinkled her nose and looked like she needed to pass gas, but I understood their excitement. I'd chased a musician or two before I knew better.

"Gertie said Cyrus will introduce us." Ellison looked to me for confirmation.

"I believe that to be true."

Ainsley clasped her hand to her chest. "Pieter is one hot hombre."

Ivy, who didn't know the meaning of hot or hombre, changed the subject. "Doesn't Julian look like the cat who swallowed the canary?"

Ellison smirked with a sibling's smug superiority. "Sure. He's getting to play with the big boys."

A noteworthy achievement. I spent half a lifetime trying to finagle my way into the big kid group. Oma called Manny and Liliane the big kids. Ainsley, Ellison, and their sister Pippa were 'the littles.' She stuck Julian, Zara, and me in 'the lost in the middles' group. Cyrus? Without a doubt, a big kid.

"What do you think, Mare?" Manny called over the engine noise. "Should Lilienthal, Inc. get a jet?"

"How would I know? Oma's the deciding vote."

Ivy huffed a little when no one solicited her opinion. Cyrus winked at me. Julian and Manny ribbed him about getting into shape before he returned to the Friday basketball games. All familial, but not too awful. Cyrus's laughter boomed through the cabin. The big kid was having fun. A reminder Greier's murder had isolated us since Imbolc. Note to self: See to it my extrovert gets more play dates.

The men returned and hovered around the table.

"Have you been following the Greier news?" Manny asked.

"Not really." I avoided it like the latest plague. "Tell me when they lock Emelia and Finley up and throw away the key." My ex-acquaintance and ex-boyfriend tried to frame Cyrus and me for murder. We hadn't thought about or discussed them in Hawaii; I wanted to keep it that way.

"I had lunch with Poppy." Manny ignored my hint, referring to the Poppenhaeger in Poppenhaeger, Falk, Awerkamp, and Duesterhaus, Riverton's leading law firm.

Cyrus's invisible antennae rose, poking my sixth sense like a sharp stick.

"Hot off the press," Julian crowed. "The police discovered a boat in Hannibal. Poppy said the luminol lit it up like a Christmas tree."

Murder, donuts, and gossip. What was Saturday morning without them?

Manny said, "It belonged to Finley's cousin. Looks like they whacked Greier in the boat."

I shuddered. Manny might not be so mafioso-cavalier if he'd seen the hammer with blood and hair on it. Cyrus squeezed my shoulder; I rested my head against his stomach.

BRACE YOURSELF FOR THINGS YOU DON'T WANT TO HEAR!

"It's turning into a real dog fight." Manny warmed to the story. "Emelia told the police where to find the boat; Finley retaliated, enlightening them about how she got the Bio-Bits and turned off the security cameras."

"Is this in the news?" I said.

"Hell, no. I had it from Poppy."

"He's defending them?" Pretty sure his wife, Charlotte, wouldn't be down with that plan.

"Again, no. Not only no, but HELL no. But he hears all the deets at the courthouse. You'll get a kick out of this, Mare," Manny said. "Emelia and Finley have public defenders."

My schadenfreude squealed into overdrive. "Emelia can't afford a lawyer?"

"She can't touch Simon's money." Manny smirked.

"The 1975 Probate Act, yeah?" I heard the grin in Cyrus's voice. "Heirs can't collect if they're responsible for the death. Or charged with it."

SOMEBODY DID HIS RESEARCH.

"She made a play for the money." Manny peered into his empty coffee cup. "There was a hearing."

"If she's cleared, she'll get the money," Cyrus said. "Some lawyer might take the case on the off-chance Emelia gets lucky."

"When Hell freezes over. Their text messages, the stuff Maren recorded on her Bio-Bit, and now the boat, they're toast," Julian said.

Me against my siblings; me and my siblings against our cousins; me, my siblings, and my cousins against the world was a Lilienthal motto. Goddess help you if you weren't in the family. Ghoulish? Harsh? As Cyrus would say, yeah.

"Looks like it'll go to a half-sister somewhere back east," Manny said. "Anyway, Poppy says they're desperate to cut a deal."

"I guess it'll go to trial soon," Julian said.

"Nah. Even public defenders try to delay." All my mystery novels said so. I glanced at Cyrus. He winked, enjoying Emelia and Finley's woes.

"They can't even come up with bail money," Manny said.

Sweet! I didn't look back on my weekend in jail with undiluted pleasure, an experience I'd happily share with those two rats.

"Poppy said you'll need to testify," Manny said. "If you need a lawyer, he's ..."

"Maren has a lawyer." The icicles in Cyrus's voice rivaled my toes. He took his role as my *Knight of Pentacles* seriously, and a hot-shot Chicago lawyer came with the territory.

I fixed a hard stare on Manny. Don't go down that road, bro; there be dragons! Manny pulled out his phone and became enthralled by the news.

Cyrus grabbed Manny's cup and marched toward the galley.

Julian squeezed my shoulder and whispered. "It's good he stands up for you. Oma said people mistake him for a scruffy poodle, but he has a Rottweiler's spirit and instincts."

Not as noble sounding as *Knight of Pentacles*, but I couldn't disagree. Not entirely. The scruffy poodle returned with Manny's coffee.

"Did you reach your lizard people goal?" Manny meant Cyrus's vacation plan to sit on the beach, soaking up the sun like a lizard. "Judging by Maren's tan, I'd say yes."

"Some people tried harder than others." I tapped my chest. "Someone else insisted on parasailing and windsurfing."

"Oh, I know. Saw the photos." Manny thrust his phone at me. "Haven't you guys seen this yet?"

The online tabloid *Tattleverse* blared the headline: *Billion Dollar Baby!*

"What the hell?" Cyrus growled.

Goodbye, Poodle; hello, Rottweiler.

> Nosey Parker. Where do you go after beating a murder rap?
>
> If you're the world's hunkiest billionaire, you grab your babi and head for paradise. Bio-Bit tycoon, Cyrus Harper, and his companion, Maren Lilienthal, recuperated from the grueling experience in a $23,000-a-night getaway on the Big Island.

Beneath the headlines was a photo of our tarmac kiss. When had we become clickbait? Other photos showed us lounging by the pool, parasailing, walking on the beach, and looking into each other's eyes over dinner.

"Where did those come from?" The heat leeched from my face.

"Damned telescopic lenses," Cyrus muttered.

> Harper was last seen leaving Riverton Courthouse after posting bail, but he doesn't always look so grim.

The photo of a scowling Cyrus leaving Riverton Courthouse had made every major news outlet on the planet. Now, the photo of us waltzing at the Beaux Artes Ball had gone national!

> Get out the tissues, ladies. The loved-up pair, unable to keep their hands off each other, gazed into each other's eyes as they waltzed at a charity ball on New Year's Eve. We have to ask, did the self-proclaimed witch put a spell on him?

I'd made my peace with the waltzing photo, but the self-proclaimed witch BS boiled my blood. Did studying the craft a year and a day and my initiation ceremony count for nothing? What would they say if I called them self-proclaimed journalists?

"Good thing they didn't get the nekkid Downward Facing Dog by the pool shot, yeah, babe?" Cyrus put me in a headlock and kissed the top of my head.

OK. Crisis averted.

Manny roared with laughter.

"There are children here." Ivy turned her laser-beam eyes on him.

Chastised, Manny asked, "How did you get Maren on a parasail? I never could."

"Told her to imagine she was riding a broomstick." Cyrus thumped his chest with his free hand. The chuckle ended, and Kilauea's lava vent was an ice flow compared to the rage in Cyrus's voice. "Where did that come from?"

I looked back at the phone. He'd scrolled past the waltzing photo to a close-up of me wearing Wallis's necklace at dinner.

Lilienthal's single-strand natural pearl and diamond necklace by Cartier once belonged to Queen Mary who gifted it to her son, King Edward VIII. Edward became the Duke of Windsor after abdicating the throne in 1936 to marry American divorcee, Wallis Simpson, and gifted her with the necklace.

After the Duchess's death, designer Calvin Klein bought the necklace for $1.2M for his young wife Kelly in the 1987 Sotheby's auction. It was auctioned again in 2007 ($4.82M) and again in 2030 ($6.5M) when the necklace came into the hands of a private collector in Beijing. A source close to the unidentified collector confirmed the $9.9M purchase by Harper.

I gulped. Every jewel thief in the world just put me on their bucket list. I'd be lucky to visit the necklace in the bank vault now.

With no throne to offer his beloved, the Duke of Windsor was profligate with elaborate gifts of jewelry inscribed with such still-mysterious baby talk as eanum pig. This leaves us wondering what sweet-nothings Harper whispered when he slipped the necklace around Maren's neck.

Cyrus punched out a text message on his phone. Smart money said the unlucky recipient was Vivica Chastain, the CEO of CPH LLC, his family office. Smarter money said she'd handle it, but it might not be pleasant.

Manny's phone made the rounds. More storm clouds gathered in Ivy's face. Julian, Ainsley, and Ellison clamored to see the necklace. I cast a pleading look at Cyrus, who shrugged. Best to get it over with. I pulled the necklace from under my sweatshirt.

"Oh my god, you're wearing it," Ainsley screeched.

"It's so beautiful." Ellison's eyes glittered. She might beat the jewel thieves to the punch.

GOBSMACKED, YET, IVY?

As I recalled, Ivy returned from her Hawaiian vacation with a mere antique jade bracelet. Wallis's necklace put Manny on the hook for one hell of a push present. She confirmed it by rubbing her baby bump.

"It was Maren's birthday, and she's fascinated by the Duchess. Did you know she owns one of her dresses?" Cyrus, with a self-deprecating shrug, jumped to my rescue. As if a second-hand dress was stiff competition for a multi-million-dollar diamond and pearl necklace. "I read somewhere Kelly Klein said, 'It is my hope the necklace will be given again as a gesture of love and will be worn often and proudly.' It was and is."

Nice try, *Knight of Pentacles*, but Ivy muttered, "We know it'll be worn often. And inappropriately."

My resolve to be pleasant flew right out the window and died, gasping for air at 30,000 feet. "What's a girl to do? Cyrus needed my help. That $13 million a day he's making isn't spending itself."

"Maren!" Ivy's Oma impersonation was on point.

My brother's coffee was full of fishbones, judging by his hacking and red face. Ainsley and Ellison hooted, proving what I long suspected. They didn't like Ivy either.

"Oh, babe, your mouth." Cyrus rubbed my head with his knuckles and chuckled. At least I'd improved his mood. "There you have it, folks. Maren Lilienthal, the most helpful woman I've ever kissed."

The Cyrus-laugh boomed through the plane, cajoling everyone to join in, even Ivy. Everyone except me. All the money that couldn't spend itself wasn't enough to erase the intrusion on our privacy. On the bright side, Oma could evaluate our relationship in the tabloids without pestering me or grilling the family.

The intercom crackled. "Ladies and gentlemen, we're making our initial approach to Chicago's Midway Airport. It's cloudy and 45 degrees outside. We'll be on the ground in about ten minutes."

I buckled my seatbelt. Thank Goddess! We'd served our time in the Hell I didn't believe in.

A POISON BOUQUET

SATURDAY, MARCH 12

No "PLEASE REMAIN IN your seat until the plane arrives at the gate" announced our arrival in Chicago. The gate came to us lickety-split. Two white SUVs with three rows of seats waited by the airstairs. A minivan pulled up to the cargo hold, and the ground crew unloaded the luggage.

Gertie, seeing the car seats for her brothers in one car, headed straight for the other. Ainsley and Ellison trailed after her, their nonchalance camouflaging their intention to stay far away from Ivy. I followed suit. Lilienthal women got what they wanted. After situating the others, Cyrus hopped into the front passenger seat and gestured toward the driver. "This is Richard Cichowski. His wife, Pat, is driving the other car. They manage me when I'm in Chicago."

"Welcome to Chicago, ladies." Richard's wild salt-and-pepper mane and beard scruff verged on homage to his boss, making me doubt how much managing transpired.

The SUV stopped at the gates. An announcement blasted over the car's audio system.

Chicago Public Health Or-
der Number 2044-6. Issued

```
and Effective February 1,
2044.


You are now entering the
Chicago hot zone. Stra-
bovirus-3, also known as
Jakarta  Panic,  is  at
Stage 5.


All individuals age two
or older in the City of
Chicago must observe so-
cial distancing and wear
a mask at all times in
any public place unless
the area has Bio-Bit and
DoorMed technology.


There are no exceptions.
Violators will be fined
$1000 per infraction.


Welcome to Chicago.
```

WELCOME, INDEED!

The message thrummed in the silence. If this was how Chicago welcomed millionaires and billionaires, what message greeted regular passengers? Beatings will continue until you put on your darn mask?

We left the airport and swung onto Cicero Avenue. Tall, silvery buildings glimmered in the distance, but this stretch of Cicero threaded through sprawling, rundown neighborhoods. Calling them dank and dour was charitable.

Gertie burrowed under my arm and pointed at the masked people lining the road. "Scary."

She rarely saw masks; in The Bluffs, even infants wore tiny Bio-Bits. These were not just any masks, either, but a panoply of animals, skeletons, zombies, and other grotesque creatures. The masks accentuated scrunched foreheads and glassy eyes.

A group of men banged metal garbage can lids. Others hoisted signs protesting Health Order 2044-6 and shook their fists. At a stop sign, a small group surged onto the road and pounded their fists on the hood of a nearby car. Their auras trended toward dark, muddy colors or dull, angry red. The last place I encountered so many angry auras was the Riverton jail.

My cousins muttered uneasily.

BE THE ADULT.

"Reminds me of the great ape sanctuary." I hugged Gertie closer, reminding her how much she enjoyed the tour. "Remember how they pounded on the bars and made noise to get our attention? They didn't like being cooped up, and that's why we gave the sanctuary money for the open range."

"Yeah, I guess." Gertie didn't sound convinced.

"By the way, someone twiddled with the garage door last night." Richard slipped the news into the silence.

NOT HELPFUL.

"Checked the cameras. Looked like kids. Ran away when I called out."

"Guess we'll need to mount lasers on the roof," Cyrus said.

He made it sound like a joke; given the street vibes, maybe not. Wasn't Chicago supposed to be the fun place? The knot in my stomach loosened when we turned onto the Stevenson Expressway and left Cicero Avenue in the rearview mirror, but I couldn't shake the angry looks.

"Did you hear that, babe?" Cyrus looked over his shoulder. "Our landscape architect is coming next week to show us plans for the spring plantings."

OURS? US? SLICK, HARPER.

Was spring planting meant to distract me? Or to establish we were in this thing together? Cyrus was an efficient guy, so likely both.

"Maren designed the gardens in Riverton. She knows everything about plants." He punctuated the praise with a dazzling smile.

"A slight exaggeration." I returned the smile, but my dazzle was a little off-point.

"Maybe you should take on the landscaper here," he said. "She talks and talks and talks, and says things like you need five-hundred cone-flowers on the east side. Like I know what a coneflower is."

"A pink perennial," I said. "Very hardy."

"See! You speak her language."

Whatever. Do the mask people care about coneflowers?

We lapsed into silence until the car turned onto Lake Shore Drive. Gertie pressed her nose against the window to see the wild waves beating against the shoreline. Buckingham Fountain with the city skyline behind it was a head-turner, and I pointed it out to her.

"It's so big!" She squealed and bounced in her seat, the masked mob forgotten.

"It's all lit up at night, and the colors change," Cyrus said. "If you're good, we'll come back. Would you like that?"

Oh, yes, she would! She'd agree to clean her room if Cyrus suggested it. She was more like me than her mother cared to admit. Ainsley and Ellison joined the chorus of yeas.

We reached Cyrus's neighborhood, reminiscent of The Bluffs with big houses, trees, and a quiet air of affluence. No iron fence with impressive gates surrounded it, but guards in flak jackets stood at each cross-street, checking tags on the cars and scanning Bio-Bits.

"A federal judge lives two houses from me." Cyrus responded to my raised eyebrows. "He's controversial and gets regular death threats. A couple years back, the homeowner's association voted for security. It increased the HOA fees a little, but well worth it. I chipped in portable Door-Meds since everybody who lives here has Bio-Bits. Seems to work."

No masked marauders here.

The streets were quiet except for women in designer athletic wear taking brisk walks. Women Oma's age led the charge; younger women followed like fishing boats in the wake of ocean liners. The car turned toward the lake onto a long, brick driveway. Trees and shrubs camouflaged a white stucco house, rendering it almost invisible from the street.

After a house tour and the much-anticipated Chicago-style pizza, everyone retired to their rooms. Recovering from travel on a private jet, unpacking, and putting up with each other was exhausting. The kids — lulled by promises of the downstairs game room with its bowling alley, slot machines, pool table, and theater — consented somewhat willingly to naps. With everyone tucked away, Cyrus led me along the upstairs gallery to the master bedroom.

AWKWARD.

Yep, awkward. Sleeping with Cyrus wasn't a big secret after I spouted off about it in a crowded restaurant, and even less with the tabloids reporting on us. But in Riverton in *my* house, we had separate apartments with our separate beds, whether or not we used them. The plane and Hawaii? Neutral ground. But going straight to the master bedroom in *his* house put me in the company of Madame Pompadour, Mary Boleyn, and Cleopatra when she visited Rome.

Cyrus shuffled from one foot to another before gesturing me into the room. "It's a little decorator."

"It's nice, but there's a lot of white." An understatement. The room boasted innumerable shades of non-offensive cream and white, right down to the duvet cover. An oriental rug and a patterned red throw on the bed provided the only color. A fireplace with a white mantle and a balcony with white fencing tipped toward romantic. In a safe way.

"We can change anything. Hell, we can change everything if you want to." Out of the blue, he'd developed the mannerisms and chatter of a cartoon chipmunk.

Nerves aside, he assumed we'd be together long enough to redecorate a bedroom. Or, knowing Cyrus, tear it down and start fresh.

So NOT READY FOR THAT DISCUSSION, ARE YOU?

I patted my sweatshirt. "What about the necklace? Every cat burglar in the world knows I have it."

"We can put it in the safe."

"Yes, please." It seemed prudent after the drive down Cicero.

He beckoned, and I followed him into the bathroom, which was grand in a decorator-safe way with three skylights positioned over the walk-in shower and a bathtub big enough for a family.

"Deep Space Nine," Cyrus said.

"Excuse me?"

"Star Trek? Old TV show? I watched it with my dad. It's OK, babe; I forgive you for being a cultural barbarian. It's like a password. Voice recognition."

A marble slab behind the bathtub slid back to reveal a safe.

"Cool."

"Isn't it? I'd love to take credit, but it was the previous owner. Who'd look for a safe in the bathroom?"

He punched a code on the keypad and placed his finger in the optical fingerprint reader. The safe door swung open. Inside, stacks of money and a gun rested on a pile of papers.

"You know how to use that?"

"The money, yeah. It's not always plastic and bank transfers; sometimes they let me handle the real thing."

"Right, your walking around money." He'd explained the concept back in Riverton in case we needed to go on the lam. "But I meant the gun."

"Down on the ranch, we shoot bottles off the fence. Sometimes, I go varmint hunting with the ranch hands. Texas, right?"

"Yep."

With the necklace secured, I returned to the bedroom and looked out the French doors leading to the balcony overlooking Lake Michigan. "Stunning. You must like water views. This place. Riverton. Hawaii."

"Guess I do." He came up behind me, wrapped his arms around my waist, and rested his chin on my head. "Yeah, every place. There's a river — at least what passes for one in Texas — running through the ranch. I can see the Pacific from the place in San Francisco, and the Atlantic in New York. Hmm, the Potomac in DC. Gosh, in London, there's Tower Bridge and the Thames. Never thought about it before now."

The Universe thumped me on the head. I was Pisces, a water sign. He was Taurus, an earth sign.

EARTH GIVES WATER PURPOSE AND FORM; WATER NURTURES EARTH. YOU CAN NURTURE HIM WHILE FINDING SECURITY IN HIS STRUCTURED, STABLE LIFE. AN EVEN TRADE.

Pisces and Taurus were zodiac soulmates and had a great capacity for pleasure.

BINGO! IT'S WHY THE SEX IS GREAT.

It made sense, so why hadn't I figured it out?

BECAUSE YOU'RE SCARED IT WON'T LAST?

"Star Trek? Old TV show? I watched it with my dad. It's OK, babe; I forgive you for being a cultural barbarian. It's like a password. Voice recognition."

A marble slab behind the bathtub slid back to reveal a safe.

"Cool."

"Isn't it? I'd love to take credit, but it was the previous owner. Who'd look for a safe in the bathroom?"

He punched a code on the keypad and placed his finger in the optical fingerprint reader. The safe door swung open. Inside, stacks of money and a gun rested on a pile of papers.

"You know how to use that?"

"The money, yeah. It's not always plastic and bank transfers; sometimes they let me handle the real thing."

"Right, your walking around money." He'd explained the concept back in Riverton in case we needed to go on the lam. "But I meant the gun."

"Down on the ranch, we shoot bottles off the fence. Sometimes, I go varmint hunting with the ranch hands. Texas, right?"

"Yep."

With the necklace secured, I returned to the bedroom and looked out the French doors leading to the balcony overlooking Lake Michigan. "Stunning. You must like water views. This place. Riverton. Hawaii."

"Guess I do." He came up behind me, wrapped his arms around my waist, and rested his chin on my head. "Yeah, every place. There's a river — at least what passes for one in Texas — running through the ranch. I can see the Pacific from the place in San Francisco, and the Atlantic in New York. Hmm, the Potomac in DC. Gosh, in London, there's Tower Bridge and the Thames. Never thought about it before now."

The Universe thumped me on the head. I was Pisces, a water sign. He was Taurus, an earth sign.

EARTH GIVES WATER PURPOSE AND FORM; WATER NURTURES EARTH. YOU CAN NURTURE HIM WHILE FINDING SECURITY IN HIS STRUCTURED, STABLE LIFE. AN EVEN TRADE.

Pisces and Taurus were zodiac soulmates and had a great capacity for pleasure.

BINGO! IT'S WHY THE SEX IS GREAT.

It made sense, so why hadn't I figured it out?

BECAUSE YOU'RE SCARED IT WON'T LAST?

"We're matching this week." Gertie's dress provided an ex
to wear something to garner his mother's approval.

I lifted my dress from the box. Also rose-colored, the s
neckline and fitted top hugged my waist. Scalloped lace pee
underneath a full skirt.

"Oh, my." Cyrus's eyes sparkled. "Not your usual color cho
tie turns you into an old softie."

"True dat. But look at these." For Gertie's concert debut, I'd
a black leather dress with puffy lace sleeves and Doc Marten
with sparkles on black leather. For myself, a black leather jacke
multi-colored studs on the collar, cuffs, pockets, and a wrapar
belt. Perfect with a turtleneck and jeans.

"Hello. There's my Maren. You'll be Gertie's hero. Speakin
clothes." He gestured toward two doors. "My closet's here. The
over there is yours. I've never used it. I don't think I've even opened
door, but Pat said she cleaned out the cobwebs. Viv called the wom.
who did my closet, and you can do it up to fit your needs."

I fanned my face and avoided the implication I need
a closet tricked out to my specifications. Both closets wer
room-size. His closet surpassed the one in Riverton, which I'
dubbed The-Shrine-of-the-Suit-for-Every-Day-of-the-Year. Clothing
organized by purpose, color, and fabric. A wall of shoes, everything
from athletic shoes to boots. A place for everything, and everything in
its place. *Hello. There's my Cyrus.*

"You are such a clothes horse, Harper. You put me to shame."

"I hate packing."

"I heard that rumor." Patting his cheek, stubble rasped against my
hand. "Like you hate shaving?"

"They're a hassle and a waste of time."

In his case, it was true. Cyrus, wasting an hour packing, was an
extravagance few could afford.

"Next week," he said, ignoring the nerves jittering around the room,
"I thought you might like to drop by the Harp Building and visit CPH
so you can meet Viv in IRL."

CPH. Cyrus Paul Harper, LLC, a company with one customer and one
customer only. I'd spent hours talking to Viv. Like a Field Marshall, she

commanded dozens of employees who tended to Cyrus and his money so "our boy," as she called him, could pursue genius stuff.

"I look forward to meeting anyone who keeps you in line."

"Afterwards, I thought we'd do a little reckless shopping to fill up your closet." He rolled his eyes. About reckless shopping or the idea of someone keeping him in line? "Jeans, sweaters, and fancy knickers. Can't forget the fancy knickers. Viv will set up appointments on Oak Street for nicer stuff."

GAH! More plans.

"Packing wastes time," he said, acknowledging and trying to forestall my panic.

"Right."

"You'll need this." He plucked an envelope off the dresser and handed it to me. Someone had scribbled my name across the front. I tore it open. A black titanium card with my name and other information laser-etched on the metal slid into my hand.

"When did I get this?" I swallowed a gulp. This card was the velvet rope of credit cards, available by invitation only to .01% of the population. I wasn't on the VIP list even before Babington demolished my inheritance.

"Says 03/44. Right under your name." Mister .01% looked as innocent as an angel in a Renaissance painting.

"Different question. *How* did I get it?"

He squirmed. "I made you an authorized user on my account."

HELLO, MADAME POMPADOUR!

"Bit of a kept woman vibe, don't you think?"

"Everything's hardball with you. We could settle the conundrum if we flew to Las Vegas and got married." He checked his Bio-Bit. "If we leave now, we'd be back in time for breakfast."

NO MARRIAGE TALK!

"You're a funny guy, Harper."

Marriage was the ultimate long-term, disaster-inducing plan in my book, and he knew it. We'd discussed my parents and the toxic waste dump they called a marriage.

"Wife is another word for kept woman." I tackled him, pushing him onto the bed, sitting on his stomach, and pinning his shoulders to the mattress.

"Bit of a compromising vibe, don't *you* think?" He gripped my hips with his hands. "We can debate it another time."

You're not getting off that easy, buddy.

"I still have credit cards. I can buy my clothes."

"Look." He wrapped his arms around me so I couldn't wriggle away. "I'm the one with the packing issue. I'm the one asking you to stock the closet. It's my problem. Why should you literally pay for it?"

So rational.

"How much do you think I'll spend on clothes?" The card literally had no limit. Rumor said someone purchased a Picasso at a Christie's auction with one. For all I knew, it's how he bought Wallis's necklace.

"Frankly? A lot." He rolled and pinned me to the mattress. After a flurry of kisses, I forgot the card and clothes. He didn't. "You'll need everything from fancy knickers to evening gowns. I most ardently admire your exquisite, albeit quirky, taste. You deserve — and I want you to have — the best. The best ain't cheap."

"You're a slick one, Harper."

"What's with this Harper business? It just started."

He caught on quickly. It was me putting distance between us and preventing a mental hightailing because plans were coming thick and fast. "Who knows? I'm crazy. Ask Ivy."

"To be fair, the crazy train runs in both directions." He gestured between us. "I'd rather be crazy with you than sane with anybody else."

Romantic? Not so much. But it suited us.

"Last night, you didn't hear what I thought I said. I didn't explain myself so well, yeah?" He rolled over like a dog when I scratched his belly.

"Go on."

"You thought I didn't want to return to Riverton. And just now, you thought I wanted you to buy clothes so I wouldn't have to go back."

"Sorry, no cigar."

"Anyway, the thing is, I'm gonna love the place in Riverton." The elaborate gestures came out. "I hope you'll love it, too. Enough to move out there with me. To a place that's ours. Someplace not tainted by Finley and Emelia. And no ghosts."

"You know about the ghosts?"

"Course I do." He made the DUH face. "Here's the thing. I travel. A lot. It's endless. Off the top of my head, I'm going to Luling in June and then on to Bilderberg. There's the Family Office Forum in Zurich in August. I'm speaking at Davos at the end of January."

A veritable What's What and Where's Where for Bil-lionaires.

"I don't want to go alone. And there's fun stuff, too. Le Bal in November."

"Get out of here! You're going to the fanciest debutante ball in the world? Are you looking for a trophy wife?" I hated the words the minute they slipped off my tongue. The implication insulted both of us.

He recovered first. "Uh, no. I hope when I have a daughter, she'll be presented."

Is that Ivy cackling? Or Oma, who opined Mr. Harper knows when a man makes a substantial fortune, one must have children to carry on the family name? Did he mention his Le Bal plans to them? Even if Oma bit her tongue, Ivy surely told him you'd make a lousy mother.

If he noticed me struggling to keep my head above water, he ignored it. "I have standing invitations to Paris, Milan, and New York Fashion Weeks. Gratitude for Bio-Bits and Door-Med making it possible for people to attend. Wanna go in September? Front row, my little fashionista?"

When it came to temptation, the devil-I-didn't-believe-in had nothing on Cyrus Harper. I consigned all thoughts about future Harper heirs to a foot locker at the bottom of Lake Michigan and gave two thumbs up to Fashion Week.

"I've been in a lonely place," he said. "Is it wrong to want a companion, a confidante, a lover? To want someone to share my life?"

"You play hardball, Harper."

"I try. I don't want us to waste time packing when we could be having fun. Plus, there are a lot of closets to fill." He shrugged as if to say *that's who I am, yeah?* "Lawrence told me success means living your life the way you want, not how others expect you to. What do you say?"

It sounded freaking reasonable. "I'll think about it."

"It'll be hard, but we'll get there." Flashing the infamous, knee-hollowing grin, he bopped my nose with the black card. "In the meantime, take the damn card. As someone said earlier today, the money won't spend itself."

My New Year's resolutions stomped through my head. *I welcome transition. I welcome growth. I welcome abundance. I welcome love. I know what*

I need. I am ready. Easier resolved than done. I started by sliding the card into my back pocket.

"We can try here and see how it works. Then, try the big house in Riverton. Step by step. One city at a time. Count me in for Chicago."

He rewarded me with a kiss. I was the voice of reason? Goddess, help us.

Richard tapped on the door, and we sprung apart. "This came for you, Ms. Lilienthal."

The day splintered. A putrid green aura punched at my face and swallowed the massive flower arrangement Richard carried. The sunlight pouring through the French doors scorched my eyes, and the tears stung. I turned my head, and my neck creaked like old stairs.

"Isn't that pretty? Who's it from?" Cyrus said.

My scalp prickled. A cloud covered the sun, and a sullen, heavy feeling crept into the room. A sour tang, starting in my stomach, crawled into my throat.

"Put the vase down. Now!" My intended roar was a mouse squeak. I gestured toward a small table. "Don't touch those flowers."

"What's wrong, babe?"

"Poison." It wasn't a wave of fear sloshing toward me; it was a freaking deluge.

Cyrus's face turned to chalk. Richard scrambled to comply.

The pain in my head twanged. "You need to wash your hands now."

"Use our bathroom," Cyrus said. Richard scurried into the bathroom. The water from the faucet sounded like a torrential downpour.

GET IT TOGETHER, LILIENTHAL. YOU'RE A WITCH. TIME TO ACT LIKE IT.

"Those blue hood-shaped flowers are Wolfsbane. Scratch your hand and touch them, they'll stop your heart."

INTERESTING CHOICE. Inner Voice became an icy wind in my soul. AND?

The tape recorder in my head turned on and babbled. "In the Middle Ages, witches used Wolfsbane in their flying ointments and love potions; they called it Mourning Widow. Those purple and green bells are Belladonna, also known as Deadly Nightshade. Touching won't kill you — you have to eat it — but it can irritate your skin."

Belladonna was rumored to be Romeo and Juliet's poison of choice. Someone had a thing against lovers because the bouquet also included the perennial bridal favorite, Baby's Breath. Poisonous when eaten, irritating to the skin.

"Who's it from? Where's the card?" Cyrus reached for the bouquet.

"Don't touch it," I shrieked. His hand froze in the air.

"It was on the front porch. No card," Richard said.

Unable to stop my recitation, I said, "That's hemlock. The one that looks like Queen Anne's Lace, except for the ribbed stems with purplish streaks. There's no antidote if you eat any part of it. It also causes a skin rash."

"Check the door cameras," Cyrus said, deadly calm. "Let's see who delivered it."

Richard hustled off.

I continued my inventory. Bell-shaped Mountain Laurel, white with deep rose spots, and so deadly children died after eating Mountain Laurel honey. The skin absorbed the fuchsia Foxglove's toxin, resulting in blurred vision, nausea, vomiting, convulsions, and death. The centerpiece was Dead Man's Bells, a dangling bulbous purple flower with a distinctive, dark checkered pattern. You didn't see Bells often, but they were a grade-1 poisonous plant.

Someone knew their deadly flowers. So many had skin reactions. I suspected the sender hoped an unsuspecting someone in this house would bury their nose in the bouquet. My phone pinged. Something compelled me to open the email right away.

To: Witch Maren
From: Alexander Filippidis
RE: Did you like your bouquet?

From one fellow gardener to another, let me say I love the Herbs & Plants spreadsheet in *BoSsBlog*. I shall be disappointed if you can't decipher my flowery message. I know Harper can't. All my best!

SOMEONE DOESN'T LIKE YOU.

Message received. My head felt as weightless as a helium balloon. My arms, legs, and feet buzzed, and the bed did a slow, lazy tilt. Black spots dotted my vision and marred the ceiling's pure white expanse.

"Cyrus, you need to see this message."

ADVENTURES OF SALLY AND MAREN

"I'm sorry, Mr. Harper; there's not much we can do." The female officer looked everywhere but at Cyrus.

POLITE, BUT USELESS.

If Evanston PD devoted as much energy to finding the jerk who left the bouquet as they did avoiding Cyrus's scowl, Alexander would be in jail already. I never imagined missing Detective Schulze, who grilled me for hours to unearth one insignificant fact. At least he was thorough.

"They left poison at our door. There are children here." Cyrus rolled his shoulders and neck. If he pinched the bridge of his nose and ran his fingers through his hair, unleashing the Kraken was imminent. I grabbed his hand and caressed his palm with my thumb.

"You can find those flowers in any garden, according to Ms. Lilienthal." The male officer exchanged a wary glance with his partner.

TRUE, BUT BESIDE THE POINT.

"She said they're not poison unless you eat them," he added. "Besides, we can't track down the perp. We got nothing. The kid who delivered the flowers lives in the neighborhood."

The security camera caught a teenager leaving the bouquet; Cyrus identified him as a neighbor. When the police questioned him, he said a tall, thin guy in black jeans, black coat, black protective mask, sunglasses, and a black knit cap paid him a hundred dollars to deliver the bouquet. No, he'd never seen him before, much less know him. There were no fingerprints on the vase, except Richard's and his.

"He's stalking Maren." Cyrus's hand twitched out of mine. "Reading her blog."

The officers stepped back. Smart move when Cyrus's eyes turned to flint, and his lips curled. He cracked his knuckles, an alarming sound that echoed off the foyer's arched ceiling and bounced up the stairway.

"It's a public blog, sir, although the email was a little creepy."

I told them I only shared my blog with a few people, but the male officer had already discounted that little factoid.

"How did he know we were here?" Cyrus demanded. "We've just arrived."

The officer shrugged. "Lucky guess."

I wrapped my arm around Cyrus's waist and leaned against him. This conversation was going nowhere, unless pissing off Evanston PD was our goal. "Thank you, officers. We appreciate your time."

"Sorry we couldn't be more helpful, ma'am," the female officer said. The guy was already out the door. "We'll have a patrol car put you on the rounds. If he shows up again, we can question him."

I thanked her again. Time to soothe the Kraken and lure him back to his lair, a task that consumed the remainder of the afternoon.

After dinner, when the kids were in bed and Ainsley and Ellison dragged Julian off to meet their sorority sisters, we sat on the breakwater patio, wrapped in winter coats and blankets, watching waves pound the shoreline. A full moon floated overhead, casting a magickal haze over the water. I slipped a glass jar filled with water on a small table to make moon water to use in any rituals I might perform during my unexpected stay here.

Ivy's teeth chattered. Cyrus threw another log into the fire pit.

Mulled wine and the fire kept me toasty, and I made a valiant effort to turn the conversation away from the bouquet and the police. "I don't know why, but this reminds me of the levees."

"Danger? Water?" Manny pulled Ivy next to him and stared up at the moon. "They were magnets for you. Since forever. Remember the time you and Sally went levee hopping?"

"Yeah, Oma almost killed me. A stand-out memory." I smothered a snort.

"A Maren and Sally story? Don't leave us hanging." Cyrus wrapped his arms around me and shared his body heat.

Operation diversion, success!

"It's a good one." Manny chuckled. "The girls weren't supposed to go to the river alone; naturally, they hopped on their bikes and rode down there every chance they got. How old were you when you tried to hop the levees?"

"Fifteen." Sally was three years into stealing and knocking back Jack Daniels. She'd mixed a lethal combo of Jack and ice in water bottles, which you might mistake for iced tea. If you didn't smell it.

"Yeah. Sounds right," Manny said.

"Pardon my ignorance, but what's levee hopping? Is it like bar hopping?" Cyrus sounded jovial, if you didn't look into his hard-as-flint eyes.

"Only because you need to be drunk to do it," I muttered. He pinched my butt.

"You ride up the side of a levee and project yourself in the air. With any luck, you land on the top of the next one. It's almost like flying, but way more dangerous. The girls shouldn't have tried it," said the brother who taught me how to do it.

"Sally was smashed," I said. When wasn't Sally smashed? I wrinkled my nose at the tangible memory of summer heat and the smell of whiskey, dead fish, and muddy water. "She had a spectacular flight, but a rough landing. Broke her ankle, although we didn't know it at the time. All we knew was she couldn't ride her bike because it hurt so much."

"Maren came straight home to fetch someone, even though she knew she was in big trouble," Manny said.

"It was a long ride home up a steep bluff, and I heard Oma's lecture the whole way."

"Snaps for Maren for being a good friend. As I dimly recall, you were grounded for the rest of the summer," Manny said.

"Yep, and it was only June."

The judgmental crease between Ivy's eyebrows stood out like a scar in the firelight.

Manny stroked his chin. "I ran into Sally a few years back. Three sheets to the wind, par for the course. She repeated the story like I'd never heard it. Said when Maren disappeared over the levee, she wondered if Maren would bail, and she said she wouldn't have blamed her."

"I'd never do that."

"Sally said after that day she trusted you with her life," Manny said.

"Oh, puh-leeze." An exasperated look flitted across Ivy's face. Ivy wouldn't trust me to hold her purse in the middle of a police station.

"My Maren is loyal." Cyrus raised his wine mug in a toast. "Guess that makes me a lucky man."

Ivy didn't puh-leeze us again, but her expression spoke volumes. We called it a night.

While the lucky man showered, my phone pinged.

```
To: Witch Maren
From: Alexander Filippidis
RE: The Perfect Evening

  Is it a night around the fire staring at the
  stars? Did you worry about getting burned
  like witches in the past, or did you think
  it was romantic? If the past is prologue,
  the latter.

  Think again, Maren. Harper's pretty, like
  the bouquet, but deadly.
```

I almost dropped the phone. Who was Alexander? I stared at the message like it was a scrying bowl that would show me the answer. A jealous ex who wanted to torment me? I called the one person who might have an answer. Sally answered on the first ring.

"Lo, you." The words slurred together, a hazard of calling after cocktail hour, but this was an emergency.

"Hello, you." I paced the room. "Do we know anyone named Alexander?"

"Alexander isn't a Bluffs name." Sally giggled. Older Bluff residents said that when someone mentioned an outsider.

"Was I ever involved with anyone named Alexander?"

"I'm not Hookup-a-pedia, Mare. Some of those guys had no names."

"What about Finley's former bandmates?" They held a grudge when my credit cards stopped financing their gigs.

"Now, you're talking a cast of thousands. Still don't remember any Alexanders."

Me either. Drunk or sober, Sally had the memory of an elephant; she'd heard every misadventure I'd ever had, no matter how fleeting, including the sad tale of the Caernarfon druid. If Sally didn't remember him, Alexander and I had never crossed paths.

"What's going on?"

"I'm getting weird texts."

"Happens to me all the time. Cyrus will know how to block them. Even old Beeb can do that."

No doubt Cyrus could fix it with one hand tied behind his back. His mad internet skills, however, might dredge up more of my checkered past from the slime.

"Beeb, honey, fix me another one," Sally said.

It was three-sheets-to-the-wind o'clock. But the question still nagged. If Alexander wasn't an old hookup, who was he?

"What else is happening?" Sally moved on from my mundane stalking problem. "Heard about the necklace. What a birthday present. When are you coming home? I so want a picture of me wearing it. Beeb, I said, top me off!"

Necklace or anchor around my neck? "End of April because in other news, Cyrus thinks we should live together, starting now."

"That's different how?"

"Technically, he's my tenant," I said. "But he wants me to move into the Timmerwilke place, and, you know, travel with him on business and stuff."

"Brav-freaking-O, but will he put a ring on it?" Sally subscribed to the Riverton code, where marriage was the pinnacle of social success. She was waiting for her parents to approve of BeeBee.

"I'm not ready." My heart leaped into my throat, almost strangling me. I tamped it back into my chest.

A disapproving hum. "Whatever! If you let him slip away, you'll get no sympathy from this girl. But, back to the present. What are you gonna do in Chicago for six weeks?"

"Shop." Wasn't that the promise I made by accepting the black card?

"I'm down for it. How about I take the train up, and we hit the shops?"

"Uh, sure. Spend a night or two. The house is on the lake. It has an amazing home theatre. Girly movie night?" Would Cyrus object? It was one way to test his patience for living together.

We agreed on a shopping plan and discussed dates. I said a hasty goodbye when the shower stopped. Shock is a man with damp hair in a cashmere robe carrying a gun.

"Are we shooting varmints tonight, Harper?"

He cocked his head and considered the question. "I hope not, but you never know."

"Let's not go there yet." Showing him the latest message was a definite no-go.

He placed the gun on the bedside stand. "I'll put it back in the safe in the morning."

"Right." I crossed the room, wrapped my arms around his waist, and pressed my face into the robe's vee. His skin was warm and moist. Bergamot's heady scent made my head spin in a way the mulled wine hadn't. I always associated Cyrus and bergamot with prosperity, forgetting bergamot's other magickal property. With the right spell, it encouraged peace and harmony.

Better work on that.

"We're here for fun, so let's get to it."

"See, told you I was a lucky man."

He swept me into an old-fashioned dance around the room. Perhaps the Greier thing made me paranoid, but how long could we dance around the Alexander flame without getting burned?

THE MAGICIAN

SUNDAY, MARCH 13

I SAT CROSS-LEGGED ON the bedroom floor, trying to meditate. Beyond the French doors, the lake morphed from cold, battleship gray to soft eggshell blue. The sunlight catching the waves created a path of diamonds from the horizon to the shoreline. The view teased me with the potential for tranquility, but tranquility slid through my fingers. Cyrus returned the gun to the safe before I woke, but its ghost lingered. The poison bouquet and Alexander's creepy messages played on an endless loop, like an old-time damsel-in-distress movie.

TRY HARDER, OR KISS BLISS GOODBYE.

"In the name of the Goddess, Lady of the Crescent Moon and Queen of Earth, bless you for the gifts of love, light, and peace. Bless this daughter of earth and guide me as I move through your world. Open my heart to your mysteries. So mote it be."

Prayer didn't stop the film and bring up the house lights.

I pulled my daily Tarot card, meaning to ask *What is my guidance for the day?* Instead, I blurted out, "What do I need to know about Alexander Filippidis?"

GOOD QUESTION.

I activated my Bio-Bit's recorder to document my interpretation and turned over the card.

I tapped my forefinger against my upper lip. A major arcana card might be a person in your life. Sometimes, when I didn't imagine Cyrus as *The Knight of Pentacles* or a Fae Prince, I fancied him as *The Magician*.

Why not? He checked all the boxes. *The Magician* was a beautiful man in his prime with dark curly hair, someone coming into his power. With one hand pointing to the sky and the other to the ground, he personified "as above, so below." Roses and lilies suggested he was committed to passion and making life beautiful. *The Magician* was the card of the inventor, the traveler, and the entrepreneur. An apt description of Cyrus Harper.

But an upside-down *Magician* was a whole different story. Older decks called him *The Juggler*, a traveling huckster or a con man playing a shell game, a trickster manipulating people. His belt was an Ouroboros, a serpent with its tail in its mouth, suggesting a continuous cycle of devouring and regenerating itself. A *Magician* reversed warned about someone who shed his skin whenever it was convenient. He was all show, no truth. What you saw wasn't what you got.

Cunning and deception! Oh, yeah. My ex-lover Finley had turned up in readings as a *Magician* reversed too many times to count. *Untrustworthy and conniving!* I'd ignored the message. The keywords popcorned in my brain and roiled my stomach.

Don't go down that road again.

The Magician reversed could appear trustworthy to gain your trust. Didn't Alexander's smarmy compliments and twisted insights scream, *Trust me; I'll save you from Cyrus?* Like Finley, he meant to keep me off balance by suggesting deceit surrounded me. My head spun. I needed to be cautious.

When *The Magician* reversed appeared in the *Wheel of Fortune* reading that solved the Greier murder, Cyrus called him the anti-Cyrus. I suspected it was still true.

I rapped my knuckles on the card. What had I expected from the reading? A reason to warn Cyrus another anti-Cyrus lurked on the perimeter? He already knew. A name and address? The cards didn't work that way. They warned about a problem on the horizon and the clues for recognizing it; the rest was up to me. I uploaded my musings to *BoSsBlog* so I could review them later.

Alexander's ghost clamped an icy hand on Inner Voice.

ARE YOU SURE YOU'RE NOT GOING DOWN THE SAME OLD FINLEY GARDEN PATH? THE MAGICIAN REVERSED IS ALSO A BEAUTIFUL MAN WITH BLACK, CURLY HAIR. HE'S TOO SMART FOR HIS OWN GOOD. WHAT GAME IS CYRUS HARPER PLAYING, ANYWAY?

Shut up! Cyrus didn't hurl insults at himself. Besides, he was with me when all these messages arrived.

GIRLFRIEND! CYRUS HAS THE TECHNICAL CHOPS TO FAKE A TEXT MESSAGE AND MINIONS TO DO IT IF HE CAN'T BE BOTHERED.

Don't and won't believe it, Troublemaker. If Cyrus wanted to get rid of me, he'd hop on his plane and go to another one of his houses. I didn't even know the addresses. So, there!

The cynical conversation came to a screeching halt when Hal, Cyrus's virtual assistant, pinged. "Time to get ready for tea, Maren. You leave in one hour and thirty minutes."

A shiver ran down my spine. Tea with Cyrus's mother and sister alarmed me as much as *The Magician* reversed.

TEA TIME

"Aunt Maren!" Gertie's whimper brought our blistering Pease Porridge Hot game to a screeching halt. "Those people are scary."

"Just a bunch of crazies. Chicago's full of 'em." Richard pulled up to The Drake Hotel. A small crowd congregated against the Plexiglass enclosing the Art Nouveau portico.

"I don't like them." Gertie put her hands against the window to hide the scary people.

Six people wore skeleton or zombie face masks instead of regular medical masks. Sunglasses concealed the rest of their faces, and hats hid their hair. A seventh man, all in black with reflecting sunglasses and a gaiter pulled over his nose, waved. My mouth went dry. A tingle started in my chest and spread to my arms and legs. Something wasn't right. I swallowed the urge to tell Richard to drive away.

IT'S NOTHING! YOU'RE MEETING YOUR LOVER'S MOTHER FOR THE FIRST TIME. JUST NERVES.

"Aunt Maren!" Tears welled up in Gertie's eyes, and her lower lip quivered. "I'm afraid."

"They're being silly," Ivy snapped. "Don't be a baby, Gertrude."

WAY TO BE A MOTHER, IVY!

"It's okay, sprout. I'm here. And Richard, too." Brave words notwith-standing, the Man in Black looked unacquainted with silliness. My spit turned to vinegar, and the blood in my veins coagulated into ice.

The car radio announced the hotel's DoorMed deemed us virus-free. A doorman in a uniform, more Buckingham Palace than Chicago Gold Coast, opened the car door. With Skeletons and Zombies afoot, I'd have preferred a Seal Team Six uniform.

"Welcome to The Drake, Ms. Lilienthal. We've been expecting you. Your party is already here."

Great. Tardiness always impresses people.

"Thank you." I hopped out. Global warming had come to Chicago; my Burberry trench coat felt like a parka. Sweat slid down my spine. I held out my arms and swung Gertie to the ground, giving her a reassuring squeeze. She buried her face in my coat.

"Hey, Maren!"

I turned. Who knew me in downtown Chicago?

The Man in Black thumped his fist against the Plexiglass. "Where's Cyrus today?"

Skeletons and Zombies peppered me with questions.

"You wearing the necklace?"

"Heading back to Hawaii soon?"

"You following the Greier trial?"

"Are you a witch?"

"Give us a smile, Maren."

"Hey, little girl." The Man in Black pointed at Gertie, who burrowed deeper into the folds of my coat. "Don't you know it's dangerous to hang out with witches?"

A Skeleton lifted her mask and spat. Saliva splattered the Plexiglass barrier. "Thou shalt not suffer a witch to live!"

I clutched Gertie's hand and dashed through the Plexiglass tunnel into the lobby.

Ivy scurried after us. "Who are those people? Does that man know you?"

Would I be running if I knew those people?

The panting doorman caught up with us. "I am so sorry, Ms. Lilienthal. I'll send security right out. A left here takes you to the Palm Court. The hostess will show you to your table."

The Palm Court was secluded and had no windows. Fine by Gertie and me. It shielded us from the Skeletons and the Zombies outside. Blinding white pillars and tablecloths kept it from being gloomy. A beautiful lime-stone fountain dominated the center of the room. A bronze urn, at the center of the fountain, held a ten-foot-tall spray of white flowers. Their faint fragrance scented the air. Gertie released her death grip on my hand and coat.

A hostess in a chic black dress wound her way through the tables. "Ms. Lilienthal, welcome to The Palm Court. Please, follow me."

Her stiletto heels clip-clopping on the marble floor and the tea drinkers' well-modulated voices wove through a string quartet's dulcet melody. It was all so civilized, making me doubt someone had spat and called me names.

Three women — Cyrus's sister, Cassandane; a short and plump woman with thick, dark hair clipped close and Cyrus's eyes and nose; and a girl Gertie's age — watched us cross the room. Our table was in a prime location next to the fountain.

BE CAREFUL. DON'T TRIP AND FALL INTO THE FOUNTAIN.

When I reached the table without embarrassing myself, I stuck out my hand to spare us fake cheek-kissing.

Oriana Rossellini's eyes focused like laser beams on me, sparing a glance at Ivy. I almost saw a word cloud appear over her head. *Why didn't Cyrus pick someone like the blonde?* Sure, every mother coveted Ivy's cool Nordic looks and never-a-wrong-step demeanor for their boy. *Tough, Doctor Rossellini. You're stuck with me. For now.* Pretty sure relationship-assassin appeared somewhere on Dr. Rossellini's CV. The skeletons and zombies could take lessons in terrifying people from her.

"Maren, dear, so lovely to meet you at last." Dr. Rossellini rose from the gold-gilt chair and went for the cheek brush despite my best efforts.

"Same," I said. At last? A reference to my tardiness?

"Don't you look lovely today?" Cassandane embraced me. "Almost glowing."

Anxiety sweating did that.

"I don't think I've ever seen you in pink."

Translation: you only wore witch-black in Austin. Wonder what she'd say if I told her *I don't always wear black. Sometimes I wear nothing at all. Witches call it sky-clad.*

Cool it.

Dr. Rossellini gestured toward the chair between her and Cassandane. Well and truly trapped, I gingerly took my seat, fearing I might knock over the crystal water goblets or send the china crashing to the floor.

Safely seated, I gestured to Gertie. "I'm twinning with my niece, Gertrude. This is her mother, my sister-in-law, Ivy Lilienthal. Doctor Rossellini and Cassandane and Harper Álvarez."

Cassandane and Ivy sized each other up. Gertie and Harper bonded at first glance. Harper, a Palm Court veteran, dragged Gertie to the fountain to look at the fish.

"Cassandane says she met you in Texas. At parties. Cassandane isn't usually a fan of parties. I can't tell you how many times she's told me parties are a waste of time."

Only the parties I attended. Not like old Gregarious the Great. Cyrus never met a party he didn't enjoy.

Cassandane gave her dark curls a shake. I recognized her *Please, Mother!* look, and I expected Oma would, too. The attempt at a conversational shift also rang a bell. "I couldn't remember the last time we saw each other."

Why would she remember? If we ever exchanged hellos at a party, we'd have counted it a lengthy conversation.

"Then it came to me. Last year's Fourth of July party at Johnson Towers. You know, the place on Lady Bird Lake."

I'd been there because I was sleeping with a resident; hopefully, I hadn't been too blasted and done something embarrassing.

"It was wonderful, wasn't it? You should have been there, Mom. Austin shoots fireworks from Lady Bird Lake, and the people who own the penthouse threw a party. The fireworks were at eye level right outside the window. And no mosquitos. Not to mention, air-conditioning is always a plus for July in Texas."

"It was trippy," I added.

"Cyrus was supposed to come," Cassandane said.

To tea?

"He was at the ranch, and I invited him. At the last minute, he decided to go to Lawrence's party. Just think, you might have met him months earlier."

Had someone drugged her? Pretty sure she'd have gone into full kamikaze mode to prevent me from meeting anyone, much less Cyrus.

She leaned toward me, her lips forming the ghost of Cyrus's contagious smile. "Cyrus should do fireworks on Lake Michigan at Harp headquarters. Host an open-air event for the public and a by-invitation-only party in the CPH offices."

YOU CAN TAKE THE GIRL OUT OF MARKETING, BUT YOU CAN'T TAKE MARKETING OUT OF THE GIRL.

"Maybe."

"You can help me persuade him."

I almost choked on a swallow of water. When had we become allies? The server brought the tea service, but I was still hacking when Harper and Gertie returned to the table. The girls might have been twins with their dark hair and eyes. Harper had the curly hair that ran in Cyrus's family, and Gertie's hair was stick straight, but the resemblance was uncanny.

"Mom, can I spend the night with Gertie at Uncle Cyrus's?" Harper said.

"Uncle Cyrus has guests." Cassandane mouthed *sorry* to me. "Gertie can spend the night with us if it's OK with her mother."

Harper, only eight, had mastered the teenage I-can't-be-lieve-you-said-something-so-stupid expression. In case her mother missed it, she added, "Our house is boring. Uncle Cyrus has a bowling alley, a theatre, and a soda machine."

And pinball machines, a pool table, a ping-pong table, and a popcorn machine. Shangri-La for kids and geeks.

"He has guests," Cassandane repeated with a stern look.

The adults stared at me. I was slow on the uptake. It was a test. One I'd already failed. Could I make amends?

"Uhm, I think it would be fine with Cyrus. He's always saying how much he misses the kids."

"Yay," Gertie and Harper said, settling the matter before they tucked into the children's tea service. They'd chosen hot chocolate rather than tea and bypassed tea sandwiches in favor of Orange Creamsicle Macarons and Strawberry Shortcake Bellini. Excellent choice.

If I so much as looked at, much less ate, the Salmon Mousse or the Thai Spiced Chicken Salad Tartlet, I'd barf. Forgoing the opportunity to make a great first impression, I sipped the Montagne Bleue tea. It delivered on its promise of a delicious blend of black tea, honey, lavender, berries, and rhubarb. What would Plaza patrons think about high tea?

Ivy sampled the tea dainties, sipped Big Ben English breakfast tea, and pronounced everything delightful. I envisioned her and her friends cooing and gossiping over tea and dressing their daughters in tea dresses to get them prepared for Cotillion. Yep, tea at the Plaza was something to pursue. I surreptitiously slipped the phone from my bag and sent a message to myself. Gah! I was turning into Cyrus.

Ivy quizzed Doctor Rossellini about young Cyrus, which ought to have been my job. Did they think less of me for the oversight?

"I was finishing my dissertation on Cyrus II when I was pregnant with him," Doctor Rossellini said. "So, I was adamant about his name. We called him Cyrus the Great, King of the Four Quarters of the World."

THAT EXPLAINS A LOT.

"I've called him that a time or two," I said.

"Have you?"

BRR.

"She was working on the dissertation long before Cyrus," Cassandane said. "I'm named after Cyrus the Great's wife. So, what else could she name our little brother but Darius?"

The server brought fresh tea while the Harper women interrogated me about the Hawaiian coffee plantation.

"Looks dreamy. Cyrus sent us the link to the realtor's website," Cassandane said.

"It would be perfect for Christmas." Doctor Rossellini took a dainty sip of tea. "The ranches are nice and all, but *Lōkahi* looks like paradise."

Christmas? Long-term planning was a Harper family trait. If the Harper women didn't have me trapped between them, I'd have hightailed it back to Riverton.

"Mother! Cyrus and Maren may already have Christmas plans."

Doctor Rossellini's and Ivy's faces mirrored my surprise at the statement. Almost as if they didn't expect us to be together at Christmas. Couldn't blame them; I had my doubts.

"Uh ... I ... uh ... we haven't discussed Christmas." *You're in big trouble, Harper. You shoulda warned me.*

"By the way, I ran into Gavin and Connor," Cassandane said in the awkward silence when the string quartet music faded. "They are so excited about The Plaza opening. You remember The Imag-i-Tron, Mom? Cyrus took the kids there at Christmas."

Did Cassandane run everything by her mother? Was I supposed to do the same?

"Oh, yes. A wonderful space. The children had a lovely time."

"Maren's family owns The Plaza in Riverton. People can rent Bio-Bits there. Everyone goes maskless the whole time, like when you were a girl."

Dr. Rossellini nodded and looked puzzled. Her expression seemed to ask, *What's your point, Cassandane?*

"Maren brokered a deal to bring The Imag-i-Tron to Riverton. It opens when? The beginning of summer vacation?"

"That's the goal." If Connor, Gavin, and the electricians could stumble onto the same page. What was Cassandane up to? Before I exploded like a volcano from the tension bubbling in my gut, I asked for directions to the ladies' room.

"I'll go with," Cassandane said. Another surprise. On the way, she said, "I know we haven't been best friends."

Understatement much? I groped for a diplomatic response. "Uh, well, different life paths."

"True, and I thought you hated children, a deal breaker for me. But seeing you with your niece tells a different story. Reminds me of Cyrus. Speaking of which..."

Yeah, speaking of which ... Was this when she told me to hit the road and leave her brother the hell alone?

"I love my brother."

YEP, GET OUT THE SUITCASES.

"If I know him, and I do, he's head over heels about you."

A brief pause when we reached the ladies' room and entered separate stalls to do our business. I fanned my face before opening the door.

She resumed the conversation at the sinks. "He started talking about a woman at Christmas; Rafael and I looked at each other and said BOOM! You're his type. Tall, exotic, and quirky. And you have the clavicle thing that drives him wild."

Clavicle thing? Damned by faint praise. I glanced in the mirror. The scooped neckline highlighted my prominent collarbone, a feature skinny people like me learned to endure.

"He's obsessed with clavicles," she said. "He told me — this is so Cyrus — clavicle comes from the Latin clavicula, meaning little key, but it also means to cradle. You know, hold gently and protectively."

Our first night together, he'd kissed his way across my collarbone, lingering and pronouncing it as fragile as a hummingbird. My cheeks caught fire at the memory, and I nodded, desperate for a witty, or even sensible, response.

"Damn. I just noticed. You look like the woman in the Chagalls," she said.

"The Chagalls?" Now I was confused.

"A Russian painter. Cyrus bought a bunch of his drawings." She shook her head. "Totally obsessed. He's been collecting them for years. They all have this woman with dark, curly hair. You could have been the model. Except he didn't know you when he started collecting them. Strange."

Strange, indeed.

"Anyway, I love my brother, but I'm not blind." Cassandane fluffed her hair, marginally less unruly than her brother's, but the Harper DNA was strong. "He's sweet and charming, but the most determined person I know."

Scruffy Poodle meet Rottweiler.

"He seems determined where you're concerned. Therefore, I hope you and I might become friends."

"Oh, me too." If my sincerity left something to be desired, she didn't seem to notice.

We returned to a Palm Court gone all a-twitter. Matrons, ladies who lunch, and ingenues (Maidens, Mothers, and Crones?) craned their necks toward our table where Cyrus, Manny, and Cassie's husband, Rafael, now sat. Their long-sleeve tee-shirts, basketball shorts, and leggings definitely didn't meet the Drake's high tea standards.

Our progress across the room cranked up the whisper volume to ten; my name and the word witch swirled through the crowd like tendrils of smoke. Some women fixed icy stares on me; others snapped photos with their phones. After an interminable time, we reached the table, and Cyrus pulled me into the chair next to him. Another spate of photos.

"What's happening?" I asked.

Cyrus and Manny exchanged glances.

"There's uh-uh a situation outside," Cyrus said. "Richard called me."

"Situation! It's a damn cluster-eff..." Manny glanced at Gertie and Harper. "A cluster-you-know-what."

"Yeah. Yeah." Cyrus dragged his fingers through his hair. "So, yeah. Viv called the security guys, and they're waiting for us. We're leaving. We've got several cars."

"Security? Like men with guns?" I asked.

"Something like that, yeah." He glanced around the room. "We need to go. It's getting wild outside. They're holding everyone in here until we leave and it calms down."

That explained the icy stares and whispers.

"What do you mean by several cars?" Dr. Rossellini said.

"Some are decoys. They're trying to throw the protestors off our tail." Cyrus raked his fingers through his hair again.

"Do you think they'll follow us?" Cassandane chewed her lower lip.

"I don't know, but we're going in different cars and driving fast. That's what the security guys suggested," Cyrus snapped.

Dr. Rossellini tapped her fingernail against the porcelain teacup. "Are you setting up a Princess Di in the Paris tunnel situation, Cyrus?"

"Not helpful, Mother."

"All I'm saying..."

"All you're saying is Darius would handle it better." He grabbed my arm and stood. "Let's go, babe."

Every eye in the room followed our departure. Whispers coiled around us like someone had dropped us in a box of serpents.

Burly men in dark suits waited at the Palm Court entrance. Four peeled away and surrounded Cyrus and me. A man in a suit and a gold hotel name badge wrung his hands and skipped alongside us.

"I'm so sorry, Mr. Harper," Hotel Guy said for the fifth or sixth time. "This shouldn't happen at The Drake. We called the police right away. The protesters vanished and returned a few minutes later. I am so sorry."

Cyrus nodded and kept walking.

Camera flashes exploded from the lobby. The staff, lips and hands clenched, had corralled the photographers into an alcove. They climbed onto tables and chairs to get a photo. The blue and red strobing of police cars parked out front intermingled with the flashes.

Outside, people shouted and pommeled the Plexiglas.

"Witch! Witch! Witch! Burn the witch!"

"Hey ho! Hey ho! Harper's gotta go!"

"Did they say. . ."

The chanting confirmed it. "Witch! Witch! Witch! Burn the witch."

"I told you it was a cluster-you-know-what out there," Manny muttered. Harper and Gertie whimpered; the pitiful sounds sliced through the pandemonium.

"Hey ho! Hey ho! Harper's gotta go!"

Cyrus leaned into me, his arm tightening around my waist, and whispered, "Keep it together for a few more minutes, and we'll be outta here. It helps if you think about pi."

"Apple or cherry?"

"Pi." He chuckled. More flashes.

"Witch! Witch! Witch!"

The chuckle died out. "3.14159265358979323846 ..."

Oh, PI!

Everyone panted to keep up with Cyrus, except for a hunky guy with a shaved head.

"Is this necessary?" I said to no one in particular.

"Hey ho! Hey ho!" A siren drowned out the chant.

"Yes, ma'am." Hunky Guy grinned and winked. "But don't worry. You'll be on your way in no time."

"Only staff can access the parking area where the cars are waiting," Hotel Guy said. "We're taking you through a restricted exit."

"Excellent," Cyrus said.

I glanced over my shoulder. Our families followed at a more sedate pace, each group with their bodyguards. Ivy and Manny shielded the girls; Rafael and Cassandane put Doctor Rossellini between them.

Hot air blasted us as we entered the kitchen. Sweat aside, it distracted Cyrus who ran a knowing eye over the fixtures and managed civilized compliments, which made Hotel Guy beam and forestalled another apology. The staff kept working, not intrigued by the group tromping through their domain.

"They're used to it," Hunky Guy whispered. "You wouldn't believe how many VIPs get escorted out through the kitchen. Last month, we smuggled out FinTech members in an armored truck."

"I see." Sweat popped out on my forehead and trickled from my armpits. Right before I melted like the Wicked Witch of the West, Hotel Guy gestured us into a service elevator, smelling of onions.

We emerged into the parking garage where two limousines with curtained windows and six Range Rovers were idling.

"Are we each getting our own cars or something?" I asked.

"No, ma'am, the limos are decoys to distract the crowd," Hunky Guy said.

Hey ho and *Burn the Witch* tolled like a faint church bell.

"Ignore them." Hunky Guy waved his hand in my face and pointed to the first Range Rover with windows tinted dark enough to be a black hole. "See, there's your escort. You and Mr. Harper are in the second car. Third car for the kids and their family. Another escort car. Fifth car for the three adults, and another escort."

He sauntered to the first limo and slapped the hood. The driver lowered the window.

"Show time. Pull up front and stop. Don't leave until Mac calls." He repeated the slapping process with the second limo. "Give it ten before heading down. When you hit the street, honk twice, and peel out. Call when you hit Lake Shore Drive."

He returned to Cyrus and me. "Ready?"

Cyrus nodded.

"It was a small crowd when we arrived," I said to no one in particular. "Just six people."

"There's more now." Cyrus pulled me into the car after him.

"Pardon me, Miss Lilienthal. Afraid we'll need to get up close and personal. I'm Beckett Smith." Hunky Guy slid in next to me, shielding me from the window with his body.

What was the etiquette here? Oma's lessons hadn't covered bodyguard protocol. "Hi, Beckett."

A guard squeezed in beside Cyrus. Another took the driver's seat; a fourth guy hopped into the front passenger seat.

"Don't worry. We've handled worse. And this car is one bad boy." Beckett patted the door. "Bullet and blast proof top to bottom. Soundproof too."

He slammed the door closed, cutting off *Burn the Witch* and *Harper's Gotta Go*.

"Push comes to shove, I've got my friend here." Beckett opened his coat; he wore a holstered gun. "The other guys are carrying, too."

"Relax, babe. These guys know what they're doing." Cyrus looked up from his phone where he'd started punching out messages. "We'll be home in about twenty-five minutes."

The car exited the parking garage into an alley. Five minutes later, we made the sharp turn onto US-41 and picked up speed. Twilight had spread over the city, casting dark, purple shadows. The preferred time for creepy crawlies, like vampires, skeletons, zombies, and other ghouls.

My phone pinged, and I jumped. Who would call or text me on Sunday? Another ping. The Salmon Mousse I hadn't eaten curdled in my stomach. A third ping.

"Someone's popular," Beckett said.

"Might be Manny," Cyrus muttered as his phone blew up.

I fished the phone from my purse. My finger hovered over the screen, reluctant to commit to a swipe. Mentally crossing my fingers, I brought it to life. I'd missed several messages.

Sunday, March 13

Alexander:

4:15 PM: Where are you, Maren?

4:16 PM: The tea service ended 15 minutes ago. Come out and play!

4:20 PM: Ah, the boy genius to the rescue. Don't be shy. Come on out. Both of you. My friends want to see you.

4:30 PM: A limo? How very hoity-toity. Can't believe I fell for that old trick.

4:32 PM: See you next time? Remember, you need to be lucky every time. I need to be lucky once.

4:35 PM: BTW. Pictures don't do you justice. You'd make a beautiful corpse.

A picture of me holding Gertie's hand as we arrived at The Drake filled the screen. Mouth open; eyes wide; panic twisting my features, I was the proverbial deer in the headlights. Sweet Goddess, I had a stalker. Only celebrities had stalkers. I handed my phone to Cyrus.

"Fuck," he said.

PROFLIGATE SON

MONDAY, MARCH 14

WITCH! WITCH! WITCH! BURN the witch!

Skeletons and Zombies capered through a hazy landscape, narrowly avoiding pools of phlegm. In the distance, flesh slammed against Plexiglass.

Hey ho. Hey ho. Harper's gotta go!

The Man in Black cackled. Fluorescent green, horizontal pupils glinted through his sunglasses. Demon eyes. Or a magician's.

Come out and play.

I jerked awake. The bright morning sunlight spilling through the French doors gave the phantoms pause. I reached for Cyrus.

Hey ho. Hey ho. Harper's gotta go!

The pillow and sheets beside me were smooth and cold. The Man in Black nodded as if he expected it.

See you next time!

My stomach knotted.

Witch! Witch! Witch! Burn the witch!

Skeletons and Zombies lurked in the hallway. Or something much worse. Alexander? I pulled the duvet over my head; my rapid breathing made it too hot to hide for long. Ivy's braying laugh snaked up the stairs and parked at the foot of the bed.

OK. CALM DOWN. PEOPLE, NOT GHOULS, ARE IN THE HOUSE.

I slid one foot onto the floor. Then another. I darted into my closet like hellhounds were on my tail, wrapped myself in a robe, and bolted. I'd rather deal with Ivy and her annoying laugh than stay here alone.

"Hey, babe, come in here," Cyrus called as I dashed down the hall.

Neither a request nor a challenge, it was a directive from someone who expected the world to snap to attention. And I did, muttering gratitude to the Goddess that he found me before the monsters and saved me from Ivy before I had coffee.

The cream-colored office welcomed me like a protective amulet. Pops of color — a navy and pink oriental rug and lemon-yellow couch — declared No Skeletons and Zombies here. Five gigantic monitors dominated a work table pushed against a bank of windows. Sunlight fumigated the night terrors.

Cyrus, purplish-black smudges beneath his eyes, spun his chair away from the table. A grin spread across his face. "Hey, there's my Kinky Bear."

His crazy attachment to my floor-length camel-colored cashmere robe reassured me the nightmare was well and truly banished.

"Can I call you Kinky Bear?" He rubbed his chin. "Is it inappropriate?"

Call me anything, just call me! "When it's just us, sure. But don't let Oma hear you."

"Definitely not, yeah." He shuddered. "When Oma's around, it'll be K-Bear."

We had different nightmares. I smoothed the robe over my hips and changed the subject. "How did this get in the closet? Did Johnny pick it up from home?"

Johnny Marlow, gofer extraordinaire, transported everything from burner phones to multi-million-dollar necklaces at Cyrus's behest. So why wouldn't he fetch my robe? Still, the idea of Johnny pawing through my closet creeped me out. I formed my objection, but Cyrus cut me off at the pass.

"Nope. Viv called Célia Lisette's, and they sent one."

Nobody needed two cashmere robes at $3000 a pop. Extravagant, but not creepy. Cyrus taught master classes in real extravagance.

"I asked her to send one to all my places."

I didn't know how many places he had, but it added up to a real obsession. "Isn't that over the top?"

"How so? It keeps you warm and makes me happy. I call it win-win."

End of discussion. The fresh coffee smell distracted me; my nose twitched. Cyrus kept a complicated-looking espresso machine in his office. Without asking, he rolled his chair to the machine and started a cup.

"Did you sleep at all last night?" I asked. The cold, smooth sheets answered the question, but it never hurt to check. He'd rubbed my back to help me fall asleep, and it took a while.

"Grabbed a couple right here. A rough one, yeah."

Patting his knee with one hand, he beckoned with the other. When I came closer, he grasped the belt on my robe, reeling me onto his lap so I faced him with my knees on either side of the chair.

"This is more like it," he said, initiating a serious nightmare-banishing spell.

One hand cupped my chin, the other burrowed into my hair as his mouth met mine. He smelled like heaven with the faint fragrance of musky oud, cedar, and patchouli, of wind and gold. His cologne ought to be illegal; it ignited something so exciting and deep, no one (certainly not me) could resist it. I was Scheherazade, and he was The Thousand and One Nights.

In a nano-second, he shrugged away clothes until his skin burned against mine in an onslaught of lips, teeth, fingers, and nails. When his palms cupped my hips, we surrendered to each other. Time, children's laughter, the buzz of conversation slinking up the stairway, and frolicking zombies and skeletons vanished. The universe itself ceased to exist. There was only us. Best banishing spell ever!

Afterward, I rested my chin on his shoulder and studied the five monitors. The coffee was already cold and useless. "What's all this?"

It was only seven AM, but one monitor scrolled endless streams of numbers in sets of four separated by periods; the second screen rolled through a list of names. Every few seconds, virtual push-pins updated locations on a world map on a third screen. The fourth screen displayed my phone messages. An expired Face2Face chat session with Viv was on the fifth.

"You were hacked," he said.

"Right. You said you fixed that after the bouquet."

"I moved *BoSsBlog* and gave you an email behind Harp's firewall, but I didn't change out your phone. Should have figured he'd hack it, too." He grimaced and grabbed a cell phone from the desk. "New phone and number; but remember, phones aren't secure."

"Back up. He hacked my phone? How?"

"Yep. We found the breadcrumbs." He bared his teeth in a silent snarl. "I imagine he's using Zeus, which routs a phone's defenses, including encryption. It puts your text and voice communications, location data, photos and videos, notes, and browsing history at his disposal. It even can activate the camera and the microphone. And you won't notice a thing. Complete remote personal surveillance at the push of a button."

"How is that even legal?"

"It's not, but Zeus insists its software and support are available only to sovereign states for law enforcement and intelligence purposes. There's evidence that's not true."

The pressure in my chest made it hard to breathe. My sweet Goddess, all my secrets were exposed to a psychopath.

"He picked up your texts to Oma and Sally. I think it's how he knew you'd be at The Drake."

"He's a real stalker." I forced myself to breathe. Someone stalking me sounded ridiculous. Self-important. Yet, Cyrus wasn't joking, and the bouquet and protestors were real.

"'Fraid so." Cyrus rubbed his eyes. "Oh, and I reset your Bit and archived and encrypted the data."

The tightness in my chest threatened to crush my lungs, yet my arms and legs felt hollow. *Witch! Witch! Witch! Burn the witch!* No, not going there. I pointed at the screens. "What are you doing?"

"Trying — not successfully — to track down Alexander."

Cyrus unsuccessful? I glanced out the window, checking for flying pigs.

"He used a different phone for each text. Even the rash of texts he sent yesterday. I told you about burner phones, yeah?"

"Yep. This guy knows about burner phones?"

"Oh, yeah. He's a clever S.O.B." His eyebrows drew together, his eyes narrowed, both a precursor to a rage you never wanted directed at you.

WATCH OUT, ALEXANDER!

"Those numbers are the IP addresses he pushed his texts through."

My face probably looked as blank as my mind.

"Every computer has an IP address. It tells your internet provider's name, city, and ZIP or area code. Anytime you go anywhere on the internet, it's like signing a guestbook. Your IP address is the signature."

"I see." Not really.

"But this guy's hacking into other people's computers and using their IP addresses." He ran his fingers through his hair and gestured at the other screens. "I traced the names and locations. Useless, yeah. He can't be in seventeen different countries."

"I didn't get that many texts," I said, trying to be helpful.

"He bounced each text to hide his location." Cyrus scowled. "He's got the technical chops, yeah. But I'll find him."

"Of course, you will." Why wouldn't he?

"There's this." His fingers flew over the keyboard, and the Face2Face page switched to *Tattleverse*.

"Her again," I muttered.

"Her, yeah." He tapped his fingers on the desk, his nervous tell. While I read, I covered his hand with mine to stop the tapping.

Profligate Son

Nosy Parker. The Roman philosopher Marcus Tullius Cicero opined: It is not only arrogant, but profligate for a man to disregard the world's opinion.

Chicago billionaire Cyrus Harper ought to heed that advice. He and his girlfriend, Maren Lilienthal, arrived via his private jet at Chicago's Midway airport on Saturday amid a severe economic downturn. Figures released last week show an 8.5% unemployment rate for the city, three points higher than the national average.

Lilienthal nailed travel chic in her $2000 Dior sweatshirt, black Balenciaga skinny jeans at $625, and Givenchy's 'Urban Street sneakers weighing in at an eye-watering $1200. Harper's newest babe appeared to color coordinate with her billionaire boyfriend, who rocked an equally expensive black sweater, jeans, and boots. With Illinois's maximum unemployment weekly payment of $533, Lilienthal's outfit cost almost twice what an unemployed worker receives in a month.

"How did they know what I wore?"

"They pay airport workers to report things." His arms tightened around me. "Keep going."

Two Mercedes GLS class SUVs, going for a cool $150k each, whisked the lovebirds and their friends away. Word on the street says Lilienthal is inspecting the Harper beginner mansion on the lake, which he purchased for $11.4 million after the Harp IPO in 2038. Who begrudges him a modest seven-bedroom love nest on a half-acre of prime lakefront real estate when we're all struggling to find a seat on the El and afford a two-bedroom condo in a high-rise facing the freeway?

She bludgeoned readers with dollar signs and taunted them with amounts guaranteed to dazzle and infuriate.

People are no longer tolerating tech zillionaires' high-handed ways. When Harper's girlfriend arrived at The Drake Hotel for tea with the Harper matriarch, protestors met the so-called witch as she entered the hotel. If she'd cast a banishing spell, the protestors proved to her she might not be the powerful witch she imagines herself to be. Lilienthal scurried inside like a scared mouse, and the hotel called Chicago's finest to chase the protestors away. The crowd remained undaunted, picketing the hotel with placards that expressed their disgust with Harper's high-handed ways and his girlfriend's new-age pretensions.

Photos showed Skeleton and Zombie protestors carrying professional-looking signs. One was a photo of Cyrus with a bull's eye superimposed over his face. The words *Witches sleep with the devil* encircled the waltzing photo from the Beaux Artes Ball. The signs blared a cornucopia of grievances and wild accusations.

Strabovirus-3: A Harp conspiracy?
Jakarta Panic makes Cyrus Harper richer!
Salem 1692: 19 hanged; a good beginning!
Proud witch hunter.
Ditch the Witch.
Witch! Witch! Witch!
I covered my ears, but the chanting didn't stop
Burn the witch! Hey ho. Hey ho. Harper's gotta go!

When I'd done the *Wheel of Fortune* reading last month and the *Judgement* card came up, Cyrus had asked, how does that card play into it? I'd blithely answered, if we can learn from the past and accept our choices have consequences, we can heal each other and rise. In my wildest imagining, consequences never came to this.

"They hate us, don't they?" A slow burn started in my stomach and inched toward my heart.

SCREW THIS WITCH-SHAMING SCRIBBLER! SCREW THE DAMN PROTESTORS. SCREW ALEXANDER, AND SCREW THE THREE-FOLD LAW.

The desire to hex someone scorched me, and Cyrus was already a five-alarm fire.

"Not necessarily. I spoke to the police." Cyrus massaged his forehead. "Those protestors were hired. Someone placed an ad for actors. Two hundred dollars for a couple hours of work. They met a guy with a panel truck in a nearby parking garage, and he handed out the masks and signs."

"Do you believe it?"

"They all told the same story, and the police located the ad. Posted on a job website."

"Is Nosey Parker behind it?"

"Can't pin it on her or anybody. A fake email was used to place the ad with a prepaid debit card. But I'm certain she knows something. I just need to prove it."

"Who the hell is she, anyway?" I screeched like a cartoon witch. "She slams you for having money, but I bet she gets paid plenty and doesn't refuse a dime. Why will no one admit to liking money, to enjoying it? It's like water. You can't live without it."

"Thank you. I needed to hear that."

I double-checked. Not even a crumb of sarcasm. I clicked the link on Nosey's name to see if her bio offered any clues.

The screen changed to a hipster coffee shop background with a superimposed watercolor portrait of a lady with an elaborate hair-do. Wearing a lilac evening dress with a black lace mantilla and holding a gold fan, she stared at the viewer; disdain distorted her delicate features. Graffiti scrawled on the coffee-shop floor said *This brain of mine is something more than mortal; as time will show.*

"Modesty isn't Nosey's strong suit."

"It's an Ada Lovelace quote, and Nosey's using a well-known portrait of Ada," Cyrus said.

"Ada Who?"

"Her father was a poet, Byron Somebody."

Ah, the mad, bad, and dangerous to know Lord Byron. An epitaph Alexander probably coveted.

"Ada's the Mother of Computer Programming," he continued. "She programmed for the world's first computer, Babbage's Analytical Engine, in the 1800s."

Interesting. Nosey's bio, like the photo, needled the reader.

Nosey Parker

A "working-class, educated gal" joined *Tattleverse* in 2041. With access to the greatest columnists and an army of gossip spiders, which she weaponized to ferret out the juiciest stories, Nosey became our most popular contributor. She maintains, "I am guilty of nothing but standing by my principles. If I ever regret my words (and I won't), I'll never regret the passion behind them." Her greatest fear is someone accusing her of trendiness. By 2043, Nosey's articles reached the gold standard of a million hits per day.

I snatched Cyrus's hand as it crept back to his tangled black curls. Kissing each long, elegant finger, I murmured, "I warned you. I can't love a bald man."

No grin answered my joke, just a wry expression. "I'm not a bad person, you know. No matter what they say, I'm not greedy. I do my part; I do my best."

He sounded as aggrieved as a child learning the truth about Santa, the Easter Bunny, and the Tooth Fairy in one fell swoop. I rubbed my cheek against his hand.

"For fuck's sake," he growled. "I'm sponsoring every school childhood nutrition program in the city. Expanded them from breakfast to lunch and dinner. Seven days a week, year-round."

"A good thing, for sure."

"I bought ten old motels and renovated each room into a micro apartment for the homeless." So much heat radiated from him, I half-expected the air-conditioning to kick on. "Not to mention, Meals on Wheels donations. I've done more than the damn government."

"Does anyone know?" He'd never mentioned his charitable work before today. If Manny knew about it, he'd have told me.

Cyrus cocked his head and considered the question. "I don't want my name plastered across the internet with a thousand vulgar stories about my generosity. That's not compassion; it's PR."

"Sure." But for Cyrus, anonymous no longer existed, as we'd discovered. "If the world doesn't know what you've done, there'll be more articles like this. I guarantee it."

A dramatic sigh led to a swipe at his hair; I stopped him mid-swipe. "I know, but I hate bragging."

"We'll figure something out; this isn't acceptable." CPH ought to have handled it and never allowed it to reach this point. I'd put Viv in touch with Uzma Chaudry, Oma's publicist, who was adept at making Oma shine without sounding braggy.

"We'll figure it out!" Cyrus's face brightened. "I like the sound of we. I promise you, I will track down this Alexander asshole to the gates of hell if necessary and make him regret even thinking your name."

"Yes, we will." I voiced my correction in the gentlest tone possible. "We'll track him down."

"We," he agreed.

Pressing against him so close my heart synched up with his, I whispered, "Hey, hey, hey, Harper's gotta stay."

"Witch! Witch! Witch. Love the witch," he said.

Ah! Transformation spells. Simple, yet effective.

BILLIONAIRE BARISTA

TUESDAY, MARCH 15

FOR A LILIENTHAL FAMILY lunch, it was civil. Gertie and the twins babbled about Virtual Reality games, dropping unmistakable hints about the basement game room. My cousins jabbered about the upcoming concert while Manny and Cyrus poked at each other about their March Madness picks. Ivy practiced her disdainful expression, not that she needed practice.

The phones exploded like IEDs. With no Oma to forbid it, the adults plucked the phones from their pockets. Manny scrolled and sucked in a breath before passing his phone to Cyrus, who never brought one to the table. (One of the little-known reasons Oma approved of him.) I leaned against Cyrus, reading over his shoulder, and choked on the soup.

"Not her again!"

Billionaire Barista!

Nosey Parker. Most people don't mix work and pleasure, but most people aren't Cyrus Harper. Dubbed "High tech's hunk," Harper recently whisked his lady love, Maren Lilienthal, to Hawaii's Big Island to recuperate from accusations of murdering a tech rival.

Simon Greier, a tech rival? Right, and the Riverton High Eagles rivaled the Chicago Bulls.

Charges were dropped after Harp Industry data pointed the finger at new suspects. Did Harper grease police palms? Or did the influential Lilienthal family pull strings? I'm just asking the questions...

Give me a break!

The loved-up beach bunnies took full advantage of all the fun the island offered, but they also toured several coffee plantations. Before jetting home to Chicago, Harper purchased the Mauna Kea Hamuka Coffee plantation and a nearby legacy estate. This gushing prose comes from a realtor website that caters to the rich and famous.

The incomparable private estate and family compound, known as Lōkahi, offers 600 feet of ocean frontage and four unique homes. Surrounded on three sides by the Pacific Ocean, an offshore reef protects it. The owners commissioned masterpieces from renowned Hawaiian artists for the home, and they convey. An international celebrity chef deemed the kitchen his favorite kitchen in the entire world! The meticulously designed and maintained landscaping will leave you breathless. Your privacy, anonymity, and security are all assured in this one-of-a-kind, historical property. The price for this gem? A cool $57 million. Harper won't need to slum in a $23K-a-night commercial property the next time a wild hair takes him to the Big Island.

Damn! Nosey wasted no time getting in the jabs.

The plantation in the heart of the Kona Coffee Belt produces up to 30,000 pounds of coffee a year and set Harper back another $24 million. One wonders if serfs, like the artwork, convey, or will it be a separate expenditure? Why shouldn't we be curious about Harper and his billions?

"Curiosity killed the cat, Nosey," I muttered.

An old brochure describes the plantation's signature coffee as having a deep, dark caramelized richness with notes of molasses, chocolate, and stout beer. Sounds delish! But don't line up at your favorite bistro just yet. Harper's spokesperson, Vivica Chastain, says Harper has no plans to continue marketing Mauna Kea Hamuka Coffee. Is it possible he doesn't want to stand in line with peasants to get his favorite brew? Can you hear Lilienthal saying à la Marie Antoinette, "Let them drink wine?"

If I ever doubted Nosey had us in her sights, this article squashed it.

"Does she know about the winery," I said.

"Probably." Cyrus growled and slammed his fist on the table, an opening salvo in an unspoken declaration of war.

My cousins jumped, and Ivy turned to Manny, who shook his head.

Cyrus stomped from the room.

The rest of us? We stuffed our faces with salad, Coconut-Tomato Bisque, and Croque Monsieur sandwiches and hoped it absolved us from acknowledging the elephant muttering into his phone from the next room.

"Real estate records are public." Manny cast a wary glance at the doorway. "Strictly speaking, the article wasn't libelous. It's all inference, and he can't do much about it."

UNLESS HE CALLS HIS BROTHER. DARIUS MIGHT DO PLENTY AND CALL IT GOOD FUN.

Please, let it be Viv on the other end of the call. On the off-chance Cyrus read my mind (which I sometimes suspected) and acted on it, I buried the Darius thought beneath mundane musings. How to fix my hair for the concert. What jewelry to wear? Time for a manicure? Take a nap and sink into oblivion?

Cyrus returned. Had he called Darius or Viv? He flashed his signature grin at the kids. Viv; he never smiled after speaking with Darius.

"Hey, guys, eat up. I downloaded the new Alien Vacation. How about we challenge these old dudes?" He hooked his thumb toward Manny and Julian. "Milkshakes for the winners sound good?"

Ivy's pitying smile chafed my last nerve. Yeah, he had a milkshake machine in his high-tech man cave. Sure, he *was* good with kids, but techies were kids at heart. Didn't prove a thing. The VR games and the milk-shake machine were total self-indulgences. Not a hint he wanted to procreate with anyone. Ivy, wearing a smug smile like the latest fashion accessory, nodded in my direction. *Not just anyone, but especially not you!*

Armageddon postponed, I excused myself and galumphed upstairs. With any luck, I'd avoid Ivy until dinner; then, off to the concert. Pregnant women, she'd announced, didn't attend rock concerts. I fell back onto the mattress, visions of Ivy and Nosey Parker spinning in my head.

GET OVER IT! NOTHING GOOD COMES FROM SULKING.

I sulked until the sun shuffled from the French doors overlooking the lake to the western windows facing the street.

Cyrus pranced into the bedroom, smacked my butt, and trumpeted, "Ready to party, girlfriend?"

I recognized the cocky "I won" grin. If it lightened his mood, I was all for it. "Milkshakes all around for your team?"

"We slaughtered them." He flopped on the bed beside me.

"Who could stand against your hand-eye coordination?" I cooed.

"Honed by years of practice on a hot keyboard."

After fretting all afternoon, I couldn't hold my tongue. "However, it boggles the mind. You went from killing rage to a virtual warrior in less than ten minutes. What did Viv say?"

His grin morphed into a smirk. "I told her we'll buy *Tattleverse* and shutter it."

"A spectacularly bad idea."

He shrugged. "Feels good."

"It confirms, in their pea brains, what they're saying about you."

"Maybe." The grin dimmed, and his shoulders slumped.

"It encourages future *Tattleverse*s to piss you off in hopes of a windfall."

"Probably."

I rubbed my nose against his. "Besides, I need you to save your pennies. What if another piece of royal jewelry comes on the market, and you decide I can't live without it?"

"Are you saying you won't throw a hissy fit the next time I give you a gift?"

"You'll do what you want, hissy fit or not. Just don't waste money on *Tattleverse*."

"I'll think about what you said, yeah." He gave me a long, satisfying kiss, and his hand crept under my sweatshirt.

I brushed the hair from his face. Too bad I couldn't brush or kiss away his *Tattleverse* aggravation. He would ponder what I said. He'd do the smart thing because that's how he operated. But the itch to retaliate would drive him crazy.

"But, for now, let's rock and roll, babe."

"Is rock and roll a euphemism for pre-concert sex, Mister Handsy?"

"Alas, no. I meant head out to the concert."

The opening band for Pieter started at 8:30, four hours from now. "I'm not ready."

"You look great. You always look great."

NICE SAVE.

"We haven't eaten."

"Pieter called and invited us backstage before the concert. I thought Gertie and the girls might get a kick out of it. We'll grab something backstage. Pieter's contracts call for freaking feasts. So, put on your fancy leather jacket, and let's hit the road."

My irritation at the day's events flooded back and scalded my tongue. With only one person in range to take it out on, I honed in like a heat-seeking missile.

"Fine." I snarled. So he could tear his attention away from VR worldwide domination and *Tattleverse* long enough to take a call and accept an invitation. But shouting up the stairs to check with me was too much to ask?

"Uh-oh!" He slapped his forehead. "I learned a long time ago when a woman says fine, it's time to run like hell."

GIVE THE MAN A CIGAR.

"It's fine," I said.

IS THAT FROST IN THE AIR? TAKE IT DOWN A NOTCH. HE'S OUT OF PRACTICE. HE HASN'T NEEDED TO COORDINATE HIS PLANS WITH ANYONE FOR A WHILE, IF EVER.

"It's not fine. I should have asked." He took my hand and kissed the knuckles. "But I'm trainable."

"Remains to be seen." I consoled myself with the apology and the promise of an Ivy-free evening. Well worth the inconvenience of dressing in a rush. He pulled me down the steps while I was still buckling my jacket. Right before we reached the bottom, he nibbled my ear.

"In case you were wondering, pre-concert sex is OK, but post-concert is exquisite." He kissed his fingertips and flicked the kiss into the air.

"I'm holding you to that promise."

"Counting on it."

Everyone had gathered in the foyer. While I'd moped away the afternoon, my cousins had transformed themselves into glamazons. Since lunch, scarlet streaks had appeared in Ainsley's tawny shoulder-length hair, and spikey black tips enhanced Ellison's pixie cut. Ainsley's black dress with gold, white, and pink stars and moons flounced six inches above her knees, showcasing legs honed by years of tennis lessons. Her glittering pink topaz statement necklace and matching earrings twinkled *look at me*. Ellison opted for an all-black ensemble with a midriff-baring tube top, a leather mini-skirt, and sequined Converse high-tops. She looked hot enough to fight off a March chill.

"Aren't you girls gorgeous?" Ivy cooed. Well-versed in how to ignite my insecurity, she extended faint praise. "You look nice, too, Maren."

I rallied. "Doesn't Gertie look adorable?"

Ivy raised her eyebrows, suggesting she'd never choose a black leather pinafore and sparkly Doc Martens for an eight-year-old. *That's why I'm the cool aunt, and you're the killjoy mom.*

"Are we ready?" Cyrus, a smart man, propelled me to the door.

ARIE CROWN THEATER

TUESDAY, MARCH 15

I HADN'T BEEN TO Arie Crown Theater since my high school history class came for the revival of *Hamilton — The Musical*. The ongoing pandemics had changed things. People with Bio-Bits had elite parking and their own entrance, designated by the gold Harp logo on a Door-Med device. Not that *we* used it; our cars pulled into a covered berth next to the tour bus.

A bright young thing in a tuxedo ushered us through the maze-like backstage. She gave Cyrus's name to the guard outside Suite B, who entered a code on the keypad. A posh voice invited us to supply our Bio Bit data. After the all-clear message, the door swung open.

A cluster of guys you'd never mistake for anything but rock'n'rollers and a smaller group of ultra-glamourous women mingled in a room rocking an edgy vibe. The vintage pressed-tin ceiling was white with intermittent sprays of black. Gray bricks with purple and turquoise streaks hinting at graffiti provided a backdrop for black tables and chairs. A banquet table laden with sandwiches, beer, and hard liquor dominated one wall.

The men checked out Ainsley, Ellison, and me. A few nodded their approval to the women's obvious chagrin.

"Cyrus, my man." A guy with waist-length dreadlocks and bushy eyebrows with multiple piercings peeled away from the crowd. "Long time. London, right?"

"Monty." Cyrus shook his hand. "London, yeah. This is Maren."

"You're the witch lady. Cool. Monty Whitecliff, Pieter's tour manager." Monty had a hearty handshake. "Pieter's in there."

He pointed to an open archway blocked by another guard. Whispers followed our progress across the room. What would Nosey say?

NOTHING NICE.

No bistro tables and chairs cluttered the inner sanctum; rock gods and their BFFs lounged on plump gray leather couches or gray chairs around ebony tables. Swaying to blues pumped out on a state-of-the-art sound system, trendy bartenders staffed the full-service bar. Chefs in full chef regalia commandeered a cooking alcove, serving up everything from cheeseburgers to Kobe steaks, pasta primavera to sushi.

Pieter rushed over to engulf Cyrus in a prolonged bro-hug. "Welcome home, dawg."

"Back at you." After energetic back-slapping, Cyrus tugged me forward. "This is Maren."

"Hey, Maren." Pieter kissed my cheek. "The girl who sent old Cy into a tailspin. Well done, you."

"Thanks." I guess. "Although he keeps me spinning, too."

"She's being nice." Cyrus hugged me against him. "Told you she was as sweet as she was beautiful."

Sweet? I couldn't remember the last time someone called me sweet.

"Is this Gertie? I've heard a lot about you. Love the boots." Pieter nodded toward her black, sparkly Doc Martens. He picked her up and summoned a flunky to take photos with her cell phone. The sparkle in her eyes rivaled her boots. He also embraced my girl cousins, who looked ready to swoon. They commemorated the occasion with more photos. They refrained from posting to social media while we watched, but I suspected it was only a matter of time.

While Cyrus and Pieter caught up, Manny and Julian cruised the bar. Ainsley and Ellison eschewed food and drink, content to bask in Pieter's presence. I made sure Gertie ate and didn't over-indulge in soft drinks. *See, Poison Ivy, I can be responsible.*

The lights dimmed, signaling the warm-up band was onstage. Our bright young thing appeared faster than a genie from a bottle. "May I show you to your seats, Mr. Harper?"

"Absolutely. My girlfriend here," he lifted Gertie's hand, "doesn't want to miss a thing."

Pieter called after us. "Hey, Marley and I are heading to Sonny Boy's later. You in?"

To his credit, Cyrus said, "Up to you, babe."

"Sure." The daggers in Ainsley and Ellison's eyes foretold death and dismemberment if I declined. "We just need to take Gertie home first."

The usher led us through the labyrinth to an enclosed box overlooking the Orchestra seats. Below us, Plexiglass partitions divided rows A through P, also reserved for Bio-Bit users, from the auditorium filled with mask-wearing fans.

Gertie had the best seat, with Cyrus and her dad on either side. She allowed me to sit beside Cyrus.

"If you need anything, press this button," the bright young thing said. "This button here controls sound."

"Thank you." Cyrus slipped cash into her hand.

Nobody paid much attention to the warm-up band, which sucked for them. After a brief interlude, a disembodied voice announced, "Chicagoland, please welcome native son, Pieter Thornhill, the 2044 Grammy Award winner for Best Album of the Year."

The crowd went wild. Gertie, Ellison, and Ainsley led the cheers in our box.

"It's good to be home." Pieter did sincere well and pumped up the crowd's enthusiasm to ninety-nine. "No place like it, yeah?"

Hmm. Had he picked up the mannerism from Cyrus? Did all Chicago guys end sentences with yeah? I lost the patter for several seconds, coming back when Pieter said, "Chicago Town."

"I LOVE THIS SONG!" Gertie shrieked.

"Me, too." Cyrus's head bobbed to the guitar chords crashing through the speaker. He and Gertie leaped to their feet, and he lifted her onto his shoulder. He boogied, and she bounced and clapped like a teenager at a rave. Her mother would not approve.

Good!

They sang along at the top of their lungs with Pieter. Julian, Ainsley, and Ellison formed a clapping chorus.

"I've lost her." Manny leaned across the vacated seats. "I'll never be as cool as that guy. Or Cyrus."

"Face it, big brother, we're the old fogeys in this group." I patted his knee. He nodded. "Sad, but true."

Even Gertie and Cyrus had their limits and sank into their seats by the fifth song. Cyrus gulped a bottle of water.

"Not bad for an old guy," I said.

"Yeah?" A wide smile. "Wanna have a go, babe? I've got one more song in me."

"Save yourself for cocoa and cookies."

"Ye of little faith." He shook his head in disbelief. I listened with my head on his shoulder. OK, not listened. I welcomed the opportunity to sit in a dark cocoon with his arm draped over my shoulder, keeping the beat with his forefinger.

". . . my friend Cyrus, another Chicago lad, is here tonight with a special lady. He tells me they have a song just about everybody in Chicagoland knows. Here to help me out is another special lady who's been in the news lately. A big hand for Marley Blue."

Marley had the same delicate features and nutmeg-colored skin as my mother and a mass of black curls to which I could only aspire. My grandfather would have killed to paint her. An electric current pulsed between her and Pieter. "Are they a thing?"

"So I hear."

Wang Dang Doodle's raucous opening filled the speakers.

Marley growled the first line into the microphone. Pieter sidled up beside her and joined in on the second line.

Cyrus pulled me to my feet, his hip bumping mine. "Let's pitch a wang dang doodle all night long, babe."

"Go, Aunt Maren, go." Gertie clapped rhythm. Her father looked horrified.

"That's my girl," Cyrus said.

Pretty sure he didn't mean Gertie. The Goddess must be smiling. The Billionaire Barista demonstrated a knack for good times that left the Lilienthals in the dust.

SONNY BOY'S

TUESDAY, MARCH 15

WE'RE NOT IN EVANSTON ANYMORE, TOTO.

Century-old red brick buildings housed a mélange of gourmet coffee shops, scruffy dive bars, artisanal cocktail lounges, galleries showcasing local artists, restaurants, and apartments. At midnight, the masked crowds ignored social distancing guidelines, crowding cheek-to-cheek and butt-to-butt on the narrow sidewalks.

Rick pulled up beside a mural of a man playing the guitar. A lighted sign confirmed we were at *Sonny Boy's Live Blues — 7 Nights*. A smaller sign read *Established 1982* and promised *Dancing*. We donned our masks for the short trek from car to door. Pieter and Marley arrived as Rick pulled away.

When DoorMed gave the all-clear, the bouncer admitted us, and we removed our masks. Sonny Boy's gritty roadhouse feel hadn't changed in the last sixty-two years. The vintage bar screamed authenticity.

A server led us to a table in the room where Elmore and the Chicago Blues Project had already taken the stage. Cyrus whispered, "The singer — that's Elmore — is a real-deal Chicago blues guy. The harmonica player is razor-sharp."

"House-rockin' blues," Pieter added.

My cousins took to the dance floor, pausing at our table just long enough to ditch their purses and jackets. Pieter and Cyrus boogied in their seats, keeping time with their fingers on the scratched oak table.

Marley leaned across the table and gestured at them. "Giddy as frat guys, those two."

I nodded, but Manny repeated his concert lament. "I am so not cool anymore. What happened to me?"

"Wife. Three kids. Another on the way." I threw back a whiskey. "It's a cautionary tale. You're becoming Pop-Pop."

"Does that make you Oma?" He snickered.

"Good come back, bro!"

From the stage, Elmore said, "Tonight, folks, we gonna give you *Fever*. Miss Peggy Lee took *Fever* all the way to the first Grammy Awards, way back in 1959. Now, we see our girl, Marley Blue, in the audience. Miss Marley, you come on up here and do Peggy Lee for us. Put your hands together, children, for *Fever* and Miss Marley Blue."

Marley made her way to the stage to thunderous applause. The slow clapping and the slashing guitar riffs lured people onto the dance floor in a nanosecond. Cyrus held out his hand and mouthed, "You give me fever."

We squeezed onto the crowded floor. His hands cupped my hips, and I draped my arms over his shoulders. Hug-and-sway, hug-and-sway to the music and Marley's seductive voice, our bodies anchored to earth as our souls moved through space and time.

"You give me fever," I said and blinked as a dozen phones flashed.

"In the morning, yeah, and all through the night," he crooned. "I'm never gonna dance with anyone else."

The cold cynic in me whispered, *it's an extravagant vow made in the heat of the dance*. The tingle warming my core argued otherwise. My fingers knotted in his hair at the base of his skull and tipped his head forward until our lips met. A kiss of obliteration or commencement. The room, the smoke, and the crowd evaporated. The music swelled. Wild electricity sizzled in my veins. I flew again like the night we waltzed at the Beaux Artes Ball. Yeah, I could get addicted to dancing with this guy. Like forever.

"You're the best, Harper."

When we returned to the table, Pieter and my brother applauded.

Three songs later, the harmonica player said, "Elmore and the Chicago Blues Project, folks. Thank ya very much. Yeah, we have what we call a tip bucket. Y'all hip? Now, ya know, the last few years been hard on us musicians with the pandemics and such. If you like what you hear and feel the need, drop some ducats in the bucket. If you don't have any ducats for the bucket, you can donate online."

He started a lonely blues wail, and servers came around with buckets and cellphones if you had an app for paying by phone, which both Cyrus and Pieter did.

During the intermission, the lead singer and the harmonica player came over to thank Pieter and Cyrus for their "ducats." Judging from the conversation and the little inside jokes, this wasn't the first time they'd met. Cell phones flashed as people took not-so-surreptitious photos.

After they left, future trophy wives in outfits a typical family could live on for a month clustered around Pieter.

WHO ARE YOU TO CRITICIZE THEIR EXTRAVAGANCE? JUST ASK NOSEY.

They came to our table under the pretext of getting Pieter's autograph, only to fake orgasmic surprise at recognizing Cyrus. They slobbered their gratitude for Bio-Bit and DoorMed making live shows possible again, declaring their lives a wasteland sans clubbing. Several girls pressed business cards into Cyrus's hand.

"Better watch out, Mare," Manny said.

"Do they wanna screw his brains out or get a job?" I said.

Manny roared with laughter.

Marley snorted. "Both."

She knew the score. Temptation strutted its stuff in this room. Paranoia resurfaced, hitting me right between the eyes. Beautiful women in short skirts tilted their heads and appraised me. *Why her? What's so special about her?* I tossed back another whiskey.

"We should have lunch soon," Marley said.

We exchanged cell numbers and promised to get in touch.

Well into the second set, servers made the rounds, announcing last call. Cyrus ordered another round. In my humble opinion, having Rick and a car waiting for us was the *best* call. Time to make that call.

WHAT HAPPENED TO THE MAREN WHO CLOSED DOWN EVERY CLUB?

Was Manny right about me turning into Oma?

My cousins, perspiration beading their faces, abandoned the dance floor, collapsed onto their chairs, and gulped water. OK, it wasn't just me getting old.

"Let's get you home, babe." Cyrus punched out a text. A few minutes later, his phone vibrated on the table. "Rick's outside."

We said goodbye to Marley and Pieter, who still nursed their drinks and rocked in time to the music. Cyrus, arm around my shoulder, wove through the crowd and cleared the path for Manny and my cousins. When we reached the door, he pulled a face mask from his coat pocket.

"Put this on. Your Bio-Bit won't help in Chicago's mean streets."

Right, DoorMed ended at Sonny Boy's door.

"You had a good time, yeah?" he asked.

"The best," I said through the mask.

We stepped into the street. The music's deafening thump faded, but my ears still buzzed. Like salmon swimming upstream, we shoved our way through a horde of masked people. After Sonny Boy's smokey heat, the night air made me shiver. Bring on the cushy leather seats, seat warmers, and a blast of hot air from the vents. "Where's the car?"

"It's supposed to be here." Cyrus looked in both directions, searching the street.

More bars and clubs closed, releasing a stream of people into the already jam-packed street. People pushed, shoved, and cursed. A girl in a black ski cap and Day of the Dead mask waved.

It's OK. It's OK. There must be a thousand skeleton masks in Chicago. From behind, someone rammed me into Manny.

"Careful, sis." Manny grabbed my arm.

"Rick, where the hell are you?" Cyrus barked into his phone.

Manny released his grip and stepped into the street. "I see him. He's way down there, still parked."

"Hey, Maren."

Day of the Dead Girl swung a small bucket, the type filled with beer during spring break on the beach. Water and ice shards slapped my face and drenched my hair and mask. My breath escaped in a hiss as I careened toward the curb and into the street. Julian grabbed me before I smacked the cement. The crowd backed up, leaving us exposed.

"You're melting!" Day of the Dead Girl screeched. "You're melting!"

"What the hell!" Cyrus whirled around and wrapped his arms around me, shielding me as much as he could. Water and ice dribbled inside my jacket, soaking my turtle-neck. I shuddered, shaking us both.

"What a world!" Day of the Dead Girl hooted.

"What a world!" echoed a Zombie with her hair tucked into a baseball cap, wearing sunglasses. Sunglasses at 3 AM? She pelted us with red beads with black spots.

I threw up my hands to protect my face and accidentally caught one. Not beads, but seed pods. I stuffed it in my pocket.

"What a world when sweet little girls like us can kill the witch. Kill the witch."

Zombie Girl flung a plastic bag at us. Thick, oily fluid soaked my jacket and splashed Cyrus's face. In the street lamps' half-light, it looked like blood.

THOU SHALT NOT SUFFER A WITCH TO LIVE.

The Zombie and Day of the Dead Girls scampered, hand-in-hand, down the street, singing *Ding Dong the Witch is Dead*.

Dozens of cell phones recorded the moment for posterity.

GUARDIANS OF THE WATCHTOWER

DING DONG, THE WITCH is dead!

Just what I needed, an earworm.

I sank deeper into the bathtub until I was up to my neck in hot water. The irony wasn't lost on me. I poked at the jagged memories, all pointing to one thing. People, who didn't know and never met me, loathed me. Was it obvious after The Drake? Yes. But when I learned the protestors were actors, my lizard brain broke into a dance with Bob Marley singing *don't worry bout a ting*. So much for lizard brains and reggae.

"You're turning into a prune." Cyrus held up my Kinky Bear robe. Although he'd showered off the ersatz blood with ruthless efficiency, he still sported a blood-red aura streaked with black. "Time to put you to bed. It's almost dawn."

"They hate me."

"They're idiots looking for their two seconds of fame."

Not to contradict him, but earlier he had barked at the police and an unlucky Harp IT guy using the phrase "dangerous lunatics." Someone had hacked Rick's phone; he never received Cyrus's text. Whoever received it sent a confirmation that looked like it came from Rick. Did anyone believe Skeleton and Zombie skanks capable of that?

"I brought you chamomile tea and a Xanax." After wrapping me in the robe, he propelled me toward the bed and rubbed my back while I downed the Xanax. My phone pinged.

"It's him." I cringed inside my robe.

"Ignore it. My guys are tracking our messages and calls. Our fuzzy brains can't deal with cranks tonight."

A fuzzy-brained Cyrus? Yikes! What next? A shift in the magnetic fields? I guzzled the chamomile tea and burned my mouth.

Cyrus patted the mattress. "Let's get some sleep."

Xanax don't fail me now!

Curled into a ball, I gritted my teeth until my jaw ached. The clock clicked toward five, five-thirty. The darkness felt suffocating. Cyrus tossed and turned. The clicking wasn't the clock, but the gears turning in his relentless (not fuzzy) brain.

"This isn't working!" When pharmacology fails, turn to magick. "I'll be right back."

Heading into my cavernous closet, I rummaged through my bag. Few options. We'd left for Hawaii in such a flurry, I'd grabbed a swimming suit, 3 pairs of shorts and tee-shirts, the sundress, and a few magickal essentials and called it good.

The Tarot deck came out first, then lavender oil (peace of mind), frankincense incense (protection and psychic awareness), and the vintage sterling silver lighter engraved with an M. In an ideal world, I'd have crystals. A crystal could boost any spell, and the Goddess knew my spells needed boosting. My kingdom for hematite (to relieve anxiety) or amethyst (to calm).

Come on, Lilienthal, if you're not witch enough to create a simple relaxation spell, that skanky Skeleton wasted her bucket of water. Get your ass out of the broom closet. Now!

I exited the closet with my tools while composing a spell in my head.

"May I ask what you're doing?" Cyrus, head propped on his fist, had turned on the bedside lamp.

"Chasing away the not-so-fuzzy thoughts so we can sleep." The clock said five-forty-five. If sleep didn't come soon, abandon all hope. "I won't allow those who wish us ill to have dominion."

How was that for bravado?

"I'd be most grateful." He nodded. I'd expected a fuss or a denial at the very least.

"Give me a hot minute to prepare." Or a hot hour or two.

STOP OVERTHINKING IT. YOU DON'T NEED FANCY TOOLS OR THE PERFECT SPELL. INFUSE YOUR INTENTION INTO IT.

I had a lot of intention.

I placed the incense coil in a small decorative bowl on the dresser and lit it, releasing Frankincense's earthy pine, citrus, and spice scents. I opened a window. Smoke tendrils rose toward the ceiling and drifted toward the open window, diffusing the leaden atmosphere. I inhaled; the air *was* purer. I envisioned a broom sweeping the negative energy from the room. The words for the spell crystallized. Time to cast a circle to keep negative energy from returning until the spell took effect.

Lacking the usual ritual items, I used Tarot cards for the cardinal points. I placed the *Ace of Pentacles,* representing north, earth, and a solid foundation, at the head of the bed. The *Ace of Swords*, the sword of truth and justice and signifying air, went on the fireplace mantle. *Ace of Wands* — fire, East, and willpower — went by the French doors. *Ace of Cups* stood for the West, water, love in its purest sense, and a connection to the divine.

Cyrus, eyes bright with curiosity, watched in silence.

"Are you ready?"

He nodded.

I stood at the foot of the bed, the circle's midpoint, and faced east. Envisioning the wind whipping around me, I found my center. "Guardians of the Watchtower of the East, Spirits of Air, I call upon you to watch over us."

I repeated the summoning for each of the remaining three guardians, visualizing crackling flames (South) and Hawaii's waves and waterfalls (West). For North, I conjured the scent of the earth after it rains. After each summoning, I traced a pentagram in the air, using my finger as an athame.

Still facing north, I searched for a connection to Earth. When I found it, I visualized a column of light reaching the stars. The circle rose with a powerful whoosh, leaving me both in the world and apart from it.

"Guardians of the Watchtowers, I bid you hail and welcome. The circle is cast. Let those within this circle exist in perfect love and trust. Blessed be." I knelt on the bed beside Cyrus. "Roll over. The tension and the ill wishes are in your neck and back."

No witchy insight there. The body knows what it knows. Sleeping beside someone for seventy-some nights revealed more than any crystal ball.

He obeyed, docile as a lamb. I reviewed my spell; it was as good as possible.

After brushing the hair from his neck, I tipped lavender oil into the small indentation at the base of his skull. The sweet floral, herbal, and evergreen smell loosened the tension in my jaw, and my teeth unclenched. I kneaded the oil into his neck muscles.

"Come sleep with me and let your troubles be. None shall pass inside this wall. No none, none at all," I chanted. The spell wasn't bad for something concocted in haste and desperation. "Release your dreams tonight and let your heart be light. Erase the foul memory. As I will it, so mote it be."

Nothing. Ugh. Why hadn't I called Talia for advice?

BECAUSE SHE'D BE SLEEPING AT DARK-THIRTY.

No one promised magick was easy, and I wasn't a quitter. I resumed massaging and repeating the spell. I persevered until the tension broke free, spewing into the air like the ash erupting from the volcano we'd seen in Hawaii. The ash sparkled with menace until incense plumes encircled it and spun it in lazy circles out the open window.

I moved from his neck to his spine. My fingers, lavender oil, and the spell elicited an occasional groan of relief. But I judged my progress by the murkiness leaching from his aura. Blood red lightened and turned brighter. When the aura turned to a clear, bright red tinged with silver, his breath slowed and became regular. He slept.

In healing him, the tension drained from my veins in a symbiotic way. I slid to the floor. Sleep yawned as a deep chasm before me, but I couldn't succumb yet. I stumbled to my feet and dismissed the Guardians of the Watchtowers, thanking and bidding them Hail and Farewell.

"The circle is open, but never broken. The love of the Goddess is forever in my heart. Merry meet, and merry part, and merry meet again," I whispered and crawled into bed, asleep before my head touched the pillow.

CY-REN SONG

WEDNESDAY , MARCH 16

Two PM. THE SILENCE in the house boomed louder than a drum. Where was everybody? My feet pounded the stairs like a herd of charging elephants. Pat was in the kitchen, cleaning up after lunch.

"Can I whip up something for you?" she said.

"Just coffee, please."

She prepped the copper espresso machine with the skill of a barista.

"Where's everyone?"

"The ladies, no clue. Cyrus and your brother took the kids downstairs for a movie." Her quizzical expression and cool appraisal pointed to Richard telling her what happened last night. *Is this girl worth the trouble?* The question came through loud and clear.

I accepted the espresso with gratitude. With it cradled between my palms, I beat feet to the theater room where three little heads, clustered on the yellow leather couch, fixated on the 325-inch television. Manny and Cyrus slouched at the bar. They looked relaxed, but the way they clenched the whiskey glasses gave it away. I kissed Cyrus's cheek.

"Good morning. I mean afternoon." His arm slid around my waist. "Sleep well?"

"Mm-hmm. You?"

He nodded. Our eyes met, acknowledging the effort of making sleep happen.

"Where's Ivy? The cousins?"

"Packing. We're going home tonight, remember?" Manny swished the whiskey in his glass. "I spoke with Oma this morning."

Uh-oh. Did the cell towers between here and Riverton ignite?

"She insists you come home, considering what transpired."

Oma barked; and just like that, Manny's stint as my advocate ground to a halt. *Lapdog!* I bit back the retort and squeezed Cyrus's shoulder. A whiff of lavender from last night's massage whispered *Stop. Think. Silence is golden.*

A frown creased Cyrus's face. "I'd understand if Maren left. Yeah, I get it, but it's unnecessary."

"I agree." I draped my arm around him in solidarity, letting my hand rest on his chest. His heart revved like a Maserati. "I have no intention of running back to Riverton with my tail between my legs because some girls bullied me."

That's right, Universe, my hightailing it days are over.

Fingers crossed.

Cheerful cartoon music filled the conversational gap.

"Be reasonable." The vein in Manny's cheek pulsed. His and Oma's fondest hope would go on life support if Cyrus showed no inclination to make me toe the Lilienthal party line. The steel rod up Manny's backside was almost visible. "Those miscreants attacked her three times since we arrived. Tell her about the seed pods and then convince me it's unnecessary."

Uh-oh, redux.

Manny, expecting a "how high?" when he said "jump," rattled the ice in his now empty glass. Each tinkle hinted at exasperation.

Wrong dude, bro.

Cyrus, unaccustomed to anyone telling him what to do, responded with a sharp, "What?"

I shifted my weight from foot to foot, regretting I'd ever rolled out of bed. Nostril flaring and teeth bared, Cyrus silently challenged my brother. I'd be lying if I said I didn't feel a little like Helen of Troy.

"Did you do what I think you did?" The steel rod in Manny's spine melted, but he tried to cover it with a nervous laugh. Nervous laugh aside, his face remained stony; he was on a righteous crusade. He talked straight at

SEASON OF THE WITCH

me, avoiding Cyrus's gaze. "I looked up those things they pelted you with. They're called Rosary Peas. Eating one seed can kill you."

"Wasn't planning to snack on them," I muttered.

"Don't be a smartass, Mare. You'll be safer at home. The Bluffs has better security."

Cyrus's face was as red and dangerous as a Rosary Pea. "You mean that place where someone broke into our house and framed us for murder? Where someone shot at us? That place?"

Yes! That place.

Manny huffed and changed tactics, sliding a tablet across the table. "You need to see this, Maren."

"Oh, fuck," Cyrus muttered. At the sound of adults misbehaving, a Gertie-giggle sailed over the sofa.

"There are children here." Manny glared.

"Double fuck. This is getting out of hand." Cyrus's voice rose several decibels, and he reached for the tablet.

I grabbed it before he threw it across the room. *Tattleverse* and Nosey. I should have known.

Videos streamed across the top of the screen. Our arrival at Arie Crown. Pieter on stage. Our impromptu Wang-Dang Doodle boogie. The *Fever* dance and kiss at Sonny Boy's. People coming up to our table. The clash with Skeleton and Zombie Girl. Somebody had followed us the entire evening. Almost like they knew something might happen.

Cy-Ren Song

<u>Nosey Parker</u>. *Siren song:* something alluring but potentially harmful or dangerous. No one says it these days, but the phrase might come back into vogue, judging by recent events.

Last night, accused murderer and tech tycoon, Cyrus Harper, and his gal pal, Maren Lilienthal, took in Chi-town's nightlife. Their first stop? Arie Crown. Cy-Ren shook their booties for Pieter Thornhill, a fellow Chicago resident and Harper's long-time friend. Is anything more heartwarming than a billionaire helping a millionaire scrape by?

Oh, gawd! Enough, already, with the murder and class-baiting.

Cy-Ren rocked out from a private, hermetically sealed box overlooking the stage. An Arie Crown spokesperson declined to comment on how much Harper laid out for the accommodation.

Afterward, Cy-Ren, Pieter, up-and-coming music sensation, Marley Blue, and their entourage showed up at Sonny Boy's Lounge on Chicago's near Northwest side. What a date night! Marley was a regular at Sonny Boy's before she took up with Thornhill.

Sonny Boy's was named after the legendary American blues harmonica player, singer, and songwriter Sonny Boy Williamson. What would Sonny Boy, a sharecropper's son, think about the serious money that changed hands so Harper could hear the blues? The cover ($200 a head) gets you through the front door if Harper's DoorMed watchdog deems you virus-free.

Now consider this, folks. If Cyrus was infected with Jakarta Panic, would we know? DoorMed controls access, and he controls DoorMed. Would Cyrus the Great deny himself anything? Ever? If you get sick and die so he can impress his girlfriend, he'll say it was the cost of doing business.

Why did this woman hate us?

Back to Sonny Boy's. Unless you want to watch the performance on an overhead monitor, you must buy a table in the room where the music happens. Harper's table for eight? A flat thousand for one set; seventeen-fifty for two. Then, there are the mandatory two drinks per person per set at $50 a pop. So, Harper plunked down $3300 before snacks. Is that the spirit of the blues? I'm just asking the questions.

DANGER! DANGER!

The cartoon bubbles over Manny's head were almost visible. *Come home now. Oma and I say so.* I didn't dare look at Cyrus. My calming spell lacked the juice to take on this blitz.

> After making a spectacle on the dance floor with their PDA and holding court at their table, Cy-Ren called it a night, but The People demanded to be heard. As the couple waited for their chauffeur-driven car, two young women doused Lilienthal with water and something that looked like blood while singing *Ding Dong the Witch is Dead*.

A photo showed me with blood running down my chin, like a vampire after a feast.

> That's right, Cy-Ren, The People are tired of your pretensions. They've had it up to their eyeballs with your gluttonous lifestyle. They're sick of your extravagance. You can call yourself a witch, Maren, but your spells can't make people forget the genuine problems of everyday life. Try to retreat into your fortress of wealth, Cyrus, and you might find pitchforks outside your window.
>
> I wish Cy-Ren no harm, folks, but I must point out the obvious or I should be derelict in my duty.

No harm? Bullshit! My tongue turned to lead; my throat became a desert. "Wow. Nosey must have a substantial expense account to pay someone to spill all those beans and take photos."

"Don't be flippant," Manny said.

"Point taken." My coffee had gone cold, but Cyrus was warm. Correction, Cyrus was boiling. "But it doesn't mean I'm going back to Riverton. Cyrus needs me here."

"Now, more than ever," Cyrus added.

"You both better come home. That reporter's practically calling for a lynch mob." The crimson stain on Manny's cheeks spread to his neck and ears. "You're crazy to stay."

Possibly. More than likely.

"I have business I need to attend to." Cyrus's jerky hand movements ended with his fist pounding the table. "I hired security. I'll do whatever it takes to keep Maren safe, but I won't let this hackette run our lives."

"Then, you tell Oma. I'm not carrying the water on this one." Manny pushed away from the bar, knocking over the stool. "Come on, kids. Time to go. Make another run through the house. Make sure you have everything."

Groans greeted his announcement.

"I said, let's go," Manny snapped. He stomped up the stairs, the kids straggling after him.

"That went well." Cyrus rolled his eyes.

"He'll get over it." I gulped whiskey from Cyrus's glass. Fire in the hole on an empty stomach. "Honest. I can't count how many visits with Manny ended this way. It means you're like a brother to him now."

"Good to know. I guess Oma's a different story."

"Definitely."

"Ouch!"

His pain was real; he'd gone all out to secure Oma's goodwill. Honest: Oma wouldn't let a lynching stand in the way of me snagging a billionaire husband, but no need to give him any ideas. There was something else I was dying (ha-ha) to know.

"Hey, did you check my phone? Did Alexander text me last night?"

He ran his fingers through his hair, so yes.

"What pearls of wisdom did he detonate this time?"

He pulled my phone from his pocket.

Alexander: Did you like Mitnick's Mungers?

Pithy. He'd attached a video of the confrontation with the Skeleton and Zombie in case I'd missed it.

"Mitnick's Mungers? What the actual fuck does that even mean?"

"It's a message for me. Mitnick was a famous hacker." Cyrus tapped his fingers against my phone, but I suspected he wanted to smash it. "In coding, munger means to destroy, usually accidentally, but sometimes maliciously. I think we know which definition Alexander prefers."

Old Alexander pushed all the right buttons. I placed my hands over Cyrus's restless fingers. "We'll get through this."

"Damn straight. You know any good hexes?"

At least we still had our sense of humor.

DOING WHAT I CAN, BABE

THURSDAY, MARCH 17

WHAT IS MY GUIDANCE for the day?

Ten of Cups! The happy family card. A couple embracing, children dancing, the rainbow of Cups arching overhead. Did it mean Cyrus and I were a family? What about those pesky dancing children? Not ours! Definitely nieces and nephews. Cyrus and I were an A++ aunt and uncle. Ask anybody, except Ivy. Or the card meant waving goodbye to my family made us happy. Ding-ding-ding!

SHUT DOWN THE CRAZY LADY TALK AND READ THE CARD.

I took a deep breath and turned on the *BoSsBlog* recorder. "*Ten of Cups* signifies true happiness and fulfillment. It's the card of happy-ever-after and domestic bliss."

Sure, it could mean those things. IF Alexander and his Mungers vanished off the face of the earth. What were the chances?

Cancel the negative thoughts, girlfriend. Listen to what the damn card has to say.

"When this card pops up, you'll find fulfillment in a relationship. It pictures the ideal life, the dream coming true. Appreciate it. Goddess knows, it entails effort, a lot of effort, but it's worth it. Also, it's telling me to consider the questions always in my head. Does he love me? The card says, yes, he adores you. Will we last? This *is* the long-term relationship card."

Too much rainbow. The crazy lady rushed back in to set things straight. "But tens *can* represent excess. Is it time to curb excessive emotions? They can leave everyone ragged and raw."

OK, but the Universe had sent an obvious message. "I need to appreciate what I have."

I stopped recording. With my hypothetical rainbow leading the way, I floated downstairs. It was all rainbows and unicorns until the sun shimmered off the too-white dining room, nearly blinding me. So much damned white. White ceiling with white beams, white shutters, white wainscoting, cream-colored walls, and a cream rug with pale pink flowers. The room reeked of decorator. Didn't the decorator know too much white can be cold, isolating, and empty or that it's associated with death and mourning in certain cultures?

Someone knew how much I loved color. A vibrant tropical bouquet with glossy green leaves and red heart-shaped blooms, orange and purple birds of paradise, and wands of pure blue ginger graced the table.

"Oh! A rainbow." I gasped. He had the idea before I drew the card. Serious magick right there. "A Hawaiian rainbow."

"Good memories, yeah?" His smile hollowed out my knees. In danger of swooning, I grabbed the chair.

Boyfriend hadn't exaggerated when he said, "Babe, I've got dishes that will knock your socks off." He'd set the table with cream-colored bone china rimmed with sapphire blue enamel and gold leaf accents. A delicate spray of gold nuggets and primary-colored dots floated in the center of the plates.

"Wow. Just wow. Where did you find these?"

"A little shop in Florence. I had an afternoon to walk around and explore. Total impulse purchase." He ducked his head as if embarrassed by spontaneity. We needed to work on that.

"Good find." I'd seen the plates in a catalog from an exclusive auction house. Limited edition. Handmade, no two alike, starting bid at six hundred a plate. His decorator wouldn't have had the imagination or temerity to suggest this set. Nope, I was looking at pure Cyrus. "They're keepers. Like you."

He rewarded me with another smile. Points to Maren for running with Happy Family guidance.

An espresso in an exquisite china cup tided me over while he served avocado halves stuffed with scrambled eggs, chives, Canadian bacon, and white cheddar. Artfully arranged plates with sliced bananas, four kinds of berries, mixed nuts, and dried cranberries were crowned with a dollop of almond butter, chocolate chips, and coconut flakes. Color me rainbow happy.

"You outdid yourself, Harper." Thank the Goddess, he was the domestic one. Left to my devices, we'd be feasting on cold scrambled eggs and burned toast.

"Doing what I can, babe." He took a bow and placed a champagne flute before me.

"Pomegranate mimosas on a Thursday morning?"

"Yeah, why not? It's St. Paddy's Day, and we Irish love a nip. Besides, the visit ended well; don't you think?" He tilted his head, considering the evidence, and nodded. "Yeah. Luck of the Irish."

"It did end well."

After Manny stormed off, Cyrus followed him upstairs. Whatever he said, Manny returned to my-brother/my-friend mode by the time the family boarded the plane to Riverton. He hugged me and urged me to be careful, but spared me another lecture. Fae prince magick? More than likely. We clinked glasses, and Cyrus took the seat beside me.

Incredible flavors burst on my tongue at the first bite. I closed my eyes to savor them.

"Watching you eat is like an orgasm," he said.

"Doing what I can, babe." My hand drifted toward him like a magnet to iron, and I stroked his face. "You know, the first time you cooked for me, I waited all evening. No orgasm, not even a kiss; nada."

"Always leave 'em wanting more."

"It's one person's opinion." I sure wanted more, like eating curled up on his lap, kissing his face between bites, and stroking his curls.

He cupped the back of my head. "I was too busy fretting to think about kissing. Worrying you'd hate everything. I pored over the menu from the minute Manny told me you were coming home. I imagined you slamming the door in my face when I asked you to dinner."

"Slam the door in your face?" Not when I saw his beautiful mouth, the full lower lip begging for a nip. It had made my stomach somersault, and I'd forgotten the word called No ever existed. TMI. "Fat chance. I was starving, dude."

"It all worked out, didn't it?" He took my hand in his. "Here we are, and I'm going to cook for you and get my cheap thrills for the rest of our lives."

Whew, going a little fast, aren't we?

Had he pulled the *Ten of Cups*, too?

Go for it, girl.

"Love you, Harper."

"Love you, too."

Happy Family card strikes again. "I know you always have a plan, so spill it while I'm in food ecstasy, and I promise not to hightail it."

"Good to know." Leaning back in his chair, arm stretched across my shoulder, he pondered the request. "Next week, I need to go to the office. There's the PSEC orientation. And I need to get with Frank and prepare for the board meeting. Honestly, I think they want me to prove I still care by showing my face."

"Sure, it's such a pretty face. A little scruffy." I cupped his chin. Its scratchiness made the softness of his lips more interesting. "I hear its owner thinks shaving wastes time."

"A truth universally acknowledged," he said. "Anyway, I thought after the week we've had, we'd hang out and relax today. Not think about they who shall never be mentioned."

"So down with that." If I never heard Nosey and Alexander's names again, it was too soon.

"Let's bowl a game or two."

Because he had a bowling alley next to the downstairs theater. Should I mention I'd never bowled?

"Don't make that face, girlfriend." He poured more champagne, this time undiluted by pom juice. "Bowling is an Olympic sport among code pigs, and I'm sadly out of shape. I'm counting on you to crack the whip."

Nice diversion, but he wasn't finished planning. Not by a long shot.

"We need to figure out which room you want for an office. Tell Viv what you need. She'll round up a selection for you to choose from."

"It's an awful bother for only a month. I can sit at the kitchen table or use your office."

"We'll be in Chicago a lot, so we should organize it now."

Along with the closet and remodeling the master bedroom, he bristled with plans.

"I connected Mab."

Mab was my virtual assistant, who was becoming the girlfriend of Cyrus's virtual assistant, Hal. Or, at the least, they hung out in the same places.

"While we're at it, pick a room for ... uh ... well, you know ... magick things."

STOP RIGHT NOW! AN OFFICE AND A MAGICK ROOM ARE SERIOUS PLANS. YOU'RE WAVING A RED FLAG BEFORE THE BULL OF FATE.

I bit my tongue. Literally. A glug of champagne washed away the blood's copper taste. OK, I asked for it. In for a penny; in for a pound. "I choose the Chinese room."

Cyrus cocked his head like a puzzled puppy. Did he remember he had a Chinese room?

"The room with the mandarin orange walls, the sea foam and tangerine Chinese rug, and the black lacquer Chinese cabinets and screen," I prompted.

"Ah. Sure, it's a nice room."

"Viv is off the hook. It doesn't need any work. I can use the cabinets for my magickal supplies." The cabinet under the east windows facing the lake made a perfect altar.

"You'll need a desk."

It was pointless to protest.

He soldiered on. "Tomorrow, I thought we might go shopping. You didn't pack for Chicago, and it's too chilly for that cute little sundress."

My brief shopping trip with Ivy and the cousins was a stop-gap. "OK, but I'll need to be back by six to talk with Uncle Ira about my proposal."

"Totally doable. I left Saturday open for the Ostara thing."

Yep, he'd agreed to celebrate the Sabbat with me, although I suspected he was leery. The last one ended with a murder charge.

"Pieter invited us to brunch on Sunday. I said I'd check with you, but I think you'll like the place. It's a 19th-century greenhouse converted into a restaurant. Exotic plants and Gilded Age menus."

"Sounds delightful."

"Cass and Rafael will be there, too."

Cassandane was going all in on her resolution to be my friend.

"Oh, I just remembered. Mrs. Mueller called to invite you to the ladies' coffee on Monday. If you go, I think you'll need a dress."

"Mrs. Mueller?"

"The judge's wife. She does this coffee thing. Like a TED Talk for the neighborhood women. Someone from U of C is talking about French and German fairy tales, and she thought you might be interested."

Invisible hands clutched my throat. Oma hosted a coffee group on the second Tuesday of every month since the beginning of time. Like Manny's basketball game, her invitation was a sign you'd arrived in Riverton. Mrs. Mueller must be the neighborhood Oma. Did she decide I wasn't just any girlfriend, or had someone (looking at you, Cyrus) lead her to that conclusion?

I stalled, trying to get the lay of the land. "Did she get you to speak yet?"

"She locked me in while I was doing the final walk-through when I bought the house." He chewed his lip. "You can always say no."

But I shouldn't. I bet, if asked, the neighborhood women would gush *Cyrus Harper? What a charmer.* Did I want to give them fodder for gossip? *The girlfriend, though. So supercilious. Witch rhymes with you-know-what.*

"Give me her number so I can RSVP. And, yes, I'll need a dress. You'll need to tell me what Evanston ladies wear to a Monday morning coffee. Remember, it doesn't make you a first-rate fashion consultant like Sally, but you'll do in a pinch."

"Understood. As long as you remember, I'm the fancy knickers expert. I have refined tastes." His laughter whooped through the room, and he leaned in for a kiss. We were on the road leading not to the bowling alley but back upstairs when his phone rang. He glanced at it. "It's Manny. Better answer."

Ugh. Maybe Manny had reconsidered his bonhomie and was ready to lecture me.

"Hello. Yeah, she's here. No, the new number is working. I think she left her phone upstairs." A pause. "Yeah? Great. I'll tell her. Thanks for letting us know."

"News?" I grimaced, my head filled with Skeletons, Zombies, the Man in Black, and Oma shaking her head in disappointment. The last image was beyond terrifying.

He poured champagne. "You have an offer on your house in Austin."

"Yee-haw!" I clinked my flute against his and gulped champagne. Oma had been carrying the mortgage for me. The fizz started in my mouth and made its way to my toes. "How much? I'm not gonna lose money, am I?"

"Manny thinks you'll net about three million. Buyer's coming with cash and wants to close in thirty days."

"Woo-hoo! I'm not a pauper anymore." Except on Planet Cyrus. Still, I boogied in my seat, waving my hands above my head.

"Any thoughts on how you'll invest the money?"

"Not off the top of my head." I sighed. On this, I suspected he and Manny were in lockstep. *Don't let Maren blow the money.* "Any advice? Besides hockey teams, where are you looking to put your money these days?"

"Here and there." He squirmed in his seat.

WHAT'S GOING ON HERE? WHY SO CAGEY, BOYFRIEND?

"Will you have to kill me if you tell me?"

"No. No. Not at all." He scraped his fingers through his hair, blinked, and cleared his throat. "Pieter's contract with his music label ends on March 31. He's not renewing, and we're starting a label called Native Son, based here in Chicago."

IS ANYTHING MORE HEARTWARMING THAN A BILLIONAIRE HELPING A MILLIONAIRE SCRAPE BY? DOES NOSEY KNOW ABOUT THE MUSIC LABEL?

"Cool. How much are you investing?" That noise? Oma clutching her pearls and hissing, *Maren, don't be vulgar.*

"We're each putting up two million. We're announcing on April 1. Big party at The Palmer House. Uh-oh." He tugged his ear and looked at the ceiling. "I should have mentioned it before now. Pieter's people are arranging it, and Viv put it on my calendar. I told her to check with George. Maybe ..."

"It's fine. I'm already here, right?" Another day on Planet Cyrus, another dress. Was this all a ploy to force me into using the black card?

"Viv and George need a regular meeting to coordinate our calendars."

Every nerve, from my eyebrows to my toes, spasmed. Were we *that* couple? I jerked my head in an approximation of a nod and changed the subject. "So, can I invest in your record label?"

"No. We might lose it all, so I wouldn't advise it." The veins of his throat popped, the pulse visible. "I can afford to lose it; you can't. I know it sounds bad when I say it's all play money for me; but what else could I possibly spend it on?"

Diamond and pearl necklaces. A coffee plantation. A winery. The big-ass house in Riverton. To name a few. "What would you advise for me?"

"First, don't take my advice. The problem with success is people think you're an omniscient financial god, and I'm not a god. Not by a long shot." He rocked in his chair and sighed.

WHAT'S GOING ON HERE?

I tapped my foot against the rug and forged ahead. "Remember when I did The *Wheel of Fortune* reading?"

"How could I forget? It cleared us of a murder charge."

"In that reading, the *Nine of Pentacles* was me." I cleared my throat. *Yes. Me.* "She created her wealth; no one gave it to her. The advice was to invest wisely and seek sound financial advice. That's what I'm trying to do. Why are you being so weird?"

A wrinkled brow and more throat clearing. "Because I don't want you to lose any more money because of me."

"Let's be clear. Babington stole your code and my money. You had nothing to do with it." For good measure, I added, "You're not Finley, for Goddess's sake. He literally took my money."

"Whatever. But if you take my advice and lose money, I'd feel responsible and say something paternalistic, which I guess I'm gonna say, anyway. I'd make it good. I'd take care of you. Now you're going to smack me upside the head or rip out my heart and feed it to the dogs."

"Am I? Last time I checked, neither of us had a dog."

"Jesus, Maren, we nearly came to blows when I gave you a credit card."

He had a point, and I'd jumped off the Happy Family train. Damn. I couldn't let it go. "So, what? You're telling me to stick the money in an interest-bearing savings account so you don't feel guilty?"

"See. No. You should invest it, but not in something risky. Like a music label." His attention returned to the fruit plate, and he pushed bananas and berries around, arranging them in tidy rows. "Look, if you're interested, I'm investing in this kid, Daniel Khati. He's developing a device for detecting deadly diseases in the first cell stages. My medical people looked at it, and it's solid. We're in clinical trials now and plan to announce early next year. If all goes according to plan, I expect to double my investment, but something can always go wrong."

"How much are you investing?" If Oma had a grave, she'd be whirling in it.

"Eighty million." He tapped his index finger against his lower lip. "There'll be a final round of funding, and I can package you in."

"I'd like that."

"OK. We can hammer out the details later." He muttered something under his breath. It sounded suspiciously like *Thank God, that's over,* but he summoned a weak grin and said, "Now, can we go bowling?"

How could I say no?

For the record, his bowling alley was a decorator-free zone. Kudos to Cyrus. Illuminated rock and roll posters lined one side of the lane; on the other side, vintage pinball machines and a rack for bowling balls and shoes. Blue, green, and purple neon lights ran along the floor. Two 1950s rocket-sled couches, blue leather with black stars, looked darn comfy. A trippy paradise for a geek of any age.

"How do you play this game?"

Shaking his head in disbelief, he said, "First Star Trek, now this; you really are a barbarian."

"You love that about me."

"I do." He patted my rear; brief financial flare-up aside, we were good again. "You roll a ball at those wooden objects, called pins, and knock down as many as possible. The person who knocks down the most pins wins."

He selected a ball for me. I wanted the black one with silver sparkles, but he chose the purple and red one, explaining the weight was much better for me. After I found shoes, he gestured up to the electronic scoreboard.

"Notice there are ten segments; they're called frames. In baseball, you'd call them innings. You get two tries in each inning to knock down all the pins."

A dubious probability. "How many points can I get?"

"Three hundred is a perfect game, which is 12 consecutive strikes. A strike is when you knock down all the pins with one try," he said. "But the average score, mathematically, is 77."

"Do you ever bowl a perfect game?" My money said yes. Cyrus hated losing, and he'd never play at something he couldn't win.

"Not often enough. Once in a blue moon."

The tart way he said "once in a blue moon" confirmed my suspicion about hating to lose even a game.

"A strike happens when your ball hits the pocket," he said. A complicated explanation of angles, where I should stand, and why I needed to throw a curved ball followed. He dove deep into calculating acceleration and contact points, using words like radius, velocity, and angular rotation speed.

"Remember I'm an English major. High school algebra was a reach for me."

"Let's just give it a shot and see how it goes."

My first try went straight into what he called the gutter. The second picked off two pins. At least I had a number on the big electronic board. He rolled a strike, and it was back to me. On the second try, my ball took out one pin.

When my turn came around again, he said, "Let's try something different, yeah."

Just like that, the game became less theoretical and way more interesting. His hands were all over me, correcting my hip alignment and the way I held the ball. Bowling turned into a full-contact sport because, with increasing frequency, he just held me. I leaned into it, breathing Oud's smoky, sweet scent mixed with the tart smell of bergamot and a whiff of sex. I sailed the ball down the alley in a haze of desire.

My game improved (a little), and his prowess declined as his interest swelled. Felt it whenever I rubbed my butt against him during the "teaching moments." After three games, my score rocketed from 30 to 72. Cyrus took a nose dive from 260 to 190. Go, Team Maren!

We made a bee-line for the rocket-sled couch, shedding clothes along the way. The cool leather warmed up pretty darn fast as we nuzzled each other like we'd never get enough. It was all glorious skin on skin, soft mouths, and bristle-y chin against my moon tattoo.

"Nothing like bowling to get the juices rolling." I ran my fingers through his hair.

"Doing what I can, babe. Doin' what I can."

NINE OF PENTACLES

FRIDAY, MARCH 18

WE WERE OK. ALL the evidence suggested we were better than OK; we were fan-fucking-tastic.

Yesterday proved we could replicate our (mostly) harmonious day-to-day existence anywhere. This morning, we checked out Oak Street, a ritzy, gated shopping area. With the temperature an unseasonable seventy degrees, well-heeled shoppers came out to play. Blissfully anonymous, we strolled hand-in-hand amongst them. Even when someone uttered *cute couple*, I didn't cringe. We topped it off at a chic café, making goo-goo eyes at each other over coffee and wine-drenched pears with rich, gooey chocolate in a hazelnut pastry.

So why was I a quivering jellyfish of self-doubt?

Mab, my virtual assistant, saved me from wallowing in that particular insecurity by replacing it with another. "`Maren, it's time for your call with Uncle Ira.`"

Face2Face and Cyrus's blazing-fast internet connected me to Uncle Ira way too fast.

He beamed. "Witch Child, thank you for indulging me on a Friday evening. I needed to get un-jetlagged."

"No problem. How was Bora Bora?"

"Splendid. We stayed at Conrad Bora Bora Nui."

Uncle Ira never explained who "we" included. The family buzzed about it and pried in vain. Good for him for keeping his private life private.

"The over-water bungalows are fabulous, and I swam with sharks. In a steel cage. Obviously." He peered through the screen. "Your Oma says you've been swimming with sharks, too."

The Lilienthal penchant for gossip rivaled Nosey Parker's. He'd know every salacious detail from the mob at The Drake to the altercation outside Sonny Boy's. Probably read the *Tattleverse* drivel, too.

"It's been rough. Nothing a facelift and a spa month can't fix." I shrugged, but my twitching eye undermined my bravado.

"Your young man needs to take better care of you. Do I need to speak with him?" He sounded severe.

BREATHE.

"He's doing what he can. He hired off-duty policemen to patrol the house."

He harrumphed, but let it go. "You got something for me?"

"I do." I took a deep breath. "You saw the proposal?"

"Walk me through it."

In Hawaii, Cyrus drilled me every day until I could have rattled off the presentation under enhanced interrogation. "I plan to make The Plaza a destination. A place people plan to visit."

"A theme park?" He raised his eyebrows.

"Not exactly, but the data says most Plaza visitors can't afford to shop at the stores."

If his eyebrows went any higher, they'd disappear into his hairline.

"The data says they buy souvenirs. You know, like tee shirts, mugs, and souvenir caps." I clung to data like a lifeline. What other cred did I have? I didn't have an MBA from Stanford like my cousin Liliane. Need I remind him I'd blown a $25,000,000 inheritance?

BEAT FEET TO THE HARD, COLD DATA, MAREN.

"I ran the numbers. Plaza shoppers don't live in The Bluffs. Ivy and Lil haven't set foot there in forever. They want to go to Oak Street here in Chicago or New York Fashion Week. We need to cater to people who actually come to The Plaza."

He frowned, but the truth was the truth.

"There's an empty movie theatre on the north end. It was quasi-renovated about a decade ago."

"The Majestic." Uncle Ira rubbed his chin, his eyes misty. "Movies there were magical."

"But they're not coming back," I said after a respectful pause. "Cyrus has this over-the-top television and theatre set-up, and Manny's kids went wild. Now, he's talking about getting something similar. Not everyone can afford a 325-inch television, but movie theatre-style entertainment in their home is in everyone's grasp. Live entertainment isn't. That's where we come in."

"Good point, but what you're proposing is damn ambitious." He'd read the proposal, after all.

"It'll work." An injection of enthusiasm? Stick with the facts, Cyrus had advised. "I sent the financials."

"Very impressive, but tell me more."

"It's making The Majestic a destination." I shuffled the papers. My slick presentation slipped out the door. "Movies aren't a destination."

His expression remained impassive. Yeah, covered that point, hadn't I?

"People still want entertainment. Look at us. Cyrus hauled our butts to Chicago for what? A concert. The cousins wheedled their way into the trip. Riverton was in the middle of Pieter's tour trajectory. He was in Kansas City two nights earlier. The interstates feeding Chicago, KC, and St. Louis, all major tour stops, run right by us. But Riverton doesn't have a venue."

"Go on."

"Our Bio-Bit agreement makes The Plaza a unique experience Arie Crown can't match. Half the people in Chicago don't have Bits. They sit in the outback, wearing a mask and separated from the stage by Plexiglass." Thank you for that tidbit, Nosey! "We can offer performances like the good old days."

"Why would big draws stop in Riverton?"

"It's a long haul from KC or St. Louis to Chicago. They might lose two nights of receipts between driving and time to set up. A Riverton performance generates more income and reaches a larger audience. Plus, people might travel to Riverton for the maskless experience."

"Who would you book with?"

"Pan American Broadway and Ticket the World."

"You've talked with them?"

"Preliminary stuff, but I didn't go into specifics. Not until I talked with you."

"Impressive."

Cyrus might have leaned on them. Everybody took his calls. Uncle Ira didn't need to know. A chill snaked over me. *It helps when people know people.* How many times had Manny, my dad, and Pop-Pop said it? It made me feel like the little match girl with her cold nose pressed to the glass.

"Do you think they were interested or polite?" he asked.

"They want to talk more."

"You're sure?"

"As certain as I can be." I paused, screwing up my courage. "Did you see the plans for converting the theatre into an auditorium? It won't be cheap."

The paper shuffling crackled over the miles. "I see that. You got funding lined up?"

"I do."

"Go for it."

JUST LIKE THAT? REALLY? OK, THEN.

"One more thing I need to run by you."

"Just one?"

His tolerant smile said I could ask a second thing, but not a third. "I had tea with Cyrus's family at The Drake Hotel."

"Madre told me. She said they were nice, even if the crowd wasn't."

The old Lilienthal gossip train chugged right along.

"More than nice." At least Cassandane was nice, although I still doubted her sincerity. "Anyway, The Drake does a tea service every Saturday and Sunday. High tea, like Oma and I had in London. Ladies in hats and gloves. Little girls in the sweetest dresses. Gertie was adorbs; I'll send you a photo. A tea service would be a hit with Bluffs ladies *and* visitors. I want to talk to The Gibraltar management about hosting one if it's OK with you."

"How many times need I say this? You set the direction for The Plaza now. Thank you for consulting me, but get on with it."

"OK." I drew out the syllables, giving him a chance to renege.

"I think we're finished here. Give my best to Cyrus. But tell him if he can't get a handle on these nut cases, I'll come up there and bring you home."

"Yes, sir." So unfair to Cyrus, but it was an argument I couldn't win; I could only ignore it.

"Keep up the good work, Maren. I'm proud of you." Uncle Ira signed off.

Nine of Pentacles, here I come. Bring on the beautiful garden with purple grape vines, the flowing golden robe, and a red beret. I'd get a falcon for my shoulder. Nine was an independent woman. She might be me. No, she *would* be me.

OSTARA TAROT READING

SATURDAY, MARCH 19 OSTARA

CYRUS WITHDREW INTO HIS office after breakfast, leaving me to my own devices. A good sign. He trusted me to be around when he emerged.

STOP THE NAYSAYING.

Stop nagging. I went to the Chinese room. *MY* room, not *THE* Chinese room. I repeated *my room* until I said it without dithering.

After my morning prayer, I meditated on Ostara, spring's return, and new beginnings. The spring part came easy; spring permeated *my* room. Mother-of-pearl cranes and butterflies fluttering around a garden embellished on a black lacquer screen. A grass-green Chinese rug was strewn with purple, orange, and yellow flowers. If that didn't scream spring, what did? As for new beginnings? On it. Wasn't I making a life with Cyrus? But Ostara also embodied the equilibrium between light and dark, male and female. Point taken. We weren't in balance yet.

I turned to my Tarot cards for guidance. A single card draw wouldn't cut it. I searched for the Ostara spread I'd tucked away in *BoSsBlog*.

"How do I balance my life with Cyrus?" I shuffled, laid out the cards, and turned on *BoSsBlog's* recorder.

1. What you need to cast off

2. What you need to bring in balance

3. What you need to bring in balance

4. What you need to bring in balance

5. What you need to focus on for balance

6. How are your intentions unfolding

7. What do you need to remember to for a more joyful and centered life

Seven of Cups reversed showed a mysterious figure scrutinizing the cups. In the first cup, a man with black curly hair, sometimes identified as Saint Michael, indicated higher powers at work. I couldn't ignore the resemblance to Cyrus. Smack in the middle, a tiny, shrouded figure emerged from a cup. Me seeking a revelation? Jewels, a castle, a victory wreath, a snake, and a dragon filled the remaining cups. Symbols for wishes, dreams, and fears? Did those shiny objects represent what Cyrus offered as a warning? For sure, the objects possessed the magick to make someone like me lose focus and chase pipedreams.

"I interpret this card to mean I'm either letting my negative imagination run wild, or the prospect of achieving my hopes and dreams overwhelms me. It's time to stop questioning what the Universe offers. Stop searching for something better when I have everything I need."

Cards 2, 3, and 4 pointed out what I needed to bring into balance. What did it say about me that it took three cards to cover it?

An upright *Ten of Pentacles* showed wealth's positive side, an established family, home life, and attainment in the material realm. *Ten of Pentacles* reversed warned about wealth's dark side. Was it a not-so-subtle reminder wealth might be a trap? My mother learned the lesson too late, and it killed her. I learned the lesson from her too early; it encouraged hightailing it.

"*Ten of Pentacles* reversed asks, *is this how you want to live*? Time to get my head straight about money and what it means to me. Complicating matters, Cyrus has so darned much money it makes my head spin. I need to deal with the ramifications of wealth."

SOLDIER ON!

In a relationship reading, the *Ace of Cups* could overflow with positive emotions, but reversed indicated repressed and unexpressed emotions. I tried to keep my feelings on the down low because I had a solid track record of getting hurt by telling someone how I felt. Had I gone too far?

"*Ace of Cups* reversed tells me not to hold back with Cyrus and get my trust issues under control so our relationship can move forward."

Nine of Pentacles. Again. OK, Universe, beat me over the head with this card, why don't you? "I can take care of myself, but doubt undermines my confidence. This card means, *Go ahead. Prove yourself, Maren, I dare you.* Time to say *Cancel! Cancel!* every time self-doubt or negativity rear their ugly little heads."

The Devil showed a naked man and woman chained to his podium. When I first started reading cards, I assumed the Devil held them against their will; Talia pointed out that the chains around their necks were loose. They *could* escape if they wanted. She also drew my attention to the horns on their heads, a sign they were developing animalistic tendencies and raw instincts, much like the *Devil*. The fire on their respective tails signified pleasure and lust.

"*The Devil* is my shadow self. He's all the negative habits, dependencies, thought patterns, relationships, and addictions standing between me and my best self."

Ugh. I knew them well.

"On the positive side, *The Devil* shows a powerful attachment between two people. But I need to be careful. We're talking about *The Devil*. This attachment can turn into an unhealthy, co-dependent relationship."

How often had I chosen instant gratification and ignored long-term well-being? After breaking up with Finley, I'd used sex to keep lovers at a distance. I'd tried it with Cyrus, too.

"When *The Devil* shows up, it's a reminder to be aware of negative influences and banish them." I meditated on that before moving on. "The *Three of Pentacles* speaks to teamwork and collaboration, indicated by the stonemason working on the cathedral per the architects' plans. When you work together, you can create something more significant than one person alone. Got it. Cyrus and I are a team. Together we are unstoppable."

I recalled how many times I'd said *we* since arriving in Chicago. Yep, making progress. Both of us.

"*The Hermit* reversed represents what I need to remember to lead a more centered and joyful life. The upright Hermit shines a bright light into the darkness, but a reversed Hermit experiences isolation, loneliness, and withdrawal." How many times had I been so absorbed in myself that I shut everyone out? The reversed Hermit's light illuminated the wrong things. "It reminds me to be mindful of Cyrus's needs and not withdraw when he tries to deepen our connection. We can respect each other's space even while supporting each other."

I meditated on the total reading. When most cards in the spread are reversed, it suggested personal upheaval. It also can signal a vortex in which you aren't taking personal control or using your power. Neither option was off the table, not with Alexander careening toward me like a runaway train.

I felt ready to tell *BoSsBlog* my conclusion, which bore a strong resemblance to a relationship to-do list.

"Stop searching. I have what I need now.

"Get my head straight about money and what it means to me.

"Don't hold back with Cyrus. Ixnay distrust so our relationship can move forward.

"Stop worrying about what people say about me being with Cyrus. I *can* fend for myself and don't need to prove it.

"Acknowledge my negative habits, dependencies, and behavior and get rid of them.

"Cyrus and I are a team. We accomplish more together than alone.

"Support each other and respect each other's needs."

Easy-peasy. Right? Not really, but I had a plan; plans thrilled the other person in this relationship. It was a start. *I want a lifetime of moments with you.* Cyrus said it, and I needed to take his word. If we'd navigated our way through murder, we could manage this. Whatever *this* was, I had a freaking plan.

Ritual for Two

Although I believed the wand chose the witch and the right tools appeared when you needed them, I'd deemed it unlikely they'd appear before the Equinox sun set.

On the way to our Oak Street shopping spree, Cyrus ferried me to a local shop where I picked up rose incense (love, protection, and happiness) to blend with Copal's warm, sweet, musky scent (fulfillment of dreams). I purchased candles, a cinnamon-scented besom/broom now leaning against the Chinese cabinet-turned altar, and smudge sticks.

On the way home, we passed a shop called Blue Moon. My spine tingled, and I made Cyrus stop. Inside, I discovered a small, free-standing circular mirror cradled by a silver crescent moon and framed by obsidian pyramids. The pyramids and crescent moon rested on a marble base with stylized gold antelopes lounging on either side. A god and goddess for my altar. A sterling silver chalice also presented itself. Ta-da! Found magick.

A bemused Cyrus observed in silence when I slapped down my personal credit card. He understood why I needed to buy my instruments with my own card.

I still hadn't replaced my athame. Thinking about it, my premonition of murder roared back, smacking me in the face. Simon's corpse with eggplant-colored bruising around his eyes. Fluid, the color of cheap Zinfandel, dripping from his ear and forming a faint pink pool around his head. My athame buried deep in his chest.

CANCEL. CANCEL. IN THE GODDESS'S NAME, CANCEL. EQUIPMENT DOESN'T MAKE YOU A WITCH. YOU DON'T NEED AN ATHAME OR A WAND. YOU CAN USE TWO FINGERS AS A SUBSTITUTE.

I had two good fingers and everything else I needed for a ritual.

While I was arranging the altar, Pat tapped on the door. "Your flowers are here."

If I had hackles, they would have risen. After Alexander's floral message, bouquets triggered free-floating dread.

CANCEL! YOU ORDERED THE FLOWERS!

Right. I leaned against the altar to steady myself. "Put them on the cabinet, please."

Pat placed the vases on either side of my new mirror.

"Thank you."

She nodded and withdrew.

With a faint, sick feeling for what I might discover, I inspected the bouquets. Thank the Goddess. The florist had followed my instructions to the letter, putting together two stunning daffodil, primrose, violet, and pussy willow arrangements. Nothing spooky. Nothing to alarm me or Cyrus.

Buoyed by what I'd accomplished, I bounced into Cyrus's office. He was hunched over a monitor. His hand was anchored in a shock of hair that looked like it had endured hours of torture.

I wrapped my arms around him and nuzzled the invading hand. "No love for bald guys, remember?"

He sighed, and his breath carried the world's weight. "Frank wants me to write an inspirational welcome for the PSEC troops. They'll be here on Monday."

"In my book, you embody inspiration."

Cyrus could inspire people to cheer and march off to certain death with a smile on their lips and a song in their hearts. March off to certain death? Ugh.

CANCEL. PULL YOUR HEAD OUT OF THE NEGATIVITY GUTTER.

"I could pound out this stuff when I was in my twenties." He emitted a soul-shuddering sigh; his lips brushed my hand. "It was easier then, yeah."

"Why?"

"Those Nosey Parker articles got me thinking. The world thinks the most important thing I'll ever do is in my rearview mirror. Inventing the Bio-Bit was a lightning bolt. Everything I do from now on, people will compare it to that. If I went to Mars, the headline would read Bio-Bit inventor on Mars."

"Saving the world is a hard act to follow."

"I wanted to save the world. Like in those old movies Darius and I used to watch with Dad."

AND DARIUS WANTS TO BLOW IT UP.

"What's left? Make money I don't need? Produce music that would get made without me?" The hand made an end run for his hair; I blocked it. "And this welcome thing. Who am I to enlighten them about bliss in security software coding? I'm almost thirty-five, and I don't know what to do with the rest of my life. What makes me an expert on theirs?"

Wowsa. It hit me like a thunderbolt between the eyes. The Tarot message wasn't only for me. Cyrus needed balance, too. "One of my therapists said basing self-worth on success is like a drug. It makes you feel good, and you'll run from victory to victory to keep feeling good."

"Let me guess," he said. "No matter how fast and far you run, you never arrive."

"Right. Worse, to avoid feeling awful, you'll need more and more."

His aura crackled. Crazy energy rolled off him like thunder rumbling in the distance. What next? Windows shattering? The ceiling crashing on our heads? A tidal wave wasn't out of the question. Intervention time.

"I did a reading this morning. Ostara is about balance since the light and dark hours are equal. The cards are smarter than me. I thought the reading was about me; then, I find you all discombobulated. It's about you, too. May I play the recording for you?"

He nodded, and I played it. Emotions ran across his face faster than lightning during a spring storm.

When it finished, he leaned back in his chair and flexed his hands. "Yeah, I see it. I said Nosey made me think. But, nah; I'm not thinking. There's the problem. I'm reacting like Pavlov's dog."

"We can discuss it walking around the neighborhood, looking for signs of spring."

We'd agreed over breakfast on a walk to reset our heads before the ritual. I miscalculated how much resetting was in order. He followed me down the stairs, his steps so heavy I checked to see if he wore cement boots.

GET CRACKING, GIRLFRIEND.

The sunny afternoon required nothing but lightweight jackets. I pointed it out as a sign of spring, which made him smile. We stopped by the flowering maple in our front yard.

"Most people don't notice maple flowers because they're so small." I gestured toward small clusters of flowers as red as his aura. "Maples are a perfect symbol for practical magick because they can adapt to different climates and soils. It's a tree of balance, and we're both in definite need of balance."

"Don't disagree," he said. "We run toward the edges of cliffs, yeah?"

"Just a little." I took his arm when we resumed walking and returned to our earlier discussion and Nosey's effect on him. The *Seven of Cups* capered ahead and inspired me. "You know, Nosey and Alexander are trying to mess with our hopes and dreams. They want to distract us. We need to move them off our radar. We need to believe we have what it takes to make our dreams happen. Think about it."

No argument, only diversion. "Hey, look. Crocuses. We had them in our yard when I was a kid. Darius called them Easter eggs."

The clusters of yellow, deep purple, and white cup-shaped flowers resembled colored eggs. Whenever he said Darius's name, he frowned, but not this time. A wistful expression flickered across his face.

"I suppose they have a symbolic meaning," he said.

"Oh sure. Rebirth and new beginnings. The usual culprits for springtime flowers."

"I like crocuses," he said with a plaintive undertone.

"We'll order corms to plant this fall, and next spring we'll have fields of crocus." *We.* I could say *we* without crashing to the ground and kicking my legs in the air like a toddler.

PROGRESS.

"Corms?"

"Corms," I corrected. "Like a bulb."

"You're trying to make me a gardener." A fake punch to my chin became a caress. "Kidding aside, it'd be nice, yeah. For Riverton, too."

"For sure. I'll get on it." We reached the cross-street with the security checkpoint. I stooped to pick the lavender-blue globes growing in the strip between the sidewalk and the street. I inhaled before handing the mini-bouquet to him. "This is Scilla. They smell like spring."

He nodded and tucked a flower behind my ear. "You're the goddess of spring."

"I wish." If I were, I'd erase the worry wrinkling his brow. I'd transform his mouth's straight, grim line into a smile.

"We'd better turn around." He nodded toward the Bio-Bit checkpoint, sending its data to the neighborhood security service. There it was, the symbolic barrier between us and the pre-Nosey and Alexander world. Eight days ago, we'd have blown past the checkpoint. Now, in an abundance of caution or paranoia, we turned around and headed home, where off-duty policemen supplemented their incomes by making sure if anyone slipped past the checkpoint, they'd come no closer.

Diversion, diversion, diversion.

"What you said about the rearview mirror ... it's only partially true." The middle part of the Tarot reading poked at me like a hot poker. "I mean, sure. Inventing the Bio-Bit is a once-in-a-lifetime achievement; but you can save the world in a billion ways. From each according to his ability, to each according to his needs."

"You know you're quoting Marx, don't you?" He ruffled my hair. "Are you trying to make my filthy capitalist head explode?"

"I could go full-on Wiccan and say as above, so below."

It drew a faint smile, which meant Nosey's comments still rankled; but he'd mastered the diversion game. "The daffodils are early this year. Probably a global warming side effect."

Good observation. I'd make him a gardener yet. "They're still pretty."

"I suppose Nosey will blame me for global warming, too." He squirmed and kept his eyes on the daffodils.

"We have to acknowledge the money. There's so much money, and it has a dark side." I poked the tender bruise because someone needed to tend to it. Money did a number on me, my mother, and, if I felt generous, Emelia. "But it doesn't mean you can't do good things. You can — Holy Hekate, I can't believe I'm trotting out this cliché — you can be the change you want to see in the world."

"I'm listening."

"Some people volunteer in a soup kitchen to feed hungry people. Oma suggested it to me when I said I wanted to help solve world hunger."

WHAT A CONVERSATION THAT WAS.

"Serving enough food to get people through one day didn't cut it for me. I wanted to do something that mattered. What do they say about teaching someone to fish?"

"It's a Chinese proverb. Give a poor man a fish and feed him for a day. Teach him to fish, and you give him an occupation that will feed him for a lifetime."

"Right. So, I found this group online called Heifer International."

"Heifer? Do you know what a heifer is?"

"I know a lot of things. You'd be surprised." I pinched him. "Anyway, Heifer's mission is to end hunger and poverty by giving animals and teaching people how to farm. They have a gift ark. You know, like Noah's Ark with two of every animal. It includes two water buffalos, two cows, two sheep, and two goats, along with chickens, rabbits, and bees. Anyway, it seemed a bargain at $5000."

"So, you donated a gift ark?"

"No, I donated fifteen. I still had money in those days. Think about what you could do."

Our stroll ended across the street from our house beneath a magnificent Witch Hazel tree. I tugged at a branch so we could inhale the yellow buds' spicy scent. *Our. We. We* were in this together.

"We need Witch Hazel trees to keep evil away."

"Heifer." He shook his head in disbelief. "Just when I think you can't amaze me more than you already have, Moonchild."

"I worked with what I found, but you? You could be The Heifer of anything you set your mind to. You can save the world again."

Before I could elaborate, an off-duty police officer rounded the corner of the house. "Hey folks, beautiful day for a walk."

"Sure is, Jim," Cyrus said. Trust him to know the name and recognize the face of every cop he'd hired.

"The guys have been wanting to thank you. The warming tent, the food, the hot coffee. It's like we died and gone to patrol heaven."

"It's the least we can do." All the Cyrus charm came out in full force.

TAKE THAT, NOSEY!

"Most people think it's enough to pay us," Jim said.

"We're so grateful you're here," I said. "I feel safer whenever I see you."

He grinned from ear to ear.

"Are the cameras working?" Cyrus said.

"Yes, sir. Not even a cat's gonna get by us." He turned to me. "Don't you worry, missus, that kook won't get within a mile of you."

Missus? I gulped.

Cyrus reiterated our gratitude, and we went our separate ways.

"I'm working on a foundation, yeah." Cyrus opened the front door, and I scooted into the house. "It could be a Heifer thing if we ever decide what to focus on."

Jealousy spurted through my veins. This time, *we* didn't include me. Who was the mysterious we, anyway? I put on my big girl panties and took the high road. "You can focus on whatever you want. You have that luxury."

"Hmm. I'll put you on the board, and you'll straighten us out." He patted my butt to speed me up the stairs.

"Yeah, right?" I reached the landing. "Anyway, let's focus on the ritual. We're going to meditate on bringing our life in balance and address it in the circle."

He sighed and agreed.

After meditating, he presented me with a gray Valentino garment bag pulled from the depths of his closet. "I know your ritual robe is in Riverton. Does this work in a pinch?"

Inside was an elegant white gown with gathered sleeves and an A-line skirt. Embroidered magenta and chartreuse flowers and black leaves were scattered here and there as if they'd fallen from a tree. The floor-length gown evoked SPRING. I'd admired it in the shop, but the $12,000 price tag jeered *Nosey will have your ass if she finds out*. Cyrus hadn't heard or didn't care about Nosey's opinion. A lesson there for me.

"It's perfect." I kissed his cheek. "In every way."

"Good. You can leave it here and not worry about packing." Some things never changed, and they shouldn't. Cyrus donned a black linen galabeya with gold, green, and red Bedouin embroidery he'd picked up in Cairo. Also, perfect.

Just before sunset, we walked hand-in-hand toward the Chinese room.

"You ready?" I paused at the doorway.

His gaze darted toward the stairs. I almost heard him calculating if he bolted, would I catch him before he made it out the front door. He gave a jerky nod. Typical first Sabbat nerves.

"It'll be fine. I promise."

We cleansed the space and each other with smudging sticks. I called the elements, raised the circle, and made offerings to the God and Goddess.

"If our path is not always straight, and our future seems cloudy, we will continue along the road where all existence comes together." Turning to face Cyrus, I clasped his hands. "On this day of balance, we discovered our life was not in balance and reflected on what we needed to change."

We took turns asking and answering each other how to bring our lives in balance. If it resembled a plan, I called it a divine one. We concluded the ceremony with a commitment to new beginnings.

"Today, the light and the dark are in balance," I said. Certainty, which was becoming more familiar the longer I stayed with Cyrus, sprouted inside me. I closed my eyes to savor it. "Like flowers bursting through the ground, we awaken in Spring. We welcome new beginnings."

Later, we nestled in bed. The lingering scent of incense and oil permeating our skin and hair made me drowsy. I was drifting into sleep when Cyrus's palm settled on my triple moon tattoo.

"The thing tonight." The words rumbled in his chest and against my ear. "I was nervous and skeptical, but it was good, yeah."

"No doubt about it. We're on a roll, Scruffy."

Take Your Girl Friend to Work Day

Monday, March 21

The car turned onto Chmod Court. The Harp Building, thirteen stories of glass shaped like a cantilevered egg, shimmered on the horizon. Rick phoned ahead, so Cyrus was waiting out front and bounded to the car.

"Thanks, Rick. You and Pat can take a break. We're going to dinner after we finish here."

"Very good, sir," Rick said.

"Hey, babe. Let's get you out of the wind." He flashed a thousand-watt smile and ran his hand over my black wool coat, tracing its colorful embroidery and tweaking the wispy pompoms along the front and hood. "The coat looks great, by the way."

"Thanks. This is quite the building."

"Hope so. Buildings can't just be concrete, steel, and glass anymore." His hands flew like excited birds, taking in the building and most of the known world. "They need intangible materials, yeah? Technology, multimedia, intelligence, and interactivity."

Whatever that meant. I nodded.

After clearing DoorMed, we entered a light-filled, three-story atrium. The receptionist, enthroned behind a curved white marble desk, nodded.

Cafés and shops lined a long corridor leading to a glassed-in plaza. Tour groups gathered around a fountain, where water bubbled over black glass and granite blocks into a black granite pool.

"Do I get a tour?"

"Sure. If you want one."

He wanted me to want to, but wouldn't say so. He'd call it bragging. I nodded and spared him.

"These guides do a great job." Cyrus ushered me into a group surrounding a perky redhead wearing a khaki skirt and a white polo shirt with the Harp logo.

The tour group dynamic changed when they recognized Cyrus. People nudged each other and tried to catch his eye. The bolder ones stuck out their hands, and he shook them.

"Welcome to Harp Industries," the tour guide bubbled and waved to get our attention. The tourists turned in her direction, albeit reluctantly. "As you know, Harp Industries, under the leadership of Cyrus Harper, our founder, invented the Bio-Bit and Door-Med technologies in response to the continuing pandemic crises."

Applause rippled through the crowd. Several people bowed Namaste-fashion in Cyrus's direction. He ducked his head, bashful as a teenager, and mouthed thank-you.

"In this building, we've taken the Bio-Bit Cybertecture even further. Employee Bio-Bits monitor their vital signs, weight, and blood pressure and can signal their doctors when necessary." The tour guide had a future as a cheerleader.

"A bit big brother-ish, isn't it?" I covered my mouth with my hand so the adoring crowd wouldn't hear.

"It's the future, babe."

I missed the next few minutes searching for a retort. I failed.

The guide talked as we walked. "We can't visit all the floors because there are several proprietary projects in the works. You'll be hearing about them soon."

My personal guide could (and probably would) make sure I saw those floors.

"We will, however, visit a prototype office, where you'll see how employees can customize their workspace," she promised. "They can choose virtual real-time scenery from around the world for their office windows.

Great idea, isn't it? On a snowy Chicago afternoon, I like to look out my window and see Tahiti."

Bumping my hip against his, I murmured, "Very cool, Mr. Future."

Was that a smirk?

The tour guide directed our attention to the glass façade. "The building's passive solar design decreases heat and lowers energy loads. Solar photovoltaic panels and rooftop wind turbines generate onsite electricity. Extensive gardens shade and cool the building."

"Neat, yeah?" he said, putting his lips to my ear.

"You know it." One thing was obvious. Boyfriend liked his projects. If this building and the weekend doldrums were any clues, starting a music label wouldn't occupy him for long. Note to self: keep him in projects or become one. "Is all this Harp Industries?"

"The first ten floors. Eleven is for start-ups I've invested in. I'll take you up there so you can meet Daniel Khati. Twelve is The Harp Foundation, which we talked about."

People leaned in, trying to hear what he said.

"We need to move along; I think we're a distraction. This way." He hustled me through the stunning greenhouse garden. I'd have to inspect the plants later.

"What's on the thirteenth floor?"

"My office and CPH." CPH was the company whose sole client he was. We rounded a corner if an oval-shaped building had a corner. He stopped at an elevator and slid his ID card into a slot. "You'll need card access for the elevators and upper floors. Here's yours. It works on every floor but thirteen."

He handed me a laminated ID card on a green lanyard with tiny gold harps.

"Hey, how did you get my picture on it?"

"Please. You think I don't have photos of you? The CPH floor uses biometrics. Viv will set you up."

Wondering why I'd go to the thirteenth floor without him and knowing better than to ask, I slipped the lanyard over my head.

"You hungry? Shall I order lunch?" he asked.

"Do you treat all your visitors like this?"

"Only VIPs." The elevator door opened, and we entered. "The chef's decent. I mean, he's not me, but he's decent."

"No one is you." I shrugged off my coat. "Thanks, but I'm full of coffee, dainty little sandwiches, and epic pastries."

"Ah, yes. Mrs. Mueller's coffee." He gestured to my red midi-dress, decorated with raw black trims and black traditional Paraguayan embroidery. "It was appropriate?"

"Lots of compliments. You get promoted to assistant fashion consultant." He'd spotted the dress on our shopping binge and reminded me he enjoyed seeing me in red.

"The ladies were nice to you?"

"Sweet as apple pie, as Oma would say. They invited me back in April and sympathized with me over recent events. Oh, and they told me at least a million times you were a sweetheart and a charmer. I smiled and blushed. So, yeah, they were delightful."

"That's a relief." He pretended to wipe sweat from his brow. "Glad I didn't need to beat up the judge because his wife was a mean girl. Nosey would be all over me."

"Hush, you'll jinx it." No poison pen texts from Alexander, and Nosey hadn't blasted out a character assassination since Wednesday. Cyrus's crack IT team was on it, but why tempt fate?

"Good point."

When we reached the seventh floor, Cyrus prompted me to try my ID card in the reader. It chimed, Door-Med read our health, and the door opened into a hive of computer beeps and droning voices. People discussing serious matters fell silent and snapped to attention.

A transformation came over Cyrus, too. No sign of the despondent guy who wondered what to do with his life. Greeting people by name, he asked about their projects. He remembered little personal details. (George was our first intern; he impressed us so much we had to hire him.) He handed out praise, but not indiscriminately. After the Cyrus-encounter, the troops stood a little taller, shoulders back, faces glowing. If Nosey saw this Cyrus, she might sing a different tune.

"This is Maren," he said like they were panting for an introduction.

When the first person said "So good to finally meet you," I almost blinked. It came to me. The world knew Cyrus and I were together. But this group gobbled up news about the Greier murder and the recent tabloid stories. After all, their future depended on him.

After a brief tour, we went to the eleventh floor to meet Daniel Khati, in whose company Cyrus suggested I invest. Super nice guy. Back in the elevator, I channeled the good girlfriend. "How's it going with the PSEC crew?"

"Good, I think. We had breakfast. HR gave them the down low on their benefits package. They seemed pleased by the upgrade. Now, they're geeking out in a lab."

"Winning friends and influencing people."

He took a bow.

Good girlfriend came out again. "Will your record label have offices on this floor?"

He beamed. "Oh, for sure. Pieter's excited that we won't look like a poor startup."

As IF!

Before heading to the thirteenth floor and CPH, we toured the mostly empty, but impressive, floor where the Harper Foundation was germinating. He waved his Bio-Bit at an ordinary glass panel; it slid back to reveal an elevator. Did he get the idea from the bathroom safe? He waved me in and pressed his face into the eye-level camera. A female voice purred, "Welcome back, Cyrus."

"Cute. Your last girlfriend?"

"I'll change it to your voice." The door slid closed; when it opened, we faced a blank wall. He repeated the wrist waving and eye scanning process.

"In the old days, my office was right off the bullpen." Nostalgia tinged his voice. "People wandered by and shared their ideas. Then, this guy we fired got all bent out of shape. He blew in and took a punch at me."

"Oh, my god. Were you hurt?"

"Nah. I'm not the pretty boy you think I am." He winked. "Brown belt, remember? But when I built this place, the board insisted I take security precautions. They put me in an office with windows eight inches thick. You can't even select the thirteenth-floor elevator without the right Bio-Bit and biometric readings. If someone unsavory hitches a ride, the inner corridor has security people, although you'd never guess it by looking at them. They say it's for my safety, but they're not afraid someone will punch me. They're terrified someone will pitch a wild ass idea to me, and I'll run with it."

We entered a corridor that might have been a sci-fi movie set. Two guys in khakis and black polo shirts with the gold Harp logo sat behind control desks. Cyrus was wrong. I instantly made them for security. Like Hunky Guy from The Drake, they were all muscle and no-nonsense. Security, I could deal with, but I needed a hot minute before strolling past the inner sanctum minions. I gestured toward a door with the Women sign. "Just gonna pop in here."

"I have a bathroom off my office," he said.

"Nah, I want to see the ladies' facilities to make sure you treat them right."

"OK. I'm straight down the hall. Doesn't look good if I lurk outside the women's loo like a perv."

The ladies' room was both high-tech and feminine. The black floor tiles, the geometrical tiled white walls, and the industrial fixtures blended with the spacious stalls and black wallpaper with red roses. Stainless steel dispensers delivered high-end soaps and lotions. I took the first available stall.

The outer door opened, and a voice drifted over the cubicle wall. "Cyrus is here today."

"Yeah, Mary saw his car in the parking garage."

A third voice piped up. "Bill saw him get in the elevator. *She's* with him."

She. AKA me. No stall doors opened. Must be make-up replenishment time.

"You think she's really a witch?" Voice One said.

"Must be." Voice Three snickered. "Has to be a spell. Who here hasn't given Cyrus the old college try and nada? Not even a coffee in the cafeteria. Remember when everyone decided he was gay, and Emory was the happiest guy in the whole USA?"

"Yeah, right before he joined the Cyrus-didn't-give-me-the-time-of-day club," Voice Two drawled. "His Babe of the Month thing convinced me he liked girls just fine."

Babe of the Month? Mr. Lonely-hearts would hear about this.

"OK, changing my vote to witch," Voice One said. "Not to mention, he's been with her for almost four months. It's a record."

"Johnny likes her. He said she's nice."

He did?

"Johnny's a newb, and he likes everybody."

"The presents. Oh my god, we could all retire on the presents he gives her."

"What besides the necklace?"

"For Christmas, he bought her a vintage Patek Phillipe watch. Set him back half a mil, and he had the lab convert it into a Bio-Bit. Valentine's Day, he gave her diamond studs; cost him fifty large, and he sent Johnny to Paris to get special chocolates."

"No wonder Johnny likes her. He went to Paris for the chocolates, and he took the necklace from Beijing to Hawaii. Cyrus gives him a day or two to enjoy the sights. She's Johnny's ticket to fun."

"I wonder if Johnny is still willing to travel. He's got a girlfriend, now."

"Wait, Johnny has a girlfriend?"

A round of titters. "Met her right after he came back from Paris. They got hot and heavy in a nano-second. Notice how sleepy he looks these days?"

"Speaking of hot and heavy, back to Cyrus. He told Viv to get the necklace no matter what it took; sky was the limit. So, the witch must have world-shaking nookie."

"Whatever! She's a scrawny little thing to be wearing such an important necklace."

They erupted in a chorus of giggles. I could have squashed them like bugs by opening the door and washing my hands, but decided to support Johnny's *nice* assessment. The outside door opened and Voice Four announced, "Cyrus is in his office."

They stampeded out. Had I been transported to the Court of Louis XIV? Would Cyrus prance out in a sun costume and declare to rapturous applause, "Le business, c'est moi?" Wait, wrong king. WWCGD? What Would Cyrus the Great Do?

The hallway was no longer empty. A dozen people bustled around, trying to look busy. Others gathered in the various offices, engaging in ever-so-important conversations, judging by their serious expressions. Pro tip: don't undercut your business mien by nudging each other and swiveling your heads in my direction when I walk by.

Nonetheless, I felt compelled to ask an office dweller, "I'm a little turned around. I'm looking for Mr. Harper's office."

The man gave me a puzzled look. The word *seriously* might have popped up in a thought bubble over his head.

Oh. My. Sweet. Goddess. Mr. Harper?

I sounded like Oma. Even the guys on the seventh floor and the Bathroom Gossip Girls called him Cyrus.

The man gestured toward the southern end of the building. "Big office at the end of the corridor. You can't miss it."

I scurried away before I confirmed his impression I was an idiot.

Reaching his office, I paused in the doorway, awestruck. Cyrus, reading a tablet, sat on a massive ebony desk. Overhead, a chandelier with metal ribbons of dark bronze, mosaic gold, and silver bore a strong resemblance to a crown. Behind the desk, illuminated cases framed antique swords mounted on what looked like gray silk. Framed black-and-white portraits of legendary jazz and blues musicians set off the black paneling. No virtual window scene for Cyrus. The Chicago skyline, Diversey Harbor, and Lake Michigan spread themselves at his feet, courtesy of a two-story window. No decorator here, this was Cyrus Unleashed. If you weren't intimidated, you weren't paying attention.

With the uncanny acuity of cats and Fae princes, he looked up. "Hello, Trouble. Come on in."

"I can see why you prefer my kitchen table to this rat hole."

"The table has a better view. Sometimes, I get to see you wearing my sweatshirt and nothing else." He patted the desk. "I could, however, be persuaded to think more highly of this office if you'd kick the door closed and consider a quickie."

Tempting. Oh, so tempting. Until I remembered the Gossip Girls and all the people with their ears to their doors. "Next time."

No one sighed more dramatically than Cyrus.

THREE LITTLE PIGS

MONDAY, MARCH 21

IF CYRUS'S OFFICE OVERWHELMED the visiting humans with its Dark Fae Prince vibe, Viv's dazzling white office intimidated them with ice. The six-foot-tall woman with the regal profile of a Nubian queen in a steel blue silk tuxedo jacket and pants, magenta blouse, and matching stilettos radiated power. By the skin of my teeth, I stopped myself from genuflecting.

Viv overlooked my tongue-tied admiration. "I thought this desk might do when Cyrus told me you chose the room with the Chinese cabinets."

Johnny Marlow, as resplendent as Viv in a navy pin-striped suit over an eyeball-burning red and orange argyle vest, handed me a photograph and description.

Classic harpsichord shape ... model of 18th-century efficiency and functionality ... multiple nooks, crannies, pigeonholes, and drawers ... elegant Chinese black lacquer ... mother-of-pearl inlay ... heirloom quality ... custom-made matching chair included.

"Beautiful." What else could I say?

"Isn't it?" Johnny gushed. He hadn't stopped grinning since I greeted him by name.

"It's a local dealer. Say the word, and it will be there this afternoon," Viv said.

"Sounds perfect."

Cyrus wiggled his eyebrows the way he did when Oma went all Boss Granny. A match-up between Viv and Oma going *mano y mano* for the privilege of orchestrating our lives would sell out Wrigley Field. A gaggle of titters begged me to set them free. My phone pinged. Hoping the distraction might save me, I swiped the message.

> **Alexander:**
> Do you like the shrine to Cyrus's genius?
> I find it ostentatious. Is he over-compen-
> sating for a lack in another department? I
> guess you'd know. BTW: I'm hurt you changed
> your number, but did you think it would
> stop me?

How did he get *this* number?

> **Alexander:**
> Gilbert K. Chesterton, said, "The man who
> throws a bomb is an artist because he
> prefers a great moment to everything."
> But Nikita Khrushchev said, "Bombs do not
> choose. They will hit everything." Who's
> right?

WTF was he talking about? Why was he talking to me?

"What's wrong, babe? You look like you've seen a ghost." Cyrus took my arm. "Do you need to sit? Some water?"

The overhead communications system crackled to life. "Ms. Betty Bit, report to facilities. Betty Bit to facilities."

Cyrus and Viv locked gazes. He raised his eyebrows, and she nodded, a short, jerky motion.

"Betty Bit to facilities, please."

The two men from the security desk, guns drawn, barged in without knocking.

"Sorry, Mr. Harper, Ms. Chastain." Guy One glanced in my direction, and his eyes went vacant. "Sorry, miss, but we need to move you folks right now. Follow me, please. You, too, Johnny."

"Is it a drill?" Cyrus tightened his grip on my arm and whispered. "Betty Bit is the code for a bomb threat."

Without waiting for the security guys to answer, he moved me toward the door. Viv and Johnny fell into step behind us.

"No, sir. Credible threat called in at 14:40. We're moving you to the panic room," Guy One said.

"Turn off your phones and any other digital devices except your Bio-Bits. Right now," Guy Two barked. "We don't want any signals detonating the bomb."

Viv reached for the light switch, and Guy Two put his hand over it. "Leave it. Could be a trigger."

They herded us into the hallway toward an unremarkable paneled door. Guy One stood guard; Guy Two fiddled with his Bio-Bit. The panel slid back. He nodded to Cyrus, who pressed his thumb to the scanner. An alarm clangor started; I covered my ears. A door opened into a narrow stairwell with harsh, blinking lights. The strobing and clanging encircled my skull like a vise. The door closed, and the alarm dwindled to a dull cacophony. A testimony to the walls' thickness?

"Shouldn't we evacuate?" I asked. WTF? WTF! How many more times this month would someone move me around like furniture because of an imminent threat?

"Afraid not, miss," Guy One said as we reached the 12th floor. "The caller wants you and Mr. Harper to come out alone. Could be a sniper situation."

"Don't worry, babe. The panic room is a bunker," Cyrus said. "It can ride out a nuclear attack."

Nuclear attack? Was that supposed to reassure me?

THIS ISN'T A BUCKET OF ICE WATER OR SOMEONE SINGING DING DONG, THE WITCH IS DEAD.

My face went numb like someone slapped me.

YOU COULD DIE HERE.

A spider of fear wriggled up my neck; my hands and feet prickled. Somewhere before the 11th floor, I stumbled and lurched forward.

"Careful, babe."

Cyrus's death grip saved me from tumbling head over heels down a hundred steps.

"What's the evacuation protocol for everyone else?" Cyrus asked.

"We've moved them to interior rooms until Site Search finishes evaluating the routes and evacuation areas for HOT items."

"Hot means Hidden, Obviously suspicious, and not Typical," Cyrus explained, a factoid I never imagined I'd need to know.

"Once we finish, we'll move them out the lakeside doors," Guy Two said.

"Harbor Patrol's already there to help with an evacuation," Guy One added. "Police and bomb squad are on the way to assist Site Search."

Bomb squad! A reminder of why we were scuttling down this secret stairway. Fear of falling had made me forget. Above us, a door banged shut.

Don't Look Back! If someone's stalking you, there's no time for looking. It's probably Site Search.

My quick, shallow breaths ricocheted off the walls like bullets. Cancel! CANCEL! CANCEL, DAMN YOU!

A sign announced we'd reached the 1st floor. I prayed for the door to open and for someone to tell us it was a joke or a drill to see if high-powered tech tycoons could follow instructions. Instead, my heart thudded in my ears so loud I'd never have heard them. A dash of vertigo and the black spots dancing before my eyes made me stumble again. Thanks to Cyrus, I only banged my shoulder against the wall.

"It's OK, babe," he said. I didn't hear him; I read his lips. "We're almost there."

We continued downward for what seemed an hour, but when I checked my Bio-Bit later the whole journey from the 13th floor to the sub-basement lasted about seven minutes. The air felt heavier as if the building's weight pressed on us. Another figment of my imagination? I hoped so.

We emerged into a long gray hall. A thick circular door with dozens of locks and bolts was at the far end. It resembled an old-fashioned bank vault.

"24-inch-thick steel," Cyrus said. "It's modeled on the First National Bank vault where the Dalton Gang made their last stand."

I wanted to acknowledge the effort he made to distract me. The words eked past the boulder in my throat. "What happened to them?"

"All the bad guys died, save one, and he went to jail."

"Good," I croaked.

Be careful what you wish for. Law of three.

Guy One gestured. "Sir?"

Cyrus pressed his finger into a fingerprint reader and his face into an optical scanner. All the gears and levers were for show; the vault door swung open with a whisper.

The panic room might have been a snazzy VIP lounge at the airport. A jumbo-sized television covered one wall before a curved sofa. A fireplace, surrounded by bookcases filled with books and video disks, occupied another wall. Open doors led to hotel-style bedrooms. Cyrus had planned to panic in style.

"Make yourselves comfortable." Cyrus gestured toward the couch. "We'll be here for a while. If you get tired, there are five bedrooms. Stake your claim. The kitchen's over there if you get hungry, and I'm suspending the rule about drinking on company time."

How could he be so calm?

"What happens if the building blows up?" My question ended on an octave that would make a soprano proud.

"We'll be here until they dig us out." He squeezed my waist. "We can survive for a year or longer since there are only six of us. I think we planned for ten to fifteen people."

Guys One and Two nodded in agreement.

"Great. When Oma and Uncle Ira catch wind of this, they'll dig me out with their bare hands and yank me back to Riverton by my hair."

"I don't think it'll come to that," Cyrus said. "Johnny, get Maren a glass of wine."

A glass? Think barrels, boyfriend. He opened the bar and splashed scotch into a crystal tumbler. Eschewing the niceties of inhaling the scent and savoring the flavor, he knocked it back like cheap tequila and poured another. We were on the same page.

Guy One and Two waved away the offer of alcohol and stood guard. Like anyone could make it through 24 inches of steel and all the bio-metrics on earth. Viv sipped a Gin and Tonic, and Johnny slouched in the corner with a bottle of Fiendish Ol' Monk ale. Getting blown into the Summerland while you were drunk wasn't a bad way to go. At least, I hoped so.

We waited.

The Ice Queen enthroned herself on the couch. If, no, WHEN we got out of this mess, I wanted her to teach me how to look stone cold while your Inner Voice screamed, *you're going to die*. Poor Johnny Marlow looked green, and his hair stood up in bushy shock waves from running his fingers through it. I bit the inside of my cheek until it bled.

Cyrus paced. Spine stiff, head lowered ready to charge, eyes narrowed, and lips curled into a snarl, the Rottweiler was out in full force. I debated showing him the texts from Alexander but decided against it. When Cyrus paced in her direction, Viv shrank into the cushions, looking ready to take her chances with the bomb. I screwed my courage to the sticking point and joined the pacing, looping my arm through his. He didn't shrug me off or bite me.

"Do you think Alexander's behind the bomb?" Stupid question. The answer was in the texts that I hadn't shown him yet.

"Absolutely," he snapped. His eyebrows drew together in a straight black line like a storm cloud on the horizon. "No doubt he's sent a press release to *Tattleverse* by now."

Made sense. Alexander and Nosey were kindred spirits. After a few turns around the room, I guided him to the couch. Miracle of miracles, he sat. Viv scooted to the other end.

We enjoyed the ersatz calm until a phone rang. Guy One picked up the receiver of an old landline.

"Landlines don't trigger bombs," Cyrus said in response to my enquiring look.

Guy One put his hand over the receiver and turned to Cyrus. "A television station received a video. They sent a copy to the police, and they thought you should see it, sir. See if you recognize anyone?"

Cyrus gestured to the gigantic television.

"Send it to PanRoom1," Guy One said.

Panic Room 1? How imaginative.

Guy One hung up the phone and faced Cyrus, making him the bravest person in the room. "The evac routes are clear. They're moving people to the lakeside evacuation areas. No tall buildings out there for a sniper shot, but they put up screens in case someone's hiding in the bushes. Buses are arriving."

"Good. At least the plan's working." Cyrus stroked his chin. "When can we leave?"

"Not until everyone's gone. In case we're talking about a disgruntled employee with a gun."

My rising hope did a nosedive. Cyrus patted my hand. A CD arrived via a pneumatic tube. Cyrus shoved the CD into the player.

The now-too-familiar Skeleton Girl rocked in a chair before a cozy fireplace that dissolved into an explosion. Her rocking picked up speed as Armageddon ensued. She opened a leather-bound book. The camera lingered on her expressive arched eyebrows and the mask with a bone-white face and juicy pink lips.

"Consistent branding," Cyrus muttered.

With the world turning to ash behind her, Skeleton Girl spoke.

> "I bet your mother read *The Three Little Pigs* to you. Mine did, but we didn't hear the real story."

"Somebody needs to go back to acting school," Cyrus said. The girl spoke with a poncy accent, but Chicago broke through.

> "Once upon a time, a poor old mother pig named America had too many piglets to feed, clothe, and shelter. So, she sent them out into the world to seek their fortune. The world was arrogant and gluttonous. Instead of art, Shakespeare, and the pursuit of happiness, we learned to accept Pieter Thornhill's imbecilic ramblings and a world governed by pandemics designed to make rich people richer."

"Dumbass." Cyrus muttered curses under his breath. I patted his knee.

> "In our world, not all piglets are created equal. Some piglets lie and cheat their way into vast fortunes, leaving us with their droppings. One piglet has a domineering attitude and insists on having his way. No matter the cost."

The image faded to a pig with curly black hair, heavy eyebrows, and a five o'clock shadow encroaching on its snout. Oof. Cyrus's knee juddered like he was sitting on an earthquake.

"In this dog-eat-dog society, you don't have to be competent to be successful. If you tell enough people you're competent and know how to influence them, people will applaud your so-called ability. So, it is with our third piglet. Suffering from a delusion of competency, he built a shrine to his alleged achievements. Like the Egyptian Pharaohs, his vanity made him believe it was his House of Millions of Years, a monument to proclaim his glory until the end of time. His house, however, like his accomplishments, is straw. Or should we say glass?"

Maybe Alexander's tactic was to make Cyrus the bomb because he was ready to explode.

"One day, a wolf came upon the straw house."

Skeleton Girl held up a drawing of an egg-shaped straw building. Subtlety wasn't her strong suit.

"The wolf knocked on the door 'Little pig, little pig, let me in!'
"'Not by the hair on my chinny-chin-chin!' cried the frightened little pig."

The pig caricature trembled, cried, and snot dripped from his nose.

"'I'll huff, and I'll puff, and I'll BLOW your house down!' growled the wolf. And he did.
"In the traditional narrative, you're told the wolf is the bad guy."

Skeleton Girl shook her head, more in sorrow than anger.

"But the real villain is the greedy pig who took all your money to build his straw house. The wolf was trying to set things straight."

Skeleton Girl dissolved into a dull red background thrumming like seismic waves. A quick fade-in followed, revealing the Man in Black, hiding behind mirrored sunglasses and a gaiter. But today, no cap covered his shoulder-length hair, the color of black licorice.

"Hello, Cyrus not the Great. Are you trembling yet? You will."

Man in Black's voice was garbled as if he spoke through a distortion machine. He'd gone stylish for his fifteen seconds of fame, wearing a silky black turtleneck under a black jacket. Cyrus had rocked that look on more than one occasion. Coincidence? I thought not. Man in Black's eyes seemed to hunt for us despite the sunglasses. Loathing and menace oozed through the camera.

"The day comes when I'll stand at your door, saying 'Cyrus, Cyrus, let me in.'
And you'll bleat 'Not by the hair of my chinny-chin-chin.' I'll huff and puff and blow your straw castle down."

The camera pulled back. The Man in Black wore a boutonniere in his lapel. Spiny, scarlet seed pods nestled against a star-shaped gray leaf with red veins.

"It's Alexander," I whispered.

"Probably, yeah." Cyrus was laser-focused on the video.

"I'll shoot your plane from the sky and demolish your factories."

"No, I'm sure." A faint whiff of mugwort, its sage-like scent well-seasoned with frankincense and cinnamon, tickled my nose. An unquestionable sign I understood the Man in Black's allusion. "His boutonniere is a Castor Bean. The seeds inside the pod contain ricin, you know, ricin; 6,000 times more poisonous than cyanide."

"What?" I had Cyrus's attention now, but only for a second.

The Man in Black nodded as if he'd heard.

"I will burn your witch, and she will no longer cast spells. On that day, you'll feel my justice."

The crystal tumbler hit the oyster-shell-colored wall, and the fine Scotch left an amber stain. "The slimy bastard is going down."

THE GARDENER

FOR THE SECOND TIME this year, I found myself in a squad car. This time, I was the victim. I didn't feel any less trapped. I closed my eyes to the budding maples and daffodils along Lake Shore Drive. Two days ago, they promised new beginnings; today, they mocked it.

Cyrus squeezed my hand until it felt bruised. He looked cool and calm; if you knew what to look for, there were signs of icy rage. He'd gone silent, forgoing his usual camaraderie with the police officers. I felt the ice pulsing through his veins and heard the whirring and clicking of his busy brain shifting to cyber-detachment, calculating an algorithm of retaliation and retribution. I shivered.

"It's gonna be OK, babe." The smile didn't reach his eyes. No bomb, the bomb squad said. At least no bombs that could destroy a building. But as sure as spring followed winter, a bomb exploded in our lives.

"Just got a text." The officer in the front passenger seat turned and peered at us through the security screen. "Said we'll finish with your car tomorrow afternoon at the latest."

Technicians were combing through Cyrus's car. Someone had smashed the window. Was there a bomb in the car? Had someone tampered with the electronics? The brakes? CPD wasn't taking any chances.

"Thanks. I'll send someone for it." Clipped and efficient. No time to waste on chit-chat when you were plotting a reprisal.

"You reckon this is the same bunch that gave you trouble at The Drake and Sonny Boy's?"

It wasn't a great feeling when the police knew about your troubles.

The officer didn't wait for an answer. "You folks need to get yourself protection."

"People at the house 24/7." Cyrus bristled. I withdrew my hand before he mangled it.

"Good. You need someone when you leave the house, too.

"Ah. Yeah. Good idea. Hear that, babe? You're getting a bodyguard?" He retrieved my hand.

Over the weekend, he'd tiptoed around the possibility. I'd rejected the idea as pointless. A bodyguard only drew attention and gave Alexander the satisfaction of knowing he'd rattled us. Cyrus caved, but today changed everything. The frost in his voice, the way his eyebrows drew together like a thunderbolt, the steel rod instead of a spine pointed to one thing. Argument was futile, and a bodyguard was in my future. His next words confirmed it.

"Maybe Beckett from The Drake. You liked him, yeah?"

"You mean Beckett Smith? We've worked with him. Good man." The officer nodded for emphasis.

"What about you?" I said.

"I'll be fine." The cocky, genuine smile returned. "Brown belt, remember?"

"When I last checked, a brown belt didn't stop a bomb."

"Don't hold back, babe. Tell me how you really feel."

The officers chuckled.

The squad car pulled up to the curb as a Chicago Hands-Free delivery van pulled away. We thanked the officers and headed up the driveway, past a bronze Volvo SUV.

"Christ on a Crutch," Cyrus muttered. He grabbed my arm and hurried me along the walk. "Cassandane. Just what we need."

"She's worried about you." I shuddered to imagine what my brother would say. I stopped short. Cyrus collided with my backside.

A simple bouquet blocked the front door. Lenten Roses formed the core of the arrangement. The midnight-purple blooms and leathery evergreen leaves were funereal. Lenten Rose was an ingredient in the legendary flying ointment and in blighting charms. The other blossom was Black Henbane.

Its pale lemon and black-veined petals and dark center emphasized the Lenten Roses' shadows. Called Devil's Eyes or the Witches Plant, witches in the Middle Ages used henbane in ritual purifications, love potions, and the ubiquitous flying ointments. Every part of the plant was poisonous, and its fishy odor alone caused some people to faint.

A fat cream-colored envelope propped against the vase bore my name. The prickling hairs on my neck told me who sent it. I expected the message to read: *Thou shalt not suffer a witch to live.*

"Freaking sympathy flowers," Cyrus grumbled. "Sorry about the bomb. Hope the flowers cheer you up."

"Don't touch it." I swallowed hard. Boyfriend needed a crash course in poisonous plants.

When he realized what I meant, the Rottweiler emerged, chewing its way through any semblance of cool. He growled. "Alexander!"

Goddess, forgive me, but if I had the wherewithal to cast a summoning, I'd put Alexander in Cyrus's path and relish the spectacle of Cyrus ripping him to pieces and hurling the bloody chunks into the lake. I sucked in the chilly evening air and let it tamp down my fury.

"This bouquet is not only poison, it's bragging. See the black flower? There's speculation Alexander the Great died from its poison. This is Alexander saying he can handle poison with impunity."

Cyrus's brown eyes turned as black as Alexander's soul.

"It's also supposed to make you invisible." I risked the fallout from his fury so Cyrus could understand Alexander's message. "Lore says a magician threw the powdered plant in the air over his head and moved unseen through enemy lines."

"We'll see about that," Cyrus said.

"He's a gardener. Alexander's a gardener, or he knows one." Why hadn't I seen the pattern before now? "No way is he choosing poisonous plants by accident. He's using them to send a message."

"He slipped up this time. I got the name of the delivery service so the police can track him." Arm around my waist, he steered me toward the backyard. We entered through the kitchen, where he instructed Rick to dispose of another poison bouquet, concluding with, "Tomorrow, we'll order hazmat suits."

Rick managed a chuckle.

Cassandane and Rafael paced the floor in the sunroom. Upon seeing Cyrus, Cassandane emitted a strangled yelp and wrapped herself around him like an octopus.

"Oh. My. God. Cyrus!" A hysterical gulp followed each word.

He patted her back. "There. There. There."

Rafael had discovered the wine cellar, and he poured a glass for me.

"I saw the damn video," Cassandane said, "and I know who he is."

WHAT?!?

It never occurred to me that the Harpers might know Alexander. I pegged him as someone from my shady past.

"It's Eli King," she said. The name came out in a gush. "It's Eli. Tell him, Rafael."

"Eli Who?" A baffled Cyrus was a rare sight.

"The programmer we fired," Rafael prompted.

Cyrus shook his head.

"Oh, for God's sake, Cyrus." Cassandane sputtered, droplets of spit flying. "You remember. He's the guy who slipped features into the code during regression test. After you told him not to. We almost missed the release date for Bio-Bit 1.0 thanks to him. It's the same guy who hit on all the women."

"The dude who tried to punch you out," Rafael said dryly, "and you decked him."

"Oh, that guy? Wasn't he a skinny blond twerp? The video guy was ripped and had straggly black hair."

"Hair dye, bro, hair dye, and serious gym time." Cassandane rolled her eyes. "It's Eli. I know it."

"Why do you think that?" Cyrus threw his hands up in self-defense.

"He always called you Cyrus Not the Great," Rafael said. He poured more wine. "All. The. Time."

"Did he?"

Cassandane shook her head in disbelief and turned to me. "Cyrus lived in a rabbit hole back then. He focused on the release date and how much money we had left. He came unglued when Eli slipped in the new code and everything went splat."

Cyrus grabbed the wine bottle from the end table and took a swig. "I'd already hit Dad up for a loan to make payroll."

"Totally focused." Rafael leaned toward me. "We had to tell him when to take a shower."

"Eli lost his stock options and tried to sue us. Do you remember?" Cassandane said.

"Oh, God. That guy was an unending whinge-fest of hard-done poor-me." Cyrus shook his head. "But why call himself Alexander Filippidis? Oh, wait, it's like a nom de guerre, yeah?"

"Bingo," Cassandane said, "and Mom's gonna kill you for not remembering, but who was Alexander Filippidis? Come on. Think."

"It's been a long day, Cass. Don't do this."

"Alexander, son of Phillip. Alexander the Great. The guy who conquered the Persian empire and defeated Darius the Great. Wrong brother, but hey, it's got a ring to it, yeah?"

"I guess." Cyrus sounded doubtful. "I never thought Eli was a clever devil, not like this Alexander."

"He was talented," Rafael said, "but obstinate, the squeaky wheel who refused to do what he was told. And he hated you because he lost millions in stock options."

"Ah." Cyrus nodded. "It's all coming back. He was a self-righteous little prick. When he wasn't whining, he was bragging about how smart he was."

"Was Eli interested in plants? Unusual ones?" They looked surprised to hear me speak; maybe, they'd forgotten I was there.

Cyrus shrugged.

With that one gesture, I saw how Cyrus's indifference to Alexander goaded him. It was festering resentment à la Emelia with the same old root of all evil. Money. If Cyrus couldn't be bothered to remember Eli, he'd damn well remember Alexander.

"How did you know?" Cassandane squealed. "He filled his cubicle and a neighboring one with plants. The kind with thorns and foul smells. Once he brought in a Venus Fly Trap and a jar of flies. It was so gross."

"Eli's your man," I said.

"We need to find him, prove he is behind the shenanigans, and let the police take control. The delivery truck might be the key." Cyrus, cheated out of wreaking his full fury on Alexander's head, sounded annoyed.

Stopping Alexander wouldn't be that easy. I felt it in my bones.

THE FATHER OF ALL CRAZINESS

TUESDAY, MARCH 22

DOWN. DOWN. DOWN THE stairway into the pit. Alarms clanged. Sometimes I was inside the noise; sometimes the noise was inside me. A rumble from the building's bowels started in my feet; it scrabbled up into my knees and chest. One by one, the steps crumbled. Air, hotter than a dragon's breath, surged from the darkness. I grabbed for the railing, but it dissolved into ash. Falling felt like flying until my arms and legs began flailing, which didn't slow down my descent into the fiery inferno.

I woke clammy with sweat. I did a spot check to reassure myself I was in our bedroom. Pale gray linen sheets. The duvet's nubby texture. Laundry detergent mingled with Oud's peppery bergamot and Roja Luxe's rose and jasmine on the pillows. The sunlight off the lake made the familiar rainbow pattern on the walls. Despite so many reassurances, my heart continued to pound because yesterday's bomb threat and long descent waited for its time to roll around again.

After meditation, prayers, and a shower, the jitters receded until their next opportunity to pounce.

WHAT DID YOU EXPECT?

A reasonable question, but if I didn't get it under control, I'd be jumping out of my skin until I was nothing but tatters. There was only one thing to do. I pulled out my Tarot deck and turned on *BoSsBlog*.

"What do I need to know today?"

I shuffled and cut the deck five times. With each cut, the breath tightened in my lungs and throat. My insides quivered like jelly. So much for tranquility. I drew a card and placed it on the floor.

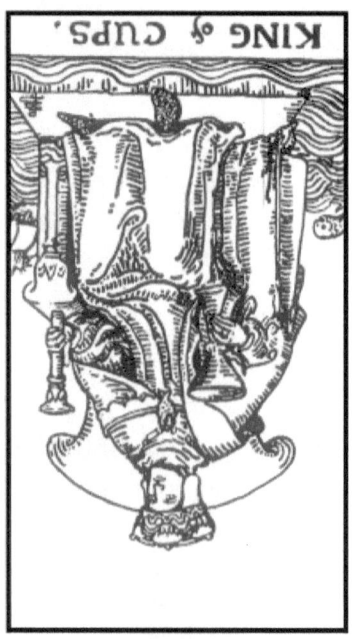

In Tarot, kings and queens represented people in your life. The *Page* and *Queen of Cups* were both fair-haired. When I'd consulted the cards about Simon Greier's murder, the *Queen of Cups* reversed pointed toward my flaxen-haired frenemy, Emelia. Under his helmet, was the *King of Cups* another blonde killer? He was if I believed Cassandane's allegation that Eli was Alexander, and I did.

Behind *The King*, the swirling green, turquoise, and gray water churned; a ship listed on the horizon. An upright *King of Cups* stood stalwart against turbulence; a reversed *King* reveled in it. He was the father of all craziness. Charismatic, volatile, enigmatic, and vindictive, he blamed other people for his failures and possessed a talent for emotional manipulation and destruction. *Alexander, are you ready for your close-up?* This card invited me to explore his soul. Sorry, that invitation was a powder keg, and no RSVP was forthcoming.

Was it my imagination, or was *The King* smirking? The room rotated faster than a merry-go-round. I shuffled *The King* back into the deck and concentrated on breathing until the dizziness passed.

YOU CAN HIDE THE CARD, BUT YOU CAN'T BANISH ALEXANDER.

Someone tapped on the door, and I jumped like a scalded cat.

"The police want to speak with us," Cyrus said.

I'd never hear that sentence without remembering the police bursting through our front door and accusing us of murder.

CALM THE FUCK DOWN! YOU'RE THE VICTIM HERE.

"Did they find him?"

Cyrus shook his head.

"Did they at least find the delivery truck?"

"Yeah, but no joy there." Cyrus pulled me to my feet. "It was a contactless delivery service. There are kiosks all over town. You take your package there, pay the fee, and pop it onto a conveyor belt. It goes into a locker; a van picks it up and delivers it."

"But there's video surveillance, right?" The smirking *King of Cups* floated before me. *Scram!*

Cyrus pulled a long face. "It's about what you'd expect. A girl in a skeleton mask and hoody. She paid for the delivery with a pre-paid debit card. You can buy them almost anywhere, and I bet she paid cash for the card, so it'll be untraceable. She walked from the kiosk, so no license plates to run. CCTV caught her entering the Purple Line station at Foster, but no sign of her in the crowd on the platform. Probably changed masks and jackets."

Damn Alexander. He was good, very good.

"Anyway, the police want you to listen to the bomb threat call." Cyrus's arm snaked around my waist and stayed there as we made the short trek from the bedroom to his office. "If I ruled the world ..."

"You don't?" I said, trying to keep things light.

A glimmer of a smile appeared. "Not yet. But if I did, I wouldn't let you listen to the recording. It's vile."

What else could you expect from someone as loathsome as Alexander? I took a seat before the monitors. "Have you heard it already?"

"Harp recorded the call. We gave the police and FBI a copy. So, yeah, I heard it."

He sat beside me, one arm around my shoulder, and fired up Face2Face. The police must have given him a direct number; the transmission went straight to a guy with clipped gray hair and a weather-beaten face.

"Good morning, again, Mr. Harper. Ms. Lilienthal, I'm Detective Murphy, and this is Agent Sanchez from the FBI." A second man leaned into the frame and nodded. "The FBI is helping with this case. We apologize for putting you through this ordeal. But if you recognize this guy, it might move things along."

My gut knotted, expecting his geniality to turn on a dime. Detective Schulze had been darn friendly. At first.

BETTER BE ON YOUR BEST BEHAVIOR, MAREN.

"Not a problem. Anything I can do to help."

"Again, our thanks," Murphy said. "Let's get to it, and you can have your morning back."

Alexander had already hijacked my morning, if not the entire day.

The detective started the recording. Whoever placed the call had climbed the Harp phone tree until they reached an actual person.

"Harp Industries. How may I direct your call?"

"I'll let you decide, Ma'am." The male voice was soft, hypnotic.

A song in the background drummed the refrain, "The revolution will not be televised."

"Yesterday." The seductive voice turned icy. "My friends visited your place with backpacks. They were in the main concourse, the shops, and the secondary hallways."

"Did they lose something? I'll connect you with Lost and Found."

"Not exactly." A chuckle worthy of a cartoon villain. "They left seven backpacks with seven pipe bombs. Seven bombs with a 500-meter blast radius."

The receptionist's gulp came through loud and clear. "I see. Yes, I see. Can you tell me where they're located?"

"No."

"Can you describe the backpacks?"

Seriously? She expected an answer? I glanced at Cyrus, who whispered, "There's a checklist of questions for these situations."

He planned for everything, even a bomb threat.

"You need to stop interrupting me. Understand?" Soft and seductive was long gone; hard and menacing took center stage.

"Yes, sir."

"If the bombs detonate, people will die. There's also a sniper with an AK-47. If you try to evacuate the building, he'll pick off people as they come out the door. Do you want that to happen?"

Alarms reverberated in my head. I sat on my hands to stop them from shaking.

"No, sir."

"I want Harper and his witch at the main entrance by 3:45, or those bombs will detonate."

"I'm not sure Mr. Harper is on campus today, sir."

"Don't lie to me. I saw Harper help the witch out of his big white Mercedes. Tell her Alexander will be respectful. I won't destroy her face. Just a clean shot through the heart. The blood won't be visible on the pretty black coat with all those cute little pom-poms. Her grandmother and niece don't need to see something like that. Do you understand?"

How many ways can he say thou shalt not suffer a witch to live?

My toes, fingers, and face went cold and numb. Alexander had been right there, almost beside us, and we didn't see him. Only Cyrus's arm around my shoulders prevented me from plummeting into a black hole.

After a lengthy silence, the receptionist said, "I think so. Can you tell me where you're located?"

"Do you think I'm stupid? Ring up Harper and tell him to get his privileged ass out here. Get a move on or people will die. Understand?"

I gripped the chair, half expecting it to disintegrate like the steps in my dream.

"I'm sorry, sir. I don't quite . . ."

"Do you know what happens when a bomb explodes? It's not pretty. Myself, I'd prefer a nice clean shot to the heart. The pressure wave travels fast and damages soft tissues, destroys blood vessels, and causes massive internal bleeding."

Cyrus massaged the knot at the base of my skull. I flinched.

"If it hits when your heart is at an isovolumetric contraction, the heart muscle walls rupture. A shock wave liquefies your insides."

The silence lasted about thirty seconds, but it felt like an hour. If the receptionist was like me, the caller's barrage of words dazed her.

"When the bomb goes off, the shrapnel comes at you ten times faster than a hurricane. It'll tear you to pieces."

"Can I do anything to persuade you ..." The receptionist sounded on the verge of tears.

"Does the company have a flower fund? It'll need one for all the funerals if Harper and his witch don't get out here." The phone call ended, and the silence was deafening. That poor girl, dealing with a maniac while we took shelter in the panic room.

"Anything ring a bell, Ms. Lilienthal?" Sanchez asked.

"I'm afraid." I choked on the word. Afraid didn't cut it; I was terrified. "I'm afraid not."

"You're sure?" Detective Murphy's no-nonsense expression sagged.

"I can't say for certain, but his voice is distinctive. If I'd met him, I'd remember. Haven't you discovered anything about him?" Unbelievable! They were counting on me and my memory.

"Not much. As I told Mr. Harper earlier, we found the phone in a trash bin outside The Harp Building. Standard burner phone. You know what that is?"

I nodded.

"CCTV caught a guy in a mask and parka tossing it. We think he wore gloves because no prints. The camera followed him into an office building, and we didn't see him leave. Probably changed clothes. An organized guy. We're interviewing people who work there, but so far, nada."

Same technique as Skeleton Girl and the delivery kiosk. Bet she and Alexander were yukking it up. *How clever are we?*

"We sent the video to Quantico, but this devil is wily," Agent Sanchez said. "We expect he wiped the digital info."

"Count on it," Cyrus snapped. "What about Eli King? Anything on him, yet?"

Sanchez licked his lower lip and tugged at his tie. "We're looking into him. He seems to have vanished about five years ago."

To my surprise, Cyrus let it drop. After obligatory words of appreciation, he clicked off and rocked back in his chair. "He's lying."

"Who? Sanchez? How do you know?"

"Rafael and I trawled the interwebs last night."

So, that's what kept him up into the wee hours.

"It's true; Eli disappeared five years ago, but Sanchez failed to mention the most interesting bit. Care to hazard a guess where he worked after Harp, but before he disappeared?"

"Not a clue."

"Information architect for Cena Babington." Cyrus steepled his fingers. "He left the company with a platinum parachute."

Focus. Forget the clanging and the crumbling staircase.

"How platinum is platinum?"

"A $72 million severance package, which just happens to be about what he'd have received from his Harp stock options. The money was all layered out to a dozen offshore accounts; then, it disappears, probably to Switzerland or the Caymans. That's CEO-level parachuting."

He would know. "That was my money she paid him with."

Cyrus winced at the reminder his code had taken part in Babington's theft.

"Why would she give him a payout like that?"

"Don't know, but I'm damn well gonna find out."

Didn't doubt it for a second. I needed to quit falling to pieces and reconsider the Universe's invitation to investigate Alexander. When Cyrus and I pooled our talents, things happened. This call made it clear we couldn't bury our heads in the sand. But first, I had one more burning question. "Do you think he intended to shoot us?"

"I don't know." Cyrus pursed his lips. "Probably not. I mean, there was no bomb, was there? He's playing mind games, trying to freak us out. Rafael said Eli did that; I don't know."

An uncertain Cyrus was almost scarier than Alexander.

HIT JOB

CYRUS RETURNED TO HIS office in the Harp Building, signaling it was safe for a couple of thousand Harp employees to come back to work and tightening the knot in my stomach.

The bomb threat had made the downstate news. When I convened the monthly Plaza vendor's Face2Face meeting, the news sat like a big turd in a silver punchbowl until I addressed it. "They didn't find a bomb. Just a crackpot looking for excitement."

If only. But the acknowledgment broke the tension.

Not taking any chances, I jumped into my plan to convert The Majestic into a venue for concerts and plays. When I dangled more potential customers, dollar signs danced in their eyes, and bombs became a distant memory. The Imag-i-Tron guys forgot to bitch about the electricians and proposed a "kids' night in" for theater and concert-going parents.

Emboldened by their enthusiasm, I put forward Sunday afternoon tea at The Gibraltar Hotel to draw in more Bluff's residents. Everyone licked their chops at the prospect. My assistant, George, smiled, a once-in-a-blue-moon occurrence. A productive call, a world away from my first one where frigid stares reigned supreme.

The day trended toward normal unless you counted the hunky guy with a concealed weapon pacing around and twiddling his thumbs. Pretty sure my morning walk and a lesson on using my Bio-Bit's panic button didn't contribute to Beckett's job satisfaction.

I ate lunch at my desk and read preliminary quarterly reports, putting off the moment when I'd use my cards to delve into Alexander. Face2Face pinged. Virtual flames blipped around Viv's name. I clicked Connect.

"Hey, Viv. You hear something from the police?" I crossed my fingers. Cyrus's team told us Alexander hacked Gertie's phone to get my new phone number. What were the police doing to catch him?

"Nope," she said. "You listened to the call, I guess?"

"Yeah."

"It was pretty bad."

YOU DON'T SAY?

The call lurked in the shadows of my brain with Alexander's message playing in the background. Any minute I expected him to jump out and screech *GOTCHA!*

"To make matters worse, another *Tattleverse* article hit the internet." Viv's tight tone and expression didn't portend sunshine and unicorns. "He hasn't seen it yet, but he's gonna go berserk. You should come up with a battle plan."

After mental cursing followed by a deep cleansing breath, I said, "Send me the link."

"Check your email."

"Give me a minute."

Will the Real Cyrus Harper Please Stand Up?

Nosey Parker. People who meet Harper say the same things. For a tech guy, he's damn good-looking. They mention his infectious smile. (Who wouldn't smile if they were the second richest person on the planet at the age of thirty-five?) His room-filling guffaw is legendary, and a key distraction from his relentless and ruthless pursuit of success.

Damn, Nosey, you started so nice.

Most early Harp employees, now coat-tail millionaires, shy away from calling him demanding, hot-tempered, unforgiving, and unflinching. Dig deeper, and a few acknowledge he can be "a real hard-ass."

"There's intense, and then there's Cyrus," one former employee said. "He set rigorous goals for Bio-Bit 1.0. It was brutal. He'd catch a nap in the office, where you'd find him 24/7. People took it as a hint to follow suit." Another former employee recalled Harper's Friday spiel. "If you don't show up tomorrow, don't bother coming in on Sunday."

"He didn't say that, did he?"

"No, no, he did." Viv shook her head. "What she neglects to mention was he only ever said it to Cassandane. It was their standing joke."

Despite the sharp elbows, or more likely because of them, Harper made Bio-Bit into a household name and a must-have for all major airport hubs and a substantial number of brick-and-mortar businesses.

Harper's heavy-handed business practices are the source of admiration, fear, and awe among business leaders, rivals, and investors. A mere rumor Harper is entering a new sector can send competitors' stock plunging. He owns a stake in several VERY large companies and sits on the boards of others, thus propagating his business philosophy.

Investors with their noses to the ground hint Harper is considering a retail venture. It begs the question. Is his liaison with Maren Lilienthal (Executive Vice-President for Development at The Plaza, an upscale shopping area owned by her family in downstate Illinois) a romance or a business merger?

Why else would he be interested in me? Is that what you're saying, Nosey?

After Monday's bomb scare, Harper is reaping sympathy in the press. It must have been terrifying for the 2300 Harp employees and several hundred visitors, but no one reported seeing Harper among the evacuees. Where was he? Did he scamper away while the bomb squad combed Harp's head-quarters, leaving behind the employees on whose backs he made his fortune?

Harper is either a good-looking charmer with a brilliant mind or corporate America's golden monster. I know where my vote will go, but perhaps we're better served by asking, "Will the real Cyrus Harper please stand up?"

Holy Hekate! I fanned my face.

"Thank goodness, he's in the PSEC meeting and forwarded his phone and email to me." Viv, surrounded by a black aura tinged with red denoting pain, massaged her forehead. "I need to warn you about something else. This morning, a PSEC jerk asked why Harp didn't buy the company before now. Said Simon Greier might still be alive if we had."

"Isn't that what you call a career-limiting question?" Cyrus was already grumpy from frustration and lack of sleep. Did I say grumpy? Short-tempered, belligerent, verging on furious didn't begin to cover it.

Viv nodded. "You'll need to calm him down, or he'll stroke out."

Or he'd forget buying and shuttering *Tattleverse* was a bad idea. We spent thirty minutes strategizing as everything in my stomach turned to acid.

"OK. I read about a couple's massage at the spa in the Waldorf-Astoria. I think it's called BonBon. Do you think they can work us in tonight?"

"PUH-leeze, girlfriend. I'll drop his name, and they'll make time. He doesn't like it when I do." Viv rolled her eyes. "But what he doesn't know…"

"Exactly. Desperate times, desperate measures. Set it up for the works. Everything on the menu."

"You probably know this, but he's particular about massage oils. He prefers the Neroli from Star Botanicals. We keep it around because it comes from Florence. As in Italy."

Goddess, please don't let that tidbit fall into Nosey's hands. "Good to know."

"I'll send Johnny to the spa with a bottle," she said. "He has a date tonight, and he mentioned they were going to a club. So it's right on his way."

"Tell him thanks and to have a drink on Cyrus." Could I do that? Viv nodded, so, yes, I could.

"Also, get us a reservation at the Peruvian place. Tantra. For 9:30. That should give us plenty of time."

"Done. By the time he gets home, he'll be so logy, you'll have to throw him over your shoulders and carry him to bed. He won't care what Nosey Parker says."

"Gotta hope. I'll pick him up. What time should I be there?"

"His calendar says he's in the meeting in room 827 until 5:30. It's an hour's drive from Evanston at that time of day." Viv massaged her forehead.

Can you catch a virtual headache? A distinct possibility.

"I worry once he starts the blow-up, nothing will stop it." Viv was a charter member of a different bomb squad.

"Not on my watch." It wasn't my first rodeo either.

With Rick and Beckett in tow, I braved rush hour traffic to the Harp Building, where a lot had changed in two days. Decorative cable fencing, ten feet tall with sharp spikes, stretched across the grassy park area between the two entrances to Chmod Court. Security guards checked under the car with a device that looked like a camera on a stick. After ensuring we were bomb-free, they asked for our Harp IDs. Fortunately, both Rick and I had them; they gave Beckett a visitor's pass after checking his Bio-Bit data. Can you say bunker?

Rick parked in the circle drive; Beckett insisted on accompanying me to the conference room. Feeling conspicuous and out of place, I fumbled with my entry card. We made it just as Cyrus exited the room in a gaggle. Manny once said, "Cyrus doesn't need to call a meeting. Wherever he is, that's the meeting." Did that make me a meeting?

"Hey, dude, you need a ride?"

As a group, their heads swiveled in my direction. Waving his hand and grinning, Cyrus said, "Looks like I have a date tonight. See you guys tomorrow."

With Beckett trailing us and Rick waiting at the front entrance, we became an entourage, if not an actual meeting. We slid into the backseat.

Once again, Beckett took the front passenger seat, explaining it was the best spot for surveying traffic to make sure no one tailed us. Rick gunned the engine and off we went.

"I didn't expect you," Cyrus said after a healthy kiss. "What a lovely surprise."

"The first of many. The stars say you need a massage."

"Don't disagree. Team-building exercises are brutal bullshit." He rubbed his temples with his fingertips. A lot of headaches going around, today. "Sometimes, I stand outside the conference rooms where no one can see me and listen. People say things they'd never say to me. Good things. Thought-provoking things. But I know the minute I walk through the door, everything will change. I almost feel their spines stiffen, then mine does."

"A massage should help. The stars also made reservations at Tantra. So, everything's coming up Cyrus."

"I do like Peruvian, but you taste better." One hand tilted my head toward him, and he nibbled my lower lip. Ignoring Rick and Beckett, his other hand burrowed into my coat and worked its way under my sweater, searching and finding the moon tattoo. His sense of direction matched his instinct for making money, and we made out like giddy teenagers, ignoring the parents in the front seat until we reached our destination.

The Waldorf-Astoria on Chicago's Gold Coast was nestled in an old-fashioned motor court with a burbling fountain to muffle street noise. Its elegant façade, steel-grey mansard roof, and jaunty royal blue awnings harkened to the fashionable Marais district in Paris's 4th arrondissement. The marble lobby, with its ersatz Greek and Roman sculptures, hinted at old-world elegance.

"Cyrus, hey." Johnny Marlow, resplendent in a black top coat resembling a knee-length tuxedo jacket over skinny blue and green tartan pants with more zippers than God, darted from the elevator and across the lobby. "I thought I might see you here tonight."

A tall, curvaceous redhead in a short skirt and skyscraper heels clutched Johnny's arm. The girlfriend the Gossip Girls mentioned? The sparkle in her periwinkle eyes reminded me of ice chips floating in Creme de Violette liquor. You could scrape frost from her smile. Warning, warning, she projected a dark brown aura. In my experience, self-centered, egoistic, and deceptive people had dark brown auras.

Be nice, Maren! Maybe she's shy.

"I didn't expect to see you," Cyrus said. "Isn't Wednesday your night at The Laugh Factory?"

"Stepin Fetchit go where Boss Lady tells him," the girl said. A dull yellow tinge ringed her aura; add jealousy and negativity to the personality mix.

Brr! A chill radiated off Cyrus.

A scarlet blush crept up Johnny's neck, burned across his cheeks, and disappeared into his hairline. "Muireann, this is my boss, Cyrus Harper."

Emphasis on boss. Buy a clue, girlie. You might be sex on a stick, but Johnny has a good thing going. He's warning you not to blow it.

"His partner, Ms. Lilienthal," Johnny stammered.

"Aw, Johnny, we've been through enough to be on a first-name basis." I tapped his shoulder and smiled.

"Aren't you sweet?" Muireann gave Ivy a run for her money in the subtlety sweepstakes.

I checked my Bio-Bit and nudged the iceberg formerly known as Cyrus. "I'd love to chat, but our appointment is in three minutes."

This was Cyrus's cue to remind me appointments started when he arrived. Instead, he gave Muireann a brisk nod. "Nice meeting you. Catch you later, Johnny."

"Sure thing." Johnny made one last desperate attempt to salvage the intro. "Hey, if you have the time, check out Loulou Bleu on the third floor and keep your eyes peeled for the Chariot de Rosé. It's a roving bar cart with rosé wines hand-picked by the somms. Good stuff."

"Sounds fun." I put my hand on Cyrus's back and shoved him toward the elevators. When the brass doors closed, he leaned against the wall and sighed. "Johnny found himself a babe. Too bad she's a bitch."

"Aren't babe and bitch synonymous?"

"You, my love, are the exception to the rule."

"Flattery will get you everywhere, but my babe credentials don't measure up to my bitchiness. Ask anyone in Riverton."

"Ah, but you're my babe and my bitch. That makes all the difference."

I rolled my eyes. "You should put those computer skills to use and check her out. Johnny's a nice kid."

"When you go babe hunting in your twenties, you don't want advice. You have to get it out of your system."

The voice of experience?

The elevator stopped on the 37th floor. A woman, wearing cropped black pants with a gold tunic, waited before massive double doors carved with a tree of life. "Welcome, Mr. Harper. If you'll follow me, your dressing lounge is ready."

Another carved door led to a room warmed by the glow of copper Moroccan lamps, soft draperies, and lounging couches. Hello, Sheik of Arabi.

"Please, help yourself to tea." The woman gestured toward a table with teapots and bowls of nuts and fruit. "We have mint, lavender, chamomile, rose, and passion flower. Before your massage, we invite you to enjoy our Himalayan salt sauna, the aroma therapy steam room, and the aromatherapy shower. We recommend using them in that order because each one is progressively cooler to prepare your body for treatment. Take your time. Jani and Michelle will be in Room B when you're ready."

We took our time, and it was so worth it. When we entered Room B, I stretched out on the massage table like an old cat in a sunny window. The flute music teased my brain into releasing the week and drifting into a universal nothingness. The notes, the fingers digging into my shoulders, and the fist rhythmically pummeling my back became one with the Neroli oil's rich, floral scent and the sage candles. They promised a place where ill-fortune never came. I forced my eyelids open and checked on Cyrus on the opposite table. He looked loose and limber, his breath even and soft. Mission almost accomplished. After dinner, wine, and mind-blowing sex, Nosey Parker could say whatever she damn well pleased.

In the Dream Room with its heated stone lounge chairs, we returned to the world while gazing at the stars in the ceiling. Slithering back into our clothes, we headed, arm in arm, for the first-floor lobby. Cyrus called Rick to tell him to bring the car; no more text messages to go astray. Did they have a super-secret password, too? I hoped so.

"Thank you. I needed this," Cyrus said. The elevator door closed, and he embraced me. Lingering massage bliss, a whiff of neroli, and a kiss lasting for thirty-six floors transformed me into warm slush. The door slid open. "We'll do this again."

"It's a date."

The lobby was empty. The desk clerk nodded. "Have a good evening, folks."

A chilly wind from the lake came through the revolving door. I shivered and leaned into Cyrus. Rick pulled up. Beckett hopped out to open the back door.

THWIP. The sound zipped past my ear with a wasp-like flutter and struck the stone with a dull thwap.

"Duck," Beckett shouted and bolted toward us, knocking us back into the revolving door and inside the lobby where he and Cyrus both sprawled on me.

"Take cover." Cyrus's voice echoed off the marble.

"Active shooter," Beckett added, in case it wasn't clear something bad was happening.

The front desk clerk ducked behind the L-shaped desk.

"OK, over there." Beckett nodded toward the reception desk that looked miles away. Behind us, glass shattered and hit the floor, clinking like ice cubes in a drink. "Duck and run."

Our footsteps clattered on the hard marble floor. I stumbled and careened toward the floor, but Cyrus caught me. The desk seemed to recede farther and farther away. Beckett shoved me, and I slid behind the desk like a baseball player heading into home. The clerk, curled into a tight ball in the L, whimpered. Her eyes darted around in their sockets.

Cyrus gestured toward the open door to an office behind the desk. "Does it lock?"

She opened her mouth, reminiscent of *The Scream* painting. Nothing came out, although she tried to speak several times before nodding. Beckett, gun in hand, crouched in the doorway until we were inside. After locking the door, the men blocked it with a desk and file cabinet. I closed the curtains.

"You two." Beckett pointed at the receptionist and me. "One in the coat closet there. The other in the john. Lock the doors and silence your cell phones. Don't open the door, no matter what, until I tell you to."

The bathroom had a sink and commode. I waited for Cyrus to join me. He didn't. I locked the door and squeezed myself into the space between the toilet and the wall. Someone turned out the lights in the outer room, erasing the sliver of light from under the door and leaving me in total darkness. My breathing muted my pounding heart.

"You know how to shoot this thing?" Beckett's muffled voice came under the door.

"Yeah."

"You guard the door while I phone the police."

Is the Universe saying it's your time to die?

Shut up! Yet, here I was, sending up a wordless prayer. *Make it quick so I don't feel it.*

I sent a text to Cyrus that he might never read.

> **Maren:**
> Love you so much.

Another went to Oma.

> **Maren:**
> Pondering what a pain in the ass I've been over the years and how you were always there for me, no matter what. Love you so much!

And a final one to Manny.

> **Maren:**
> As sisters go, I've been a jerk. Sorry our visit ended on a sour note. Love to you, Gertie, and the boys.

Not even imminent death inspired me to reconcile with Ivy.

How long did I hug the toilet like it was my best friend? Eternity sounded about right. A loud pounding on the outside door startled me into banging my forehead on the toilet tank.

"Law Enforcement. Anyone in there?"

Cyrus and Beckett whispered to each other. I couldn't make out what they said.

"Is anyone there? This is Lieutenant Aristides Gomez with Chicago Police. I'm conducting a room-to-room search."

Nothing.

"I'm slipping my business card under the door. You can confirm my identity by texting CPD."

More whispers, a long pause. Beckett said, "There are four of us."

"Hey, babe. You can come out now." I opened the door, and Cyrus helped me to my feet.

"Are you OK?" the voice at the door said.

"Yep."

"OK. Unlock the door. Step back to the center of the room. Keep your hands where I can see them."

I wobbled my way to the center, as unsteady as I'd been the first time I wore three-inch heels. The men moved the desk and file cabinet. My heart drummed, alternating between relief the ordeal was over and panic we'd been tricked into opening the door to a killer. I licked my lips and gripped Cyrus's arm as Beckett unlocked the door.

Gently disentangling me, Cyrus said, "Not yet, babe. They might think we're hiding something."

The door swung open to three silhouettes with long guns. My world tapered into a narrow tunnel with a bright light.

IS THIS THE LIGHT AT THE END OF THE TUNNEL WHEN YOU DIE?

Someone flipped on the overhead lights. I sobbed. No angels. Just two men and a woman in green fatigues and black flak jackets with POLICE stenciled in white, a SWAT patch, and nametags.

"Clear," one shouted.

"Anyone injured?"

Beckett shook his head. His gun was no longer visible. Good thing. The officers might have shot us.

"We're going to continue our sweep. Y'all lock the door. Someone will be back to get your statements. Especially yours, Mister Smith."

After the final all-clear, we checked into the five-bedroom Presidential Suite and waited for the police to interview us. Better not to let the press, crowded on the street, know that once again we'd been "victimized."

"It will encourage the crazies," an officer said.

Beckett paced and reiterated what had been a whispered conversation during the siege. "I'm sure no one followed us, and the gunman was on foot. It's not clear to me that you and Ms. Lilienthal were the intended targets."

"You're calling it a coincidence? Seriously?" My eyes rolled so hard they got stuck in the back of my head.

"Seriously," Beckett said. "Someone looking for a cheap thrill. Someone trying to blood-in to a gang. Happens all the time in Chicago."

Cyrus nodded and dropped onto the sofa, head in hands.

I sat beside him, head on his shoulder, and whispered, "Next time I try to relax you, it's popcorn in the basement. It'll be cheaper and less exciting."

He turned his head, his expression raw. "I am so damned sorry I brought this on you. Maybe you should go to Riverton until I sort it out."

Not bloody likely. "Nah. I'll cast an invisibility spell, and it'll all be tickety-boo."

He patted my hand. "You're a peach."

Later, after the police interrogation, but before I fell asleep, my phone pinged for a text message.

> **Alexander:**
> Exciting evening, wasn't it? Bet you're thinking it's unfair he's in the revolution's cross-hairs.

I did. Although seeing Alexander in the nice SWAT team's crosshairs seemed more than fair.

> **Alexander:**
> Harper's no civilian, no innocent. He's a general at the heart of America's global financial empire.

Enough, already!

> **Alexander:**
> You up for a war, little witch? If not, get the hell out of Dodge while there's still time.

You know what I'm up for? Bringing you down, you rotten coward. Fuck you, the horse you rode in on, and the Three-Fold Law that forbids it.

WHAT THE CARDS KNOW

THURSDAY, MARCH 24

THE NOTORIOUS *THEY* INSISTED Tarot can't (or won't) answer yes or no questions, so don't bother asking. Every rule had an exception. What was the worst outcome? I'd break the Tarot? Not if I set the parameters. I'd ask my question and draw a single card. An upright card equaled yes; reversed meant no.

"Is Alexander in Chicago?"

Eyes half-closed, I shuffled and cut the bulky deck three times. Three times is a charm. A single card rolled over my knuckles and onto the floor. My breath hitched.

So, yes, Alexander was in the city. But *The King of Cups* again? A repeating card was a message from the Universe.

YOU'RE NOT LISTENING TO WHAT IT'S TELLING YOU. YOU'D DAMN WELL BETTER RSVP TO THE INVITATION TO LEARN MORE ABOUT ALEXANDER.

Message received; but the most important thing for now, in my humble opinion, was finding him. Sure, Cyrus was on the lookout. But Alexander was one slippery needle in the proverbial haystack, and Chicago was a 300-square-mile haystack.

The cards might shed light and give Cyrus a place to start his search. I meditated on the problem and created a compass spread, using *The Magician* as the significator to represent Alexander.

I concentrated on one question. "Where in Chicago is Alexander?"

North was *Two of Wands*, a dark-haired man in a red robe and hat. He literally held the world in his hands, and he resembled Cyrus, who had a red aura and a home on Chicago's North Shore. *Two of Wands* always had a coherent action plan, explored options, and plotted the path ahead, accounting for all possibilities and potential challenges. Unless another card contradicted my interpretation, *Two of Wands* made our house the northern boundary of the search.

A blindfolded figure sitting before a vast body of water surely symbolized Lake Michigan to the East of Chicago. *Two of Swords* reversed often signified a stalemate, suggesting an inability to choose a direction or being caught between a rock and a hard place. Perhaps information overload and other people's observations had overwhelmed us, and we needed to listen to our intuition.

Two of Pentacles reversed signified the South and more water. Did water bind Alexander on three sides? That made no sense to me, given my understanding of Chicago's geography. In a traditional reading, *Two of Pentacles* suggested balance and good things, but I always saw someone dancing like crazy as they tried to keep all their balls in the air. Reversed made the juggler even crazier and the struggle to not drop the balls harder. Was the key to finding Alexander in his distractions? Curiouser and curiouser!

The *Knight of Wands* rode toward the West. He wore full armor and a yellow robe decorated with salamanders (associated with fire). Fiery red plumes flowed from his helmet. The fire symbolism contradicted the water in the other cards. Plus, the background was hot, dry, and barren, with three pyramids soaring in the distance. Kemetic witches who made ancient Egypt their focus called the West the Land of the Dead. Certainly, Alexander was fixated on death. Moreover, *the Knight of Wands* was bold, disregarding the consequences and venturing into unknown territory to further his mission. He laughed at danger; danger made the mission more exciting. This knight could be charismatic and impulsive. The *Knight of Wands* checked all the Alexander boxes.

My old buddy, *The Tower,* warned me to expect the unexpected, the lightning bolt. It forecast an event that shook you to the core. *The Tower* stood at the heart of the reading and symbolized Alexander's actual location. The burning building represented chaos, upheaval, and destruction. People plummeting toward the ground embodied desperation. False assumptions, mistruths, illusions, and blatant lies ran rampant whenever *The Tower* appeared, and no one escaped as I'd learned firsthand. Wherever Alexander was, it didn't bode well for us.

I rocked back on my haunches and considered the reading. Three cards showed water, and water surrounded the *King of Cups.* What did it mean? How could water surround Alexander on three sides? Three cards were twos, which symbolized partnerships. Only *Two of Wands,* the Cyrus card, was not reversed. A hint at Cyrus and Eli's fractured relationship? A relationship Cyrus hadn't even realized he was in? What was I missing?

"What else should I know about Alexander?" I pulled another card.

Seven of Pentacles in the upright position was a good card. I tended to see something more literal. It confirmed he was a gardener, but he was a twisted gardener who tended a poisoned garden. Somehow, his garden was a key to locating him.

I printed out black and white Chicago maps and passed the afternoon trying to suss out Alexander's location from the clues. I lost track of time until Cyrus returned from the office, all but prancing into the room.

"You look mighty smug, Scruffy."

"Oh, I am. I most certainly am." He dropped to the floor beside me and pumped his arms into the air in a V for Victory. "My support of Senator Patel has proven worthwhile."

Patel was the Senior Senator from Illinois. Cyrus answered my question before I asked.

"He's on the Banking Committee and Appropriations." He steepled his fingers in a reasonable imitation of a cartoon villain. "So, he has insight into the Babington investigation."

"Pray, share."

"He couldn't come right out and say it, but they're investigating Eli or Alexander or whatever the hell name he's going by." He thumped his chest.

"According to chatter the intelligence community picked up, Alexander seems to have had shady dealings with *Die Basis*."

I flew my hand over my head, signaling a fly-by.

"The Base. It's a paramilitary group dedicated to violently overthrowing the capitalist system. They also train extremists in the skills to create real-world violence. Our friend not only gave them money, but he also trained with them."

"This makes you happy. Why?"

"Because they'll lock him up forever when they find him, which I intend to help them do." His eyes looked into the distance, no doubt visualizing the press scrum on the day they captured Alexander. He gestured to the Tarot spread and the dozen are so discarded maps. "Oh, I hope I didn't interrupt. What are you doing?"

"Trying to help you locate our personal terrorist." I rolled my shoulders, but the tension stayed put. "I'm afraid I'm still mostly in the dark."

"Tell me what they say. We can work it out together. We're good at that, yeah."

I explained my compass spread and what I'd gleaned. "Some of it makes sense, but the whole being surrounded by water on three sides, if I interpret the cards right, doesn't add up unless he's sitting in the middle of Lake Michigan. The desert to the West makes it impossible for him to be in the lake."

"I see why you're confused. Your maps lack geographical details." Cyrus rubbed his chin and fell silent, then pulled out his phone and pulled up a colored, geographical map of the Chicago area. "You didn't grow up here, and the black and white maps aren't showing it, but you're not taking the Chicago River into account."

Amateur mistake. I took the water scenes too literally, imagining only vast bodies of water.

"Look at this. See, you've got the Lake on the east, so side one. Now, look right here; The Confluence splits the river and runs into the Lake by Navy Pier. Kinda cuts the city into North and South, so a second side. But the main channel keeps flowing south, running along the Stevenson Freeway. You call it I-55. That's the third side."

"Fair enough. But what about the wasteland?"

"Industrial areas and blight. When we drove in from the airport, you saw it. A wasteland, yeah?"

How could I forget my initial impression of Chicago? Well, worse things had happened since then. "So, we've whittled down from 300 square miles?"

"Yeah, by half, if we're lucky." He closed his eyes. "If I've learned anything from Darius, it's that people use old industrial buildings for nefarious purposes. I need to focus on them."

"Look for greenhouses," I said.

He raised his eyebrows.

"He's a gardener." Something akin to glee fluttered in my chest, and I punched Cyrus's arm. "The bouquets, the boutonniere, even the Rosary Peas were freshly cut. Not shipped on a truck from somewhere. Those plants are out-of-season and non-native. He has a poison garden, and he's growing it in a greenhouse."

Cyrus tapped my nose. "Clever girl. I think you've earned your dinner. Rick picked up Thai. The Green Papaya Salad with carrots, cherry tomatoes, and lime-tamarind dressing is to die for."

Later, after we'd gone to bed, he brushed the hair from my face and asked, "Inquiring minds want to know, why did you decide to learn Tarot?"

"Did I never tell you?"

"I know Talia taught you, but what made you seek her out?"

"My mother read Tarot. Her grandmother, my great-grandmother, Maramawit, read tarot and taught her."

"I've never heard you mention a grandmother named Maramawit."

"I never met her, only saw photos, but she was my grandfather Yonas's mother."

"Yonas the artist?"

"The very one. The cards were always around, and my mother promised to teach me when I became a woman, which to her meant my first period. She promised to start teaching me after she and my dad returned after a retreat."

My throat felt full and tight. A shrink told me the opening between the vocal cords swells up because your body is trying to protect you so you don't tear your lungs. I called bullshit. It's the pain seeping from the place where you buried it.

The quivering in my lips made my next words shaky. "She never came back."

Cyrus pulled me into his arms, making the soothing sound my mother made when I had nightmares. "Hey. Hey. I'm sorry I brought it up."

"No, I wanted to tell you. I never told anybody, not even Talia. After the plane crash, Oma searched the house for the jewelry and stuff, of course. But I only wanted my mother's cards and hid them in my underwear drawer. Oma would have had a hissy if she knew I took them. Superstitious nonsense in her opinion. When Talia offered the course, I knew I had to take it. For my mother. And, yes, Oma had a hissy, but she didn't find out until much later." A long, shuddering sigh escaped, but the weight in my chest lifted. "I guess you could say I'm a hereditary Tarot reader."

He hugged me tighter, and his lips brushed my forehead. "Thank the Goddess. We'd be in a pretty pickle if you weren't."

KNOCK ME OVER WITH A FEATHER.

SPELLBOUND

FRIDAY, MARCH 25

"ARE WE ALL SETTLED?" I braced for an onslaught of whinging via Face2Face symphony-level sound.

George nodded, but the Imag-i-Tron guys dithered. Gavin cast a surreptitious glance at Connor.

"Geeze, guys! It's electrical work, not the Nobel Peace Prize. The Plaza uses union electricians; read the contract." They had a Texas-size aversion to unions that gave me a Texas-size headache. "Do you want to open this place or not?"

They blinked. Gavin cleared his throat. "Yeah, let's move forward."

Before they reconsidered, I said, "Great. Let's light the place up and schedule inspections for May 2. Did we approve Milo's ad budget?"

George nodded.

"Grand opening on point for June 1?"

Connor said, "Yep."

"We're done here. For today, anyway. Same time next week." I held my breath. No one grinched. *Thank you, sweet Goddess.* Not one to tempt fate, I signed off.

"Well done, Girl Boss."

I jumped. Cyrus was supposed to be shepherding PSEC employees into Harp culture. "What are you doing here, Boy Boss?"

"A: We live here. B: I gave the troops the afternoon off to play in the lab, Ms. Slave Driver," he said. "Their eyes and mine were glazing over."

"What a nice guy."

"I am." He ducked his head in a show of modesty. "Since we're both free, I'm taking you to The Block."

"Huh?"

"The art museum at Northwestern." He held out my coat, and his expression brooked no objections to his plan. As we headed down the stairs, he called out to Pat. "We're eating out, so don't bother with dinner."

The nice guy was making a day of it, but my old jeans, black boots, and a turtleneck under a black and white button-up cardigan didn't scream dining out. "Should I change?"

"Nah. Unless I'm mistaken, and I never am, that's a Chanel logo on the buttons of your sweater. Chanel is always the right choice, yeah?"

Unimpeachable logic. Mr. Nice Guy told Beckett to take the afternoon off, assuring him he, Cyrus, had it covered.

I elbowed him in the ribs. "Dude, I am not an *it*."

Beckett cracked a smile when Cyrus winced and nodded. Points to my lethal elbow.

A sleek, sexy, steel-gray Aston Martin sat in the driveway. I stopped short. "What's this?"

"The SUVs are getting too recognizable, so I had Johnny pick this guy up for me."

Johnny had the most coveted gofer job in the world, globetrotting with multi-million-dollar necklaces in his carry-on and tooling around Chicago in a sports car he could never afford. Dollar to a donut, he swung by Bitch Babe's place and gave her a spin before handing over the keys. "If you're aiming for inconspicuous, this car screams 'Don't look at me.'"

He rolled his eyes. "Tinted privacy windows. We're invisible, babe."

Uh-huh.

Ever the gentleman, Cyrus opened the passenger door for me. The two seats, nestled into what resembled a fighter jet's cockpit, had sixteen-way adjustments, according to Pilot Harper. The burgundy leather seat engulfed me and smelled like a new car. I stroked the buttery leather and the wood console. "Nice."

"You like?" Cyrus slid into the driver's seat. The car started with a throaty vroom.

"Oh, yeah." The engine subsided into the low rumble of a contented tiger, and we were off.

"We'll drive back to Riverton instead of flying."

"Woo-hoo. Road trip." I imagined cornfields whipping by at warp speed and startled cows mooing their appreciation. "Good thing you hate packing. This bad boy doesn't look suitcase friendly."

"As it should be," he said. "We can stop in Woodhull. There's a café with the best pie."

"I never say no to pie." Five minutes later, before we completed our road trip itinerary, we roared into The Block Museum's parking garage. "Remind me why we're here again."

"An exhibit called Spellbound. It's all about magic, ritual, and witchcraft." He turned off the engine, and the silence hurt my ears. "Thought it might be right up your alley."

"You're the best, Harper." I leaned over the console and kissed his cheek.

When we arrived at the third-floor exhibition hall in the glass, steel, and limestone museum, the door was locked. "It's closed."

"They're still setting up; it opens on Monday." He tapped a text on his phone. "Ramona called and asked if we wanted a preview. She'd read you were a witch."

"Who's Ramona?" The question covered my discombobulation that total strangers knew I was a witch. Sure, Nosey's articles were out there, but I'd convinced myself normal people didn't read them.

SERIOUSLY DELUSIONAL; YOUR BROTHER READ THEM, DIDN'T HE? WHO'S MORE NORMAL THAN MANNY?

"Ramona Whitney. She's the director of The Block Museum of Art. Nice lady."

"How do you know her?"

"I'm on the Board of Advisors."

A surreptitious internet search on my phone confirmed it. *Cyrus P. Harper, Chicago Illinois, Appointed 2040, Chairperson, Harp Industries, Art Collector. (MS Computer Engineering '34.)* Made sense. Only morons wouldn't make a billionaire alumnus a board member, and I doubted if morons ran the university or its museum. Another search confirmed my not-so-wild guess. It was ranked 9th among the American universities and had the 10th largest university endowment in the country. Faculty and alumni included Nobel Prize laureates, Pulitzer Prize winners, Rhodes

Scholars, MacArthur Genius Fellows, American Academy of Arts and Sciences Members, Supreme Court Justices, and the guy with wild hair who might have saved civilization with his invention.

The director opened the door. "Welcome, Mr. Harper. Welcome, Ms. Lilienthal; I'm Ramona Whitney."

She locked the door and sized me up. I returned the favor. Her younger, less experienced cohorts shuffled through The Lilienthal Museum in Riverton, using it as a stepping stone to jobs like this one. She aced the artsy, yet conservative, look that appealed to board members. Gray hair pulled back in a sleek bun, tribal jewelry; a black, grey, and beige shawl jacket (handmade fabric dotted with tonal tufts of soft fringe) over a black silk tee and loose black pants. Everything about her appearance conveyed one sentiment: you can trust me to spend your donations wisely *and* creatively.

Social amenities discharged, she turned her attention to Cyrus. "I ran into Grayson at the Art Institute."

"Grayson Harris is my Collections Manager," Cyrus informed me. I assumed Grayson didn't collect bad debts; he was probably a preppy guy who helped refine and preserve the art that made Cyrus an *Art Collector*.

Ramona clasped her hands to her chest. "He told me about the Miró. How exciting! Will you bring it to Evanston? Or will it go to the freeport?"

"I'm afraid I'll have to pay taxes. It's going to my place in New York. I'm such a peasant, I thought it would go well with the Calder mobile."

Ramona struggled to maintain her composure at such a pedestrian point of view. I labored to swallow a snort. He pinched me, and the snort escaped.

"I'm sure they're complementary," she said.

Good save, Ramona! Then, she pivoted, proving her suitability for her position.

"I'm so excited to show you this exhibit." She led us into a gallery. "These intriguing objects give us insight into how our ancestors used magical thinking to cope with the unpredictable world around them, a topic I'm sure you're quite familiar with, Ms. Lilienthal."

"Certainly." Particularly when it came to Alexander's savage unpredictability. Maybe something in the exhibit would help me find and stop him.

The intriguing objects included a unicorn's horn, exquisitely engraved rings, medieval magick tomes, and commissioned works by contemporary artists in keeping with the Spellbound theme. The informational placards avoided condescension about pagan beliefs, always a plus.

Cyrus studied a silver and lead heart-shaped case that contained a lock of hair. "Love spell?"

"More likely a binding spell." If I could only get my hands on Alexander's hair ... nope, wouldn't go there. The sudden, distant hum of a vacuum cleaner in another hall made me jump. Thinking of Alexander did that to me.

GET A GRIP. THE DOOR'S LOCKED, AND NO ONE KNOWS YOU'RE HERE.

Cyrus took his time, studying each object as if committing it to memory. When he asked questions and Ramona answered, he double-checked with me, sometimes adding, "You'll need to explain this to me later, babe."

With each question, it became clear Cyrus wanted to understand me in a way no one ever had. I asked myself, not the first nor the last time, how lucky could I get? If its pesky sister question (how long can your luck last) reared its ugly head, I had a banishing spell at the ready.

In the final exhibit, videos recreated the confessions of accused witches with authentic historical backgrounds. The actresses displayed realistic bruises, jagged haircuts, and panicked expressions as interrogators mocked and insulted them. My heart and throat constricted, and I shivered. *Thou shalt not suffer a witch to live.* The more things changed, the more they stayed the same. *Ding-dong, the witch is dead.*

In the video, the inquisitor tied a witch's arms behind her back and fastened weights to her legs before hoisting her into the air. Her shoulders snapped and popped as they were pulled from their sockets, and the blood-curdling scream echoed in the empty exhibition hall. It was practically a how-to manual for someone like Alexander. I cringed and clutched Cyrus.

Ramona's nonchalant appraisal of my reaction made my toes curl. Fight or flight? Fight kicked in.

In the coolest possible voice, I said, "I hope these films teach people that judging other people by narrow-minded standards is not only morally wrong but brutal. Like animals, not people."

HA. MADE HER FLINCH.

"That's the hope, yeah. Doesn't mean we need to see it." Cyrus took me under his arm and rubbed my neck. Thanking Ramona Whitney, he hustled me outside. "Sorry, I didn't know about that part. If I had ..."

"It's OK. I should have expected it. A bit of panic."

"Understandable, given what we've been through. Are you up for dinner, or should we go home?"

"Dinner, please. We can't let the awful world run our lives, right?"

"Right," Cyrus said.

The Aston Martin's growl as we roared from the parking garage promised *no witch hunter can catch us, and they'll be damn sorry if they try.* By the time we reached Los Tacos del Diablo, I'd stopped shaking.

"The best tacos in Chicago," Cyrus said.

"The Devil's Tacos. Are we selling our souls?"

"We're getting the better deal," he said.

Door Med cleared us. A collage of devils painted like a stained-glass window decorated the foyer. It had a banner reading *Hell is empty; all the devils are here*. I concurred with the sentiment until the delicious aroma of warm tortilla chips seduced me into thinking a world that invented tortilla chips and dip couldn't be all bad.

The hostess scurried up. "Welcome back, Mr. Harper. It's been a while."

"Too long," he agreed. She led us to a booth. Day of the Dead artwork and devil statues were everywhere.

"So, will you trust me to order?" he asked.

"You're never wrong about food. Go for it."

Without hesitation, he ordered mango cider for me and habanero cider for him and rattled off an order without checking the menu.

I fiddled with my napkin and took a deep breath. "Any Alexander news?"

"Rafael found a bank account in the Seychelles. A few million." A dark cloud crossed his face. "I'm still trying to find greenhouses and nurseries on the southside. It's going slow, and I rather doubt he's operating one as a legitimate business."

I swallowed my disappointment.

The waitress returned with the cider, chips, and *Ceso Fundido*, melted cheese with chorizo and peppers.

"Got an update from Jack today." He dipped a chip into the melted cheese and offered it to me. The light and crunchy chips lived up to their smell, and the *Ceso Fundido* might be the gods' greatest gift to humankind. "Things are moving along."

Jack was the foreman for the Timmerwilke House — excuse me, Harper House — renovation.

"In other good news," he said. "The Williams are on-board. They'll move into the guest house on April 1 and oversee the move from Chestnut House, so send them a list."

"Wonderful. Grace will have it tickety-boo in no time." My grandmother's long-time housekeeper suggested her son and his wife as caretakers for the Timmerwilke house; the four-bedroom guest house was part of their compensation package.

"I'm so ready to go home. Look." He pulled out his phone to show me photos. "They finished your greenhouse."

The last time I saw it, it was nothing more than a glass cottage sitting next to a brick pile. The photo, taken at night, showed rope lights, twinkling like stars, outlining a fairy castle roof. "Amazing."

"Look at the labyrinth." The original inner courtyard had been a dull concrete outdoor eating area. At my prompting, we'd transformed it into a walking labyrinth with a meditation fountain at the center. Over three hundred plants, representing the seven chakra colors, lined the slate pathway. A retracting glass roof ensured a year-round garden. Maybe Alexander and I weren't that different. *Cancel. CANCEL!*

"It's more wonderful than I imagined."

"Isn't it? We could use some labyrinth meditation time, yeah?"

Indeed.

"The kitchen's finished, too. The stove came in last week." He zeroed in on a sixty-inch Thermador professional range and lovingly recounted its many features.

"Impressive."

"One makes do and gets on with it," he said with an affected British accent. "Don't you think they did a marvelous job with the cabinetry? Look, they finished the butler's pantry and the first-floor wine closet."

"Beautiful." The original cabinetry was beyond saving, so he'd had it recreated.

Our waitress presented two taco plates and *elote*, grilled corn on the cob smeared with chilis, garlic, and lime.

I took a bite and nodded my approval. "Can your fancy stove dish up something this tasty?"

"I'll do what I can, babe." He swiped at his phone and handed it back to me. "I know you're not a kitchen witch, so I won't bore you with stove and fridge talk. What about this?"

The photo showed a Moroccan-style bathroom with indigo-blue tiled walls. Flanked by carved console tables, the lattice canopy over the bathtub drew the eye upward to an elaborate, coffered ceiling with a gigantic copper chandelier. Green leather chairs on a tribal rug with a geometric pattern in bright tangerine, blue, green, and white formed an intimate seating area.

Cyrus reached across the table and swiped to a second photo. More indigo tiles framed a sequence of arches, forming a corridor to a shower. The shower's geometric tiles looked hand painted and picked up the colors in the rug.

"Stunning." I enlarged the picture. "Are you already planning our next vacation?"

"Nope; it's ours."

It took a minute to register what he meant. "You mean this bathroom is in the Riverton house?"

"Yeah. This, too." The photograph showed a bedroom from *One Thousand and One Arabian Nights*.

"Oh, my."

"You don't like it?" Alarm tinged his voice.

"No, I love it. And I love you for remembering I was pining for a Moroccan bedroom." I reached across the table and squeezed his hand. "You don't need to be so darn nice to me, you know."

"I do." His expression grew serious. "I promised you a good time, and it's been anything but."

"Not true. A certain Alexander who shall remain nameless has been a pain in the butt. But I don't go tooling around Evanston in an Aston Martin with just anyone, you know. I have standards."

"Standards are good." He flashed the grin that turned my knees to water and my thoughts to things best not mentioned in public. "Just so you know, I'm determined not to screw things up with us."

"You won't." Screwing up relationships was my superpower.

"We're going to make this work,"

Did wanting something make it so? If so, I wanted it with all my heart and soul. "Yep."

We laced our fingers together as if making a pact.

"Anyway." He cleared his throat. "I imagine you feel isolated up here. Mrs. Mueller isn't exactly your cup of tea ... or coffee. So, I changed the date of Sally's visit and invited Sally, BeeBee, Talia, and Zeke to the music label announcement. Sally and Talia are coming up early so you all can get in some shopping. I want you to get something special for the party."

"You're the best." My fingers tingled with the desire to cup his chin and kiss him long and hard. "How do I ever show you I mean it?"

"By not hightailing it?" He kissed his fingertips and pressed them to my lips.

"Doing what I can, babe."

After the third cider, he said, "I got other good news today."

"Spill it."

A dazzling smile, so the news must be more than good. "Heard from the NHL commissioner this morning. They approved my bid for the Chicago Blizzard." The grin spread from ear to ear.

"You waited all this time to tell me?" I punched his arm. He didn't talk much about his ambition to own a hockey team; when he did, a fire ignited in his eyes and his voice.

"Yeah." He made a deprecating gesture. "Didn't want to seem like a rodomont."

"Excuse me!"

"A braggart."

"Ah." I didn't know much about sports, but Manny said acquiring sports franchises approached the tenth circle of hell. Money (loads of money) was just the beginning. The NHL Board of Governors had to give their approval. Their criteria were close to alchemy, but the murder accusation had put Cyrus behind the puck. So, getting their approval merited a little bragging. I summoned my brightest smile. "Way to go, babe. I know how much you wanted this."

He wriggled like a kid on Christmas morning. "Yeah, I did."

"They'd have been fools not to go with you." I wasn't blowing smoke, either. "However, inquiring minds want to know. How much does a hockey team go for these days?"

He shifted in his seat. "You'll read about it, so I might as well tell you. Less than ten figures because they're not a great team. Yet."

"Real numbers, pretty boy."

"Yeah, OK. I negotiated down to $973 million."

Whoa!

"And you didn't buy two teams, you tightwad?"

"They're not a great team, yet," he repeated. "But they will be. We'll bring the Stanley Cup back to Chicago, but they need a solid core of great players and the talent to surround them. The core won't come cheap, and I have a floor and ceiling on salaries mandated by the NHL. We'll also need a better coach, an arena, and a team plane."

Hands were flying. He was all but licking his chops in anticipation. Boyfriend had his project.

"I love me a good hockey game, babe. It's non-stop action. Those guys are tough; the game is in their blood, and their blood is in the game. You know what I mean?"

I did not, but I nodded anyway. It didn't take Tarot cards to predict I'd be boning up on hockey soon.

We downed two margaritas to celebrate. Maybe, just maybe, the car should have been self-driving, but we made it home, where a gaily wrapped package sat on the bed.

"You have to stop." I poked at the package. "You spoil me. Pretty soon, I'll be out of control."

"That's my goal." He rubbed his chin. "Confession. While technically this present is for you, I'm the chief beneficiary. Also, it's something I promised you on the plane, but it's taken longer to find it than I imagined. So, arriving tonight is happenstance."

"Any more excuses?" I plucked the elaborate bow from the package and draped it over the bedpost. Inside a cloud of tissue paper, I discovered four corsets. One was standard dominatrix black leather. The other three were feminine and vintage. Embroidered oak leaves and wheat ears on a maroon silk corset. Paisley satin in shades of pale pink, cream, and tan. Cream, pink, and green embroidered flowers on black velvet with cream ribbons. "Four! Bit over the top, wouldn't you say?"

"I couldn't decide, and why should I?" He shrugged. "Something for every occasion?"

"No doubt. I'll give it to you, Mr. Harper; contrary to what you think, you know how to show a lady a good time."

"I promised I would."

And he'd delivered, so I grabbed his shirt collar and pulled him toward me for a soul-searching kiss that left us both gasping. "What's your pleasure, big guy? Kinky leather, sweet pink paisley, red silk, or black velvet?"

"Honestly?" His expression communicated spellbound in anybody's dictionary. "Big fan of all of them. You choose."

"Very helpful." I nuzzled his chest and inhaled the rich, spicy scent of Oud. When the marketers claimed it acted as a carnal catalyst, they knew what they were talking about. "No complaining. You live with my choice."

"Yes, ma'am." He nodded obediently.

The black velvet corset with ivory ribbons and embroidered with delicate flowers in carnation pink, ivory, and moss green called to me, although I'd never considered myself a pastel flowers and ribbons gal. I snatched it from the bed.

"Good choice." His expression turned to panic. "Hey, where are you going?"

"My closet. You get to see the finished product, not how I get there. It won't be sexy or even dignified." Right before I closed the closet door, I glanced over my shoulder and added, "The occasion calls for fancy knickers, which are in here."

"Two thumbs up for fancy knickers." He sounded so relieved I wondered if he'd believed I'd abscond with the corset.

Shrugging off my clothes: easy-peasy. The fancy knicker selection was limited, so I didn't have to mull it over. A black thong with geometric cut-outs, lace trim, and three adjustable hip straps more than compensated for rejecting the kinky leather corset.

I learned why Edwardian gentlewomen considered a ladies' maid a necessity, not an extravagance. My modern hands fumbled with the ten thousand (OK, an exaggeration, but not much) minuscule hooks on the corset's front. I struggled for several minutes, but the hooks refused to line up much less hook. I twisted this way and that; at one point, I stretched out on the floor and did strange acrobatics that left me exhausted and a little sweaty. Not in a good way. But the hooks remained unhooked.

"You better appreciate this, Harper," I muttered and congratulated myself for seeking privacy. Had I said undignified? My contortions were downright mortifying. Where was Sally, the walking encyclopedia of kinky undergarments, when I needed her?

Ready to admit defeat and grovel for Cyrus's help, I noticed a wall-mounted tablet. Cyrus had one in his closet so he could refer to a spreadsheet of his suits, shirts, shoes, and probably underwear. When had he decided I needed one, too?

Don't look a gift horse in the mouth.

In two seconds flat, the internet steered me to The Gothic Garden Corset Lady and her instructional video on fastening "the busk." (Yay. New vocabulary word.) Gothic Garden Corset Lady warned me not to start with the top or bottom hooks because the busk can act like a hinge and make you lose control. I did not want to even imagine what that meant.

The hooks were called knobs and loops, which made sense; you were supposed to start with the second to the top knob. I folded the fabric back and used my thumb to keep the knob straight and push it through the loop. I did pretty well until I reached the bottom knob, which refused to go in the loop.

Gothic Garden Corset Lady anticipated this issue and assured me it was quite normal. She suggested sticking my hand (palm out) inside the corset and grabbing the bottom to help the knob along. Yeah, right. Like there was room. How skinny were those women, anyway? One undone clasp did not keep me from dancing a victory jig.

I checked the results in the full-length mirror. The corset's rigid structure pushed up my boobs and gave me cleavage for the first time in forever. Even better, the corset and the thong straps framed the triple moon tattoo between my hips. Somebody was a mighty lucky boy, even if I smelled like I'd run a marathon.

After the floor shenanigans, my hair looked like someone had pulled me backward through a bush. I combed it with my fingers. Like Cyrus would notice my hair?

When I exited the closet, he'd already shed his clothes. If Michelangelo were alive today, he'd have a new model for his David. His eyes lit up at the sight of me, and he beckoned. I scooted across the room. He dangled Wallis's necklace from one forefinger and twirled the other one, signaling me to turn around so he could fasten the necklace around my throat. The pearls slid over my skin, warm and mysterious. The pearl and diamond pendant nestled in the hollow of my throat. It rose and fell with my pulse.

His dazzling smile hit me like a lightning bolt before his lips grazed mine. He tasted spicy, like habanero cider and chili peppers. His fingers toyed with the pearls before skimming across my clavicle, murmuring, "Delicate as a hummingbird."

He dropped to his knees, his hands cupping my hips. One thumb caressed the tattoo spanning my stomach from hip to hip. He kissed the full moon. His chin stubble against my belly's tender flesh ignited a deep, dizzy thrumming. I fisted his hair to brace myself.

"Let's get kinky, bear." His words vibrated against my skin, and we collapsed on the bed.

A-hexing We Will Go

Saturday, March 26

Who loves a lazy Saturday? This girl!

Sleeping in. Late coffee and oranges in a sunny chair, as recommended by Wallace Stevens, although it wasn't *Sunday Morning* and my fuzzy robe didn't qualify as a peignoir. A stroll around the neighborhood before the forecasted rain blew in. Sheer perfection.

Halfway through our promenade, Cyrus called on his persuasive powers to cajole me into helping him decorate and furnish the Riverton house. He proposed splitting the downstairs. The foyer, drawing room, dining room, great room, and conservatory for me. He volunteered for the kitchen, breakfast room, billiard room, and library. He had a way of making it sound reasonable.

"Do I have a budget?" He looked at me like I'd started speaking Martian.

"Whatever it takes to make it cozy," he said. "I'll send the blueprints and pictures so you can get started. Grayson will send the catalog for the freeport. Several pieces should see the light of day, and you have a great eye for art."

How much art resided in those international storage facilities? Guess I'd find out soon enough. "Won't you need to pay taxes to get them out?"

He shrugged. "What're you gonna do?"

As far as he was concerned, it settled the matter. A question popped out of my mouth. "Would it bother you if I asked Oma for decorating advice?"

His eyes widened and a bark of laughter escaped. "Whoa. Never expected that. You know I admire your grandmother. If it doesn't bother you, why would I object?"

"Would it bother me? I don't know. Don't know why I said it either. But she has exquisite taste. Guess I'd rather have her inside the tent pissing out than outside pissing in."

"Your decision, love. You can always fire her." He chuckled at the thought of someone firing Oma.

Dark clouds blanketed the sky and ended the discussion. For now. We skittered into the sunroom ahead of the first fat droplets.

Douce Ambiance, Django Reinhardt's gypsy jazz guitar music, filled the sunroom. Sweet ambiance indeed. Cyrus sprawled across the sofa, head in my lap, tablet propped against his knees. Before he started responding to emails and toiling over the Harp board meeting agenda, he forwarded blueprints, photos, and a request to Grayson for the art catalog.

I combed through his curls with my fingers and watched the storm brewing over the lake. Lightning flickered in the east, stark against a gray sky growing ever blacker. Thunder crackled, the sound as soft as waxy paper.

"This is nice," Cyrus said. "Thank you."

"For what?" I brushed a rebellious lock of hair from his forehead.

"I never spent time in this room." His eyes didn't move from the tablet, multi-tasking like a boss. He resolved issues marked Hot! and Stat! with a tap or swipe. "I came home from work and either went to my home office or straight to bed. Sometimes I might fiddle around in the game room or cook. The rest of the house didn't exist for me. But this room is pleasant. I enjoy being in here, so thank you for reminding me we have a sunroom."

We was not a scary word.

"Doesn't mean you can't change it."

Had I scowled? "I love it. I was thinking *Douce Ambiance* is the perfect song for this room."

If I changed something, would it reassure him I was committed to making this work? Different lamps? Nah, I liked the Tiffany "spider" lamps with arachnid veining spread over a mottled golden glass shade that cast a warm glow over the room. The sofa? Cream wasn't my favorite color, but it worked in here. The antique Persian Heriz rug picked up the colors in the lamps and stained-glass windows. Nope, nothing to change.

Wait! Plants? The room needed big plants. Palms and hanging ferns. Orchids for the corner table. Come Monday, I'd ask Beckett to take me to a nursery. The conundrum resolved; I resumed storm-watching.

"Hey, check this out." He handed me his tablet, showing an article from *Art News* Grayson had forwarded to him.

Abebe Self-Portrait Could Break Records at Sotheby's

A self-portrait by Yonas Abebe is set to break records at auction this fall. Sotheby's will offer Abebe's *libē nefisē 2011* (*My Heart, My Love*) in New York this November. The work is expected to fetch $30 million — over three times the artist's current auction milestone of $8 million, notched in 2035. The soon-to-be-auctioned painting depicts the artist gazing pensively at the viewer; superimposed on his forehead is an image of a woman.

It comes to market after being held for 20 years by a private collector in Texas. The seller purchased it in 2024 at Sotheby's for $1.4 million, against an estimate of $800,000. Prior to that sale, it belonged to the estate of Parisienne writer and critic Adèle Archambeau, Abebe's wife, and believed to be the woman in the portrait.

Describing the work as "emotionally bare and complex," Sotheby's chairman Gianni Rossi said in a statement that *libē nefisē 2011* is "a defining work by one of the few artists whose influence transcends the world of fine art to pop culture and beyond."

"I have a small print of his at the New York apartment," Cyrus said. "Grayson wants to know if we want to bid on this one for the Riverton place."

"I'm not keen on having Adèle take up residence." I chewed my lower lip. My grandmother Adèle, whom I'd never met, dismissed my parent's marriage and offspring as too white-bread and lacking imagination. She didn't reach out when my parents died, nor when Yonas died. Her lawyer conveyed Yonas's will and the paintings he'd bequeathed to Manny and me. We learned of her death and her will leaving her entire estate to Société Protectrice des Animaux from the *Wall Street Journal.*

"OK." A sharp glance and nod. Cyrus understood when something upset me and didn't prolong the agony with questions.

The trees swayed as the wind coming off the lake picked up. A young willow bent over, trying to touch its toes. The rain pattering on the roof kept time with Django playing *Manoir de Mes Reves*. Manor of My Dreams? Coincidence or Cyrus's hand at work? He moved on to the next message.

"Viv's getting theatre tickets for my parents and wants to know if we're interested. The *Mamma Mia* reboot."

"Computers reboot, Super Trouper; musicals revive." I ruffled his hair. "I've read good things about it."

"I'll take that as a yes, Dancing Queen." His fingers flew over the tablet. "OK, Hal, play *Mamma Mia* Broadway soundtrack." *Honey, Honey* came over the speakers, and he returned to his messages.

The wind picked up, and waves crashed against the rocks. Lightning crackled, picking out different colors in the stained-glass windows. The rain went from pattering to drumming on its way to hammering. The music couldn't compete. A good day to be curled up on the sofa with your lover.

Cyrus cut loose with curses. The hair rose on my neck, and I held out my hand for his tablet. When he wasn't forthcoming, I snatched it.

A photo of us, hand-in-hand, leaving Dior on Rush Street last week captured Cyrus's exuberant head-thrown-back-body laugh. But he wasn't laughing now.

Cy-Ren Shopping Spree

Congratulations, Nosey. You paid attention the day the teacher taught alliteration.

> <u>Nosey Parker.</u> Who said if shopping can't buy happiness, you don't know where to shop? The phrase didn't originate with Cyrus Harper and Maren Lilienthal, but it might have. We spotted them engaging in retail therapy. Were they trying to forget accusations of murder in Lilienthal's hometown or protestors chasing them from The Drake?

Jerk, and it was actors, not protestors.

> Murder aside, Lilienthal is the type of girl you'd expect to see on Harper's arm. She has breezy, contemporary good looks. In her designer clothes and jewelry costing more than most people earn in a lifetime, she exudes casual, upscale elegance and bolsters the image Harper wants to project. But there's nothing casual about the serious money it takes to cultivate that image, an image I'm sure Harper is happy to underwrite. With her Woo-woo beliefs (she calls herself a witch), she's the perfect foil for Harper's faux serious-boy-genius mien. She plays the billionaire's girlfriend role to perfection.

WTF! Why not paste a scarlet W for Witch and Whore on my forehead and march me through town? Cyrus was punching keys on his phone like a prizefighter.

> With a dual pedigree of old Midwestern money and NYC art scene (she's the granddaughter of Ethiopian painter Yonas Abebe), she buffs Harper's nouveau riche glare to a fine patina. Is that why he's thinking about acquiring her grandfather's over-priced painting at auction in the fall?

The article linked to the *Art News* story. Viv's soft voice threaded through the thunder, assuring Cyrus she'd find out who leaked the painting story.

> The scion of a semi-famous sub-Saharan artist might earn Harper bragging rights over his mentor, Lawrence Freeman. All the so-called Oracle of Luling has to show for *his* money is an aging rock star's ex-wife. If Maren gets uppity, Harper can always remind her that in the month in which she lost her "inherited" fortune, he increased his net worth by $260 million.

Double oh boy! Enough damn dog whistles to start a riot in an animal shelter. Nerd. Kook. Pretentious. Fake. Tradition versus Tech. Yes, my grandfather was Ethiopian; ergo, I must be uppity. And a gold digger. Publicly castigating a woman was popular even before the first witch trials. I braced myself, half-expecting to see literal smoke coming from Cyrus's ears.

Outside, Zeus hurled a lightning bolt. Any second, Thor might lob Mjölnir across the sky and start Ragnarök, the end of the world. I massaged Cyrus's neck. The world hurtled toward an extinction-level event that even Viv couldn't stop.

THINK FAST!

My glance fell on *Evanston Today*, the only printed news source in Evanston. An ad was face up. I checked the store hours. "Hey, we need to get a move on if we're going to get to Fred's Cosmic Rock Shop. It closes at four."

Cyrus turned, a bewildered expression stealing over his face, and Viv took a breath.

THINK FASTER!

"Crystal therapy for the house. Remember? Make the house mine as well as yours." I poked his shoulder.

He'd count saying I was making the house mine as a victory and move heaven and earth to make it happen. That's why we braved a torrential downpour to get to Fred's Cosmic Rock Shop on Main Street, Evanston, which, given the weather, was empty. DoorMed cleared us.

Cyrus looked wary as we picked through the quartz.

"This is rose quartz." I handed him a stunning Himalayan quartz cluster, radiating a soft pink glow. The crystals were large, and the terminations were nearly perfect. According to the signage, it came from Mount Meru.

"What's Mount Meru?"

"In Hindu mythology, it's a golden mountain standing in the center of the Universe. It's also the axis of the world and the abode of gods. The Himalayas are its foothills."

"So, it's not real." He sounded grumpy. "How can they claim the quartz comes from there?"

"There's a mountain called Meru Peak." I struggled to find the right tone. Not too meek, not too emphatic. "No one's ever summited it. By the way, that's not an invitation for you to try. Anyhoo, it makes these crystals rare. Workers carry them off the mountain in backpacks."

The bell over the door rang, but no DoorMed greeting followed. A man wearing a rain hat, dark glasses (in a rain storm?), a black pandemic mask, and a black calf-length rain slicker scurried into the store. Did central casting call for a stereotyped villain who turned out to be the grandfather next door?

"OK, I got all that." Cyrus studied the rose quartz. "But why exactly do we need a $1700 pink rock?"

"For peace." His eyes glazed; I reeled him back. "And the bedroom. It's the stone for lovers because it improves the female libido."

"A bargain at twice the price, I guess." He carried it to the counter where the clerk engaged him in a conversation about the fossilized dinosaur tooth, holding pride of place on the counter.

"Carcharodontosaurus," the clerk said. "Might have been bigger than a T-Rex. This tooth's a beauty. See how lustrous the enamel is? The dark reddish-brown color is a desirable coloration for fossils from the Kem Kem Basin."

The tooth transfixed Cyrus; more to the point, it was a snit tranquilizer. As I evaluated the Gwindel Smokey Quartz, also from Mount Meru, Black Rain Slicker sidled up to me. The slicker dripped water, making a puddle.

RUDE!

Cyrus and I had the decency to leave our umbrellas by the front door, and there was a coat rack there, too.

"Not the best day for rock hunting, is it?" He stood too close, reminding me how close Alexander had been before the bomb threat.

WHO'S BEING PARANOID?

OK then, his forced jocularity grated. I gave him a brisk nod and edged away.

"I guess I came to the wrong place." Ignoring the hint, he closed the gap between us. "I was hoping to find boulders for my yard. Do you know where to find those?"

"Sorry. Not from around here." *Cyrus, where are you? Save me. Ha-ha!*

No help from that quarter. Cyrus was hanging on every word the clerk dropped about the Carcharodontosaurus tooth. If it distracted him from Nosey, it might make a nice paperweight. I smiled politely and moved on to the chunks of green malachite. The guy followed me. It's not paranoia when someone is really following you.

EVANSTON. MIDDLE OF THE DAY. CYRUS BETWEEN YOU AND THE DOOR.

"That one looks like a green brain," he said. "Not sure I'd want it in my house."

"Different strokes," I muttered and returned to the quartz section.

Following me, he handed me a tourmaline quartz with black needles running through it. It was a brutal, yet beautiful, stone. "I hear tourmaline quartz is a hexing stone. With the right spell, you can cause confusion and pain with it. What do you think?"

I THINK I WANT YOU TO VAMOOSE.

"Anything's possible."

"I suppose so. But what do you think?"

"Excuse me." I couldn't count how many impromptu crystal conversations I'd had in other shops. None felt as icky as this one. I scurried to Cyrus's side. "Hey, babe, I need your help picking out the smokey quartz."

We picked out twelve Smokey Quartz stones, two for each exterior door and one for each corner of the sunroom.

"These are for?" Cyrus asked.

"Security, patience, and permanence." I did a discreet survey of the store. The icky guy was gone. How did he slip out without me seeing him? Better tune up my alarm antennae.

"Who can be against that?" Bemusement erased the last vestiges of rage from his face.

HUZZAH, QUARTZ!

He whipped out his credit card when a smiling Fred (if there was a Fred) rang up our purchases.

Crystals and a Carcharodontosaurus tooth: $8238.43.

Saving the world from Cyrus's wrath: Priceless.

Money *can* buy plenty of things. For everything else, there's magick and crystals.

You wanna see Woo-woo, Nosey? I'll Woo-woo the hell out of Cyrus and save your worthless tabloid neck. You good with that?

On the way home — there! I'd called it *home* — Cyrus turned up the volume for the *Mamma Mia* soundtrack, and we rocked along with the beat.

We were making pizza when the doorbell rang. I opened the door as a Chicago Hands-Free Delivery truck backed away. A small package wrapped in Tiffany blue paper with a white ribbon and bow sat on the doormat. A card addressed to me was tucked under the ribbon.

"Get this present-giving under control, Harper."

My lofty principles didn't stop me from ripping open the package. My breath turned to ice and chilled me to the bone. I dropped the tourmaline quartz. It clattered on the brick stoop. Fingers shaking and against my better judgment, I opened the note.

Dearest Maren, I can't decide if you listened to your grandmother about not speaking to strangers or if you're just plain rude. The new car's nice, BTW, although ostentatious. Bet it set the boy billionaire back a pretty penny. Anything to get laid, I suppose. Did you find the right crystals? I am reminded of Leviticus 20:27. A man also or a woman that hath a familiar spirit or that is a wizard (or a witch?) shall surely be put to death. They shall stone them with stones so their blood is upon them.

Oh, man! I needed to listen to my gut when it warned me about people. Icebergs big enough to sink the Titanic clogged my veins. I rubbed my arms until my fingers ached, trying to dislodge them. Nope. Still there. Alexander was creeping closer and closer, close enough to stab me today. What would happen when he found me alone?

HOLD MY BROOM!

SATURDAY, MARCH 26

"YOU OK, MA'AM?"

The question catapulted my thoughts back to the front porch. How long had I been zoned out? Long enough for the misting rain to become torrential. A puddle around my feet soaked my socks up to the ankles.

"Ma'am. Did you drop this?" The officer guarding the house held out the quartz. It thrummed with malevolence.

"Drop it."

"Begging your pardon, ma'am. I didn't quite catch what you said."

I thought I'd shouted. Apparently not.

YOU CAN'T JUST LEAVE IT OUT HERE. DEAL WITH IT.

I held out the box, unwilling to touch the crystal. Unperturbed, the officer dropped it in the box. So, had Alexander only directed the malice at me?

ALEXANDER HAS NO MAGICK.

His intentions might be strong enough to make up for the lack.

"Hey, babe, I thought you got lost." Cyrus stepped outside and wrapped his arms around me. "You're soaked."

The raindrops plopping from the overhang shimmered like tiny crystal balls that I didn't dare look into for fear of seeing something horrific. I whispered so the officer couldn't hear.

"Alexander hexed me." I raised my voice and said, "Thanks, officer, just woolgathering and watching the rain."

Cyrus pulled me inside and closed the door. I showed him the box and the note. Calling the police was useless. Did the note constitute a threat? Didn't matter. It came from the contactless delivery service, so we could assume it was untraceable. Cyrus's guys might try, but they'd fail.

We pretended I never uttered the word hex. I placed the box in a ring of salt on an out-of-the-way counter to contain its negative energy. We prepared the pizza in silence. Just your average billion-aire-with-his-own-built-in-brick-pizza-oven Saturday night. The chatter in my head was deafening.

THE BASTARD HEXED YOU.

Who's being paranoid now?

The fireplace beneath the pizza oven emitted a cheerful glow. Cheerful until I remembered Alexander would shove me in it, like the wicked witch in *Hansel and Gretel*.

When only pizza bones (aka crusts) remained on our plates and the wine bottle was empty, Cyrus broached the silent elephant in the room. "So, what shall we do about this?"

"Hold my broom. I'm tired of playing Ms. Nice Witch with this jerk." I tried to smile, but my lips flattened across my teeth, becoming a snarl. "Not again. If Emelia and Finley had been half as competent as Alexander, we'd be in prison or dead. You know it's true. Never again."

Cyrus blinked several times.

"I'm going to hex him back into the Stone Age."

His mouth twitched between an indulgent you're-kidding smile and a frown before he coughed up a strangled laugh. "What about the Three-Fold-Law thing?"

"What about it? Am I not allowed to defend us?" My shoulders curled up around my ears.

COOL IT, LILIENTHAL. HE'S RIGHT. YOU ALWAYS STEW OVER THE LAW. IF YOU CURSE SOMEONE, BE PREPARED FOR IT TO FLY RIGHT BACK AT YOU.

Call me prepared.

Cyrus turned sideways, presenting his arm and shoulder as if he expected me to reach across the table and rip out his heart. An image of the silver and lead heart flashed before my eyes. Given the chance, I'd bind Alexander's black heart faster than a speeding bullet.

"You should call Talia."

"She'll be here on Wednesday."

"I meant you should talk with her before you hex anyone." He squeezed my hand and shifted in his chair.

"Good idea." I'd never hexed anyone; I'd only read about it. His sigh of relief echoed in the tense silence.

We filled the dishwasher before finding excuses to withdraw to our separate offices. I hesitated half a second before Face2Facing Talia. When she came on the screen, candles formed a halo around her head. She looked ethereal. Celtic electroacoustic music played in the background, conjuring images of the open skies, magick, and running barefoot across meadows. The serenity lasted a second.

"Hello, dear." Her smile was beatific.

WHY CAN'T YOU BE MORE LIKE HER?

"Hope I didn't disrupt a cozy evening." My semi-apology didn't ring genuine even to me.

"Not at all, just having a think. How are you? Cyrus mentioned your troubles when he called."

She adjusted the music's volume and peered into the camera. She was reading my aura.

I tilted my head, giving her a better view.

"Not great, I see," she said.

"It's getting worse. Someone hexed me." I brought her up-to-date with Alexander's latest gift and note.

"As you know, I believe hexing is real, but it's rare." She leaned forward, her eyebrows drawing together. "People with hexing knowledge have better things to do. Effective magick — for good or ill — requires words, desire, and will."

"This guy wants to kill us, and he's not someone you can dismiss. I need to squash him before he succeeds." My righteous anger burst into flame.

BREATHE. IN. OUT. SMELL THE ROSES AND BLOW OUT THE CANDLES.

Talia leaned toward the screen with a soft, sad smile. "When the world comes after us, using magick to rectify the situation seems reasonable. But wait before throwing any counter-curse. Being pissed isn't a good reason; it might make things worse."

My fist slammed the Chinese desk, making files bounce and hit the floor. "Trying to kill us is a damned good reason."

"Maren, Maren, Maren. Have you seen your aura? It's dim and cloudy. You're radiating negative energy." She sighed and held up a mirror.

My dark violet aura had muddy brown patches. "I see it, but my aura isn't the problem. That psycho is."

"If there's a hex, shield yourself and break it." Her self-control made me want to scream. "I can help with that, but I will not help you cast a hex. Do you understand?"

So effing reasonable.

That's why Cyrus suggested calling her. But reason didn't cut it when you were grappling with an irrational monster. I scrubbed at my burning eyes with my fist.

Get a grip. You need her help.

"A good start. Sure." The words almost choked me.

She walked me through creating a mirror spell to bounce the hex back to Alexander. Apparently, it did not violate the Three-Fold Law in her opinion.

"Do you believe I don't have the juice to hex him?"

"I'd never question if you could do it. The question is, should you send all that negative energy into the Universe? It will come back at you. As Confucius said, 'When you embark on a journey of revenge, dig two graves.'"

"Right. Right. I get the point." But I didn't cross revenge hexing off the list either.

"Good. I recommend an aura cleansing to remove those dark spots. Balance your chakras while you're at it."

I nodded. I didn't need novice lectures.

"Also, keep up your daily spiritual practices. Ground and center every day. Have you been practicing shielding? No? Now's the time. I also suggest cleansing and warding the house; the grey quartz will help. You'll be fine. I know it."

With Alexander in the world, the chance of fine was zero.

"Remember, Mercury is going retrograde in two days with its turbulent and disruptive vibrations. If nothing I said persuaded you, it's not a great time to hex. Expect the unexpected and take the time to reflect and meditate. Then choose your next step with care."

"I'm tired of being careful; I want to go a little apeshit."

She kissed her fingertips and pressed them to the screen. "Bright blessings from above bind Maren with love. Goddess who loves us all, watch over Maren tonight; guide her words and actions so she may do what is right. Drive away all harm and fear, so only goodness and light surround her. In the Goddess's name, as I will it, so mote it be."

After bidding her farewell, I collected everything needed for the repelling spell. Necessity being the mother of invention, I improvised and prayed Cyrus didn't emerge from his lair to investigate. I crept up to his office door twice to make sure. He was conferring with Rafael.

After one last check, I locked the Chinese room's door and created a salt circle to contain the magick and protect myself. Burning frankincense cleared the atmosphere before I cast a circle. I wrote the banishing spell on paper.

Inside and out, front and back, bounce the curse back to Alexander, back to Eli, and banish it so it can never come again.

For shielding, I placed the smokey quartz on the four corners of the Chinese cabinet I used for an altar. The spell required two silver bowls filled with black salt to protect me and repel negativity. I'd worried I might need to improvise with lava rocks from the garden mixed with regular salt. Lucky for me, someone was a gourmet cook. Inside a box labeled Black Flakey Sea Salt were jet-black pyramid-shaped flakes of salt, distilled from the Mediterranean and blended with activated charcoal. Perfect.

I positioned my newfound mirror in a bowl and poured the black salt around it. The mirror's silver crescent moon, cradled by obsidian pyramids, honored the Goddess and imparted extra strength. I placed the banishing spell and the hexed quartz in the other bowl facing the mirror, poured black salt over them, and lit a white candle. If the quartz emitted negative energy, it would hit the mirror and bounce back to Alexander.

"Alexander, born as Eli, I cast you out. You are not welcome here. I cast out your spell and extinguish its power. Let fire and salt cleanse you from this house and place your fate in the hands of the Goddess."

Closing my eyes, I visualized the Man in Black retreating further and further, backing out the door of Fred's Cosmic Rocks, out of our house, and out of our lives. I visualized the reflected candlelight carrying the negative energy from the quartz toward the mirror and bouncing it away.

"I cleanse our home of your evil. We are safe. The hex you placed on me, I return it to you three-fold. As I will it, so mote it be."

Success was a fizz of energy, a sign I had cast the right spell at the right time. A good sign, but an unfulfilling one. Like eating two crackers when you're starving. My implacable craving for vengeance growled for more.

Maybe I never had any intention of stopping with a repelling spell because I'd collected everything I needed for a hex. The circle still held, so I jumped right into creating a crude poppet from a white napkin and kitchen twine. Alexander's hair or nails would be more effective, but I had to make do. I drew his hat, sunglasses, and mask on the napkin with a black marker. I wrote Alexander Filippidis in red ink on the poppet's chest and bound it with more twine.

IS REVENGE WORTH YOUR TIME AND ENERGY? YOUR TIME IS VALUABLE. ALEXANDER HURT YOU AND DESERVES TO SUFFER, BUT YOU DON'T DESERVE FOR HIM TO TAKE UP ANY MORE OF YOUR TIME. GET ON WITH YOUR LIFE.

Unless I prevented it, he wouldn't stop. A match stuck inside the poppet's body would cause his plans to go up in flames. I sprinkled vinegar on the poppet to sour his life and pressed thumbtacks and staples into the cloth to cause him pain. Oh, yeah; I'd created an ugly little bugger that resembled Alexander's soul if not Alexander himself.

THE CURSE CAN REBOUND.

I KNOW. They say stabbing a poppet is as satisfying as causing actual harm to your enemy. I called BS. My intention was real. I wanted to cause as much psychological and physical harm to Alexander as he'd hurled at us. Fair is fair.

I carved his name into a white candle. Since I didn't have an athame, my fingernail sufficed. I carved the triple moon into the candle to put my power behind it. After placing the candle on a platter, I lit it.

"O Goddess, on this night, send the power of fire to protect us from those who wish us physical, mental, or emotional harm. Let no harm or fear come to us. As I will it, so mote it be."

The candle's flame, an angry red without a trace of gold, blazed like a comet. I saw it as a sign, and it banished all doubt about what I was doing.

While dangling the bound poppet by a string over the candle, I chanted. "As this poppet burns and withers in the fire, so may Alexander's heart burn and wither. Let anyone who seeks to destroy us be confounded and put to shame. Let anyone who seeks to hurt us be turned back and brought to confusion. May our enemies' path be dark and slippery and their lives be as chaff before the wind."

Without thinking, I'd expanded my curse to include Mitnick's Mungers. Well and good. As Oma's housekeeper said, "When you see a cockroach, there's never just one."

"Let destruction come upon them unawares; and let the trap Alexander set for us catch them all so they fall into destruction. I curse you, Alexander, by day; I curse you by night; I curse you with all my might. As I will it, so mote it be."

The candle flame skyrocketed. Yes! It worked. I recited the hex three times.

After the third utterance, the flame spiraled like a tornado, and shock waves radiated from the circle's center as the curse gathered strength. It gushed from the room like blood from an open wound, searing the triple moon tattoo on my belly. A heartbeat later, gooseflesh popped out on my arms and legs. My head spun, and I sat down hard.

Qualms and doubts, thicker than flies, clotted the air, making it difficult to breathe.

YOUR ACTIONS WERE RIGHTEOUS. IT'LL BE FINE.

Exactly, a witch has the right to defend herself, and Alexander started it. Sweet Goddess! I sounded five years old.

I rocked back and forth for several minutes before I brought down the circle. My breath remained shallow and fast, and I panted like a dog. A dull, cramping ache started in my feet and inched up my calves and lower back. My ears throbbed; the pressure disoriented me. Amateur mistake. I hadn't grounded before raising the circle, and now my energy was turning against me.

I took a deep breath or ten, touching my chest over where my heart pounded. Nothing. I rubbed my hands, tapped my thighs, and tensed my muscles to shake off the excess energy. It muffled the ache, and the pressure dissipated but didn't disappear.

Feet apart at shoulder width, I took deep breaths and imagined a glass orb overhead. It tipped, pouring a warm golden stream, thick as honey, over me.

BREATHE!

A soothing balm percolated through my scalp and into my brain and down my throat before pooling at the base of my spine, where it lapped at the ache.

BREATHE!

The warmth and weight oozed into my legs and feet before boring deep into the earth, passing rocks, tree roots, and different layers of minerals until it hooked into the Earth's core and anchored me.

BREATHE! FEEL THE CONNECTION AND LET IT GROUND YOU.

The jangling nerves and aches faded; composure crept back. I focused on the present, but the grittiness of what I'd done clung to me.

I drank straight from the bathroom sink faucet before cleaning my face, behind my ears, and my head, hands, and feet. Fresh clothes erased the last vestiges of the gritty sensation. I slunk to Cyrus's office, hoping he'd keep me centered. A wild laugh halted me at the doorway.

"*Die Basis*? Jesus, bruv, that's serious shit you stepped in."

Darius! Let the hex repercussions begin.

"I never worked with 'em myself, being the capitalist they profess to hate. No objections on their part, mind you, but I'm not gonna sell someone the gun he'll use to shoot me."

I banged my forehead against the door frame.

"Can you help me find this guy?" Cyrus raked his fingers through his hair and sounded fraught. He had to be desperate to let Darius see his apprehension.

"Don't worry, bruv. I'm on it." An empathetic Darius terrified me. "Kudos to Maren's cards. If he's in Chicago, he'll go to ground on the Southside. It's a No-man's-land these days. Someone will know where he is. And, I know the people who know the people. Believe me, someone will spill the goods if the price is right. No matter what they say, there's no honor among thieves."

"I appreciate it."

"What are brothers for?" Again, with the empathy. "Keep searching for the greenhouse, and I'll circle back when I find something. Between us, we'll put the pieces together."

The Three-fold Law was a rough beast slouching towards Chicago to give birth to my worst nightmare.

"Hey, Maren." Darius laughed. "I see you lurking in the doorway. Get in here, girl, and say hi."

Cyrus spun around in his chair; he looked as guilty as I felt. A curt nod acknowledged our guilt and made a promise not to discuss it.

WITCHES JUST WANNA HAVE FUN

WEDNESDAY, MARCH 30

"WHAT'S MY LIMIT?" UNLIKE Cyrus, Viv might give me a straight answer.

Viv cocked her head; Face2Face zoomed in on her puzzlement. "Your card doesn't have a limit."

"Right. Right. But what does Cyrus think is reasonable for me to spend? I don't want to overstep." Finley taught me an unforgettable lesson. When someone crossed the money line, there was no coming back.

Viv clucked. "If I tote up how much that boy spends on clothes, I'd say the sky's the limit."

Unlike that boy, I wasn't spending *my* money. It crossed my mind not to use the black card, but that would cause another type of ruckus. I felt my eyebrows drawing together in a scowl.

"Not that he doesn't know the meaning of the word limit," Viv hastened to assure me. "When he decided he needed a ranch, he wanted it yesterday or the day before and expected us to move heaven and earth to find one, but he was firm on the price. '$45 million, Viv,' he said. 'Not a penny more.' If he has an opinion on how much you can spend, we'd know."

"OK." Not helpful. And I was miserable at setting limits. "Anyway, thank you for making appointments for tomorrow."

"No problemo. You're all set at Chanel and Dolce & Gabbana in the morning." She flashed a conspiratorial grin. "I drop our boy's name; they get stars in their eyes."

"Don't you mean dollar signs?"

"That, too. Also, I booked you at Triangle D'Or after lunch."

"Golden Triangle? Is that anything like the Bermuda Triangle?"

"Ha-ha. Cyrus said you were into vintage, and they have the best. They're at every estate sale on the Gold Coast. If you want designer vintage, they got it."

I'd miss rooting around for the lucky find, but I'd waited too long to shop for Pieter's big party. Sally and Talia had arrived this morning to help me put the pedal to the metal.

"I'm not their ideal body type." Viv chuckled and glanced down at her ample bosom. "But a little thing like you, you're their dream customer. Oh, and you have a reservation at Artella for 1:30. It's the hot spot for ladies who lunch."

Ladies who lunch reverberated like funeral bells. Manny was right; I was becoming Oma. Or worse, Ivy. If I had any doubt about it, the call to Oma about helping furnish the Riverton house removed it. She accepted the invitation with alacrity and almost giggled while prophesying the fun we'd have.

"Cassandane, Dr. Rossellini, and Ms. Blue will join you," Viv said.

"Excellent." Cyrus wanted to blend our lives, and Viv made it happen. I didn't mind it as much as I thought I would.

"If you run into any problems, I'm a phone call away. Ciao."

"Oh, my god, you have people." Sally, curled up on the sofa in the sunroom and cradling a wine glass, chortled. "First the hunky bodyguard, now the efficient lady arranging your reservations. Next thing you know, you'll be saying I'll have my people get in touch with your people."

No joke. On Monday, George divulged he and Viv had booked meetings on the first and third Mondays to coordinate my schedule with Cyrus's, but they had their limits. No one booked a come-to-the-Goddess meeting, so Cyrus and I tiptoed around our Saturday night sins. With no messages from Alexander, Darius, and Nosey, we cherished the silence. We had no illusions. The consequences simmered beneath the surface, waiting for the right moment to erupt.

"Didn't you cast a prosperity spell right before you left Austin?" Talia said, derailing my downward spiral into remorse and repentance.

"I recall something like that."

"It seems to have kicked in."

Cyrus's prosperity wasn't my prosperity.

DON'T SPOIL THE PARTY WITH FACTS.

Talia stretched, basking in the late afternoon sun coming through the stained glass. "This room is lovely. So tranquil."

Tranquil until Nosey Parker or Alexander slithered from beneath their rocks.

"The plants bring in the outside," she said.

Despite everything that happened over the weekend, I'd remembered to get ferns, palms, and orchids for the sunroom. Two points to Team Maren.

Sally switched from wine to Jack Daniels long before the sun set and Cyrus waltzed into the sunroom. She hopped up from the couch and threw her arms around his neck. "Dude, you're looking good. Mega thanks for flying us up here. Trippy."

"Glad you enjoyed it." Cyrus squirmed and raised his eyebrows when he spotted the half-empty bottle of Jack on the side table.

LITTLE TOO EARLY FOR HIS TASTE.

Out of my control. She'd gone upstairs and returned with the bottle. Once upon a time or two, I'd tried taking it away, but it never worked.

Breaking free of Sally, he bent over to kiss Talia's forehead. "Good to see you."

"Same." She patted his cheek, her face drawn into sympathetic lines.

He squeezed next to me on the couch and whispered, "Having fun, K-Bear?"

"Mm-hmm." I poured wine for him as a small reward for not making a scene.

"Am I escorting you ladies to dinner?" He turned to me for confirmation. "Or is it bachelor sandwiches for me?"

"I asked Pat to make something simple. An easy evening for everyone." I kneaded the rigid muscles in his neck.

"Isn't that interesting?" Talia said. "Both your auras became brighter and clearer the instant Cyrus came into the room. Now, they're coming together from the Surya chakra."

She had a knack for provocative diversions, although Cyrus's eyes went blank.

"Surya is your emotional center," I said. "It's below the heart, slightly to the left."

"It's like a string connecting you," Talia said. "First, it was white blooming to violet, a spiritual connection. Now, it's settled into a clear blue, which means you're aligned with each other."

Pat announced dinner, cutting short a chakra lesson. We feasted on Pasta Primavera, crusty rosemary and black pepper rolls, and a Soave wine.

Sally, who'd emptied the bottle of Jack, slugged back the wine without appreciating its fresh almond aroma and lemon palate. Talia covered Sally's conversational deficiencies with anecdotes about Bell, Book, and Candle customers. "The Bio-Bits are selling like crazy. I can't keep them in stock."

"I can't wait to see what else you've done with the store," I said.

"When do you return to Riverton?"

Cyrus moved the wine out of Sally's reach. "After the board meeting at the end of the month."

"We'll be back for Beltane. How are plans coming along?" I said.

Talia frowned. "Developers bought the grove we've used for the past decade. New suburb. The bulldozers moved in last week. Ironically, they're calling it Spring Woods. Looks like we'll use our backyard."

"Your backyard is enchanted," I said. Talia had planted and cultivated it for the last two decades. If you were looking for the perfect backdrop for Shakespeare's *Midsummer Night's Dream*, look no further.

"It's so small." She sighed. "And the neighbors are nosy."

True. In her neighborhood, the houses pressed against each other.

"There's always our place," Cyrus said. My mouth dropped open. "There are bushes and iron fences on three sides and a river on the fourth. Privacy won't be a problem. I'll have Jack give you a fob for the gate so you can check things out."

"Oh, that would be a lifesaver. Thank you."

"When is Beltane?" Sally slurred, coming out of her torpor. She turned her empty glass around in circles as if more wine might magically appear. Cyrus moved the bottle to the floor beside his chair.

"May 1," I said.

"Tickety-boo." Sally pumped her fist in the air. "You'll be back in time for the May Babies Ball."

Because so many people around my age had May birthdays, a blow-out party a decade ago had become an annual weekend event hosted by Sally's partner, BeeBee, at his river camp.

"Oh, man. I haven't been to a May Babies Ball since I moved to Austin. You know who else is a May Baby? This guy!" I nudged Cyrus with my shoulder.

BETTER GET CRACKING ON THAT BIRTHDAY PRESENT; TIME'S RUNNING OUT.

"Gonna be trippy." Sally's words ran together. "BeeBee built a big old dock for his boat. I am so down for skinny skiing. What about you, Mare?"

"Nope. Still too cold." Nothing against skinny dipping, but I preferred getting naked in well-maintained heated pools, not on skis behind a boat in the muddy Mississippi in May. If Sally was driving the boat after an evening of party-hearty, count me out, times two.

"Party Pooper." She stuck out her tongue. Cyrus looked relieved.

Sally rambled about May Babies Balls past and present, a garbled trip down memory lane. Talia and Cyrus's tolerance faded into finger-tapping and watch-checking. Mid-sentence, Sally's head drooped, held up by her hands planted under her chin.

"Hey, Sal." I rose and tapped her shoulder. "C'mon. Bedtime."

I helped her negotiate the stairs. She stumbled on the top step, nearly sending us head over heels into the foyer. When we reached the bedroom, she collapsed onto the bed. Deadweight made it impossible to undress her. Wasn't the first time she'd slept in her clothes, and her stretchy leggings and loose shirt were almost pjs. I removed her shoes and covered her with a spare blanket.

When I kissed her cheek, the alcohol fumes made my eyes water. A bottle of Ghost Mojave was on the dresser. I spritzed her, covering Jack Daniels with a floral woodsy smell that reminded me of violets, and murmured, "Hey, girlfriend, this is getting out of hand again."

When BeeBee arrived on Friday, we'd have another little talk. After I returned to Riverton, we'd visit her parents, lost in their alcoholic haze, and achieve nothing. Eventually, we'd persuade Sally to enter rehab under the guise of a spa vacation. If the past was prologue, she'd stay long enough to dry out. The cycle would begin again. Utterly predictable; utterly heartbreaking.

"Sweet dreams, princess." I sighed and rubbed my chest. My mind skipped ahead, already preparing for the next relapse. *Cancel! Cancel!* "We'll get through this, and there won't be a next time, OK?"

If I told a big enough lie, I might believe it. I slipped from the room.

Talia was alone in the dining room and sipping tea. "I gave Cyrus a hall pass. Told him we had witch business."

"Do we?" I sank into a chair and poured a cup of tea. Honey-scented steam filled my nose.

"Always." Her mischievous grin was infectious, but it turned serious. "I guess we've all been here before. With Sally."

"Yep." No point in dissembling. Talia had counseled me through Sally's first intervention.

"She started drinking on the plane." Talia shook her head. "Sad. She has such potential. I hear good things about Sage Recovery Villa. A high priestess runs the program. Equine therapy, guided meditation. They have everything."

"It won't help someone who refuses to see the problem."

"Can BeeBee reason with her? He seems to adore her, so I'm guessing he wants the best for her."

"For now." BeeBee's high school crush and his secret belief he didn't deserve Sally had carried him this far, but when would he say enough?

"Let's focus on you," Talia said. She reached across the table, her spirit as warm and comforting as hot chocolate on a frosty night. "Did you cleanse the house?"

"I did and put smokey quartz at the entrances."

"Good, good. Now, let's place wards around the house, shall we?"

"Can't hurt." Working magick with Talia made me tingle in anticipation.

We checked the Smokey Quartz stones, and Talia pronounced their potency and my magick strong. "But for protection from someone wishing you harm, you can't overdo it."

It was a perfect opportunity to confess to casting a hex. Instead, I nodded and followed her to the sunroom.

We sat cross-legged, facing the lake. I focused on my breathing, seeking the connection to the ground beneath the floor and the water beating against the shoreline. When I found it, energy flowed into my core, slow at first, but picking up like water blasting through a kinked hose.

"Breathe the energy into the room. Imagine a barrier of earth and water encircling us and the house." Talia's voice, soft and mesmerizing, surged through me. Each exhalation strengthened the barrier.

A spectral grove of Honey Locust trees sprouted, nourished by Talia's magick and the soil and flood we invoked. After willing the trees to grow to their full height of seventy feet with trunks three feet in diameter, we focused on strengthening the dark brown, scaly trunks covered with large, purple-brown, three-part thorns. Perfect. If thorns protected Sleeping Beauty for a hundred years, they'd keep Alexander from our castle.

"Very good," Talia said. "Now, make your intention clear, and we'll bolster it with our will."

"I invoke this shield to protect our home from darkness. Let no negative energies or entities with ill intentions enter our home. Protect all who dwell here. No dangers or ills can befall us when we are within its magickal protection."

"May the Goddess bless this home. As we will it, so mote it be," she finished for me.

The protection exhausted me. I bade Talia goodnight and stumbled upstairs. Cyrus, a tablet propped against his knees, was reading in bed. I brushed my teeth, washed my face, and donned sweats before climbing into bed and snuggling against him.

"Hey, Kinky Bear. Did you get your witch business taken care of?" One arm circled me and drew me even closer. I rested my head against his shoulder.

"Oh, yes. Talia was all about witch business. You know, witches just wanna have fun." No need to mention she thought our house needed more protection. "What are you reading?"

"Frank's presentation to the board. In theory, he's updating us on the strategic plan implementation and the major performance indicators, but it's a word salad." Cyrus shook his head and put the tablet on the bedside table. "He looked good on paper, but it's not translating to action. I can't hold his hand forever. We'll invite him to pursue other opportunities."

"No second chance?"

"This was his second chance." Cyrus tapped his forefinger against his lip, eyebrows drawn together. "Sometimes I wonder if the idiot knows the meaning of strategic plan or performance indicators. Well, he'll be somebody else's problem soon enough."

He cracked his knuckles and bared his teeth, a prize fighter getting into the ring. Yikes! Here was the Cyrus caricatured by Nosey Parker.

He turned on a dime. "So, where's lunch tomorrow?"

"Artella."

He went silent, checking the database in his brain. "Nice place. The loggia has gold vaulted ceilings and the original herringbone brick floors. I think, or I remember someone saying, it was a central garden courtyard of an art school. The dining room is an atrium with fountains, chandeliers, and olive trees."

"Sounds cool."

"Their wine cellar is in the loggia, and it's halfway decent." He cleared his throat. "So, what can we do for Sally?"

"We? We can't do anything?" As much as I hated to admit it, I couldn't lie. "I've tried, but her family doesn't see the problem, and BeeBee won't cross her. She thinks she's fine. So, it's back to rehab sometime soon, and a brief respite before it starts all over again. Seems like the breathers are getting shorter and farther apart."

"What a waste." He puckered his lips, shook his head.

I was losing my friend, and all the magick and money in the world couldn't save her.

MUSIC MAKES THE WORLD GO ROUND

SATURDAY, APRIL 2

WE'VE ALL SEEN IT. Tuning in to an awards ceremony or surfing the internet, we recognize the familiar, almost ubiquitous, image. A big black limo pulls up to an actual red carpet. Plexiglass shields restrain fans, photographers, and the latest virus. The limo doors open. A cacophony of flashes, applause, and the crowd greets the beautiful people in breathtaking outfits by shouting their names. They sail by, unperturbed, regal as swans. For a moment, we imagine we're those people. Am I right? The reality is somewhat different.

Our car pulled up to the Palmer House, and Beckett opened the door. The flashes popped right on cue. Reporters and photographers bellowed our names before our feet hit the red carpet. I scrutinized the crowd, searching for Zombies and Skeletons; the flashes reflecting in the Plexiglass made it hard. The guy in a black fleece caught my eye, but he was too portly to be Alexander. Was the tall woman dressed in camouflage Nosey Parker? A dozen cameras zeroed in, ready to turn any misstep into public humiliation. I froze, certain I'd fall flat on my face.

"I got ya, babe." Cyrus offered his hand and pulled me from the car.

"Maren, look this way," the photographers bayed.

Not bloody likely. Like a butterfly emerging from its chrysalis, my public wings were still wet. Beckett stepped between me and the crowd while I gazed adoringly at Cyrus. The flashes went wild.

"Cyrus, why didn't you buy Pieter's old label instead of starting one? Is it a vendetta?"

Cyrus smiled and said nothing.

"What about the bomb threat, Maren? Did you and Cyrus skip out before anyone else evacuated?"

Do NOT grimace. They'll call it a guilty look.

I stared straight ahead and denied them the money shot. At least they didn't know about the bunker.

"Cyrus, any comment on the Three Little Pigs?"

Did they have a death wish? But no, he kept smiling.

"Maren, who are you wearing?"

At last, a question I could answer. I flashed a thousand-watt smile. "Vintage all the way, baby!"

Kudos to Triangle D'Or. They came through with a fifties cocktail dress in black velvet overlaid with sheer black lace in a floral pattern. They also steered me toward elbow-length black leather gloves, an industrial-looking black patent leather belt, and black hose with the same floral pattern as the dress. Wallis's necklace made its debut tonight, and the cameras zoomed in on it.

Because Pieter advised him not to be a boring billionaire, Cyrus rocked jeans and an embroidered midnight-black velvet dinner jacket. With sleek—and, yes, sexy—black suede boots with tapered toes and stacked Cuban heels, boyfriend was made for strutting.

I scanned the crowd again. Still no Skeletons or Zombies. Pieter's PR team withheld news of tonight's shindig until late this afternoon; Alexander and his Mungers wouldn't have had time to get out an ad for a mob.

"What a trip!" Behind me, Sally giggled, and Talia murmured to Zeke. I didn't dare turn around. The photographers would frame the shot so it looked like I turned my back on Cyrus. They'd blast the photograph around the world and scream, 'Trouble in Cy-Ren Paradise!'

Door-Med cleared us. Doormen in top hats and black coats with scarlet lapels, cuffs, and pockets opened the doors. We stepped into the two-story lobby's hushed elegance.

"Breathtaking." Talia clasped her hands.

An understatement. The vaulted ceiling looked bigger than a basketball court. Art Déco murals reminded me of a modern Sistine Chapel. Huge 24-karat gold winged candelabras designed by Tiffany & Co glittered in the soft light. (I read the Palmer House's history this morning.) The marble-topped tables, velvet seating, and plush oriental rugs were palace-worthy.

We crossed the lobby and climbed a grand marble staircase straight from the *Phantom of the Opera* set.

"I feel like I'm in a movie." Sally kissed BeeBee's cheek. "Honey, you could be the next Alec Chastain."

With BeeBee's red hair, black-on-black western suit, and a black cowboy hat embellished with silver and turquoise, he resembled the current bad boy of action films. In the up-and-coming starlet role, Sally wore a sparkling black column dress adorned with pink and purple sequins and black opera-length gloves. No one would guess she'd slept off a bottle of Jack, rising just in time to get ready for the party.

"We're in the Empire Room," Cyrus said. "Back in the 1930s, it was a supper club. Musicians traveling between New York and LA stopped over and performed here."

"Perfect venue. Your choice or Pieter's?"

"Mutual," he said. "Judy Garland, Ella Fitzgerald, Louis Armstrong, Harry Belafonte. They all performed here. So did Peggy Lee."

"*The Fever* lady." I'd listened to the song about a million times since Sonny Boy's. Every time, the euphoria of dancing with Cyrus washed over me. Even Nosey, ice water, and fake blood couldn't ruin it.

"Right you are." He kissed my cheek.

Beckett halted at the Empire Room's black French doors. "I'll be here if you need me."

Designed in the High French Empire style, the room paid homage to the Paris Opera. Gold-leafed ionic columns and friezes sparkled under crystal chandeliers hanging from massive ceiling medallions. A stage with billowing ivory and scarlet curtains dominated the back wall, and two raised daises with ornate gilt railings were at either end. A jazz band played on the stage.

"It's like stepping back in time," Zeke said.

Snugging me against him, Cyrus murmured, "Hear that music? Tonight, we're gonna dance until we wear holes in our shoes."

"Good deal."

The beautiful people, clustered on what would become the dance floor, swarmed us. Correction, they swarmed Cyrus, reminding him when they'd last met at a charity ball, after party, or celebrity-fueled bashes around the world. With their faces so familiar from magazines, internet sites, music videos, and movies, no one needed an introduction. Jewels sparkled, catching the light as the beautiful people embraced, cheek-kissed, and raised champagne glasses to their lips.

The women were flawless; I suspected a few were charter members of Cyrus's Babe of the Month Club. Operating on the *no harm no foul* principle, they greeted me with dazzling smiles and included me in the no-need-for introductions category.

"I've been dying to meet you," gushed the rising Country Western singer in the skin-tight, gold lamé sheath.

The Oscar-winning actress in silk paratrooper pants and a corset top resembling a spider web gave me the once-over. "So that's the famous necklace. It's yummy."

"Great dress," said the wife of the lead singer of the band Finley wanted to emulate. "I adore vintage. It's so much more satisfying than Rodeo Drive's same-old, same-old." Without waiting for a response, she said, "When you and Cyrus come to LA, I'll turn you on to some killer shops."

Not *if* I came to LA with Cyrus, but when.

"Don't you want to kill that Nosey Parker bitch?" The infamous female rocker gave me a sympathetic hug. "When I was in labor with my last critter, she bribed a delivery room nurse. If Jed hadn't spotted her and grabbed the phone, my twat would be all over the internet."

Eww! Cyrus meant it when he said, "Good thing they didn't get the nekkid Downward Facing Dog by the pool shot."

Talia nudged me and gestured with her eyebrows at Sally, circulating like a Queen Bee. The beautiful people took it for granted she was in their club.

Cassandane emerged from a nearby cluster of people. "Let's grab a seat. This crowd can be a bit much."

We took our table on a dais. Dinner service didn't come too soon. With all the chit chat, I'd missed hors d'oeuvres.

The Gilded Age décor notwithstanding, the room exuded an edgy elegance. Tables swathed in burgundy linen enhanced fine bone china with a crisp black and gold band. Each table boasted an individual ice sculpture, shaped into a vase and holding a single trumpet-shaped calla lily. Some lilies were white and others a rich eggplant color. The vase rested on an ice block, with corners carved into candle holders for flickering black candles.

"This bash makes the Beaux Artes Ball look like a kegger," Sally said.

Always the romantic, Cyrus winked and whispered, "Never. I thought it was a fairy tale or a dream come true."

Servers in black and white, carrying trays on an uplifted arm, arrived. The jazz band's music made the perfect backdrop. I peeled off my gloves and tucked into the barbequed strip-loin with spring carrots, crispy rice, and cornbread crumble. When the band paused between numbers, ice tinkled against crystal water glasses accompanied by the soft drip of melting ice sculptures.

"The people you met tonight will take your calls now," Cyrus said.

"Why will I call them?" I didn't see many BFF prospects in the room.

"To ask them to include The Majestic on their schedules."

Oh! After my call with Uncle Ira, I congratulated myself on my business acumen. I had a lot to learn. Arching my eyebrows, I asked, "Will Native Son take my call?"

"I'll always take your call, babe." He squeezed my knee under the table. "Fair warning; I can be a tough negotiator."

With a gentle elbow to the ribs, I whispered, "Big talk, big guy. Whip out fancy knickers, and you crumble like a cookie."

His whooping laugh reverberated through the room. He leaned in to whisper. "That's our little secret. I have a reputation."

People leaned toward us, trying to eavesdrop. Unbelievable.

Servers delivered espresso and confectionery bites, including gold-dusted truffles and chocolate-dipped fruit followed by champagne. The jazz band ceded the stage to Pieter, looking cooler than cool in boots, slim-fitting trousers, and a collarless shirt accessorized with an embroidered bib. The clink of glasses and cutlery became thunderous applause.

"Thank y'all for coming to our little shindig." Pieter jerked his thumb toward our table. "Be sure and thank Cyrus for hosting. After the bill arrives, he and Maren will have to save up for Devil Dawgs."

Laughter erupted from the Chicago crowd, and heads swiveled in our direction. I guffawed along with Cyrus, who'd promised to take me to his favorite hot dog place.

"Love ya, brother." Pieter bowed in our direction. "So, if you've been listening to the gossip, which of course you haven't, you know I'm here tonight to announce our music label, Native Son."

Pieter's speech hit all the buzzwords for this crowd.

Artistic freedom. Clap.

"Louder, please." Pieter's cocky grin dazzled the crowd. "Or as the great John Lennon said, 'The people in the cheap seats, clap your hands. The rest of you, rattle your jewelry.'"

Clap. Support for a national treasure, a truly American art form, the Blues. Clap.

Promote musical innovation. Clap. Clap.

First contract offered to Elmore and the Chicago Blues Project and Marley Blue. I stopped counting the claps.

"Now, a few words from someone who shares my commitment to great music. Someone who needs no introduction, my lifelong pal and music enthusiast, Cyrus Harper."

Cyrus took the stage.

"Thank you, Pieter." He waited for the deafening applause to wane. "My mother says music makes the world go round. As always, Mom knows best, right, Cassandane? Without music, our lives are impoverished no matter how rich we are. Music connects us with other people and with something deep within ourselves. The two things I can't live without both start with M. Music and Maren, yeah."

Another head swivel; not all the speculation stayed in people's heads.

"When Pieter and I started discussing Native Son," he said smoothly, as if he hadn't unleashed a flurry of gossip and conjecture. "We envisioned a world that supports musicians, particularly those in the jazz and blues tradition, so they can create amazing music and connect with their audience. We had one goal above all others: to nurture the Blues and Jazz community, which has had very few resources and even fewer local institutions to support them. Before we lost this most American art form, something had to change. We believe we can be the change."

He earned a standing ovation from the politically correct music crowd. Oma encouraged her granddaughters to buy a clue and act like astronaut wives: Happy, Proud, and Thrilled. She'd be pleased with my performance tonight. If there was an astronaut sister role, Cassandane nailed it.

"Finally, a word or two for my friends in the press." The audience, well-acquainted with press antics, laughed. "This isn't about Pieter. It's not about me. It's not a beauty or a popularity contest. It's about the music and only the music."

"Well done, Mr. Harper," I said when he returned to his seat.

"Why thank you, Miss K-Bear," he said with an exaggerated southern drawl.

The party swung into high gear when the Chicago Blues Project took the stage. Pieter and Cyrus leaped to their feet, pulling Marley and me onto the dance floor. They opened a floodgate where all the too-cool-for-school people hit the dance floor in a tidal wave.

As always, dancing with Cyrus was a mystical sexual experience that I wished would last forever. In the music and movement bubble, problems faded to nothing more than a faint insect buzz. No Nosey poking her beak into our business and pontificating on what we did wrong. No Alexander threats. My family's weighty expectations disappeared in a magical poof. When we danced, the world spun at the right speed.

Jed, the intrepid delivery room camera snatcher, tapped Cyrus's shoulder and held out his hand. He spun me around twice before grilling me about my musical interests. For the first time in forever, I appreciated my ex-boyfriend mansplaining music to me; I held my own with Jed.

Others cut in. The same two questions came thick and fast.

Are you a professional witch?

"Obviously."

Do you fly on a broom?

HAR-DEE-HAR-HAR! SUCH A WIT.

"I only fly on planes, and Cyrus has a big one."

Jezebel, Brunhilda of Austrasia, and Maren Spliids

Saturday, April 2

PEOPLE OVERLOAD AND MY bladder demanded I excuse myself. I left the party and headed toward the ladies' room. A male server, with heavy make-up, a sleek raven-colored ponytail, and matching mustache, asked if I needed anything.

Life in the spotlight meant you couldn't pee without someone noticing. "Just the ladies' room."

"I'm sorry. The one on this level has developed some plumbing problems." He directed me to the so-called Ladies' Parlor in the lobby.

As I floated down the marble staircase, my heels muffled by the runner's deep pile, I relived my childhood Cinderella-leaving-the-ball fantasy. Cinderella, however, didn't have a Beckett waiting at the bottom of the stairs. He sprang to attention, circumventing the glass slipper quest. Where was the fun in that?

"Just a biology break." I gestured in the direction of the Ladies' Parlor. "It's right behind the bar. I'll be fine."

"Cyrus won't like that," he said.

"We won't tell him, will we?"

He ignored my exaggerated sigh. Seriously, peeing shouldn't be a major security issue.

"Pretty please!" I repeated it until I annoyed the snot out of him.

He nodded, but I could tell the concession didn't thrill him. The poor guy walked the iffy line between a sulky me and a raging Cyrus. I dashed off before he reconsidered.

Tucked behind the lobby bar and down a dim hallway, it was almost like they didn't want anyone using the Ladies' Parlor. Chatter and music faded. The air cooled and became less charged with the scent of candles and expensive perfume.

The heavy door boasted a stained-glass window with the words Ladies' Parlor; I'd found the right place. Inside, plush chaise lounges and floor-to-ceiling mirrors ruled. Crystal chandeliers, natch. Marble fixtures and gilt. Enough soaps and lotions to stock an upscale department store. Bonus, the place was empty, a near miracle for a ladies' room. I lingered after doing my business, checking my hair and make-up, admiring my outfit, sampling various lotions, kicking off my heels to rest my arches, rolling around on a chaise, and reverting to my teenage prima donna self. Honestly, I enjoyed the solitude where no heads turned in my direction. I closed my eyes after five minutes on a chaise. The world drifted away.

"May I help you?"

I scrambled to my feet. My shoes were under the chaise, and the marble chilled my toes through the flowery hose. A poor second to my blood running cold.

The server who'd directed me earlier leaned against the arched doorway, blocking the exit. "You've been in here so long, I was worried."

THAT'S NOT CREEPY.

Up close, his heavy make-up, well-defined cheekbones, and knife-sharp jawline didn't disguise a weasel face.

CREEPY + 1.

"Thank you, I'm fine." Please go away.

"Interesting party you're missing. A lethal combo of rich people and corporate music."

Oh, gawd! I'd heard the corporate music screed often enough from Finley, my ex-boyfriend. Next, this guy would natter about how "the man" squelched true talent and innovation. Namely, his.

AT LEAST YOU HOPE THAT'S WHAT THIS IS ABOUT.

"You disagree?" He winked. "As Harper's witch, you'd have to, right?"

I smoothed my dress and stared in the mirror, hoping he'd take the hint. Hoping my intuition was wrong.

"Your dress is très chic. Unlike the costume you wore at the Beaux Artes Ball. Aren't you a little old for rebellion?" It hit me like a hammer to my skull. I recognized the voice from the bomb threat tape. A Mitnick Munger.

I turned from the mirror. He did a little Charlie Chaplin dance reminiscent of the emcee in *Cabaret*. Any minute he'd break into a chorus of *Money! Money!*

"Did you enjoy shopping with your friends, Maren, dear? Sally should drink less. Such a pretty girl, but she won't go the distance if she keeps it up."

Maren, dear? Who said that? *Sally. The Beaux Artes Ball.* He was no mere Munger! My breath caught on the knot in my throat. I was face to face with Alexander! *Beckett, are you keeping an eye out for me?*

"Nothing? Cat got your tongue?" His ice-blue eyes glittered.

Although thin, he filled the door frame, making it impossible to slip past. My heart fluttered, then skipped a beat. Right now, I'd give a million dollars for the Taser I used to carry in my purse.

"No one is coming. We've been sending people away. Plumbing problems, don't you know?"

He'd read my mind, although it might not have been that difficult to guess what I'd been thinking/hoping.

"Now would be the perfect time for magical charms." He had a crooked smile, his lips curling like a serpent across his face. "Maybe they'll do you good, although I doubt it. Sure, you twisted Harper into a pretzel, but I'm made of stronger stuff. I bet you know about Jezebel. Wasn't she a witch like you?"

Squaring my shoulder and clenching my fists, I took a step toward the door. He called my bluff and stood firm.

"They threw her from a window, didn't they? Horses trampled her, and dogs gnawed on her bones. They spread her remains on the ground like horse dung."

The room did a slow spin. The screams and joint-popping from the Spellbound video reverberated in my head. I backed up, leaning against a mirror to keep my balance.

"What about Brunhilda of Austrasia? You know about her?"

"Nope." A quick survey confirmed the only way out was through him. Or darting into a stall and hoping the door held firm until someone came looking for me. If there were Mungers directing people in another direction, neither seemed a good choice. I could spray his eyes with the complimentary hair spray. No, too far away.

"She called herself a queen, but her army called her a witch. They tied her feet to wild horses and tore her apart limb from limb and burned her. Grim, huh?"

His eyes gleamed. He found the story more exciting than grim.

"You've surely heard about Maren Spliids since you share a name."

"Can't say I have."

STAY CALM. BECKETT WILL BE HERE ANY SECOND. HE WON'T LET A MUNGER STAND IN HIS WAY.

Hope so. If Beckett said I told you so every day for a year, I wouldn't pout.

"She's Denmark's most notorious witch. Seventeenth century. Married to a successful tailor. A guy named Didrik, her husband's competitor, accused her of witchcraft. Didrik claimed three witches woke him up one night. He said he didn't know two of them, but he recognized Maren."

He spat out my name like a curse, but the diatribe sounded rehearsed. Like he stood before a mirror and practiced poking needles into me.

"Didrik said they held him down, and Maren blew into his mouth. The day after, he was sick and vomited up a moving object. He showed it to the priests and the bishop, and they declared it unnatural. Her husband finagled an acquittal. Do you think Harper would save you?"

I tried to squeeze past him. Long fingers with black symbols tattooed on the knuckles shot out and wrapped around my wrist.

"Back off." I jerked away. Only Cyrus had permission to touch my wrists.

"Whoa. Feisty girl." He chuckled. "Back to my question. I don't think he would. Harper's only interested in saving himself."

Like he knew anything. Not that long ago, Cyrus threw himself between me and a bullet.

DON'T ARGUE. YOU'LL ONLY AGGRAVATE HIM.

"Interesting story, but my friends are waiting for me."

"Don't go. It gets more interesting."

Not really; I already knew the punch line: burn the witch. I bet he called every woman a witch — old, beautiful, odd-seeming, mouthy, sexually liberated, and (particularly) powerful women. Women sent men like him into an unholy rage.

THOU SHALT NOT SUFFER A WITCH TO LIVE.

My mouth lost all its spit. My face in the mirror looked like I'd painted it white. If I didn't get out now, I might never make it. I took two steps toward the door. "Excuse me."

"Wait." He stuck out his foot when I took a third step, nearly tripping me. "The story isn't over. Didrik didn't give up, and the king brought Maren to Copenhagen and tortured her. She confessed and accused other people of witchcraft. The judges said, 'We find her a sorceress. She will suffer fire at the stake.'"

DON'T LISTEN. HE'S TRYING TO SCARE YOU.

And doing a damned good job of it. Plus, his voice was as hypnotic as a snake charmer's. The quivering in my gut traveled to my limbs.

"They executed Maren the next day." His obvious excitement pierced my eardrums. "The priest took pity on her. He gave her alcohol to steady herself and tied a bag of gunpowder on her back to make death quicker. They tied her to a ladder and threw the ladder into the fire. Ka-boom!"

The ka-boom echoed off the marble floors and mirrors.

I rubbed my arms to stop the shaking and touched the Bio-Bit I forgot I was wearing. I kept rubbing to hide my search for its panic button. Pressing every button, I hoped for the best.

"Still nothing to say?" If it was possible, his eyes got wilder and crazier.

"You think a witch is a villainess who hexes you or wreaks havoc or lures people to their demise?" OK, I had hexed him, but he pushed me to it. "But the root of the word witch is healer, someone who helps people."

"You can't help Harper, and he can't save you; you know that, right?"

PLAY ALONG!

Wasn't that the advice you read in every magazine? Play along until you get a chance to escape. My dignity wouldn't allow it. "I guess we'll find out, won't we?"

WHERE THE HELL ARE YOU, BECKETT?

"Poor, silly girl. A pity you're mixed up with Harper. Wasn't there a nice boy in that little town of yours?"

"No one as nice as Cyrus."

His cool, appraising stare made me squirm. "You have more gumption than I gave you credit for."

"Forgive me if I don't thank you." Gumption made me frosty and dismissive instead of squealing like a rabbit.

He threw back his head and laughed. Not a healthy, join-me chuckle, but an off-putting snicker like he'd drowned a bag of kittens. "You're wasting yourself on Harper. He'll grind you down into a simpering clothes hanger."

"I beg to differ."

"Honestly, would you be with him if you hadn't lost your money?"

Honestly? Maybe not. I wouldn't have returned to Riverton to meet him. I recalled his confession about setting up a "chance" encounter in Austin. What would that have been like? Good, I imagined. Our chemistry had been instantaneous and packed a wallop. I refused to share that with this monster. Let him think his monster thoughts. "I didn't lose my money. You and Cena stole it, Eli."

Surprise flickered across his face so fast I doubted if I saw it. Did he know how much power knowing someone's name gave to their enemies? If I escaped his trap, he'd learn. He scoffed, a patronizing sound if I'd ever heard one, and so predictable.

"I'll make you a one-time offer." He stepped forward. I didn't yield an inch. His odor, a cloying musk, turned my stomach. I swallowed the sick; wouldn't give him the satisfaction. "You walk away right now. Catch a plane or train back to Riverton. Change your locks and never see Harper again. Do that, and I'll call it even between us."

HA! YOU DON'T KNOW AS MUCH AS YOU THINK, MISTER SMARTY PANTS! NO ONE LOCKS THEIR DOORS IN THE BLUFFS.

WHERE IS BECKETT?

"No."

His lips curled, a moue of disappointment, ridicule, or whatever. "What? No money for train fare?"

"You think I have gumption but no brains? Is that it? You think I can't figure out the second I step outside the hotel, your Mungers will grab me. Thou shalt not suffer a witch to live, isn't that your motto?" My blood turned to liquid fire. I planted my feet, thrust out my chest, and raised my arms as if I was drawing down the moon. "The dark ages are over, motherfucker. Try burning me now and see where that gets you."

In retrospect, not the best way to defuse the situation, but he retreated a few steps, compensating with a patronizing chuckle. "Now, now, Maren, what's stopping me from taking you?"

Time started and stopped. One heartbeat lasted an hour, and the next disappeared in a flash.

Beckett, we're running out of time here!

"Because you'd have to drag me, kicking and screaming through the lobby. Might cause a rumpus. No. If you're going to kill me, do it right here, right now. Not in some dark alley."

He shook his head as if I'd disappointed him. "Maren, dear, there are many ways out of this building."

The door flew open, and Beckett zoomed through it like one of Cyrus's hockey players, knocking Alexander against the wall. He grabbed my shoulders, and I became the hockey puck, sliding through the door and down the hallway into the lobby bar.

Beckett caught up and threw me over his shoulder, barking at servers and hotel guests alike. "The fuck out of the way."

People turned to stare as he deposited me on a bar stool.

"Sit right here, and don't move," he barked. "Anyone comes near you, scream like hell. Cyrus will be right down."

Before I could agree or even catch my breath, he headed back toward the Ladies' Parlor. I hoped he'd pound Alexander's head against the marble. I stood up, longing to see that happy moment.

Sit right there!

My legs, as hollow as paper straws, shook. I sat right there.

"Whiskey," I croaked.

Beckett returned about the same time Cyrus reached the bar. Beckett shook his head. "Gone."

I downed the whiskey in a single gulp. The fiery sensation stiffened my spine and loosened my tongue. "I didn't see him come out."

"A panel in the ceiling opens into a crawl space." Beckett looked grim. "This wasn't spur of the moment; it was planned."

3-2-1. Cyrus exploded.

AFTERMATH

SUNDAY, APRIL 3

DÉJÀ VU ALL OVER again. The scenery varied, and the cast of characters now included my Riverton friends, Cassandane, and her husband. Yet, here we were in a penthouse suite recounting Alexander's latest transgression. Solemn detectives took copious notes while Cyrus raked his fingers through his hair in a way that suggested he might pull it out by the roots. Yep, we were definitely in rerun land.

Sally and Talia took turns patting my hand or knee and telling me I was doing great. Great? Every thirty seconds, hysteria welled up inside me, ready to erupt like a volcano.

NINETEEN DAYS. YOU CAN MAKE IT FOR NINETEEN DAYS.

After the Harp Board Meeting on the twenty-second, we'd pile into the Aston Martin and head to Riverton like bats from hell.

I'd never wanted to return to Riverton as much as I did right now. Or maybe once, on a Friday afternoon three weeks into my freshman year; I hadn't made any friends and faced another lonely night in my dorm. I'd hopped on the evening train; Oma sat me down in the kitchen, prepared her special peppermint hot chocolate with imported French marshmallows, and told me I was a Lilienthal and needed to buck up. It worked.

Tonight, I yearned for Cyrus to whisk me away to his castle inside a fully gated community and ply me with Concha y Toro from his wine stash. I'd do a tranquility spell, and everything would be better. That was the dream, anyway.

"I want to go home. Now." I interrupted the interrogation.

Sally squeezed my knee, and resentment bubbled up like sinister champagne. How dare she? Tomorrow, she and the others could hop on Cyrus's jet and go to Riverton and safety. Cyrus and I didn't have that luxury at the moment.

Cyrus stopped pulling his hair and jerked his head in my direction. Poor word choice. He thought I meant Riverton, judging by his look of betrayal. I did, but he didn't need to know that.

"I don't want to spend the night in this hotel when we have a perfectly good house thirty minutes away."

The detectives shuffled their tablets and feet. One cleared his throat. "If I understand correctly, this guy knows where you live."

"Cyrus, take me home." I nodded at the officers and forced a polite smile. "I have my bodyguard, and we have round-the-clock security."

With security, Beckett, and Talia's protection spell, I assumed I'd be safe; I'd been wrong before. The magick word *home,* meaning *Evanston,* cast a spell over Cyrus. We hit the road ten minutes later.

The next morning, my head was fuzzy enough to wonder if I'd had another nightmare. The buzz of conversation downstairs and the vibrato of Sally and Talia insisting I return to Riverton disabused me of that notion. Nightmare or not, I promised Cyrus we'd get through this thing together, and I intended to keep my word.

I fortified myself with my morning Tarot question. "What do I need to know today?"

Don't lecture me about blissful ignorance! When I was already in freefall, a yappy little dog warning me not to step off the cliff wasn't much help. I shoved the card back into the deck with extreme prejudice and stomped toward the living room.

My friends were clustered on the sofa while Cyrus paced before the fireplace. Sally clutched a Bloody Mary, mostly consumed. Damn it. I hadn't talked with BeeBee yet. Too late now. He'd think I was hysterical because of last night, and he needed to take Sally's situation seriously. I'd make it a priority when we returned to Riverton.

"Looks like you folks are about to hit the road." I smiled like the world was my oyster.

"Talia and I think ..." Sally said.

"I know what you think; it won't happen. I'm sorry you all got involved in that scene last night. The first Alexander encounter is a shocker."

Cyrus followed an I-told-you-so nod with a shaky laugh. After convincing them I'd be fine, and that, yes, we'd be back in Riverton in one piece and in time for Beltane and the May Babies Ball, I deserved an Oscar. By the time they were bundled in the car and off to the airport, I was ready to crawl back to bed and pull the covers over my head.

Cyrus sat on the sofa and patted the cushion. I curled up beside him, my head on his shoulder. Outside, the springtime sun glistened on the Red

Bud tree's purple flowers. A fresh scattering of green grass encroached on the wintery brown. How did the Universe permit someone like Alexander to exist on such a perfect day?

"Talked to the police this morning," Cyrus said. "Looks like someone hacked into the hotel's HR system and made it look like Philipp Alexander had worked there for about six months. Had a time card, W2 with a social, and an ID badge. All false. He signed up to work at the event on March 14. They're showing his photo, the one in his HR file, to staff, but so far no one remembers working with him."

Alexander twigged I'd be there before I did; Cyrus told me about the party after Pieter's concert on the fifteenth. "Clever bastard, isn't he? I suppose he did the ice and flower arrangements, too."

"They came from Four Finches. We use them for all our events. Anyway, I talked with Darius."

Another déjà vu all over again moment. Darius was a moral issue for another day. "Did he find out anything yet?"

"Still talking to people, but he mentioned something that already occurred to me. He said I had a busted pipe, and that the leaks were coming from inside Harp. Makes sense, I guess. Eli was one bad apple, and maybe he spread the rot."

"Anything's possible."

He sat down, then bolted upright and continued pacing. Pinching the bridge of his nose, he pushed out slow, deep breaths "Darius thinks it might be Viv, which would never have occurred to me."

"Well, he's wrong. Zeus zapping you with a lightning bolt is a lot more likely than Viv betraying you."

"I don't want to believe it." He rubbed his chest over his heart, which must be broken at the mere thought. "She's been with me since the beginning. But hell, she knows everything. About Hawaii, Wallis's necklace, when we'd arrive in Chicago, the concert, your visit to the office, our appointment at the spa, the thing about your grandfather's painting. You name it; she knows it."

Too many suspicious coincidences, for sure, with last night being icing on the suspicion cake. But Viv? "She adores you."

"She planned last night's event, right down to the seating chart. Hell, she knows most things before I do." His voice thickened, and the veins in his throat pulsed. Rage? Tears? Anybody's guess.

The Fool flashed before my eyes. GAH! I'd totally misinterpreted the message.

It's not always about you, Lilienthal.

One step away from the abyss, *The Fool* wasn't malevolent; he was blissfully careless. The white rose in his hand symbolized innocence. Most days, his mouth worked ahead of and independently of his brain. Without thinking, he rushed in to reach his heart's desire.

"It's Johnny," I murmured.

Cyrus scoffed. "He's a kid."

"He knows what Viv knows and runs all over the world for you."

"Sure. But he doesn't have a conniving bone in his body." Cyrus lapsed into hemming and hawing. He'd had an hour or four to come to grips with Viv's possible treachery. He wanted to exonerate her, but not at Johnny's expense.

"I don't think he's in league with Alexander," I said.

Another memory newsflash. Sparkling periwinkle eyes like ice chips in Creme de Violette and a frosty smile. The dark brown aura of a self-centered, egotistic, and deceptive person. What was her name? Maryanne? Maureen? Muireann, her name was Muireann, and she was sex on a stick.

"Not personally; but he might tell Muireann things when they're all bow-chicka-wow-wow," I said.

"Bow-chicka-wow-wow. Babe, you never cease to amaze me." A tentative smile grew into a snort of laughter. "I *need* to know more about ... bow-chicka-wow-wow. Maybe a demo. But, seriously? She was a bitch, I'll grant you."

"A bitch who didn't like us on sight. I'm not bragging, but it usually takes someone at least an hour to dislike me." Voices outside a bathroom stall. *Johnny has a girlfriend. Met her right after Paris, and they got hot and heavy in a nano-second.* Amusing at the time. It was right under our noses, and we missed it. Like so many things. "Get him over here right now. What if she's a Mitnick Munger?"

Mitnick Munger cut through Cyrus's skepticism. He was on the phone like white on rice. "Hey, Johnny. Sorry to disturb you on a Sunday, but can you drop by the house? We need to talk. Why don't you bring Muireann with you? We can have a drink or two. Four is great, yeah."

Amazing. Cyrus looked and sounded as innocent as a newborn. We had an hour, and he followed me upstairs to strategize while I dressed.

"She won't come."

"When did you whip out your crystal ball?"

Ouch. "Wild ass guess."

Turns out, I was right. Johnny rang the doorbell at four on the dot. The lovely Muireann was not on his arm when Cyrus led him into the living room. I poured him wine and gestured toward the empty glass. "Weren't we expecting Muireann?"

Johnny blushed. "She got a call while I was showering. Family emergency. Funny thing, I didn't even know she had family in Chicago."

I gave Cyrus a knowing look. OK, a gloating smirk.

"I don't think it was that. Actually." Johnny took a seat across from me. "The way she acted at the hotel probably embarrassed her."

I nodded sympathetically and didn't believe even for a minute she was embarrassed.

"Hey, the big party was last night, huh? How'd it go?"

Johnny gave off a puppy's wiggly energy. He was either innocent or a stone-cold villain. I voted for the former. In any case, his question made a perfect segue.

"Mostly great." Cyrus prowled the room like a panther. "But we had another Alexander run-in. He tried to kidnap Maren."

"Oh, gosh. Are you OK?"

All my life, I'd heard the phrase "eyes wide as saucers." I'd never seen it IRL until today.

"A bit shaken." I flapped my hands, a visual representation of my state of mind.

"Gosh. This is getting spooky." He scooted to the edge of his seat and leaned forward, the picture of concerned innocence.

"The thing is." Cyrus stopped prowling and towered over Johnny. That wasn't intimidating or anything. "The kidnapping wasn't spur-of-the-moment. There's evidence he knew we'd be there, and he'd been planning for weeks. Someone at Harp is leaking info."

"What? No way." Johnny's furrowed brow and headshaking emphasized his disbelief. "Nah. Impossible."

"There are too many coincidences," Cyrus said.

"Who'd do that?" His head swiveled between Cyrus and me.

"We think it's Viv," I said, following our strategy.

"Viv? Not a chance." His voice cracked, and he shook his head.

"Then someone with access to Viv's calendar, her computer. Someone who overhears everything." The muscles in Cyrus's neck corded, and he cracked his knuckles. "Do you know anyone like that, Johnny?"

Johnny's wine glass slid from his fingers, but he caught it before it hit the floor. His mouth opened, but nothing came out.

"Quit torturing him, babe." I leaned toward Johnny and patted his knee. "Did you let things slip to Muireann?"

Johnny's eyes widened from flying saucers into Saturn's rings. A light clicked on as he put the pieces together. My heart ached for him, although I'd paid the price for his indiscretion. As Cyrus said, he was a kid. In the throes of new love, I'd have done the same. Finley's ghost hooted in agreement.

"You want my resignation, I guess."

"Not necessarily." Cyrus patted Johnny's shoulder. "But I need to know what she knows."

"Yeah, sure. Give me a sec, OK?" His head drooped, and he rubbed his eyes with his fingertips. A heavy sigh opened the floodgate of times, places, and confidences, confirming that Alexander knew exactly when and how to barge into our lives.

"At least he never breached Harp data," Cyrus said. "One disaster averted."

"I'm so freaking sorry. I thought it was really sweet. She was so interested in my job. The women at work think I'm a goofball. It was nice that someone seemed fascinated by what I do."

The bathroom gigglers didn't realize that they'd molded and shaped him bit by bit until he was a pushover for Muireann.

The flame in his cheeks could have ignited the second Great Chicago Fire. "She ... she ... uh liked, you know, doing it in semi-public places. Like the elevator at the Waldorf-Astoria, the night we saw you. So sometimes ... uh ... we ... uh used the office when no one was around."

Ah, the old bow-chicka-wow-wow working its dirty magick. Cyrus grinned at me. Yeah, that was an invitation, all right.

"I caught her trying to get into Viv's office, but you know Viv is a real Nazi about locking things down. Lucky for me, I guess. Gosh, do you really think Muireann's in league with the Alexander guy?"

Young love and hope sprang eternal. After we called the police and they went to talk to her, they reported the apartment was empty. It was scrubbed down and cleaned; not a fingerprint, hair, or eyelash remained. A professional job, the detective said. As for Ms. Muireann Deighan, she did not exist.

Johnny looked like his favorite pet died on the day he learned there was no Santa Claus. On a positive note, he kept his job.

THE MAN WHO HAS EVERYTHING

I WOKE IN A panic. No Skeletons or Zombies. No Alexander. Nope, just Mab, my virtual assistant, cheerfully reminding me about Cyrus's upcoming birthday. How hard could it be? Besides, it might be a relief to focus on something besides Alexander's next move and our lack of progress in finding him.

I pulled my tablet from the bedside table and ran an internet search: gifts for the man who has everything. The inadequate results did nothing to appease the heebie-jeebies.

Private jet membership? A non-starter for the man with his own jet.

A personal message from a celebrity? They called him all the time.

Flying lessons? Given my family history, not a chance.

A Montblanc Boheme Royal pen covered in 1,400 diamonds? A bargain at $1.5 million, but I'd never seen him write anything that didn't involve a keyboard.

He already owned an Aston Martin.

A week on a research vessel in the Antarctic with a carbon offset? He'd love it, but he'd also expect me to go with him. Not bloody likely. The itinerary made me shiver and pull the duvet around me.

A Globe-Trotter bespoke steamer trunk with a crafted mini bar and compartments for shoes, a drawer to hold up to eight watches, and leather-covered hangers for bespoke suits. Mr. I-Hate-Packing could roll it out once a year on his birthday and dust it.

Three pages into the search, my bleary eyes fell on the Dom Perignon Rose Gold Limited Edition.

Now, you're talking.

The description was a love poem to champagne. "Pleasing and tantalizing in every way. The brilliant amber liquid, tinted pink by small dot-shaped bubbles, makes a wine enthusiast's heart beat faster. The taste progresses with strength — tense, radiant, and sharp — and finishes with a spicy note. Each bottle of this coveted elixir is a piece of art plated with rose gold."

Sounded right up Cyrus's alley. After checking with Viv to make sure he didn't have a bottle or ten stashed away somewhere, I sent a message to George to find a bottle. He called ten minutes later.

"It's almost fifty-thousand a bottle." His voice was stiff with shock.

My salary from The Plaza had piled up in the bank; I also had money from the sale of my house. "Go for it. If you can find two bottles, get them."

So far, so good, but I wanted to dazzle Cyrus. Give him something no one else could. Where was the genie in the rose gold bottle when you needed one?

One genie coming up. Didn't his collections manager dangle a Yonas Abebe painting in his face? You know he wanted it. Who has one?

This girl, that's who. Manny and I inherited ten of Yonas's paintings, and Oma was the trustee for the collection until we both turned thirty. I had Oma on Face2Face in a hot minute.

"What a coincidence. I was about to call you, dear." Curled up on the sitting room couch with the sun streaming through the leaded glass windows, the peach silk wall covering bringing out the creaminess of her skin, and holding a delicate tea cup, Oma looked like she was sitting for a portrait. Her serene expression meant she still hadn't heard about Alexander's latest shenanigans. I sent a silent thank you to Sally for not blabbing.

"Great minds," I assured her.

"You asked my opinion about the Imari china." I'd been running decorating ideas by Oma. As I told Cyrus, her taste was impeccable, and it made her happy. "It's a good choice, both bold and traditional. I haven't seen such a complete collection in several years. Snap it up, and I'll leave mine to you in the will."

I swallowed a smirk. To my certain knowledge, Ivy had decorated her dining room in anticipation of inheriting Oma's Royal Crown Derby Old Imari china. "I put a hold on it; I'll pull the trigger as soon as we hang up."

"Excellent. Now, did you decide about the Pierre Jeanneret dining table? You don't think Cyrus will find it pricey?"

"I showed him the photos, and he said yes. It's on the way to Riverton, as we speak." Not denying it, I felt smug about snagging a piece from a UNESCO World Heritage Site. The choice impressed even Grayson, the Collections Manager, who called it a design icon, embodying the pure idea of mid-Century Modern. A bargain, he said, at a quarter of a million dollars.

Oma clapped her hands in a lady-like way. "Lovely. Now we need to find the right silver."

"Let's leave that for another day. I have a favor to ask you."

"Who are you, and what have you done with my Maren?" She beamed. The only thing that might make her happier was a big fat diamond on my left hand. Not today, Oma; not today.

"Do you recall Yonas's painting called *Daughter Fruit — Helene and Maren*? It might be cataloged under the Amharic title *yēseti liji firē—hēleni ina mareni*. Do you know the one I'm talking about?"

Oma wrinkled her brow. "I believe so."

"I want to give it to Cyrus for his birthday."

"Oh, Maren. That's quite a valuable painting. I don't know if you keep up with the art news, but Sotheby's..."

"I know. *My Heart, My Love* is up for auction. Cyrus wanted to buy it, but I said no. I don't want Adele in my house." My house? That slipped out, but Oma's invisible antennae went up.

"No, I agree. *Daughter Fruit* is more appropriate." She tapped her forefinger against her lips. "I'm not sure how Manny would feel about it."

"He always said *Daughter Fruit* was mine." Manny wasn't the problem. I couldn't imagine Ivy allowing Yonas's "ethnic" paintings in her house, but she'd fight tooth and nail to keep whichever ones I wanted. Oma was supposed to arbitrate any disputes, and Oma's word was law to Ivy.

The well-manicured forefinger continued stroking her lower lip. She tilted her head, studying my face. She paused and said, "What if it doesn't work out?"

It meant Cyrus and me. Her hesitation was an old superstition; Oma believed if you spoke your fear, your words gave it life. It wasn't any more preposterous than me thinking that giving Cyrus the painting might also ease his fear of me hightailing it.

"He'll have a great painting, and I'll have significant jewelry."

Concern still flickered across her face.

"I don't think that will happen."

WHO IS THIS SELF-CONFIDENT WOMAN? WHAT HAPPENED TO MAREN?

"I mean, I can't say for certain, but my cards aren't pointing to a disaster of Finley proportions."

Oma winced; she always did when I mentioned Tarot or Finley. Both stabbed her sense of propriety in the heart. To cancel her negative thoughts, she shook her head, saying, "A call to the Family Office should take care of it."

I hadn't spoken with anyone in the Lilienthal Family Office since I'd withdrawn my money in a huff after they discovered Finley's embezzlement; Ivy camped out there, asking questions, bringing muffins, anything to ingratiate herself. But only one person could give the command to jump and expect them to answer, "How high?"

"It might be helpful if you spoke with them first. Let them know I have your approval."

She sighed. "Of course, dear. I'll instruct them to do whatever needs to be done to make it ready and draw up a legal transfer of ownership. When is his birthday?"

"May 13, and you're the best, Oma." I blew a kiss at her and gave her something she'd like even better than a kiss. "We're looking forward to coming back to Riverton and having our Saturday evening dinners with you."

Her expression softened. "Yes, I've been missing them. When are you returning?"

"The Harp Board Meeting is April 21 and 22, and we plan to leave the next morning."

"Excellent." A crafty look stole across her face, letting me know I was about to pay the price for my favor. "I hope you remember our Lilienthal ladies' tea in May."

"First Friday, yep." I squirmed. I'd missed the February, March, and April teas because of jail, Hawaii, and Chicago. Something told me I'd better make May come hell or high water.

"It might be nice if you were the hostess. Your aunts and I would love to see what Cyrus has done with the old Timmerwilke place. My goodness, I don't think I've been there since Ms. Timmerwilke's last Christmas party back in '23. It was showing wear and tear even then. What do you think, dear?"

I thought I'd rather die, but royal commands had less force than something Oma thought might be nice. "Sure, the downstairs is finished. Not sure what furniture will be there."

"We'll make do." Her voice dripped honey.

"Absolutely." The thought I might rather face Alexander than the women of my family zipped through my head. Cancel. Cancel.

Be content with surprising the man who has everything.

After I hung up, another call came in hot on its heels. The ID said Oriana Rossellini. Cyrus's mother looked like she'd spent the morning sucking on lemons. That couldn't be good.

Breathe. In. Out. Smell the roses and blow out the candles.

I plastered a smile on my face, hoping she wouldn't notice I was still in bed, and sprinkled sugar on my tongue. "Good morning, Dr. Rossellini."

"Good morning, Maren."

We exchanged pleasantries about the weather and our health before she came to the point.

"Cyrus thinks you should be involved in the Thursday activities for the board member's partners."

Set chirp level to high.

"Oh, right, the one at Alinea. I've read the reviews, and the block concept sounds so intriguing."

The restaurant's thematic "blocks" comprised gourmet offerings that filled the table with custom ceramics and centerpieces. Normal people might call blocks courses, and Harp had booked a five-hour, 18-block meal with wine pairings in The Gallery. For me, the description of the charred arctic char glazed with maple syrup before a hard sear that created a delicate candy-like snap made the short leap between intriguing and drooling.

"That's in the evening." The corded muscles in Dr. Rossellini's throat loosened. "I host a lunch in The Cathedral Room at the University Club of Chicago. For the board members' domestic partners."

Got it! The keyword in "I host" was *I*. She thought I was hijacking her luncheon. How did I let her know such things held no appeal for me without insulting her? I summoned a puzzled smile. "Totally not on my radar. Cyrus has been so busy, I guess he forgot to mention it."

Sour lemons. Obviously, he'd mentioned it to her. "We'd love for you to attend."

Attend, not host. Worked for me.

"So many have expressed an interest in meeting you." Disapproval dripped from every syllable.

Egads! The matrons were attacking from all sides. I plugged a pre-recorded, Oma-dictated message into the empty slot in my brain. "That sounds lovely. I'd be delighted to join you."

After a long survey that took in the rumpled bed, my hair clipped into a messy bun, and the sweats I'd slept in, she said, "Excellent. Attire is business casual."

Message received.

A Nosey by Any Other Name

Saturday, April 9

ALEXANDER FELL QUIET. No Zombies and Skeletons lurked in the shrubbery. The wards around the house hung tough, and we kept our heads down. Cyrus and his IT team chased Alexander across the dark web, unearthing where he'd been, but not where he was. Nor did Darius discover the greenhouse location.

All in all, Saturday shaped up to be a lazy day, and I welcomed the reprieve. The sun came through the sunroom's stained glass, creating cheerful patterns on the wall. While Cyrus finished the week's paperwork, I browsed my vision boards for feathering our Riverton nest. Each image was linked to an auction house, the freeport, or a store. Oma snookering me into hosting the Lilienthal Ladies Tea lit a fire under my butt. I passed my tablet to Cyrus.

"What about these for the dining room?"

I'd discovered twelve chairs with oval eye-shaped backrests from a Danish designer. The teak and black leather chairs had the same elegant simplicity as the Jeanneret dining table.

While he gave the chairs the once-over, I filled him in on the art for the dining room. "I told Grayson to pull the two Dali paintings and the Egyptian bronze and wood ibis statue from the freeport."

He looked up and smiled. "I like those Dali paintings. They're not what people expect from him. These chairs remind me of the Eye of Horus, so the ibis fits right in, yeah? You should look at the mummy case, too."

Hadn't thought of it that way, but sure. "So, the chairs are a go?"

"I'd say so." He rubbed his eyes. "Did Grayson send you a photo of the Bugatti sofa? I mean, it's art because you sure as hell can't sit on it, but it's super cool."

I combed through the ten thousand emails from Grayson until I found the Bugatti sofa email.

```
From: Grayson Harris
To: ML
Re: Bugatti Sofa

Carlo Bugatti's superior pieces were com-
missioned by several Royal Houses and the
great estates of America and Europe. This
magnificent piece from the 1900s came from
a Rothschild home. Bugatti's visual vocab-
ulary is evident in the floral motifs,
metal inlays, Islamic references, Japan-
ese-influenced painted decorations, ani-
mal skins, copper embellishments, ornate
fringing along with delicate hand-turned
finials. To create the pewter inlays, Bugat-
ti poured liquid pewter into hand-carved
walnut before hand-finishing it.
```

"Wow! It's stunning." The powerful, almost primitive piece, in cream and black walnut with painted floral motifs in brick and gold leaf leaped from the email.

"I thought it might go in the foyer instead of the usual nouveau riche grand piano that neither of us play," he said.

"Sounds like a plan."

At four-and-a-half feet tall and nine feet long, the Bugatti would make a jaw-dropping addition to the massive foyer. I shot off a yes to Grayson. So far, Cyrus and I had agreed on everything about the house, except Yonas's My Heart, My Love painting, which I hoped Daughter Fruit would remedy.

My work for the day finished, I drifted off to Your Love is King, a sultry jazz song that Cyrus had played for me several times. He said it was about a woman orgasming while her lover performed oral sex. Sweet dreams.

"That bitch is going down." Cyrus's roar ripped apart my little amatory reverie.

I pulled myself into a sitting position. "What?"

He handed me his tablet.

Cyrus Harper: Philanthropy and Employee Prosperity

<u>Nosey Parker.</u> Andrew Carnegie said about philanthropy, "He who dies rich dies disgraced." Cyrus Harper is on track to die disgraced.

No, no, no. The day had been going so well.

Most people can't comprehend the difference between a million and a billion. One million seconds is about 11 days. One billion seconds is about 31 years. Last year, Harper had 102 billion dollars. Mind-boggling.

In a recent puff piece, The Wall Street Reporter lauded Cyrus Harper's philanthropic efforts for 2043, saying the billionaire donated almost $32 billion to charities and scientific and cultural institutions. They waxed poetical about his generosity, and the amount was staggering until you do the math. Harper scraped by on a mere $70 billion. He probably had to dig into the sofa cushions for loose change to buy the Duchess of Windsor's pearl and diamond necklace for his girlfriend.

Don't you have better things to do, Nosey?

Wait, you say. Harp Industries is a perennial top runner in "The Best Places to Work" with above-average salaries and benefits. Stories abound of Harper's coattails dragging the original Harp employees from the middle into the millionaire class.

He held up his hand to prevent me from saying anything. "Don't worry. I'm not going to buy Tattleverse because you were right. That would just be a reward, but I'm gonna tear Nosey's life apart."

I kept my head down and read the rest of the article.

> Harper, like most company founders, didn't stay put after he cashed in. He resigned from day-to-day operations. A clever way to avoid employees. It's like crossing the street to avoid the homeless and panhandlers. He took his leave shortly after an employee at a company-wide meeting asked him, "What advice do you have for the rest of us who want to become wealthy?"

"I left a year later," he grumbled.

> "You develop a product or a service people want or need," he responded. "You make the world better and create jobs."
>
> "Easier said than done," the employee muttered.
>
> Harper then asked, "Who here feels rage toward the wealthiest one percent? I know I did."
>
> Several employees raised their hands.
>
> Unleashing his notorious cackle, Harper asked, "How many of you wish you were in the wealthiest one percent?"
>
> Laughing, everyone raised their hands.
>
> "You see my point," Harper said.
>
> I reached out to Harper, but his spokesperson, Vivica Chastain, said, "Mr. Harper isn't interested in responding to or being judged by people he doesn't know."

Cyrus squeezed the bridge of his nose. "I said that a long time ago when I was young and stupid."

"You can't undo the past." I massaged his shoulders, trying to loosen muscles tight as a drum. "But you and Viv need to practice saying, 'No comment.'"

"True." He leaned back against the cushions and slapped his hands together. "I'm done with Nosey. I'm unleashing the lawyers. They might not win, but they'll tie her in knots for years and cost her a fortune."

"Why did you wait so long?"

A flush crept up his neck into his cheeks. The notorious cackle mentioned by Nosey turned into a strangled laugh. "I try not to be a bully."

"Uh-huh." I scooted closer and patted his knee. "Sometimes it's unavoidable. She crossed a line, and now you'll do your worst."

"Yeah?"

"Absolutely." I wouldn't mention it now, but when we returned to Riverton, he was meeting with Uzma Chaudry, Oma's publicist. I'd given Viv her name, but nothing came of it. Time to take matters into my own hands.

"If you don't mind, I think I'll go make phone calls."

I nodded my approval. Lawyers were fine and all, but I intended to help them along with a sour jar spell concocted for Ms. Nosey Parker. While Cyrus revved up his lawyers, I collected ingredients for the spell and sent Richard out to buy what I couldn't find.

When we went to bed, I set the alarm on my Bio-Bit for 2:45 AM. The spell would be stronger if I cast it at 3 AM, the witching hour. Turns out, no alarm was necessary. I couldn't fall asleep, anyway.

When I stood before my altar after performing a cleansing ritual, doubt swarmed around me.

STOP THE GUILT TRIP! A SOUR JAR IS NOTHING LIKE A HEX; IT'S DEFENSIVE MAGICK. IF SOMEONE ACTS VILE, WHAT WITCH WOULDN'T TRY TO SOUR THAT PERSON'S LIFE AND MAKE THEIR OWN SWEETER?

I placed the open jar on the altar and added Black Mamba Hot Sauce, which came with a warning about its potency. "Let Nosey Parker's tongue be blistered for the grief she causes."

I added brass tacks I'd found in the basement; as they rusted, they'd corrode Nosey's vituperative musings. "Let Nosey Parker's negativity return to her and disintegrate her success.

"Let these mustard seeds cause misunderstandings and the poppy seeds cause confusion, chaos, and nightmares for Nosey Parker." I added the seeds to the jar. For good measure, I added my old friend, black salt, to absorb Nosey's negative energy and poisonous vibes so they didn't rebound on us.

After writing the intention I'd been composing all afternoon in my head, I rolled it into a scroll and placed it in a bottle before adding vinegar to sour Nosey's life and make the nails rust faster. I screwed on the lid and wrapped the jar in aluminum foil so no light penetrated the jar, a symbolic way to fill Nosey's life with darkness and despair.

A burning black candle sealed the jar. I centered and drew on my power, whispering my intention, "Let your cruelty and viciousness follow you all your days. If nothing but slander from your lips does fall, then let them speak nothing at all. By air, earth, water, and fire, may your life be as sour as I desire. I summon the power that belongs to me, so that as I will it, so mote it be."

Nosey should start sensing my intentions right away, but it took seven days of lighting black candles and repeating my intention to deliver its full punch. So mote it be.

TALES OF THE CLOSET ORGANIZER

TUESDAY, APRIL 11

ORDINARY DAYS ARE A gift. The balm of nothing special worked better than charms or Xanax. All calm on the Western Front until Mab reminded me that the closet organizer would arrive after lunch. Mr. Planning, whom I remembered kissing my forehead while it was still dark, struck again. He planned to spend the day at Harp. Goddess forbid I should waste *my* time. I was sticking to the house like glue to avoid Alexander and his Mungers, and he knew nothing was on my calendar. What else did I have to do besides light my black candle and reiterate my intentions to make Nosey's life as miserable as she made mine?

GUT UP AND GET OVER IT.

Sherry from Ms. Placed Professional Organizing made more notes than a general planning world conquest, all in the vain hope of making me as organized as Cyrus. We all have dreams. I remembered to tell her (you'd be proud of me, Cyrus) I'd need an extra-tall space for evening gowns.

"Already in the plan." Her perky smile terrified me and gave Oma a run for the money in the intimidation sweepstakes. " Do you think you'll keep most of your ballgowns here in Chicago?"

A hoot escaped my traitorous lips.

"Sorry. Give me a second to process that statement. I'm pretty sure even my grandmother never used most and ballgowns in the same sentence." I cackled again, channeling a nervous hyena. To squash the giggles, I inhaled the smell of baking cookies. Pat was on a baking spree, a bit of sympathetic magick to sweeten our lives.

Sherry's face scrunched up trying to puzzle me out. "Mr. Harper's on several boards and attends galas and charity events all over the country. All over the world, actually. He has evening clothes in every residence and on the plane."

A given for Mister-I-Don't-Like-Packing. That strange tipsy sensation washing over me was an acknowledgment that Cyrus might believe I plumbed the depths of his soul, but a thousand people, like this girl, understood his life and needs a thousand times better than I did. *Cancel.* "I think we'd better plan for ballgowns in every closet."

"This might help." She handed me her tablet. "It's the design for your closet in Riverton. I was just there, you know."

I didn't know.

"Oh, my." The space was large with glass closet doors along two entire walls and a window seat running beneath three ceiling-height windows. A brass, star-shaped Moroccan chandelier with multicolored glass panes hung over an island with drawers on either side.

"That's a lot of drawers for underwear." Particularly the teeny-tiny bits of fluff that Cyrus preferred. She made a note that probably logged that underwear storage was a new concept for me. I didn't enlighten her that underwear itself was also a new concept. She and Cyrus were on their own on that one.

Nonplussed, she continued, "Moroccan fabric covers the walls, and the Roman shades are the same fabric, as you can see. The island, floor, and woodwork are walnut. We could modify the design for this closet as a blueprint for the other residences. Adjusting for size."

"Excellent idea." We made progress, sketching out designs for this house, the Texas ranch, the penthouse in NYC, a condo in DC, a charming flat in London, and the place in Hawaii. By the end, we were on a first-name basis, as you were when someone sorted your underwear.

"They set up your credit card to transmit data to your closet computers so you don't need to enter anything when you buy something."

Presumably, she meant the black card Cyrus gave me. I could circumvent the system if I didn't use it.

"Your purchases will log to the residence where you send the item, and you can sort by color, designer, clothes type, shoes, purses, etc. FYI, Grace Williams helped scan your clothes at Riverton when we were organizing your closet, so the tablet is set up there."

I nodded. What else could I do or say?

"Mr. Harper finds it efficient." She had the uplifted eyes and beatific smile often found in paintings of martyrs who gave their lives for well-organized closets.

"I bet he does."

"I can show you how to disable it." An acrid whiff of desperation filled the air.

"Thanks; I'm good." Chastened by my snark, I invited her for tea in the living room. Pat served fresh macarons filled with fig preserves, blueberry lemon thyme jam, or apricot and lavender jam.

After the first bite, she threw her head back and moaned. "Oh. My. God. These cookies are heavenly."

"I'll miss Pat's baking when we return to Riverton."

"It's a lovely little town," she said. "You grew up there, right? I understand the house Mr. Harper restored is close to yours. Did you know the family?"

"I did. That house was my idea of a fairy castle when I was ten."

"And mine when I'm thirty-two." She nibbled another macaron. "The labyrinth in the courtyard is brilliant. You designed it, I understand. Whenever I'm in Paris, I take the train to Chartres to walk the labyrinth there. I hope you don't mind I walked yours."

"No, I'm honored." I unfocused my mind to see her aura. It was indigo, associated with the third-eye chakra. Interesting. People with indigo auras are intuitive. A useful gift when you're reorganizing people's lives.

"I bet you can't wait to move in, even if today's news came as a relief. That despicable woman seemed to want to make your lives pure hell."

Huh?

Her eyes widened. "Oh, didn't you know? *Tattleverse* gave Nosey Parker her walking papers. They finessed it saying she was pursuing other opportunities, but everyone knows what that means."

I sipped my tea, which tasted like nectar from the gods. Other opportunities. Lawyers. Sour jar spells. Whatever worked. The bitch got booted. Hail and farewell.

A Brother Like No Other

We picked over dinner. The caramelized pancetta and fennel salad and the Paella with sausage, chicken, shrimp, and muscles didn't receive the attention they deserved. Even the Clos de L'oratoire des Papes wine didn't divert us, although Cyrus nodded his approval when I complimented its orange blossom aroma.

"It makes no sense." He pushed the Paella around his plate. "The lawyers didn't serve *Tattleverse*. She works from home, and they're still looking for her address so they can send the cease-and-desist letter."

Although Cyrus had been prepared to go in with both guns blazing, his legal team advised starting with a warning cease-and-desist, citing character defamation and libel. I ran my finger around the rim of the wineglass. "We're not the only people she writes nasty things about. Maybe someone else is suing."

His fingers went into tapping mode, turning the dining room table into a keyboard, a sure sign he was processing something he couldn't quite articulate. When I brought up Sherry from Ms. Placed Professional Organizing and declared I liked her, he nodded. We'd hit the conversational doldrums.

When we finished pushing food around, I cleared the table and returned with macarons, the universal comfort food. Cyrus took one bite and sunk into quiet contemplation. His phone vibrated on the table, louder than a machine gun.

"Darius," he said.

That merited at least five macarons; I grabbed a handful as I tiptoed toward the kitchen.

"Maren, darlin'." Darius's voice filled the room and stopped me in my tracks. Sometimes I loathed Face2Face.

"Howdy." I leaned against the doorframe, trying to look nonchalant. Why did Darius put me on edge?

OH, LET ME SEE, ARMS MERCHANT, DEATH DEALER, AND THE SNARKIEST PERSON YOU EVER MET.

"Glad I caught you both," he said.

I stole back to the table and sat next to Cyrus. Darius wore a dinner jacket over a white collarless shirt. He'd draped a dark, polka-dotted scarf around his neck for a little panache. It declared he wasn't afraid of bold sartorial choices. He exuded as much glitz as the Belle Époque facade behind him, a veritable forest of Ionic columns and gold frescoes with crystal chandeliers.

"Monte Carlo?" Without waiting for a reply, Cyrus got right down to business. "Any news on the Alexander front?"

"I expected you to call me, bruv." Darius shook his head at a server with a tray. "You ever been to Monte Carlo, Maren? We could put your Tarot cards to good use here."

My turn to shrug, although it might be fun to hit the casinos and dress up like a Bond girl to Cyrus's double-oh-seven.

THE NAME'S HARPER. CYRUS HARPER.

"I'll bite. Why would I call you?" Cyrus said.

"Nosey Parker, duh." Everyone should experience a man with an eye patch rolling his good eye at least once in their life. "Seriously, Cyborg, use that brain of yours for something other than pushing around zeroes and ones. How do you stand it, Maren?"

"Get to the point," Cyrus said.

"Aren't you a little curious why that trash tabloid kicked her ass out the door? No, don't answer that. Here's the skinny. I found a snitcherella who claimed that Alexander and Parker were the same person. Now, I'm not gonna give credence to whispers in my ear after a few drinks."

"No, of course not," Cyrus muttered.

"As it happens, *Die Basis* records what they call confessions, acknowledgments that you're the sneaky SOB who has the guts to be a gol'darned terrorist." Darius seemed to be enjoying himself. "*Die Basis* is also perpetually cash-poor. I let it be known there'd be a couple of bricks for Alexander's tape. *Et voilà, c'est fait.* Turns out, he confesses to being Nosey Parker."

"They'd give him up for two-hundred grand?"

"Didn't even try to negotiate." Darius blew on his fingertips. "No need to pay me back unless I lose big tonight. I was appalled, naturally, that such a stellar publication employed someone with terrorist connections. Cherqi — you remember Cherqi; he took us falcon hunting in Egypt. Cherqi made *Tattleverse* aware of the situation. Bing, bam, boom, Nosey was out. I assume *Tattleverse* will inform the appropriate agencies of their discovery. If not, well, it's a service I'm glad to offer."

It made sense. Another thing we'd missed. We needed to get better at protecting ourselves.

"Are you any closer to finding him?" Cyrus asked.

"No one appreciates the work I do." Darius sighed as dramatically as Cyrus. Their similarities fascinated and terrified me. "I'm homing in on him. Need to tug a few more strings. Just a SWAG, but I predict your Alexander problem will be in your rearview mirror by the end of the month. Now, if you'll excuse me, Ines is waiting. *Adieu, mon frère,* unless you decide to hop in your jet and join us. That might be fun. A little *fête en famille, oui*?"

His laughter hung in the air after his image faded.

"Does he always have that much personality?"

"Sometimes more." Cyrus rubbed his forehead.

"Do you believe that story? It's an enormous coincidence."

"I believe Darius is in Monaco. Everything else is open for debate. Oh, one more thing. I need you to enlighten me about bow-chicka-wow-wow before my head explodes."

That was the most reasonable thing I'd heard tonight.

SOMETHING FISHY

GOOD FRIDAY, APRIL 15

"WHY ARE YOU STILL here? Shouldn't you be cheating on your taxes or something?" Cyrus was making espresso and slathering peanut butter on toast.

"K-Bear, get your slander straight." He pulled a severe expression and wagged his finger. "I don't cheat on taxes; I hire minions to do it for me."

"Yes, sir." I saluted. At least we still had our sense of humor.

"Do you have anything special planned for today? Any meetings?"

"Being a benign Witch Boss, I canceled everything and gave George the day off." I sipped the espresso and bit into the toast. Manna from heaven! "Oh, man! This isn't regular old peanut butter."

"It's Pecan Honey Butter. There's a shop near the ranch, Rustlin' Renee's I think it's called, that makes it from local pecans and honey. Once you taste it, you never go back."

"You are a walking, talking, cooking encyclopedia." I pointed at the bread and toaster. "More please."

He complied. "It's been a hard couple of weeks, yeah? I thought we'd do something fun today. Make it a great Friday, not just a Good Friday."

"Count me in. You have something in mind?"

"I thought we might hit the Aquarium and grab a bite to eat."

I clapped my hands. "I haven't been to the Aquarium since ... gosh, I don't know since when."

"We have tickets for the Beluga Encounter. I remember you whinging you were too short to swim with whales back in the day."

"Get outta here!" I waved my arms in the air and tapped my feet. "You're the best."

He acknowledged the truth in that.

After we parked the car in the Aquarium lot, I bounced to the octagonal marble and terra cotta temple to aquatic life. Its columns, formal staircase, and glass dome topped by Neptune's trident made it a Beaux Art masterpiece, a fact Oma had impressed upon me during childhood visits.

When Door-Med cleared us, a woman in a power suit advanced and held out her hand. "Mr. Harper, Ms. Lilienthal, welcome. I'm Dana White, the Aquarium's Chief Development Officer."

Cyrus didn't seem surprised by a personal welcoming committee. Part of life as Cyrus. I wondered if I'd ever become so blasé.

"You'll be seeing the Belugas at 1:45. I hope that time's convenient for you. They're in training now, and we like to keep them on schedule."

"No problem," he said.

What if he'd said it's a problem, yeah? Would Dana White move heaven and the Beluga training schedule? Bet she'd try.

"We thought we'd do a little exploring," he said.

She basked in his smile, shaking herself back to reality to say, "My assistant can give you a tour, if you'd like."

"Thanks, but I know my way around. Can't even count how many school field trips here."

"That's right." She cooed. "I'd forgotten you grew up in Chicago. Let me take your bag, and I'll have someone take it down to the locker room."

She took the backpack holding the spare clothes we'd wear under waterproof waders and gave us directions to the locker room. "If you get there at 1:30, you'll have time to change. Call me if you need anything."

Cyrus took her card, thanked her again, and gave me a personal tour of the most popular cultural attraction in Chicago (according to him.) I'm not sure we took in all 1500 different species of fish, marine mammals, birds, snakes, amphibians, and insects, but we made a serious dent in the list.

Every few minutes, I asked, "Is it time for the Belugas yet?"

"I see where Gertie gets it." He wrapped a restraining arm around my neck. "Although she's fairly restrained compared to a Maren who shall remain nameless."

I pinched him.

Eventually, at long last, finally, his tour ended at an enormous sign.

MEET THE BELUGAS WHERE THEY LIVE

STAND SIDE-BY-SIDE WITH A TRAINER ON AN UNDERWATER LEDGE IN CHEST-DEEP WATER

COME FACE-TO-FACE AND EYE-TO-EYE WITH A BELUGA

IN THIS 75-MINUTE EXPERIENCE, YOU'LL STEP INTO A MAGICAL WORLD FEW HUMANS HAVE VISITED

I jumped up and down.

"Calm down, K-Bear, you'll scare the whales."

In the locker room, we donned wool socks, leggings, and a short sleeve tee-shirt before wiggling into a flattering one-piece brown, neoprene wader that came up to our chests. With attached boots, they weighed about a million pounds.

"Lookin' good," Cyrus drawled. "I hear Dior will have a line of these next season in the hottest colors."

"Smart ass."

Before he could respond, someone knocked. A woman in a wet suit entered.

"Hi! My name is Stephanie."

She reminded me of the Harp tour guide. Hopefully, there wouldn't be a bomb in the whale tank. Fingers crossed.

"A friendly reminder, no jewelry or artificial fingernails." She did a quick once over and nodded her approval. "Today you'll meet Tootega, which is an Inuit name for a female deity who walked on water. But first, have you worn waders before?"

"Salmon fishing in Alaska, yeah."

I shook my head.

"I want you to practice walking in your waders." She looked at me. "We'll be in chest-deep water on a ledge. Trust me, you don't want to fall into the deep part of the tank. Swimming in waders is next to impossible, and the water is 55 degrees."

Walking was a polite term for my old lady waders' shuffle. After a few minutes, she decided I was as good as I'd ever be. We lumbered into the backstage pool area where trainers worked with the whales. Stephanie advised me to lower myself into a sitting position on the edge of the tank. The water lapping against my bare arms was crazy cold. When she decided we'd acclimated, she invited us onto the underwater ledge.

"No squealing." Cyrus had a death grip on my arm, probably a self-defense mechanism to avoid diving into the frigid water to save me when I stumbled. "You don't want to spook the whales."

Large white ghosts moved under the water. I suppressed the urge to squeal and stood motionless; if they retreated to the bottom for the day, I'd surely die. Stephanie told us about Belugas and the Aquarium programs to help them, but I couldn't tear my eyes away from the whales.

"At 10 feet 2 inches, Tootega is our smallest Beluga, but she's still growing." A hand signal brought a whale right up to the ledge; Stephanie rewarded her with a fish. "Go on. Give Tootega a hug!"

With Cyrus holding the suspenders on my waders, I scooched toward the whale. Tootega rose from the water and embraced me. Her skin felt like a peeled hard-boiled egg, if an egg was all muscle covered in a thick layer of blubber. She put her face against mine and gave me a big, squishy kiss. Tears came to my eyes. If I was a helium balloon, I'd be floating somewhere around Mars.

"Look, she's smiling at you," Cyrus said. I embraced the whale again.

Stephanie rewarded her with another fish. "She's a happy whale. From the time she was a calf, she's been playful and interactive with the trainers and other whales."

The large bulge on Tootega's head wiggled and changed shape. Cyrus stroked it. "Is this her brain?"

"No. It's what we call a melon. It directs and changes the frequency of the whale's sound waves. They use it for echolocation."

I caressed Tootega's melon; it was spongy.

"Old-time mariners called Belugas sea canaries." Stephanie signaled Tootega to show off her vocal repertoire of whistles, calls, chirps, clicks, and clangs.

Following Stephanie's example, I stuck my hand into Tootega's mouth and patted her tongue. The 1,100-pound whale seemed to enjoy it. When Stephanie encouraged me to reach my hand in again and tickle the roof of Tootega's mouth to see what sound she would make, I was happy to give it a go … and even happier to hear a squeak rather than chomp-chomp.

Turned out her suck was worse than her bite, and I grasped what fish and squids' final moments must feel like. Yowsa!

I could have spent the next hundred years stroking the whale and listening to her sounds. Tootega reminded me magick still lived in the world. Magick set everything right and spoke to an innate goodness that I'd forgotten with everything that had transpired. An overwhelming, all-encompassing love washed over me, the same feeling that brought me to the Goddess.

Tootega slid back into the water. Her peace and joy passed into me, pushing aside the rowdy ghosts of my past. As if sensing where my thoughts traveled, she rose — belly resting on the ledge, head bobbing — and embraced me and chirped. *Where the ocean ends, our stream begins.* The message came through as clearly as any Shakespearean actor emoting to the audience. I sent my humble gratitude to her.

Message received, she dove deep into the pool's chilly darkness, only to emerge with a saucy tail flip. Like every right-thinking female with eyes in her head, she flirted with Cyrus, batting her eyes, hugging him, and finally planting a kiss.

The booming Cyrus belly laugh rumbled across the training tank, bounced off the rocks, and echoed like a megaphone. I hadn't heard that laugh since Hawaii, although it was the mannerism that first attracted me to him. Forget pheromones. A good belly laugh had me at hello. That too was the Goddess at work.

I directed my Inner Voice to Tootega. *Thank you for sharing the wonder of your beauty. Today, because of you, I vow to banish the fear that builds barriers between me and those I love. You filled me with your strength, peace, and confidence.*

Tootega winked and blew me a kiss.

All too soon, it was time to say goodbye.

"I could stay here all day," I said. "And all night."

"Your teeth are chattering, and your lips are turning blue." Catching sight of my surely plaintive expression, he added, "No. Absolutely not. You cannot take a whale home."

Stephanie laughed, but a little uncertainly. Who knew what a billionaire might do, right?

I tossed a final tasty (aka smelly) fish into Tootega's mouth as a farewell offering, looked her in the eye, and said goodbye. Tootega whistled, dived deep, and surfaced, towering over us for almost thirty seconds. With what sounded like laughter, she squirted water from her mouth, drenching me.

"She likes you," Stephanie said. "She wants you to come back and play again."

"It's a date." On the way back to the locker room, I chattered like a chipmunk. "She was amazing. So powerful, yet gentle! So playful."

Words like magick, phenomenal, awesome, and incredible fell like rain. Back in the locker room, I jumped on Cyrus, wrapping my arms around his neck and legs around his waist.

"Hey, girlfriend, save some enthusiasm for later."

"Thank you, thank you, thank you. I don't know why you're so nice to me."

"Pure selfishness, I assure you. When you're happy, I'm happy." He buried his face in the crook of my neck, his breath warm against my chilly skin. He set me down and smacked my bottom. "Now, get dressed. I'm starved."

We went to a Spanish restaurant. After perusing the menu, I thanked the Goddess that my metabolism worked at warp speed, otherwise hanging out with Cyrus might lead to a job as the circus fat lady.

The waiter brought a bottle of red wine, which the menu claimed was succulent and boasted blackberry and black olive scents. Cyrus sniffed, sipped, and nodded his approval. "I like this place. It used to be an old warehouse."

"It cleans up good. Like you.

"Cute." He hunkered in his chair and put on his serious face. "You liked the aquarium, yeah?"

"It was super."

"They asked me to join their board."

"One of a literal dozen invitations, I'm sure."

"I'm not vain enough to think they came to me for my scintillating insights into aquatic life."

I snorted.

"I like the aquarium fine, but you'd make a better board member than me. You have a genuine interest, and you'd liven up their yearly gala. It's a yawn."

"They want you."

"No, let's be clear. They want my money. They can have it. I just won't be on their board. You will."

"What, did you make them an offer they couldn't refuse?" We'd watched an old movie called *The Godfather*, and Cyrus said it was the line everyone remembered.

"Of course."

"First, tea with Mrs. Mueller; now this. Are you trying to make me respectable?"

"Only if you want to be. I like you fine, just the way you are." He poured more wine. "But there are people on the Board you should know. Like Charles Derning, the CEO of Ticket the World. Marilyn Dutta, the Chairperson of Broadway Days. Useful for your Plaza project, yeah. So, no, I don't care if you're respectable, but if you're serious about becoming *Nine of Pentacles*, I'll do everything in my power to help."

I sipped the wine and pondered how to say 'yes, thank you' without repeating 'you're the best' for the millionth time. Perhaps the best way to thank him was to finish the sour jar spell. Tonight, I'd burn the last black candle, and tomorrow I'd toss the jar into Lake Michigan, drowning Nosey's discord for all time.

A HOLLY, JOLLY EASTER

SUNDAY, APRIL 17

I TWISTED AND TURNED before a full-length mirror, second and third-guessing my choice. The loose-fitting dress with the vibrant Indian pattern of rose, blue, and green on cream had Oma's approval. When I texted her a photo, she responded with *Lovely, elegant, and spring-like.* In Oma-speak, it meant thank God it's not black. It might alleviate Dr. Rossellini's qualms about what I'd wear to the University Club luncheon. Fingers crossed.

On to the next earth-shattering decision. With or without the matching belt? I ran my hand down the dress; the crepe de chine skimmed my hips and felt silky-smooth. No belt allowed me to indulge in the Easter feast with gusto. Another Dr. Rossellini placating gesture.

Major decision three. Should I wear Wallis's necklace? A bit much for a family gathering. The other choice was the vintage Cartier gold necklace Oma gave me for my 21st birthday. There was only one way to wear a necklace, thank the Goddess.

Another mirror check confirmed I looked presentable. Why did my stomach roll like Lake Michigan on a stormy day? Would I make it through the family gathering without stabbing myself in the foot? If fashion possessed any magick, I might. I returned to staring into the mirror, searching for ways to up the magick ante.

Cyrus wrapped his arms around my waist and nuzzled my neck. "How do you do it?"

"Do what?" Match the green in my dress to the color of my face whenever I considered a whole day with the Harpers en masse?

"Be a good sport about this," he said after another nuzzle.

Ha! If you only knew. The award for Best Actress in a Supporting Role goes to ... Maren Lilienthal in Easter with the Harpers.

"The Easter Bunny left something for you." He handed me two plastic eggs, the type starring in a gazillion Easter Egg hunts.

"The Easter Bunny must be one busy fellow." The eggs rattled when I shook them. "Which one should I open first?"

"The yellow one."

"Trying to spoil my appetite?" The egg contained two foil-wrapped chocolates, which I shared with him.

"And risk my mother's wrath? Not bloody likely."

The pink egg rattled when I rolled it around in my palm. I took my time opening it. Instead of chocolates, it contained a pair of dangling earrings with buds and flowers in diamonds, pink sapphires, and green Tsavorites.

"Did the bunny pick the dress to go with the earrings or vice versa?" Cyrus had given the dress two thumbs up on our shopping spree. Why had I fretted over it?

Get a grip, Lilienthal; it's Easter dinner, not the Inquisition.

"The bunny is a discreet fellow; we'll never know."

"Uh-huh. Not even for a kiss?" I replaced my gold ear studs with the new pair. A stray sunbeam made them sparkle.

"The bunny is stalwart and resists all temptation," he said. "Are you about ready to go?"

"Need to put my hair up. It hides the earrings."

He snorted, recognizing a stall when he heard one.

I twisted my hair into a loose knot and secured it with a clip. "See?"

He conceded the point but hurried me into the car. Even with a last-minute hairstyle change, we still reached the gray-stone high-rise on the Gold Coast before noon. We took the elevator to the penthouse. Emerging hand-in-hand into a black-and-white marble foyer, we almost stumbled over Rafael, blocking the door and looking as cheerful as the endless monologue in my head.

"Happy Easter." Cyrus ignored Rafael's glum expression. "Sent you out to the woodshed already, did they? Did you spit hot cross buns across the room or something?"

Rafael's smile of acknowledgment barely reached the corners of his mouth. "I thought you should know ..."

My stomach clenched. What had Alexander done now?

"I wanted to call, but your mom and Cass said no way. They conceded I could warn you only if I promised to stop you from leaving." Rafael's words tumbled over each other in a waterfall of anxiety. "So, please help me keep that promise."

"Chillax, man." Cyrus clasped Rafael's shoulder with his free hand. "What's up?"

"Darius is here. Flew in last night."

WHAT?

Cyrus froze. His hand, the one holding mine, went limp.

When he called from Monaco, he never mentioned a visit. Was it arms dealer secrecy, or was Darius naturally duplicitous? Or both? Wait, he grinned like a Cheshire cat when he said a little *fête en famille, oui*? A sly hint about an Easter family reunion?

"That should make Mom's Easter. Her baby bird is back in the nest." Cyrus's hand found mine again. "Word of advice, K-Bear; if Darius shakes your hand, count your fingers afterward."

Did he think I needed a warning?

"There's more." Rafael took a deep breath. "Ines is with him, and she's pregnant. About ready to pop."

Whoa. I'd never seen an expression like that on Cyrus's face. My interpretation? The Easter Bunny laid a big fat egg, and it wasn't filled with diamonds and sapphires or good chocolate.

"A baby? That's the worst decision of the last century." Cyrus tucked my arm under his and dragged me towards the door. "Let's get this shitshow started, babe."

His twitching revved up my misgivings. After three or four steps, my tremors synchronized with his. I cast a small blessing. A candle, a feather, or the hair from everybody's head would help, but I'd make do with channeling and focusing compassion on the Harper family. I did a quick visualization. *Happiness with you abide this Easter-tide. When its hours depart, leave its peace within your heart.*

Rafael trailed behind us, muttering. "I did my part. I warned him. Don't I get a thanks?"

"He didn't punch you," I whispered over my shoulder and repeated the silent blessing.

"Point taken."

Omne trium perfectum: Everything that comes in threes is perfect. Three was an essential number in almost every magick system beginning with the Egyptians. I repeated the blessing and concluded with So mote it be.

The family had gathered in the massive living room with its Chinese screens and oriental art. Glass doors led to an enormous patio with a mind-blowing lake view. I tore my attention away from the view and smiled. Doctor Rossellini, her family arranged around her, returned my smile. The children fiddled with their Easter baskets; Cassandane twiddled with her necklace. Darius sat on the floor, head against his mother's knee; she ran her fingers through his long black curls. He was an eye magnet with his pirate eyepatch and a mustache and goatee outlining the full lips I'd found irresistible on his brother.

A slim older man with the signature Harper curls, going gray, and a five o'clock shadow tended the fireplace. He left the fire and came to us.

"Welcome to our home, Maren. I'm Paul Harper, this scamp's father." He ruffled Cyrus's hair. "My wife, you know. Cassandane and Rafe, and their tribe. Darius is there, and Ines is napping. Darius, manners?"

Like a peacock, Darius rose and displayed his plumage. A loose blazer in a handwoven textile with blocky purple, blue, yellow, green, and red stripes and ornamental stitching over a plain white cotton tee shirt. The same handwoven textile appeared as artistic patches on loose jeans. Blue suede and leather steel toe-cap boots buttoned over his ankles. The ensemble telegraphed a message: young, hip, and dangerous.

"Maren, darling. Great to see you in real life and at a decent hour." Stepping over everyone and everything, he embraced me, planting a kiss on my cheek. Like his brother, he smelled good enough to eat. The many-layered scents of black currant, honey, myrrh, oud, and cinnamon exuded Herculean sex appeal.

A harrumph escaped Cyrus. I dug a subtle elbow into his ribs.

"Bruv." Darius embraced Cyrus with the backslapping bonhomie I'd seen in *The Godfather* movie. "What am I going to do with you? Mom's been telling me about what's going on. Can't stay out of trouble, can you?"

BEST ACTOR IN A SUPPORTING ROLE GOES TO DARIUS PHARRE IN I DIDN'T HAVE A CLUE ABOUT THE TERRORIST STALKING MY BROTHER.

"Can't let you hog all the trouble, yeah?"

Darius's boisterous laugh parroted Cyrus's. They were two sides of the same coin. The light and the dark. Or dark and darker. The jury was out.

Paul brought mimosas and Bloody Marys. I slugged back a mimosa and took a chair by the fireplace. Before Cyrus grabbed the one next to me, Darius slid into it. If this were a movie, Cyrus might have taken Darius's place at their mother's feet, but he chose the white loveseat next to his father. Rafe took the children to the terrace to test their Easter pinwheels. At first, the conversation was light, what you'd expect at any family gathering, catching up on the latest news, memories, and light-hearted ribbing. Paul suggested the men of the family have a Star Trek night. There was general agreement that Cyrus's big-ass television on Tuesday night was the perfect venue.

My relieved sigh was poised to take off when Darius asked, under the general conversational hum, "Do I scare you, Maren?"

HELL, YES!

I pretended to consider my response. "Should I be afraid?"

Darius leaned back and stretched his arm across the side table to pat my hand. "I don't think so, but George Bernard Shaw described people like me as profiteers in murder and mutilation. I've been called the supersalesman of death because I sell arms to anyone who offers an honest price. Unlike my competitors, I don't stoke wars. Humanity can stumble into war all on its own."

"Just an honest salesman trying to make ends meet?"

"That's about the size of it."

"Don't you, on principle, have a problem making money on smashed brains and shattered limbs?" I glanced at Cyrus, who'd made his fortune saving lives.

"Principles have nothing to do with it. I leave principles to Cyborg." Darius grinned, nodding at his brother's scowling face. "I sell to good men and bad. What they do is on their soul, not mine."

"So, are people terrified of you?" I asked, circling back to his original question.

"Of course they are." Darius chuckled. "I mean, I can't take out an ad in the Wall Street Journal, like my bruv, to tell people where to get their biological weapons, chlorine, sarin gas, or missile launchers. I can't do Black Friday sales. So, I put a gun to their heads and tell them I'll kill them if they don't do what I want. The joke's on them. I'm a pacifist. I just sell this shit; I don't use it."

I didn't believe it. Not even for a minute. The intense gaze beneath the heavy-lidded good eye and the ripple of taut muscles beneath the expensive clothes conjured a panther. Not one of those slow-moving beasts who spent their life in the zoo's Big Cat Sanctuary, but the one stalking and ambushing prey in a tropical rainforest's dense foliage. Darius, swift and ruthless, would kill you before you saw him coming.

"Quit scaring her." Cyrus cracked his knuckles. "I can fuck up a relationship all by myself."

"Cyrus." Dr. Rossellini's voice snapped like a whip.

Darius's grin broadened. "Now that you're so damn rich, it'll be harder. I doubt if I could steal Ines away now."

Silence descended over the room.

"Bet old Cyborg forgot to mention my wife used to be his girlfriend."

WHOA! WHEN WAS HE PLANNING TO MENTION HER?

Cyrus shrugged and looked into the fireplace. No one looked at anyone. I visualized ruby slippers and clicking my heels three times to take me somewhere else.

Ines appeared in the doorway as if she'd been waiting for this introduction. Judging by her sly, coquettish expression, I was sure of it. Her sacral chakra aura was the deep, cloudy orange of egotistical sexuality. The deep purple rim around the orange aura spoke to a high kink level, someone who took it to the borderline of weird fetishes and near-dangerous experiences. Which explained Darius's attraction. But Cyrus?

"*Bonjours mes chéris et Joyeuses Pâques!* Happy Easter." She was hugely pregnant, so huge it seemed like we should rush to the hospital. Cassandane had called it. Cyrus had a type: tall, dark, and quirky. In a fringed black silk caftan, she still exuded gothic femme fatale vibes. The caftan's deep vee emphasized the clavicle thing that drove him wild. Her blue eyes lined with black, porcelain skin, and jet-black hair cemented the impression.

"What have I been missing? Ah, Cyrus, you are here. *Bien. Bien.* I worried you would not come." She stressed the last syllable of every word and the last word in every sentence, giving her English a soft French lilt.

After a dramatic swoop across the room, she planted a kiss on both of Cyrus's cheeks. Like a mythical Medusa, she turned him to stone, and Darius grinned like the Cheshire cat. She turned her cool, appraising stare on me. "This is your petite Maren?"

If she meant to put me in my place, it worked. My dress, selected after so much agonizing, shifted from lovely and elegant to pedestrian and plain. My body felt lumpy and clumsy; I'd fall flat on my face if I tried to stand.

"I have heard so much about her from *mon prince des fées noires.*"

My college French was rusty, but had she called Darius her dark fairy prince? It was getting weirder by the second. I clicked my heels together. *There's no place like home. There's NO place like home.* I needed to hone my teleporting technique.

Dr. Rossellini announced it was time to eat. Cyrus, shaking off his Sphinx impression, sidestepped Ines to take my arm. As he pulled out my chair from the dining table, he whispered. "Sorry about that."

Not good enough, boyfriend.

"We'll talk later."

Ines and Darius dominated the table with talk about their forthcoming parenthood. It was a girl, the tests said.

"I want her to be born here," Darius said. "So Mother can be with us."

What about Ines's mother? Did she not count? Dr. Rossellini smiled. Cassandane caught my eye and rolled hers.

"We shall call her Aurélie Régine," Ines said.

"Our golden queen." Darius kissed Ines's cheek.

Gaining control of her eye rolls, Cassandane asked, "When are you due?"

"Next Sunday," Ines said.

Even I knew it was dangerous for Ines to travel so near her due date. Darius picked up on the disapproval going around the table.

"Our doctor flew in with us."

That brought an end to the baby chit-chat. Throughout the meal and during the egg hunt on the terrace, Ines relayed amusing anecdotes about and asked questions directed toward Cyrus. She nudged him with her shoulder or tapped him with her long, blood-red nails. The man with a memory like a steel trap developed amnesia and fidgeted.

Only once did Ines direct a comment at me. "*Je suis déçu, petite Maren. What is the word I am thinking, Darius?*"

"Disappointed." My French allowed me to fumble my way around Paris after an all-night party and to recognize someone patronizing me. If she called me petite Maren one more time, I'd demonstrate my facility with other French words, beginning with *merde* and ending with *putain.* Or a casual *va te faire foutre* (go to hell).

"*Oui.* Disappointed because I think we might see the gorgeous necklace Cyrus bought for you. We read about it, *oui.*" She clasped Cyrus's arm. "If you had given me a present *comme ça,* I think I might not have noticed how pretty *mon mari* is."

Was she hinting she'd like to resume their relationship? I never imagined Darius and I would share the same headspace, but I was almost certain my face mirrored his WTF expression. Dr. Rossellini hustled us inside for her special Easter dessert, Persian Date Cake.

Darius and I were the last to leave the terrace. An accident, no doubt. Still stewing over Ines's jabs, I blurted out, "Did you have something to do with Muireann's disappearance?"

The eyebrow behind the pirate patch rose. "I don't know a Muireann."

"Johnny Marlowe's girlfriend. The one pumping him for info and passing it on to Alexander. Nobody's seen her."

"Ah. That Muireann." He shrugged. "She was careless in the company she kept. If I knew her, I'd have put a gun to her head before she disappeared. Karma, yeah? But if I meet her ..."

The wind gusted, but that wasn't why I shivered.

"It's getting cold. Shall we go in?" He took my arm. End of discussion.

The hours of stilted conversation crept toward evening. After the children, smelling of soap and shampoo, presented themselves in pajamas for goodnight kisses, Cyrus announced he was beat. We started the long process of extricating ourselves.

The family walked us to the door. Cyrus's fast clip showed how much he wanted to be gone. Cassandane took my arm and whispered, "Typical Harper family shenanigans. At least there wasn't a brawl."

During the leave-taking, kisses and hugs were exchanged. Darius did a cheek-to-cheek kiss, whispering in my ear. "Don't get your panties in a twist about this Alexander guy, yeah?"

"What?"

"It'll be over soon." With a wink and grin, he sashayed toward the living room, where Ines waited with a smirk.

The promise burned like a shot of whiskey and fueled the ride home. But I forgot Alexander, and I had one question for Cyrus. Only one. "Why didn't you tell me about Ines?"

"Didn't seem important. It's the past."

Did Aston Martin offer a factory refresh to restore fine Italian leather when your girlfriend's head exploded? We were about to find out.

He drummed his fingers on the steering wheel and forged ahead. "When Darius came on the scene, Ines and I were over each other, but we didn't have the gumption to finish it."

Uh-huh. I'd used that one myself. "Darius doesn't seem to think so."

"That's Darius. Lots of drama, yeah?" He kept his eyes glued to the road, making it impossible to guess what he might be thinking. "I'd quit my job and was working on the Bio-Bit in my parents' basement. No money for nights on the town, weekends away, or presents. Didn't go down well; Ines is a high-maintenance gal. Two days after they met, Darius whisked her off to Monaco. Made it easy to end things. I owe him big time for that one."

What did he say not that long ago? *When you go babe hunting in your twenties, you don't want advice. You have to get it out of your system.* Was that what was going on here? In any case, as far as Cyrus was concerned, end of discussion. I begged to differ.

"So, what happened to no more secrets?" We'd made that promise after I learned about Babington using his code to steal money, and we'd renewed the vow several times.

He sighed and dragged his fingers through his hair. "Swear to God, Maren, I didn't think about it. I haven't thought about Ines in a long, long time. Seriously."

"Seriously, we will talk about this."

"Yes, we will. Just not tonight."

Again, that air of finality. My heart sank.

"Know this." He reached across the console and squeezed my knee. "I can't live without you. I don't want to. I love you more than life itself. Give me a little space to get over my embarrassment."

"Your embarrassment?"

"I didn't want and didn't expect you to find out this way, yeah." Another hand swipe through his hair.

I didn't stop him and entertained the malicious thought of imagining him bald.

"It's not a point of pride that my younger brother made off with my girlfriend. Like the way you feel about Emelia and Finley."

"Ouch. But at least we talked about that. And Manny didn't marry Finley."

"Fair." More steering wheel drumming. "Even if we don't hash it out tonight, rest assured; the subject won't be far from my thoughts."

A clear signal we would not hash it out tonight, and we didn't.

EXPECT THE UNEXPECTED

MONDAY, APRIL 18

"WHAT DO I NEED to know today?"

I craved reassurance from the cards, not knowledge. *Ten of Cups* (aka the happy family card) or *The Lovers* would be acceptable and mitigate last night's Ines revelation. I did breathwork and waited for my office's peaceful vibe to take effect before pulling a card.

If I'd pulled the *Knight of Pentacles* or *The Magician*, I could have convinced myself the card was about Cyrus and been pleased with the message. My instinct and previous experience with the *Knight of Swords* pointed to someone else. The *Knight of Swords* was quirky, entertaining, and dressed distinctively. He had a big personality and thrived on drama. Always prepared to fight, the *Knight of Swords* rarely took responsibility for the fallout. His intelligence allowed him to talk his way out of trouble. No, not Cyrus, although I suspected he could go there, but chose not to.

This knight, sword brandished and feet planted in the stirrups, was in full battle mode; even his horse was on the brink. In the background, storm clouds formed. Strong winds from the right bent the trees. The knight charged to the left, directly into the wind, unafraid of opposition. His sword slashed at the clouds and extended beyond the card's boundaries, suggesting his mission went beyond ordinary limits. Fixated on his goal, he was prepared to cut out his enemy's heart. If he couldn't release his anger and energy, he might burst.

Who fit that description to a tee? Darius.

The background was bleak, like the landscape I'd seen in the spread asking for Alexander's location.

Don't get your panties in a twist about this Alexander guy, yeah. It'll be over soon.

I contemplated the card and searched *BoSsBlog* for notes I'd made from past readings. In an entry dated almost five years ago, I'd written the *Knight of Swords'* message was 'expect the unexpected; tempestuous times are ahead.'

Hadn't Talia said the same thing when warning me about casting a hex during retrograde? Mercury was still in retrograde for another two days.

I've been called the supersalesman of death.

My skin prickled with a million pins and needles, and an iceberg lodged itself in my gut. Darius hadn't shown up with his pregnant wife in tow because he wanted his daughter to be born in America or to please his mother.

I put a gun to their heads and tell them I'll kill them if they don't do what I want.

He was here to take on Alexander. I scrabbled across the floor toward my phone, still on the charger. Cyrus needed to know.

Before I reached it, the man himself burst through the door, his hair wild, his eyes wilder. "You gotta see this, babe."

I yelped. The unexpected had begun.

He grabbed my arm and hauled me toward his office.

It's Over, Baby Blue

Monday, April 18

Dozens of streaming news sites filled the monitors, and chatter blasted from the speakers. Reporters with solemn expressions spoke into the cameras. Breaking News banners told me everything I didn't want to know.

> Shoot out on the Southside
> Chicago Carnage
> Shots Fired; SWAT on-site

Cameras panned a shadowy street. The timestamp read 5:45 AM CST, almost four hours ago. Headlights from a nearby highway did nothing to dispel the murk. A grave reporter spoke straight into the camera.

> "The city's much-vaunted high-efficiency LED lights, sold to voters as a crime deterrent, are almost nonexistent in this part of town."

A halo of blue flashing lights encircled another talking head.

"Shortly after 5 AM, this station learned about an armed conflict in progress on Chicago's Southside. Although it's eerily quiet now, our news crew arrived as an ambulance, sirens blaring, pulled away."

"Who's in the ambulance? Did they say?" Dread settled over me like fog. I took a seat and waited for him to utter Darius's name.

Cyrus shook his head.

"CPD has cordoned off an area and set up a command post near the Kaos & Sons warehouse. SWAT teams in body armor and carrying M4 A1 carbines are checking their tactical gear."

"Who's Kaos?"

"Who else but Alexander?" Cyrus combed his fingers through his hair and paced before the monitors, a general checking his troops.

"Oh. Oh! Him? You're positive?" I wouldn't be the first to bring up Darius's name; that's for sure.

"Pretty certain. Harp's phone lines were blowing up, and the operators were pulling out their hair. Threats, reporters, police, families, you name it." Cyrus rubbed his forehead. "This place didn't click when I trawled through possible hideouts."

EXPECT THE UNEXPECTED.

"Alexander got through to Viv about 8:15. He was screaming how he'd make me pay for shooting up his building. Didn't want to take any chances, so I evacuated *my* building. I alerted Beckett and our security and got here as fast as I could."

Not the most romantic way to confirm I was a priority, but I appreciated it.

"Anyway, looks like there was an altercation." Cyrus stretched; his shirt pulled up to reveal a gun holstered around his waist. It looked smaller than the one from the safe, which meant he owned at least two guns.

ARE YOU SURPRISED GIVEN WHO HIS BROTHER IS?

Panic revved up my heart, giving the Aston Martin's engine a run for its money. "Are we shooting varmints today, Harper?"

"You never know. I might have gotten a taste for it after shooting up a warehouse."

It's sarcasm, witch; deal with it. Naturally, Alexander blames Cyrus for anything and everything that happens to him, but it doesn't follow Cyrus is responsible.

Thank you, rational brain! After all, Alexander had shady associates who might not wish him well. Still ... there was the gun. Correction: guns. And Cyrus knew how to use them. Hadn't Oma said people mistook him for a scruffy poodle, but he had a Rottweiler's spirit and instincts?

So, where's your gratitude? Thank the Rottweiler.

Before I could chew on that thought, an excited anchor broke into the newscast.

> "John, someone inside the warehouse is online with us."

The Breaking News banner updated.

> Inside the Besieged Southside Warehouse

"Fantastic. They're making him a martyr." Cyrus flopped into the chair next to me. I grabbed his hand on its way to his hair and held onto it for dear life.

Alexander's cadaverous face and stringy black hair materialized. Behind him, old laptops and monitors were haphazardly attached to walls and shelves and suspended from the ceiling. Equipment too ancient to identify, coffee mugs, fast-food containers, and piles of papers and magazines spilled from the nooks and crannies. The edifice looked one healthy breath away from collapsing.

I'll huff and I'll puff and I'll blow your house down.

His black velvet shirt with a deep vee exposed a chest as white as a drowned man's face. Steepling his fingers, he gazed into the camera for what seemed an eternity. His eyes were as cold as a shark's eyes. He shook his head as if in sorrow.

A fluttery feeling rose from my stomach into my throat. Come on, drama king. It's going to be hateful, so spit it out.

> "Thomas Jefferson said, 'With a little patience, we shall see this reign of witches pass over and their spells dissolve.'"

His deep, smooth voice underscored his earnestness. I twisted my Bio-Bit around my wrist.

> "That may have been true in Jefferson's time. Back then, those strange women had witchcraft only on their tongues. But when a witch possesses the power of technology and money, hell lies even in the blink of her eye."

If my power was as strong as he claimed, did he think I'd let him whine about it on the news? Cyrus flinched; my nails had gouged four bloody crescent moons into his wrist.

> "Consider what Cyrus Harper and his witch wrought. Let's start with the character assassination of a journalist who dared criticize them. The pair hounded Nosey Parker into hiding. Or worse. As we all know, they skipped out of a murder charge downstate."

Bullshit! But he sounded so reasonable.

> "This morning, the Harpers shot up my warehouse."

The Harpers. The phrase stuck in my throat like a fishbone. Is that how he referred to us when he wasn't calling me Harper's witch? Somehow, I doubted it, but at least he didn't say the Harper brothers. Reporters might not make the connection. I twisted my Bio-Bit with renewed vigor, welcoming the stinging sensation as it scraped across my skin.

> "I offer temporary housing to people down on their luck and a hand-up by paying them to work in my greenhouse."

Such a humanitarian. How much did he pay them to harass me?

The camera shifted to another room. Hydroponic towers of plants flourished under multicolored LED grow lights, stretching as far as the camera could see. Not a window in sight, not a single clue that a greenhouse existed. No wonder Cyrus missed it. Air and water pumps emitted a symphony of gurgles, beeps, drips, hums, and growls. Oh, yes, Alexander was a master gardener, and his poisonous greenhouse exceeded even my wildest imaginings. The camera cut back to Alexander.

> "These are dark times when, not content with their ill-gotten gains, out-of-control billionaires lay siege to our homes and businesses."

Cyrus's phone rang. He wiggled his hand from my clutches to answer it. "I'm seeing it, yeah. No, damn it, I won't respond. No, Viv. I won't feed his ego."

Alexander nattered on, reaffirming he was good; we were bad. A smile twisted his mouth, and my wrist burned like someone set fire to it. Cyrus unbuckled my Bio-Bit and tossed it on the computer table. A band of raw red flesh encircled my wrist. He made an espresso for me.

"Give your wrist a break," he said and turned his attention back to the news.

> "As long as a single breath remains in my body, I will fight the enemies of the people."

My brain went fuzzy like I'd eaten something cold too fast. The Tarot compass reading flashed before my eyes. *Two of Pentacles* juggled like a crazy man. I felt as helpless and blind as the *Two of Swords*, waiting for the waves to crash over me.

The news cameras panned in real time to a three-story brick warehouse with a flat roof. Chicago's skyline, as ominous as a lightning bolt ready to strike, hovered in the distance. The sepia-drenched freeways and deserted lots surrounding the warehouse morphed into the wasteland into which the *Knight of Wands* charged, and the *Knight of Swords* was waiting. The flash-crack of gunfire illuminated and shattered a window. Impossible to tell if the shots came from the inside or not.

The room tilted; my vision went dark around the edges.

HOLD ON TO YOUR BUTT.

Cyrus squeezed my hand. "Breathe, baby, breathe."

I inhaled and exhaled and chased my breath with a gulp of tepid espresso. How long had this newscast been going on?

A slow pan down the street showed workers huddled behind cars, dumpsters, and any place offering rudimentary shelter and a good view. A reporter found someone to grill. The interviewee shuffled and alternated between ducking his head and flashing a self-conscious smile.

> "We get here around 3 AM most days to load the trucks."
> "Do you know anyone from Kaos and Sons?"
> "Just to nod to. We see them mostly in the afternoons."
> "Did you see anything suspicious this morning?"
> "Oh, yes, sir, a group surrounded that there warehouse. They looked like police, and they had guns. We stayed inside after that with the doors locked until y'all arrived."

A salvo of gunfire ended the interview.

Onlookers scrabbled deeper into the shadows. SWAT took up positions. A breathless reporter crouched behind her station's van so the camera crew could capture the station's logo.

> "We received word that a group identifying themselves as Mitnick's Mungers fired shots at the police. Our crew caught this conversation between officers."

A crackly voice, clearly a radio transmission, came through the speakers.

"Send all the ammo and support you can muster. We're gonna need help down here. We're taking gunfire."

The reporter paused so the audience could contemplate the gravity of the situation.

"We talked with officers, and they deny firing into the warehouse in the early hours of the morning. Hopefully, they can convey that message to the warehouse occupants so they'll surrender. There's no possibility of Mitnick's Mungers winning this battle when Chicago sends in its stormtroopers."

"Stormtroopers! Oh, that's not inflammatory or anything. Next, we'll hear I bribed the police into attacking." Cyrus cracked his knuckles, paced the room, and settled back into his chair after making two more espressos.

LET THE SEETHING COMMENCE.

As if to make amends for their hyperbole, the newscasts recapped what they knew, which wasn't much. The soundtrack to their coverage was sporadic gunshots, but not the Armageddon the police hinted at in their call for help. Cyrus, eyes narrowed and focused, slouched in his chair.

I indulged in a brief fantasy. The Mungers, at last seeing the error of their ways, would surrender. I salivated over the prospect of them denouncing Alexander to the Feds, who'd frog-march him off to a black ops site where they could interrogate him for bomb threats, stealing, leading children astray, attempted kidnapping, and a million other greater and lesser charges.

YEAH, HAPPY THOUGHTS.

I stifled a cackle when I imagined a look of shock replacing his habitual sneer. Would television cameras capture the moment? I regretted not learning how to scry; it would have opened up a portal with a front-row seat.

An anchor interrupted the endless regurgitation.

"We've learned the man in the earlier broadcast calls himself Alexander Filippidis, real name Eli King. According to an unnamed source, he's the man we heard recently threatening to bomb Harp Industries."

"You an unnamed source now, Harper?"

"No comment."

"I'll take that as a yes."

He raised his hands in a gesture of innocence. "What? I haven't left the room even to take a piss."

Like that would stop him, but someone else knew. Someone who'd love being an unnamed source. Someone named Darius.

The reporter spilled a lot of beans about Alexander. His sad saga at Harp Industries, his association with Cena Babington, the bomb threat, his harassment history, and his association with *Die Basis*. The "unnamed source" left no stone unturned.

GOOD ON YOU, UNNAMED SOURCE, AKA DARIUS PHARRE. LIGHTEN UP, LILIENTHAL. WE'RE ALL THINKING IT.

"Oh, Christ." Cyrus slammed his fist into the chair's arm. "He's hacking into the newscasts."

Indeed, Alexander returned in all his gothic glory. A singer wailed in the background, warning someone called Baby Blue that it was all *OVER. Fini. Terminado. Erledigt.* If only. Alexander licked his lips.

"This one's on you, Maren. Harp Industries and Bio-Bits are modern demons. You and Harper worship gold and silver idols. I offered you a chance at redemption, but you refused. Your love of gold caused this loathsome moment. You are a Jezebel, worse than poison to men's souls. Destruction follows in your wake."

"Are you fucking kidding me?" My screech echoed off the wall and scraped my throat raw. Compared to this, Nosey's slurs and the Riverton police perp walk were playground heckling or morning coffee with Ivy. "Blame the witch? Why do men do that when they don't get their way?"

"Not all men." Cyrus, face red as his aura, had scooted to a computer; his fingers flew over the keyboard.

"I tried to rally the masses for a Last Stand before you and Harper attacked us. But they were waiting for a white knight to save them. I let them in on a little secret, Maren. There's no white knight."

"Where the fuck is the crazy bastard?" Cyrus pounded the keyboard. "Nothing's coming out of that warehouse."

I braced myself for the moment he used the gun on the computer. It passed.

"Sometimes I ask, what if I'm wrong? What am I doing this for? What's the point if we're going to die, anyway? You die, and it's over. Sometimes, I can even feel sorry for you, Maren. You and me, we're pawns in the greatest psyops operation ever. So, what's the point? Then, I remember, it's a war. It's raging on all fronts. Someone must confront the demons, or we're all lost."

Breaking News cut into Alexander's oh-poor-me tirade.

"About ten minutes ago, police called for the occupants of the warehouse to come out with their hands up. In response, a man on a megaphone shouted obscenities, calling out police and Chicago businessman, Cyrus Harper. At this time, we can't identify the man. A comparison of the voices suggests it wasn't Alexander Filippidis."

A multitude of emotions ran across Cyrus's face faster than the Breaking News banners. Rage. Disbelief. Bitterness.

The police issued another surrender ultimatum.

> "Colin, we have another communique from inside the warehouse."

I braced myself for another dose of Alexander and placed my hand on Cyrus's arm. Instead, Muireann blinked into a webcam and cleared her throat.

> "I have a message from our leader, Alexander. We want our comrades to know you are not slaves or cannon fodder. You were not created to work, produce, and impoverish yourself to enrich an idle exploiter like Cyrus Harper. You are better than that. You don't need to support the boss who does no actual work, but profits from yours. We're talking about you, Harper."

Cyrus rolled his shoulders and head as if limbering up for a brawl. When had that third espresso appeared? Time was becoming disjointed.

"Don't pay any attention to her," I said. He didn't respond. I told myself he hadn't heard me.

> "Chicago is the product of modern capitalism."

Muireann's lips quivered, and sweat broke out across her forehead. She'd figured out that it's a lot easier to be brave and confident when you hide behind a besotted boy.

> "It's unfit for human habitation. Because you're human, rise and destroy it."

She lifted her fist in a mock salute. A disembodied reporter's voice came through the screen.

> "The police are lobbing tear gas canisters into the warehouse windows, and they're tossing them back at us."

Cameras bumped and jostled, showing police had already donned gas masks. The reporters scrambled away from the slow-moving yellow-tinged clouds, grappling for their gas masks, water bottles, and other relief means.

Gunfire erupted.

"There's so much smoke and shooting. It's impossible to tell if you're safe or not. Bystanders have pulled back, and the rest of us are keeping our heads down and our fingers crossed."

A Munger sent another defiant message.

"Workers of the world, join us! You have nothing to lose but your chains! When we hang Cyrus Harper and his witch, we'll use the ropes and spells they sold us."

"Paraphrasing Marx and Stalin. That's inspiring." Cyrus shook his head. "Not an original thought among them."

"We're hearing from police sources they're about to employ pyrotechnic tear gas canisters, which burn like fireworks. They dispense chemicals more quickly and get hot enough that they can't be picked up and thrown back outside."

"That's no good," Cyrus muttered. "They could start a fire."

Teargas canisters hit the windows and bricks. As Cyrus predicted, flames flickered inside a first-floor window.

"Surely they'll come out now." This had gone far enough. Alexander's innuendos had done their job. Chances were good if Cyrus and I poked our heads out the front door, we'd be tarred and feathered. What else did he hope to achieve?

An enormous ball of smoke and flame erupted from the warehouse. The explosion coming from the speakers rattled our windows. Footage from inside the warehouse streamed onto the screen. The Mungers continued shooting even as smoke and flames rose behind them. Hacking and coughing mingled with the crackle of flames and the wah-wah-wah of an alarm somewhere in the building. Were they going to choose suicide over jail?

The warehouse belched smoke. Flames spewed into the street.

As this poppet burns and withers in the fire, so may Alexander's heart burn and wither...May my enemies' path be dark and slippery and their lives be as chaff before the wind.

Had I uttered those words? A dull heaviness washed over me. Covering my face didn't drown out the alarm or the sound of flames.

> "Mommy!"

Muireann, only moments before so defiant, scrabbled across a bare wooden floor, followed by a trail of fire. The picture shifted to outside the warehouse. Fire illuminated her in a third-floor window.

LET DESTRUCTION COME UPON THEM UNAWARES; LET THE TRAP ALEXANDER SET FOR ME CATCH ALL OF THEM SO THEY FALL INTO DESTRUCTION.

She perched on the ledge against a backdrop of hellfire. The flames wormed toward her, licked at her hair, and danced along her shoulders. Arms spread like useless wings, she plummeted head over heels. Flames swelled inside the building and gushed from the windows. Lights from the cameras and police cars strobed like lightning.

It was *The Tower* card. Unavoidable chaos and destruction. Something you shouldn't wish on your worst enemy. Yet, I had. I gulped espresso.

EVER MIND THE RULE OF THREE!

During the holocaust in progress, a tray of sandwiches appeared on the table. My stomach growled. A snotty voice in my head reminded me it was rude to eat at a time like this. Alexander dominated the screen again, causing a knot in my throat that only coffee could slip past.

> "Let every tramp arm themselves with a revolver or knife and enter the homes of the idle rich. Stab or shoot them. Exterminate them without mercy or pity."

The image burned from the corners inward, like someone setting a match to parchment. His disembodied head floated against a maelstrom.

> "Farewell, a long farewell to all my greatness! This is the state of man: today he puts forth the tender leaves of hope. Tomorrow, it blossoms and bears his blushing honors thick upon him. When he thinks his greatness is a-ripening, there comes a frost, a killing frost that nips his root. Then he falls, as I do."

The screens went black.

OF COURSE, DRAMA KING WOULD QUOTE SHAKESPEARE.

I wanted to spit. Kill them all and let the Goddess sort them out.

The news resumed, and the reporters glommed onto the arrival of the Chicago Fire Department. Police held them back. Despite the inferno, the shooting continued, much of it methodical, but some gunfire seemed random.

The reporters informed us the intense heat was igniting ammunition. As the explosions continued, sky cams showed thick clouds of black smoke. A news drone came in close; the camera caught two Mungers, hard to tell their gender, who made it to the flat roof and waved their arms with increasing desperation. We learned Chicago Air Rescue was coming for them.

The drone pulled back to document the rescue. By the time Air Rescue arrived, flames licked at the roof. I scooted forward in my chair, clinging to Cyrus's hand. A wind came off the lake, pushing the helicopter toward the wasteland. It fought its way back.

> "We're speaking with Lieutenant Schmidt with the Fire Suppression and Rescue Division. How difficult is this rescue maneuver?"

The camera shifted to a firefighter with gear that was not out of place for a combat zone

> "The air around a fire makes for a hazardous ride. The closer you get to the fire, the greater the risk of the chopper losing power. There's no hardware that's easy for scared civilians to use, but still safe enough they won't get dumped while we reel them in."
>
> "What about that nifty basket the Coast Guard uses? Isn't that pretty simple? Crawl in and hang on?"

The lieutenant didn't roll his eyes, but he came close. A piece of equipment that looked like an oversized shopping basket flashed across the screen.

"Not as simple as it looks. You still need a trained rescue specialist to control the basket. There's always a chance the basket will start spinning out of control, and that's Mr. Toad's Wild Ride."

Cyrus leaned toward the television, rubbing his hands and muttering. "Wild, yeah."

Rocking back and forth and tapping my knuckles against my teeth, I tried and failed to imagine myself swinging out in the open air while a helicopter chopped the air into a frenzy. Nope. Couldn't imagine it. Windsurfing had nearly stopped my heart.

After this fright, the pair on the roof might realize following Alexander wasn't smart. I hoped so. It would make my curse a little easier to stomach.

Minutes crawled past as the helicopter battled the wind to get into position. A mating dance ensued; the helicopter sidled up to the building, only to be rebuffed by wind and flames. After several tense minutes, the helicopter closed in and held steady long enough to lower the basket.

The basket crawled toward the rooftop. It wove through thick swirls of gray and black smoke. When the wind blew away a patch of smoke, the dark blot of the rescuer in the basket became visible. My lungs burned in sympathy with the fireman and the Mungers breathing the smoke and flames.

A wind blast sent the basket careening away from the warehouse and over a small, empty parking lot. Yep, definitely Mr. Toad's Wild Ride. Several grueling minutes ticked by as the copter struggled to return the basket to the target area.

"Fire's getting worse," Cyrus said.

I'd been so focused on the basket's fate, I didn't notice flames dancing along the roof's perimeter. They leaped into the air like excited dogs. The basket descended another excruciating foot, maybe two.

"Do you think this will change them?" I gestured toward the pair huddled on the roof. It was probably only the camera angle, but they looked like frightened children, not Zombies and Skeletons.

"Who's to say? They're fanatics, and I doubt their minds work like ours. Once you go down that path …"

His voice trailed off as a collective gasp came from every news stream. The basket dangled a few short feet above the pair, but the roof collapsed into the building and flames exploded, its fingers reaching toward the basket and helicopter.

The helicopter veered; the basket arced and swung in a way that made me sick to my stomach.

The buzzing in my head transformed whatever the newscasters said into gibberish. But I didn't need to hear it said; no one could survive a drop into the inferno.

Grasping Cyrus's hand and pressing it to my heart, I recited a blessing.

"May the blessing of sunlight shine on you. May the blessing of the rain wash your Spirit clean, and leave there a shining pool where the blue of Heaven shines. May the blessing of the earth rest lightly over you. May your soul be on its way to the Goddess. Now, may the Lady bless you and bless you kindly."

Hypocritical? Yes, but I clung to my pretensions of being a decent human being.

EXPECT THE UNEXPECTED, PART 2

MONDAY, APRIL 18

A FULL HOUR LAPSED, an hour in which Cyrus and I sat in stunned silence before police permitted firefighters to tackle the blaze. By then, flames had destroyed the warehouse and damaged two adjacent buildings. Eyewitnesses professed shock and horror at the destruction. Everyone mentioned how an enormous ball of flames erupted and threatened to engulf the entire block. They replayed the almost-rescue and the Munger pair's fiery descent into hell about a million times.

"A member of Chicago SWAT spoke on the condition of anonymity. 'The massive attack turned dingbats into martyrs.'"

"Somebody's going to find himself in sensitivity training." Cyrus's hand tightened around mine.

"The police shot an estimated 1200 rounds of ammunition into the warehouse, and we witnessed the fiery deaths of three occupants as they tried to claw their way from the inferno. Will the rubble yield more bodies? Almost certainly. The rubble is still smoking; we won't know how many for a while."

An harm ye none had battled throughout the day with my hunger to hurt Alexander. To be honest, I wasn't that sorry. Horrified, yes; sorry, not so much. Was it the lingering effects of Mercury Retrograde? Never heard it was a side effect. But when you strayed so far from your professed beliefs … Some time — not today, no not today — I'd go deep into my shadow self and grapple with the morality of my thoughts and actions and their consequences. Not an undertaking I relished.

> "Why did they follow a madman who called himself Alexander Filippidis, who ranted against a local businessman and his girlfriend?"

I cast a guilty glance in Cyrus's direction. He rubbed his forehead and shook his head. Was he, too, wrestling with guilt over and satisfaction with today's outcome?

> "We now know who Alexander Filippidis was/is. At an earlier news briefing, the FBI confirmed the reports from an anonymous source that identified him as Eli King, a former Harp Industries employee, whose founder he lambasted throughout the shootout. We further confirmed King was behind the bomb scare at Harp Industries on March 21. What we don't know, however, was if the flames consumed him along with his followers."

I plucked a sandwich from the untouched plate and took a mouse nibble before sloshing more coffee into my stomach. Cyrus pried the cup from my hand and set it out of reach. "The acid from all that coffee will make you sick, K-Bear."

I took another nibble.

> "The man taken away in an ambulance in the early hours of the standoff died of gunshot wounds at a local hospital. No word yet on his identity."

The burning sensation in my stomach rivaled the flames on the screen. I grabbed a water bottle, glugged it, and retched.

"Some yogurt?" Cyrus rubbed my back.

Beckett tapped on the door, saving me from Cyrus, the lunchroom monitor.

"There's a gentleman named Darius Pharre at the door," Beckett said.

I swallowed hard to keep from retching again.

"He says he's your brother, and you'll want to speak with him. He's clean; I patted him down."

Not a phrase you expected to hear on Monday afternoon in your own home. But I hadn't expected anything that happened today.

Cyrus ran his fingers through his hair; I was too tired to stop him. "Yeah, sure. I'll be right down."

Beckett nodded and disappeared.

"I won't be long," Cyrus said. "It's time to shut down the news, yeah?"

I shook my head. Cyrus sighed and drifted from the room like a ghost. The news, sounding more like 1692 than 2044, replayed Alexander's favorite screed of not suffering a witch to live.

A somber newsreader gave the sermon of the day.

> "So, here's what's happening at 6 PM. The gunfire has stopped, and the flames are out. But a big question mark still hangs like smoke over Chicago's Southside. A burned-out warehouse contains at least seven bodies, based on images broadcast from inside the warehouse during the shootout. Early reports from Chicago Fire say the bodies are so charred, their gender, much less their identity, cannot be determined without testing. What else will we find?"

"Crazy day, yeah?"

I flinched.

Darius, decked out in upscale cat burglar black, lounged against the doorframe, looking like Hollywood had costumed him as a commando in a predawn raid. His good eye glittered with excitement. "Some real crazy shit. May I come in? Cyborg said it was OK for me to say goodbye. Ines and I are going to jet."

I gestured him inside and rocked back in my chair. "You're leaving?"

"Yeah. Hvar Island is calling to Ines." He grinned as if we shared a secret. "Make Cyborg take you there. Beaches and bays, lavender fields, olive groves that are practically prehistoric, and vineyards. Cyborg likes vineyards."

"What about the baby?"

"Oh, she'll come when she comes. We travel with a doctor, and there's a hospital suite on the plane. Never know when you'll need it." He winked, conjuring images of bleeding bodies carried onto the plane to be mended while ferrying them to a country with a non-extradition treaty.

"Did you start it?" We both knew what "it" was.

"Darlin', I told you I sell that shit; I don't use it."

Sure, and he had a bridge to sell me. Maybe he didn't fire a single shot, but he'd been there to oversee the action. His nostrils flared as if he smelled gunfire, teargas, and the acrid aftermath of the fire, a perfume that he exulted in.

"It's over, baby girl. You can quit looking over your shoulder now."

"Do you think that's OK?" I gestured toward the video of the building belching flames, the strobing blue and red lights, and the hubbub of newscasters. Over it all, Alexander shrieked *Harp Industries and Bio-Bit technology are modern demons* and *Thou shalt not suffer a witch to live.*

"I've seen worse. There was that time in … damn, where was it? But I digress." His dismissive shrug suggested that what I saw was the first circle of hell, and he lived somewhere past its ninth circle. "The point is, I told you it would be OK, and it is. The bastard deserved it."

"Did the guy who died in the hospital deserve it? Did those kids?"

"Tough luck for those kids, but actions have consequences."

His casual dismissal chilled me and fed the haunting realization that the same thinking underpinned my hex.

"The guy who died," he said. "I don't know this for sure, but I'm thinking war was his business. Only dead men ever see the end of war."

A smile tugged at his lips. Persistence was futile. He'd never give me a straight answer. Yet, he enjoyed playing with me like a cat with a mouse between his paws, so I persevered, trying a different tactic. He might slip.

"I don't know how anyone tracked him down. Cyrus tried so hard."

"True. True." His grin widened. "It turned out your cards pinpointed his location. Cyrus didn't find him because he was looking for a standard greenhouse. I've seen *Die Basis's* greenhouses with grow lights and towers for growing weed and poppies. You need cash to fund a revolution against capitalism. If he'd looked at electric usage, he'd have seen a big electric arrow over that place."

A confession without a confession. "What do you think he'd have done if he'd found Alexander?"

"Interesting question." Darius seemed to ponder it before shaking his head. "What goes on in my brother's big, beautiful brain is a mystery. Whenever I think I've figured it out, boom. I'm mistaken. Maybe ask your cards? No? Don't want to know? Smart. But what about you, witchy woman? You look quiet and sweet sometimes. But I know you can be wild and crazy, cause Cyborg likes a little wild and crazy. Is there something you want to tell me about what goes on in *your* brain?"

LET IT GO, MAREN.

I couldn't. "Every witch has more than one side, including the side you hope you never see."

"Bravo." He clapped his hands. "I need to vamoose. We'll catch up another time, but you take good care of my brother, yeah."

He was gone.

"Here's the latest on the Southside shootout..."

High-tech Moriarty

Tuesday, April 19

Magick, like nature, is amoral. It flows like water, seeking the path of least resistance. Sometimes, you can burn a forest of incense, light a thousand candles, cast a million spells, read the cards until your eyes fall out, and the worst still happens. After all, witches are only human, with humanity's limitations and flaws.

Did I regret hexing Alexander? Honestly, no. Like many witches, magick changed my life, healed old wounds, and helped me claim my full potential, which Alexander wanted to destroy. Historically speaking, witches hexed as a last resort. Alexander pushed me right there, and my rage against him had been as incandescent as the fire that destroyed his warehouse. When I cursed him and the Mungers, my intentions were never unclear.

For every witch who argued the Law of Three was silly and outdated, I had one word: *physics*, Newton's Third Law of Motion. For every action, there is an equal and opposite reaction. You send out shit; shit comes right back at you. *Omne trium perfectum*. Three was the perfect number, the number of harmony, wisdom, and understanding, which you'd receive after a good dose of Newton. So, there it was. If innocent people died because I hexed Alexander, I regretted that. Next time, I'd craft my spells with greater care.

What can you do when your flaws and limitations take center stage? You prepare for the next challenge. First, you cleanse and heal yourself and those around you; you love and allow yourself to be loved. You try again and promise to do it differently by asking for help and learning from your mistakes.

I started by consulting the Tarot. "What is the first step in my journey?"

Five of Swords. The guy holding the swords looked smug as if he took pleasure in defeating his enemies. I sure understood that feeling. The clouds looked like ripped fabric, suggesting the battle wasn't over, no matter what he thought. His red shirt and leggings spoke to his energy and ego like Cyrus's red aura. The green tunic suggested naivete born of entitlement. Both of us, guilty as charged on that score. Five was the card for mankind and experience on the earthly plane. The card demanded I consider what we'd gained after this recent battle. What lessons could we learn?

To open my mind, I used a centering technique. Holding my right hand before me, I traced its outline with my left forefinger, forward and back, until my breathing slowed, dropped from my chest into my belly, and deepened. When I emerged from the meditative state, I turned on *BoSsBlog's* recorder.

"The battle we've been fighting since we arrived in Chicago is over, but we didn't win the war with how the world sees us. We may never win it, but continued fighting will be stressful. If we leave the battlefield with dignity and grace, we can preserve our self-respect. We can stop Nosey and Alexander's ghosts from living rent-free in our heads."

I'd need time to digest that thought, but Mab, my virtual assistant, reminded me it was time to prepare for a press conference.

We drove in silence to the Harp Building where PR flacks and stylists swarmed over us like ants over a picnic basket. They curated our clothes, our hair, and even the color of my nail polish. I'd never get back the hours wasted dithering over my make-up and hairstyle: a sleek bun, smokey eyes, and natural lipstick.

"We don't want them to call you a glamazon, but people will want to know who you're wearing," a doe-eyed girl said.

SEVERAL PEOPLE BURNED TO DEATH, BUT EVERYONE WANTS TO KNOW WHAT YOU'RE WEARING?

I rattled off the fashion deets.

"Cyrus will make a statement, but they'll have questions for you," another flak said. "Because Alexander mentioned you so often."

He handed me a tablet with suggestions on how to answer the expected questions. I studied it as if I were taking final exams, but reserved the right to edit the answers. There were photos of the burned-out building; a few showed corpses.

"Is this necessary?" I turned to Cyrus.

He shrugged. "They think someone will show them during the Q&A, and they don't want us to be surprised."

No matter how many deep breaths I took, I couldn't change the reality of those photos and what Alexander, Darius, and I had wrought.

"He was a bad guy," Cyrus said. "If they want to blame us, they will. Meanwhile, we'll get on with our lives."

It sounded like my guidance from the Tarot. I tried one more breath. Nothing. "I guess sometimes you have to put on the pointed hat, pick up your broomstick, and show them who you are. Come on, Harper. Let's do this thing and get past it."

Cyrus held out his hand. Brave words notwithstanding, I grabbed his hand like a lifeline.

We, your average young couple targeted by a terrorist, stepped into the elevator. The lobby's darkened glass walls thwarted peeping Tom reporters. A line of CPD officers stood ready to push the crowd back. The doors opened, and we stepped outside into a beautiful spring day that contradicted yesterday's horror.

"Cyrus! Maren!"

A volley of our names and camera clicks pelted us. The shouted questions were brutal.

"Cyrus, could you have done anything to prevent yesterday's tragedy?"

"Cyrus, why did Alexander hate you so much?"

"Maren, do you think witchcraft caused Alexander to go berserk?"

"Cyrus, what do you know about the men who started the shooting?"

We ignored the worst questions, did our dog and pony show, and read the results that evening.

High-Tech Moriarty?

With the iconic egg-shaped Harp Building in the background and looking boyish in a brown-and-blue plaid sports jacket, turtleneck, jeans, and boots, Cyrus Harper addressed the warehouse conflagration that left at least seven people dead and destroyed a city block on Chicago's near Southside.

It wasn't a Nosey tirade. The anxiety I'd been denying evaporated.

"Maren and I," Harper said, referring to his companion, Maren Lilienthal, "are saddened by the unnecessary loss of life and property. No one watching yesterday's news can remain unhorrified by what Eli King wrought."

Not a lie. Exactly.

Eli King is the man who identified himself as Alexander Filippidis in a video attacking Harper as a murderous capitalist. The video was online during the shootout, leading to speculation King/ Filippidis was among the dead who have yet to be identified by the Cook County Coroner.

Did they need another recap? The news stream repeated those factoids as filler for its 24/7 cycle. They wouldn't cease until the next big story exploded.

When asked if he hoped King was dead, Harper sidestepped the question.

"Actions have consequences," Harper said. "Make no mistake, no matter how long or loud King railed against entrepreneurs, he was one, an entrepreneur of violence, a vicious extremist who tore things down instead of building them. He manipulated events and deployed smokescreens to confuse people. He was a technical genius who employed his skills in pursuit of revenge, chaos, and violence. In short, Eli King was the Moriarty of Technology."

Cyrus wrote every word of that statement and delivered it with earnestness. Surprised? He had a way of speaking, and not every sentence ended with 'yeah.'

Harper referred to Professor James Moriarty, the arch-enemy of Sherlock Holmes. The world's most famous detective acknowledged Moriarty's genius in *The Memoirs of Sherlock Holmes.* "He is the Napoleon of crime, Watson ... He is a genius, a philosopher, an abstract thinker. He sits like a spider in the center of its web, but that web has a thousand radiations, and he knows well every quiver of them." Does this mean Harper acknowledges the technical superiority claimed by King/ Filippidis in his tirades? Harper wasn't saying.

Now my turn on the grill.

Maren Lilienthal, Harper's girlfriend, who was often the target of King/Filippidis, accompanied Harper. Lilienthal gave a fashionable nod to her well-known witch persona with antique silver and ivory earrings depicting a moon face. She further accentuated the witchy-vibe in a black Burberry slim-fit trench coat with a nipped-in waist over a white tee shirt with black crescent moons and black crepe gaucho pants. Red Stella McCartney boots, selling in local shops for over $1500, were her only nod to color.

Points to the PR flacks for calling it.

Asked if she was a witch, Lilienthal smiled. "You say witch like it's a bad thing. I'm a practitioner in the Wiccan tradition."

"People say Wicca is a practice for over-privileged, over-sexed, white people," one reporter observed.

"Then I'm two out of three." Lilienthal might have been referring to her bi-racial family background. "But honestly, all religions have their issues, and mine's a young religion with problematic origins and problematic followers."

"So, are you proud to be a witch?" the same reporter asked.

The PR flacks told me to be prepared for that question. I was, but not the way they expected.

"I am. Witchcraft empowers women by bridging the gap between the divine and oneself. For me, witchcraft is about embracing and trusting my intuition. Margot Adler said 'The first time I called myself a Witch was the most magical moment of my life.'" Lilienthal paused and smiled. "That was true for me until I met Cyrus. Now that was real magick."

Not bad, right?

> Asked about the couple's immediate plans, Harper flashed his signature smile and said, "Go home. Fix dinner. Knock back a couple glasses of wine and, hopefully, get a good night's sleep."
>
> They ducked into the Harp Building, ignoring a chorus of questions. Eli/Alexander anticipated that as well. "They will try to retreat into their money, which makes them careless and keeps them together. You can be sure they expect other people to clean up their mess."

WHAT? YOU DIDN'T THINK THEY'D LET YOU OFF THE HOOK WITH-OUT ONE ZINGER?

The last line was a definite icicle to the heart, a sure sign the war would continue. Had exposing ourselves to the mob been worth it? The ant-hill of PR flacks and stylists who'd swarmed over us said yes. They sent Cyrus texts insisting readers would see the journalistic outrage for what it was. A bid to sell more news. I wondered.

Cyrus made dinner, and I quaffed more than a couple glasses of wine. On the fourth or fifth refill, he placed his hand over the glass.

"A bite to eat, yeah?"

I popped a stuffed mushroom into my mouth. "It's never going to end, is it?"

He paused, midway through whisking eggs for an omelet. "In the past, when they pestered me, it lasted a week or two. I laid low, and they found another victim. We'll go home right after the board meeting. Reporters won't get through The Bluff's gates, and it'll blow over."

Home. I liked the sound of it. "We're driving, right? And stopping in Woodhull for pie."

"Absolutely. Pie makes everything better."

Two of Cups

Friday, April 22

The world kept spinning, forcing me to shake off my post-Alexander gloom and doom. I lunched with the Harp Board members' domestic partners and smiled through the five-hour, 18-course dinner with the Board and those same partners. Dr. Rossellini nodded her approval. One critic down.

We'd head to Riverton in the morning and resume our lives there. I set up in-person meetings with Plaza tenants, coordinated with a caterer for my family tea, and checked with Grace Williams to see if the house was ready. Oma would be proud.

Mab reminded me it was Beckett's last day. I found him in the kitchen. After all we'd gone through, saying goodbye brought a lump to my throat. "Hey, guy. Thanks for everything. I'm gonna miss hanging out with you and evading fanatics."

"Same here." He grinned and feigned a courtly bow. "If you ever need a bodyguard, give me a jingle."

"Deal." We hugged.

"Thank Mr. Harper again for the bonus. It was unnecessary, but much appreciated."

We exchanged more pleasantries before I spared him and returned to my office.

With my tasks checked off and no Alexander to worry about, I rediscovered an old hobby: tormenting myself. Riverton wasn't "home free." I'd be living with Cyrus under my family and Riverton society's eagle eyes. How could we move our relationship to the next level with that pressure dangling over our heads like a sword? I pulled out my Tarot deck and shuffled and cut the cards until my fingers ached.

SINCE YOU WAITED UNTIL THE LAST MINUTE, ASK ALREADY.

"What should I know about living in Riverton with Cyrus?" I turned on *BoSsBlog* and pulled *Two of Cups*.

A union of opposites.

Negotiation and balance.

Passion and protection.

A declaration of love.

Hell, yeah! Count me in. The garlands around their heads symbolized success and love or maybe success *in* love. One could only hope.

The woman wore the *High Priestess's* colors; the man wore *The Fool's*. Together they signified a new relationship. If I counted the days since we met, I came up with a grand total of 138. Not a lengthy relationship by anyone's standard, even mine; but there was something deep and true about Cyrus, something I'd never experienced. Everything in the card signaled intention with the promise of love, emotional support, and domestic bliss. A relationship green light, if I'd ever seen one.

GET TO IT.

If our time in Chicago hadn't been an undiluted pleasure, we'd end it on a high note and get the *Two of Cups* ball rolling. We'd never had our Duke and Duchess dress-up dinner at home that we planned on the plane. Time was running out.

First step, planning a menu with Pat. Second step, rummaging through Cyrus's closet. He had *so many* black-tie options, although Oma decreed black tie meant navy because black can look dusty. Goddess forbid Cyrus should ever look dusty. I chose a navy dinner jacket with shawl lapels, a pleated white shirt, and navy trousers. I wrote a note explaining he needed to change into these clothes before coming home. I zipped everything into a garment bag, which Mr. I-Hate-Packing likely never used, and called Viv.

Johnny answered. "Oh, hello, Maren. Viv's in the board meeting."

"Ah, of course. Listen, I need a pick-up. Cyrus must get something before he leaves the office."

"I'll do it." Johnny volunteered faster than a speeding bullet, revealing he still considered himself in the dog house. He was, but it would work out. Hopefully, Muireann's treachery had left him with only a small amount of grief.

"Sounds good. Any time you're ready. No need to knock. It'll be the garment bag in the front hall coat closet. Thanks, Johnny."

"Sure thing. I'm on my way, and I'll station myself outside the conference room and make sure Cyrus doesn't slip out."

I thanked him again and offered a silent prayer that he'd heal.

Step three, shake off the lingering negative energy, which made me feel out of balance and full of toxins. The pink quartz I'd purchased was cleaned, charged, and ready. I gathered everything else I'd need for a spiritual cleanse.

I ran hot water into the bathtub and added Epsom salts, quartz, and lemon and orange peels. While it ran, I brewed passionflower, chamomile, and lavender into a soothing tea and set the cup by the bathtub. Moon water was more effective, but you worked with what you had. After deep, calming breaths, I stepped into the water.

Tea and the pink quartz drained the tension from my spine. I slipped deeper into the water until it reached my chin. The sun, dappled by the hanging ferns, poured through the skylights. The cascading light pulsed through my veins and muscles, sluicing away the noxious remnants of the last forty days. When the last drib of negativity disappeared, I showered the salt from my skin.

Centered, aura-cleansed, lotioned, and perfumed, I retrieved an Oscar de la Renta cocktail dress from a closet that was getting fuller and more organized by the day. The A-line silhouette was crafted from layer upon layer of diaphanous black tulle, printed with bouquets. Shimmering sequins and beads embellished each flower. Glinda the Good couldn't out-sparkle me. I wore the diamond studs Cyrus gifted me on Valentine's Day and Wallis's necklace to let him know I appreciated *all* his gifts. I pulled my curls back into a low roll and secured it with an Egyptian Revival hair comb. Strappy black sling-back heels completed the ensemble. Duchess Wallis, eat your heart out.

Patricia left dinner in the warming oven. I took a bottle of wine into the sunroom. It had a different vibe at night, the spectacular lake view reduced to the sound of waves pounding the shoreline. The golden glow of the Tiffany "spider" lamps with their arachnid-veining kept the darkness at bay. They channeled Grandmother Spider, the Native American deity who protected and nurtured humankind, guiding us along our paths with her magick.

Cyrus found me curled up on the sofa, down half a bottle of wine, and nestled in Grandmother Spider's gentle magick. Wind-blown hair, just-out-of-bed stubble, and a tuxedo made a killer combo and plucked me from my reverie. *Thank you, Grandmother Spider.* I crossed the room for a kiss. "Hey, rock star."

"Hey, Moonchild." He twirled me around and whistled. "You are the most beautiful sight I've ever seen."

"Doin' what I can, babe."

He grinned at my impression and poured himself a glass of wine, which he raised in a toast. "May we grow old together with our heads resting on one pillow."

How did I respond to such a perfect sentiment? In doubt, turn to Shakespeare. I raised my glass. "So are you to my thoughts as food to life."

We kissed, tasting the alchemy of wine changed by each other's lips. He pulled away.

"I hope I know where this is heading. But first, we better talk about something important." He led me back to the couch and sat at my feet. After two healthy swallows of wine, he took my hands in his.

Serious business afoot. Had the cards misled me? Had a new Alexander popped up?

"The Board's voted to provide security for us."

OK, hadn't expected that.

"We had security." It went without saying we didn't need security in Riverton.

"And we'll have it still. Do you know what a PPO is?"

"Nope."

Another swallow of wine. "Personal protection officer. They're saying after everything that went down, off-duty police officers aren't enough. They want a team of Becketts, around the clock, wherever we are. Well, they're not just wanting it. They're demanding it because the stock would plummet if something happened to me. Or so they say."

"It's a pain, but probably a good idea."

"Glad you think so because they insisted you have PPOs, too."

"What? Why me? Alexander's gone, and I don't own any Harp stock."

"They know I'd do anything to keep you safe, so it's a financially prudent decision." He stared into the wine before turning his dazzling smile on me. "Hey, it's not all bad. You'll get a defensive driving course where you can run over pretend people. We can paint Ivy's face on them. You'd like that."

I would. He pulled me down into his lap, his hands doing things to distract me. Damn, he knew this body of mine too well, and I liked it.

"Viv ordered you a Paprika-colored armored Porsche. I think they're called personal security vehicles." His hands flew around me as he described it. "Armor and bulletproof glass that can stop an M16 point blank. Ballistic steel roof and floor, so no worries about grenades or landmines. Hell, even the gas tank, radiator, and battery have armor."

"Sounds heavy. I bet it goes all of five miles an hour."

"Zero to sixty in five seconds. Top speed of 175 mph. You like to drive fast." He grabbed my hands and made driving motions and speed noises.

"OK, I get it."

"There's a woman who'll be working with us, Camilla Nightingale..."

"Nightingale?" I hooted.

"Nightingale." He looked stern. "Trained in deadly force, so watch your step, missy, and get a handle on those giggles. She's going to be our chief security officer. She's coming to Riverton to evaluate what we need. I know you didn't sign up for this."

I didn't remember either of us signing up for it. The world was harder to navigate since the morning I'd outrun an overweight Druid in the Cardiff airport; but here we were. His eyes narrowed, and the worry line between his eyebrows deepened, a sign that the possibility of me hightailing it worried him. Not that long ago, he'd have been right, too. All these domestic plans would have scared me as much as Alexander. Better nip his qualms in the bud.

"Sometimes you have to bow to the inevitable. But Nightingale? Her name's Nightingale?"

He tweaked my nose. "Trained in deadly force. Don't you forget it."

I did my best. It was easier when you cocooned with your lover; the lights were low; and the wine was excellent.

"I'm getting used to this, you know?" I tugged at an unruly curl and nibbled his earlobe.

"Glad to hear it." He rubbed my spine. "When I was at university and ran by this house, I imagined whoever lived here was the happiest, luckiest bastard in the world. The first time I walked in, I waited for it to hit me. I was that guy, but I still wasn't."

"No?"

"No. It was still just a house. But tonight, when I walked through the door and you were here, I knew I'd come home and was the luckiest bastard ever."

A knot formed in my throat. "We're not so different. This last month I learned we can be anywhere. Here. A hotel. A blanket on the beach, but if we're together, it's home."

He squeezed me hard. "Good. I need you with me. No, I want you with me. It's not enough to catch up when we happen to be in the same place at the same time. I don't want to open the door and shout, 'Honey, I'm back. Let's make up for lost time.' Because my home is wherever you are. Like right goddamn now, Duchess."

Wow.

"Just so you know, I don't want to hightail it. When I'm with you, I'm where I want to be."

"HAL, play *Can't Help Falling in Love with You.*" He pulled me to my feet. The speakers filled the room with music.

I pressed my cheek against his. We stepped into the song, reaching out for the next step with our toes and landing on solid footing.

Without a broom or plane, we flew.

ACKNOWLEDGMENTS

First of all, thank you to my readers. Without you, nothing is possible. If you liked *Season of the Witch*, please leave a review.

As always, many thanks to the best critique partners ever, J.K. Miles and Ellan Otero. Also thanks and overwhelming gratitude to Susan Peers who keeps my Tarot readings real.

Finally, thanks to my family and many friends (you know who you are) who keep me going.

ABOUT MICHALEA MOORE

I've been a reader and writer all my life. There's even a photo of me on the potty chair reading a picture book. I taped stories written in crayon on my grandmother's front porch. I wore out the pages of *The Road to Story Land*.

My home away from home was the Public Library. The children's reading room was in a turret, and I was the Queen. I checked out three particular books so often the library told my mother I was depriving the other children. They limited me to checking out those books to once a month with no renewals. What were the three books? *Girls' Book of Famous Queens*, *Cleopatra of Egypt*, and *D'Aulaires Book of Greek Myths*. Thus began a life-long love affair with reading, powerful women, Egypt, and mythology. Later, when writing became my passion, what did I want to write about? You guessed it.

I'm lucky because I've always had jobs that allowed me to earn a living by writing. I started by writing commercials for a local television station, spent several years writing grants, and finally became a technical writer and editor. No, I didn't write the great American novel during that time, BUT I learned plenty about writing that my creative writing classes didn't cover. The most valuable lesson? You can't wait for inspiration. Sometimes, you just put your butt in the chair and write whether or not you feel like it.

What else about me? I have two adult children who inspired me. I love to travel, and some of those places make their way into my novels. I have interests that also pop up from time to time in my fiction: Egypt, gardening, magic/heka, and romance and mystery novels to name a few.

ALSO BY MICHALEA MOORE

THE MAY BABIES BALL (BOOK 3)

"Watch your thoughts, they become your words; watch your words, they be-come your actions. Watch your actions, they become your habits.
Watch your habits, they become your character. Watch your character, it becomes your destiny." – Lao Tzu

The Wheel of the Year turns to Beltane. Returning to Riverton after the tumultuous events in Chicago, Maren and Cyrus celebrate the union of The Green Man and the May Queen with Maren's mentor and coven. They move into a house Maren once called a faery castle. Cyrus's renova-tions and the gardens they're creating promise a faery tale happy-ever-after. They also anticipate the annual May Babies Ball at a local river camp where Maren's old friends honor the people born in May. This year, Cyrus is one of the May Babies, signaling his acceptance into the Riverton community.

A true faery tale seems in the offing, but the original faery tales were dark and bloody. Maren discovers the body of her best friend in the river in the early hours of the morning after the Ball. Originally deemed a tragic accident caused by too much to drink, the police discover some clues hinting that something more sinister is afoot. Old enemies join forces, and fears divide the town into factions. Are other party-goers in danger? Are Maren and Cyrus targets, or are they the perpetrators?

The *Judgement* card advises Maren that "judgment day" is at hand. But for whom?

Available at https://bit.ly/42moA2t
Or from this QR code:

www.ingramcontent.com/pod-product-compliance
Lightning Source LLC
Chambersburg PA
CBHW020902200626
46814CB00001BA/139